"Laura Wiess boldly goes where oth
(A. M. Jenkins, author of *Damage* an
splendid and unforgettable mu

LEFTOVERS

"Like her equally gripping debut *(Such a Pretty Girl)*, Wiess's suspense story delivers an outsize jolt of adrenaline. . . . Wiess's clear insight . . . and her layered storytelling bump up the 'best friends against the world' theme to a much more challenging playing field."

—*Publishers Weekly*

"The climax is explosive, but it's the feisty heroines who will resonate more."

—*Kirkus Reviews*

"A riveting story. . . . I love this book."

—Laura Fitzgerald, author of *Veil of Roses*

"Dramatic and disturbing . . . a captivating book that will keep you turning the pages."

—TeensReadToo.com

"Reading Blair and Ardith's story is like scratching a mosquito bite—you can't stop scratching until it bleeds. And as much as it hurts, you won't be able to put *Leftovers* down until you finish it."

—Lyn Seippel, Bookloons.com

"Strikes just the right balance between hope and despair, and Meredith's will to survive and ability to take action in the face of her terror are an inspiration."

—*KLIATT*

"*Such a Pretty Girl* is a riveting novel and Meredith is a wholly original creation: a funny, wise, vulnerable girl with the heart of a hero and the courage of a warrior. This gut-wrenching story will stay with you long after you finish the last page."

—Lisa Tucker, author of *The Cure for Modern Life*

"Beautifully written and painfully real. Laura Wiess has crafted a gripping story that is heart-rending—and important, with a capital 'I.'"

—*New York Times* bestselling author Barbara Delinsky

"Gritty yet poetic, gut-churning yet uplifting—a compelling, one-of-a-kind read."

—A. M. Jenkins, author of *Damage* and *Out of Order*

"So suspenseful you'll wish you'd taken a speed-reading course. But slow down, because to rush would mean missing Laura Wiess's wonderfully precise language, her remarkable access to Meredith's darkest emotions, and a shocker of an ending, which you'll want to read twice."

—Tara Altebrando, author of *What Happens Here*

"Spellbinding. . . . We need more characters like Meredith in our world and more authors like Wiess to spin them into heartbreaking, enchanting heroines."

—*TeenVoices*

Also by Laura Wiess

Leftovers
Such a Pretty Girl

Available from MTV Books

how it ends

laura wiess

POCKET BOOKS   MTV BOOKS

New York London Toronto Sydney

Pocket Books
A Division of Simon & Schuster, Inc.
1230 Avenue of the Americas
New York, NY 10020

First MTV Books/Pocket Books trade paperback edition August 2009

POCKET and colophon are registered trademarks of Simon & Schuster, Inc.

For information about special discounts for bulk purchases, please contact Simon & Schuster Special Sales at 1-866-456-6798 or business@simonandschuster.com.

The Simon & Schuster Speakers Bureau can bring authors to your live event. For more information or to book an event contact the Simon & Schuster Speakers Bureau at 866-248-3049 or visit our website at www.simonspeakers.com.

Manufactured in the United States of America

10 9 8 7 6 5 4 3 2 1

Library of Congress Cataloging-in-Publication Data

Wiess, Laura
  How it ends / Laura Wiess. —1st MTV Books/Pocket Books trade pbk. ed.
    p. cm.
  Summary: Sixteen-year-old Hanna learns about life, love, happiness, and pain when she finally starts dating the boy she has had a long-time crush on, and when she discovers the complicated truth about her beloved Gran.
  [1. Coming of age—Fiction. 2. Interpersonal relations—Fiction. 3. Dating (Social customs)—Fiction. 4. Old age—Fiction. 5. Love—Fiction. 6. Country life—Fiction.]
I. Title.
  PZ7.W6372Ho 2009
  [Fic]—dc22   2009012785

ISBN 978-1-4165-4663-4
ISBN 978-1-4391-6422-8 (ebook)

For
David C. Gold,
who knows that
a dream goes on forever.

Acknowledgments

I've said it before but it still holds true: When it comes to support, guidance and insight, I could get no luckier than with my agent Barry Goldblatt and my editor Jennifer Heddle. Thank you both for everything.

I owe a lovely debt of gratitude to Louise Burke, Anthony Ziccardi, Jacob Hoye, Lisa Litwack, Regina Starace, Johanna Farrand, John Paul Jones, Erica Feldon and Kerrie Loyd at Simon & Schuster/MTV Books for their hard work, enthusiasm and expertise.

Heartfelt thanks to Stewart Russell, and to Lou, Nancy, Bud, Connie, Jess, and Jake Winters, who not only made me welcome and taught me how to build a respectable fire, but generously continue to share their knowledge, humor and lives with this former flatlander.

Sincere thanks to the Wiess family, Pat Schaal, Barbara Gauch, Bonnie Verrico, A. M. Jenkins, Shelley Sykes, and Dave Gold for the love, friendship and support.

I'm very grateful for the privilege of having known Carol Bon, Florence Sellner and Julia Battyanyi, strong, uncommon women who left their own indelible imprints on this author.

The deepest curtsy, given with love, goes home to Bill and Barbara Battyanyi, Suzanne Dial, Paul Pinaha and Scott Battyanyi for always believing in me, no matter what.

"I would not willingly peel back the scar tissue protecting the deepest chambers of my heart and reveal the bruised hollows pooled with the blood of old wounds—the terror comes just thinking about it—but now, facing darkness I am left with no choice.
I love you, and because of that I am going to try and raise the dead."

—Louise Bell Closson, *How It Ends*

And they all lived happily ever after . . .

It happened painfully and without warning, this sudden turning of the heart.

It happened as you stood so small and stoic beside me in the driveway, waving as your mother pulled away in her car and then your father in his, your thin, sun-browned shoulders squared, your chin up and your dark gaze riveted to their leaving, oblivious to the clean morning breeze, to shy Serepta, the youngest of the strays, meowing and twining round your bare ankles, and the glittering pink and gold beads of your new Princess Barbie bracelet rattling a hollow farewell.

Your wave never faltered, Hanna, not even after those cars disappeared around the wooded bend and left you behind, watching and waiting as if certain the steadfast devotion in your farewell would somehow guarantee their return.

But it didn't, it couldn't, and the road remained deserted, each empty passing second wilting and finally stilling your faithful, fluttering hand.

"Well," I said briskly, picking up your Princess Jasmine overnight bag. "I think it's time for some chocolate chip pancakes. What do you say?"

"My stomach hurts," you mumbled, fingering your sparkly bracelet.

"It'll feel better with pancakes in it," I said.

"Grandma Helen?" You looked up, chin quivering and doe eyes stricken with tears. "This is not a good happily ever after. I'm t-t-too sad."

It was then, Hanna, as I gazed into your forlorn little five-year-old face that fierce longing surged and, catching me off guard, wrenched free.

You sidled close and touched my hand. "Are you going away, too?"

"Oh, sweetheart, no," I said, and in that heartbeat the bond was formed, the promise made, and the emptiness inside of me was filled with the rush to comfort and protect, to earn this trust you put in me, *me,* no blood relation, the *Grandma Helen* a courtesy title given by your parents to the childless lady in the neighboring farmhouse with a passion for books, stray cats, and hungry deer, who fed the birds and loved a creaky old man named Lon who sang Beatles' songs and still had shoulders strong enough for a little girl's piggyback rides. "No, Hanna. Wild horses couldn't drag me away."

You sniffled. "I don't know what that means."

"It means you couldn't get rid of me if you tried," I said, gently swinging your hand. "Come on, let's go find us some breakfast." I led you across the thick grass still glistening with dew, under the smooth gray branches of the copper beech tree, and into the little strip of woods that signaled the end of your property and the beginning of mine.

"I think I might like pancakes," you offered, flip-flops slapping as you padded along the smooth pine-needle carpet, Serepta swatting playfully at your heels. "Hey, when we get to the meadow can we take the deer path past the pond?"

"Absolutely," I said and paused to lift you over a fallen hemlock.

"Look," you said, eyeing a good-sized hole in the mossy, crumbling trunk. "A lion might live there."

"Or a skunk or a raccoon. They're wild, so don't ever try to pet them, but they won't hurt you if you just let them be. Live and let live, Hanna." I took your hand, leading you out of the tree line and into the meadow. "One deer path, coming up." It was almost too painful, this giddy joy at sharing the everyday miracles in my world and the solemn way you soaked it all up as we stopped to consider the zigzag flight of an iridescent dragonfly, the chirp of a startled chipmunk, and the hoofprint pressed in the mud at the edge of the pond.

"Do wild horses take the deer path, too?" you said, pulling free and crouching to study the honeybees buzzing over great drifts of violets and white clover.

"Not anymore," I said. "They might have, though, a long, long time ago."

"Back when you were a little girl?" you said, shading your eyes and squinting up at me.

"It's possible," I said, lips twitching.

"Oh." You paused a minute, absently petting the cat, and then picked three violets. "You know what, Grandma Helen? I think when you were little, and your mommy and daddy went away and left you, you were sad and cried, and they came back and made pancakes with *lots* of syrup and you all lived happily ever after again, right?"

And it was then, with a crown of sunlight shimmering in your silky brown hair, the hawk circling high overhead, and your hand reaching up to offer me the tiny bouquet, that I said, "Right," and told you the first of so many terrible lies.

You practically lived with us that summer while your parents—struggling, bewildered, and unhappy—tried to figure out why the life they'd planned wasn't the one they ended up with.

It was very peaceful here then—Lon and I hadn't yet sold that section of acreage on the other side to that liar who said he loved the country and then, once he owned the property, tried to destroy every living thing on it, so this stretch of road was just my house and yours, meadows and woods. Sound carried far in the darkness, Hanna, and in the daylight, too, so when bitter disappointment got the best of your parents and echoed out over the clearing, I would find some reason to call and invite you over just to get you out of the battle zone.

I have to give them credit for catching on quickly and trying to spare you the worst of it, though, because after my first few phone calls, the roles reversed and more often than not it would be your mother calling and asking if you could visit me for a while.

I always said yes, of course, because I could hear how much it cost her to ask, but even more than that, the sight of you trudging through the field grass toward my back door, whether you were smiling and stuffing your pockets with acorns or plodding along like you didn't have a friend in the world, filled my heart like nothing else.

I would grab some cookies and hurry down the deer path to meet you, Serepta and any number of other strays following along. The moment you saw me your face would light up, and I would smile and wave because truly, is there anything as wonderful as feeling safe and loved?

I gave that to you, Hanna, but make no mistake: You gave it to me, too.

We would meet under the big old catalpa tree by the pond and, if you were especially blue, would sit side by side on the old wooden bench in the flickering shade of those huge, heart-shaped leaves. Sooner or later, if I waited long enough, you would reveal yourself in questions.

More often, though, you would ask me to tell you stories about when I was a little girl. The first time you did this I panicked and immediately let go of your hand. You didn't notice my shocked with-drawal; you were too busy rattling the knob of a door I had sealed shut years ago, asking if I was always good or if I ever got into trouble, how I got punished, if I'd had my own bedroom, lots of friends to play with, and if I'd hated peas just like you did.

Your bright chatter gave me time to recover, to breathe deep and force myself to stop and *think* instead of turn and hurry away. That was the closest I ever came to leaving you and I would have if I was still only your babysitter, would have made some excuse to your par-ents about aching bones or being too busy to watch you and disap-peared from your life, but I wasn't just Mrs. Schoenmaker anymore, I was your Grandma Helen and there was a price to pay for keeping that title.

So while I could never tell you the truth, the more I listened, the more I realized I didn't have to. You weren't probing for secrets or judging me; no, all you wanted were happily ever after tales to blunt the sharp edges of your own uncertain days, so I wove you stories of an idyllic childhood with stern but kind parents and loyal, mis-chievous best friends, of getting into trouble and the crafty ways we wiggled out of it.

"You *never* got into trouble?" you said, wide-eyed.

"Well, maybe sometimes, but if you look hard enough, there's always a way to get out of it or around it." I stopped but you begged for more, held out your cupped hands, and so I obliged, filling them with sunny days romping at my grandparents' farm, climbing trees, and saving baby animals, of the fun I'd had in school, glorious fam-ily Thanksgivings, and fuzzy little tuxedo kittens in my stocking on Christmas mornings.

I told these lies and you soaked up every word, eyes glowing and face rapt as if you were there, too, as if we were equal in age and em-barking on those merry adventures together.

My house became your second home, and even after your parents reconciled and you didn't need to be sent to me anymore, you still came regularly because you wanted to, because I made sure there was always something fun to do or read or talk about, something good to eat, interesting questions to ask, and satisfying answers to find.

And of course we had our adventures.

We sat like statues on the bench under the catalpa one June day and watched as a new fawn, dainty and curious, sauntered to within six feet of us. She paused, her wide, black velvet eyes unblinking, ears high and nostrils twitching, gauging our presence, and then, fluffy white tail waving, turned and danced away.

You stared after her in awe and said, "I never saw a real fawn close up before. A wild one, I mean."

"Beautiful, wasn't she?" I said.

"Wow," you breathed.

We spent your tenth birthday eating egg rolls and combing yard sales in pursuit of some elusive, unidentified treasure and it wasn't until late in the day that we stumbled upon the item you'd been secretly searching for: a chair of your own for my living room. The one you wanted was vintage, a wide, sturdy overstuffed monstrosity in an unsettling currant-and-forest-colored tweed and didn't match anything I owned, but you loved the brass nail heads pounded in along the arms and the plush six-inch fringe along the bottom, so we jammed it halfway into the trunk of my car and drove home at a crawl. Lon almost popped a disk hauling it up the porch steps and we had to take the front door off its hinges just to get the thing inside, but it fit perfectly opposite my reading chair by the window, creating a cozy little nook with a view past the bird feeders to the pond and became Serepta's favorite new ambush spot.

When you were thirteen we went grocery shopping and the object of your crush, a cocky teenage produce boy with bleached hair and a pierced tongue, was there. He was tending the root crops, unloading onions, neatening turnips, stacking bags of potatoes, so I sent you over to pick me out three nice yams. *"Yams?"* you whispered, as appalled as if I'd said *extra-large tampons*, but the lure of him was too strong, so off you went in blushing agony, arms folded across your chest, walking too fast, eyes too bright, lost in the exquisite torment of feeling too tall, too stupid, too hopeful, and too embarrassed to be with an old lady, hating your outfit, your hair, and the squeegee squeak your boots made crossing the polished floor. You couldn't bring yourself to look at him, not even when he shifted to make room for you, only snatched three enormous yams from the middle of the pile, causing the tubers at the peak to descend in a tumble and scatter across the floor.

You froze, mortified.

"Nice going, Ace," the kid drawled. "Any more like you at home?"

Your eyes filled with tears.

"Great," he muttered, setting aside a crate of onions. "They don't pay me enough for this kind of shit." He dropped to all fours, groping under the display for the errant tubers and giving you the chance to rush back to me, throw the yams in the cart, and run out to the car.

I wanted to slap him for his careless cruelty, to ask him if it really would have cost so much to smile at a child with such stars in her eyes, but I didn't, of course. Instead, I discovered that you were mad at *me* that day, me and those stupid yams for making you look foolish. I tried to explain the idea of keeping your composure even when you were embarrassed so no one would ever know you felt small and vulnerable, but you were either too young to get it or too busy replaying the tragic humiliation to listen, because your thundercloud expression never lightened, and so I swallowed my hurt and resorted to a stop at Rita's Italian Ice for coconut gelatos. By the time we were done eating, most of the storm had passed and the sun showed signs of peeking through again.

When you were fifteen and not coming around to visit as often, I unearthed my old red bicycle from the cobwebby corner of the barn, and huffing, puffing, and wobbling, ringing the old *tink-ching* bell on the handlebars and wearing a violent purple scarf, mirrored shades, and my yellow winter hat with the ridiculous crocheted daisy earflaps, warbling "Dear Prudence" and looking like the village idiot, I rode in circles around your house until you staggered out the front door, weak with laughter, and begged me to stop before anyone saw me.

"Not until you go for a ride with me," I called, and then, "Oof!" as a vicious rut sent me jouncing over a rock and you into fresh gales of laughter. "Har, har. What a wretched child you are. Come on, where's your adventurous spirit? Are you really going to let me have all the fun?"

You started down the steps, eyes sparkling and the crisp breeze stirring your long hair, and then stopped, biting your lip as if you suddenly remembered having fun wasn't all that simple anymore, and as you hesitated on that threshold, Hanna, time shivered and for a moment you were no longer a confused adolescent still wearing a granddaughter's smudged and rosy glasses but a tall, beautiful young woman whose naked gaze welled with tears as the cold autumn wind tore the brittle, heart-shaped leaves from the catalpa and I gripped the handlebars, silent, paralyzed, and unable to wave as the rattling bicycle carried me past.

ᑴ ᑴ ᑴ

We never went for that ride together or any other and we never spoke of why not, but something important had changed, and for the first time in years, I remembered what it was like to be lonely.

And that heart which was a wild garden was given to him
who loved only trim lawns.
And the imbecile carried the princess into slavery.

—Antoine de Saint-Exupéry

Chapter 1

Hanna

This is not exactly the exciting new high school experience I had in mind.

I'm a month into St. Ignatius, a regional, parochial school nine miles from home and I still don't know what I'm doing, where I'm going, or how I'm supposed to be.

Plus, this is the ugliest uniform in the world. It's true. I would like to know what girl-hating hag cursed us with knee-length brown plaid polyester skorts, long sleeveless vests, and baggy yellow polyester blouses.

I wish Crystal's parents had transferred her here, too, instead of keeping her in public school. Then we could be miserable together.

Oh, and I definitely need new shoes. Mine are loser wear.

Sigh.

I'd still rather be here with five hundred new kids, though, than stuck with nobody but the same boring, cliqued-out crew from junior high. They move in huddled masses just like they did in ninth grade, and seeing that makes me feel like some kind of intrepid pioneer striking out on my own.

Hanna's big adventure.

It's scary but I kind of like it.

(Cue Grandma Helen's voice) *Back straight! Stand tall! Look 'em in the eye! Smile! Never let 'em see you sweat!*

(Cue my voice) Be brave, Hanna.

School would be a lot easier if I had a partner in crime.

I miss Crystal.

I've done some research and found that most of the older girls' uniforms are way shorter and tighter than mine. I asked someone about it and she said that's because everybody hems them up and takes them in. They wear killer heels and black panty hose, too. All against the rules, but most of the nuns are old and slow, so even if one tries to snag you on a dress code violation, you can usually outrun her before she IDs you.

Turns out only us lame sophomores wear long, baggy uniforms.

Time to convince Gran to do a serious overhaul on this hideous skort.

Well, it took whining, pleading, and begging but she's hemming my skort even though my father said he didn't spend three hundred dollars on a uniform to see it turned into something too small to wear to the beach. I said everybody wears them that way, and he said (of course), *Come on, Hanna, if everybody else jumped off the Brooklyn Bridge . . .*

He is so tiresome sometimes.

My mother laughed and told him it was just history repeating itself because *she'd* gone to parochial school, too, and had a uniform just as ugly, and she'd always rolled her skirt up at the waist because feeling ugly was no way to spend your whole high school career.

My father just looked at her and shook his head like she was hopeless.

She laughed again and tickled him in passing. He told her to quit it but I could tell he was trying not to smile.

I love it when everybody's happy.

Oh my God, I'm in love.

Seth Kobilias.

I must have him.

He's a junior, beautiful, sexy, sweet, and I found out that Bailey, the girl he really loved last year, broke his heart so now he supposedly parties hard and goes out with a lot of different girls because he was too hurt and doesn't want to be again. He plays guitar, too, and hangs out in the courtyard.

I need to make the courtyard my new hangout ASAP.

I never felt anything like this before. I love his eyes and his smile and his hair and just everything. He's really tall, blond, and a little skinny but it looks perfect on him. He even makes a uniform jacket and tie look hot.

He hasn't noticed me yet but I can change that, I just know it. Good thing Gran Helen hemmed this uniform. Now at least when he *does* look at me, he'll be able to tell I'm a girl.

Also, I hung out with another sophomore named Sammi Holloway who I think might be my next partner in crime. We're pretty different—she's thinner, flatter, richer, and sleeker than me, and next to her I feel like nothing but flyaway hair, frayed edges, and loose ends—but she cracks me up bad and so far I like her a lot.

I think we could have great adventures together.

Life is very exciting these days.

I took too many classes. I have to drop some right now. They're interfering with my chance to meet Seth. The days are rushing by and I'm not getting anywhere because of all these stupid classes! I tried to dump algebra and physical science but Mr. Sung in guidance won't let me. So maybe journalism and . . . what? There's nothing else I can get rid of. I don't mind dumping journalism; it's all about facts, and who needs facts when imagining what could happen is so much more satisfying?

I kept creative writing but dropped journalism so now I have an extra free period *and* I just found out that for some reason my name isn't on the sophomore Mandatory Community Service list. Yay! I probably should be worried about this but I'm not, and I'm *sure* not bringing it up. I can use the time for my Seth quest. I'll just make it up next year or something.

I love a good computer glitch.

My parents went on a date last night—which kind of freaked me out because the last time they did that was like two years ago, and right after, they argued about growing apart—so I went down to Crystal's and we passed the time hanging out with her older brother and his friends. They were full of compliments and if I didn't like Seth so much, I probably could have found myself a boyfriend.

I hope he appreciates this sacrifice.

Oh. My. God.
Seth noticed me today. For real. And it was good.
No, better than good.
Great.
I was caught in a stream of kids changing classes, flowing down the right side of the hall, and there he was, heading toward me in the stream on the left side, ambling along, head and shoulders above the crowd, laughing at something somebody said and kind of scanning oncoming traffic as he walked.
I looked at him right as he looked at me and I swear time stopped.

He held my gaze for like a full three seconds, then smiled this sweet little sideways smile and lifted his chin in a *Hi.* I smiled back and then we passed and he didn't break the connection until he was almost past me.

He saw me. Out of all the hundreds of other people in that hall, it was *me* that he smiled at. Me!

These teachers take their classes way too seriously. I mean, I'm fifteen; I have like another *seventy years* to worry about zygotes or circumferences or whatever.

I wish I could just learn what I'm interested in, which would be creative writing, psychology, and nature stuff. And not biology. I don't want to hack open dead animals; I want to study them alive and healthy.

If I ever have to take biology, I'm boycotting carving up dead things, and too bad about the grade. If anybody makes me do it, I'll just throw up on purpose every single day all over the lab until they let me out. I don't care. I will not mangle dead animals.

Gran won't mind. Heck, she'll probably give me a medal.

(Cue Gran's voice): *No, Hanna, we don't kill spiders; they're the perfect natural insect control. Careful, you almost stepped on that beetle. Look, the spring fawns are out frolicking on the lawn!*

Yes, she actually uses words like *frolicking.*

She is so embarrassing sometimes. (I would never tell her that, though. It would hurt her feelings too badly. Actually, I'd better call her soon or else her and Grandpa will show up at school or something just to make sure I'm still alive.)

Anyway, what I really need is less classes and more free time. How else am I supposed to develop into a sociable, well-rounded human being if I never have the time to get my hands on Seth?

Sammi's doing trash pickup along the roads with a bunch of other kids for her community service, and yesterday some lady in a Lexus stopped and asked if they were from a juvenile detention center because usually only prisoners from the county jail pick up garbage, but they wear orange jumpsuits so everyone know they're prisoners out on work detail.

Sammi, being tired, disgusted, and a smart-ass said *they* usually wore brown plaid uniforms and wouldn't get released unless they completed their mandatory service, too.

The lady looked righteous and said, *Well, I don't know what you did to get into this situation, but I certainly hope you've learned your lesson,* and drove away.

Sammi said it was funny but also pretty humiliating, and next year she's just gonna stuff envelopes or something instead.

God, I'm glad I escaped this.

I've been sitting out on the curb in the courtyard in my free time, pretending to read or page through my notebooks but really watching Seth from beneath my hair and trying my hardest to will him to come over and fall in love with me.

So far, it isn't working.

I *am* learning him, though, by watching and listening, and sooner or later that's got to be worth something. I've already discovered that he smokes Marlboros, loves *South Park,* and is a killer flirt when he's high. He also seems to be addicted to bitchy girls with long nails, ankle bracelets, and cool, you-can't-touch-this smiles, which is kind of depressing.

"Hey," Sammi said, plopping down on the curb beside me. "Anything good going on?"

"You-know-who likes ankle bracelets," I said glumly.

"So?"

"I hate ankle bracelets," I said.

"I like them," she said, leaning back on her hands and turning her face to the sun. "I think they're hot."

"I don't," I said. "They remind me of shackles."

She snorted, amused. "Oh, c'mon Hanna, you can't tell me that if he walked up to you and said you'd look hot wearing an ankle brace-let, you wouldn't go right out and get one."

"No," I said, irritated, and then, "You're a pain in the butt, you know that?"

"I love you, too," she said, smirking and bumping her shoulder against mine.

Chapter 2

Helen

"It's pretty quiet around here these days," Lon says, pulling out a chair at the kitchen table and easing down into it. He's been outside cleaning the gutters and his arrival carries the mingled scents of hand soap, damp soil, and cold, matted greenery.

"Mm-hmm," I say and ladle him out a big bowl of vegetable beef soup from the pot simmering on the stove. I set the bowl in front of him and, ignoring his searching look, head for the pantry to see if the last of the summer tomatoes have ripened yet.

"Heard from Hanna?"

"Not since I hemmed up her uniform," I say without turning.

"That was back in September," he says.

"Was it?" I say lightly, as if I wasn't aware of every single empty second. "Well, I imagine homework and such is keeping her busy. She'll visit when she gets a chance." I wait, but other than a quiet exhale Lon is kind enough not to take it any further, as he knows it will only make me feel worse than I already do.

Most days I deal with Hanna's absence by trying to keep busy: baking muffins, feeding the birds, enclosing the porch in clear heavy-duty plastic, setting up the heat lamps and readying the stray-cat condos for winter, raking leaves, and stapling new PRIVATE PROPERTY/NO HUNT-ING signs on the trees along the wood line. When those tasks fail to distract me, I remind myself that it's normal for her to want to socialize with new friends rather than spend all her free time dancing attendance on an old one. It's a bitter pill, though, and doesn't go down well, so I've taken to calling Melanie Thury, Hanna's mom, once or twice a week just to chat.

"Aren't you going to eat?" Lon says.

"In a minute," I say, holding the pantry door frame and stepping carefully down into the chill darkness.

"My soup's getting cold," he says.

"Then start without me." I reach up and finding the pull cord, yank on the light.

The bare overhead bulb isn't fancy but it does the job, revealing rows and rows of wooden shelves stocked with cabbages, buckets of carrots in sand, yams, potatoes, kale, garlic and onion braids, and of course, the tomatoes.

At the end of the season some gardeners pull the entire tomato plant from the ground and hang it upside down to let the green tomatoes ripen on the vine. I've never taken this shortcut as I figure no matter how well you shake the roots there will always be dirt and bugs left clinging and brought inside. My way takes longer but I'd rather go plant by plant, fruit by fruit, examining each for bite marks or spoilage, filling my buckets and then carefully lining each tomato up on the pantry shelf beneath sheets of newspaper so they can ripen at their own speed.

I lift the first sheet of newspaper. It rattles and I realize my hands are trembling again. This has been happening more and more lately, and I don't know whether it's low blood sugar or just old age smirking at me from around a shadowy corner, but I have no intention of letting it win, so after I eat I'm going to do more reading through my natural home remedy books for causes and cures.

"Hey, Helen, I'll make you a deal," Lon calls. "If you bring me back one of those big, juicy beefsteaks, I might be persuaded to split it with you."

It's his tone, teasing and tinged with the memory of a younger man's mischief, that coaxes my first smile of the day. "Oh, really?" I abandon the small Rutgers tomato I was considering and move farther down the shelf to where the massive beefsteaks lie. "Will I have to do anything R-rated to seal this deal?"

"No," Lon says, sounding startled.

"Then forget it," I say, and at his snort of laughter, pick the biggest, ripest tomato we have, hide my trembling hand in my apron, and head slowly up out of the darkness and back into the bright, cozy kitchen.

Chapter 3

Hanna

Seth's best friend is a junior named Connor, so to get closer to Seth, I said hi to Connor twice today in passing. He looked pleasantly surprised the first time and said hi back the second. This is progress.

Then Connor just *happened* to be outside my English class when I got out and walked me to my locker. We passed Seth, and I really didn't like the looks they gave each other, like a thumb's-up from Seth to Connor that he was walking with me.

This is not good.

Later on I dodged Connor by changing hall routes and ran into Seth in the courtyard by himself. There was no way I could just go up to him so I headed over to my regular spot on the curb and he said, teasing, "What, you don't want to talk to me?"

So I went over and it turned out he was getting high and offered me weed but I lied and said, No, it gives me hives. (Weed at school. Right. Like my mother wouldn't rip my head off and take it bowling if I ever got caught getting high at school. Especially a school my father keeps wondering if he can afford to keep me in. No, I'm not losing my chance at Seth just for that.)

Anyhow, Seth said something about Connor, like he was trying to find out if I liked him and I said, "He's okay," because I didn't want to talk about stupid Connor, I wanted to make *him* like me.

He finished getting high and said, "C'mon, let's go into the cafeteria, I need something to drink."

I really didn't want to lose my chance alone with him but what could I say? So we went, with him being silly and messing my hair up on purpose, and me walking slow to make it last and praying nobody was in the cafeteria, but of course Connor was, along with a bunch of others.

So what did imbecile Seth do?

Brought me right over to Connor and with a big dorky grin said, "Don't say I never gave you anything."

And then he went and sat at a different table with stupid senior Nutria Cerelle, who had great blond bed head but also wicked knock-knees and, although nobody seemed to realize it but me, a name that meant a giant swamp-dwelling, orange-toothed *rodent*.

What a stupid day.

"Gran called earlier," my mother said when I dragged myself in the back door and dumped my books on the kitchen table. "She said to tell you that she's pickling the green tomatoes tonight so you should be there by six."

"Well, I can't go tonight," I muttered, peeling off my coat and slinging it across the back of a chair.

"Why not?" my mother said.

"Because I already made plans," I said, opening the fridge and hanging on the door. "Why don't we ever have anything good to eat?"

"Eat a banana," my mother said.

"I hate bananas," I said, scowling and closing the refrigerator.

"You'd better call Gran and tell her you're not coming," my mother said. "Don't just leave her waiting, Hanna. She counts on you."

"I know, I won't," I said and, grabbing my purse, headed up to my room.

But I did because I knew she would try to talk me into coming, and I didn't want to go and that made me feel guilty. I mean, I pickled the tomatoes with her every year, and yes, I loved the steamy scent of hot vinegar steeped with fresh dill and pickling spices and how she always sent me home with a giant jar of my own, but I wasn't really in the mood to pickle anything but myself so I went down to Crystal's instead.

There was a keg party in the woods behind her house so I drank two beers, and spent the rest of the night flirting with some karate guy I never met before who showed me how to flip people and actually did a move and put me down real gently right in a pile of leaves. Twice. He was cute but his goatee worried me. Plus my parents would probably have heart failure if I ever brought home an eighteen-year-old with two-foot dreads and a giant FUCK tattooed on his biceps.

Yup, not gonna happen.

Well, that's just great. While I was being tossed around by karate guy, Seth and Nutria the Rodent became a couple.

Sammi and I were standing in the courtyard when the Rodent-mobile pulled in, and Nutria and Seth got out. They held hands and walked over to her friends.

"Stop staring," Sammi whispered, kicking me in the ankle. "Here comes Connor."

And of course the first thing out of my mouth was, "I thought Seth didn't want to go out with anybody because he didn't want to get hurt again." And Sammi gave me this *Arghhhh* look, but too bad. I was so freaked at the sight of the Rodent flicking back her bed hair and Seth smiling down at her that I wanted to throw knives at them.

Connor gave me a funny look. "Yeah, well, I guess he changed his mind."

Then he said his parents were going away for the weekend and he was having a party and we were invited if we could get a ride there. He lives in the same town as Sammi, which is about six miles from me. Seth lives fourteen miles away. The Rodent lives in Seth's town. Of course.

I hate my life.

Chapter 4

Helen

I don't know if it's the waning daylight, the inevitable withering of all things green, or the relentless approach of hunting season, but I've been getting up early before Lon, tending the woodstove, and brewing strong, sweet cups of apple harvest tea to try and hurry the dawn. I sit by the window and, with Serepta curled up in Hanna's empty chair, watch the pale sun top the trees, the cardinals and mourning doves picking at the cracked corn sprinkled beneath the feeders, the does and their yearlings drinking from the pond, and beyond that, at the greatest distance, Hanna heading down her driveway to wait for the bus.

"There she goes," I murmur, and Serepta's ears twitch but she doesn't open her eyes, so there are no witnesses to the tears gathered in mine. I wave at Hanna's back and it's meant as a greeting but feels like a farewell.

I wish spring was melting into summer now, instead of autumn hardening into winter.

I said that once to Hanna when she was twelve and she took my hand and pulled me up out of my chair, led me outside and around the property, pointing out how pretty the sun was in the clear blue sky, the vibrant scarlet of the sumac, and the fun of kicking up crunchy fallen leaves. We gathered pocketfuls of acorns and, like amateur Johnny Appleseeds, tossed them into the woods, picked catmint bouquets to hang dry in the pantry, and watched a monarch butterfly gliding on the breeze.

"It's a female," Hanna said as it swooped low and fluttered around the few remaining goldenrod in flower. "You can tell because she doesn't have those two dots on the bottom of her wings. I wish we had more for her to eat. It's such a long migration . . ." She stopped and looked up at me. "Hey, Gran . . . do you think she knows she's not going to make it?"

"I don't know," I said after a moment.

Hanna nodded slightly and turned her gaze back to the butterfly still searching the fading goldenrod for nectar. "I think she does," she said softly. "I think she can feel it, you know? Inside of her, I mean. Like instinct. I think she knows she's not going to make it all the way to Mexico before winter hits but she's trying to anyway."

"Why do you say that?" I said.

"Because it's fall instead of summer and the air is cool instead of hot, and it takes longer for her to warm up in the morning just so she can fly because the sun isn't as strong," Hanna said. "She has to use more energy to find food, and the days are shorter so she has to find a safe place to roost before dark, which means she can't cover as many miles in a day as the monarchs who migrate in July and August can." She glances at me. "You gave me that book on them last Christmas, remember?"

"Yes," I said and tried to smile but couldn't.

She looked back at the butterfly. "She's brave."

"Valiant," I murmured and the word was bittersweet.

We watched in silence until the monarch finished feeding, and when she flew off, gliding to conserve energy, I heard Hanna whisper,

"*Vaya con Dios,* little one." And then to me, "Do you think sending good wishes with butterflies is stupid, Gran?"

"No," I said, shading my burning eyes and watching until the butterfly was almost out of sight. "I think it's perfect."

Dear God, I miss my times with her so much.

∽ ∽ ∽

The school bus finally crawls to a stop in front of Hanna's house.

I watch her board, then make my way back to the kitchen to coax a second cup of tea from the leaves in the filter. Open the kitchen curtains and set up the coffeepot so all Lon has to do when he wakes is come down and turn it on.

He surprised me with that small kindness back when we were first married and we've been doing it ever since.

Making coffee isn't a difficult task—not a task at all, really, especially not for a part-time waitress—but this morning I go through the motions hating the way my hands shake, this weakness that comes and goes at will, the muscle cramps, and the way my feet have taken to twitching like those of a cat in the throes of a dream.

If it was earlier in the season, I would have gathered wild skullcap and experimented with brewing a tea, and if money wasn't so tight, I would do as my natural-healing books suggest and buy blueberries for the antioxidants, pineapple for the enzymes, and cashew butter for the proteins and B vitamins. I would try supplements like glucosamine and chondroitin for my aching joints, grape seed extract to help circulation, and maybe even gingko to strip the fuzziness from my thoughts.

But money *is* tight, and while we're not going to starve, for the first time ever I regret giving away all those tomatoes, peppers, and zucchinis this summer instead of making myself can or freeze them. I only preserved half of the crop this year because canning alone wasn't nearly as fun as canning with Hanna for company, and so now I'm grateful that we still have as much fresh, good food stocked in the pantry as we do.

I'm still not ready for winter; I hate driving to work in the snow, the slick roads and icy steps, hate having to walk the deer path alone in the cold, gray dusk, and the long, bleak days with no company but my own thoughts.

And I worry about the heat.

Lon can't fell the dead trees or cut, split, and stack wood like he used to, but we need at least five cords to make it through, and I don't know how we're going to get them. The house has electric baseboards but the cost of running them has become too high and so the wood-stove in the living room will be our only source of warmth.

We could buy a cord or two and maybe barter for the rest, find someone looking to make money selling firewood and offer him our dead trees providing he splits our half of the wood, too. I can probably stack it if I move slowly and don't push too hard.

Or we could impose on Wes, Hanna's father, to help, but I hate to do it. He works such long days and what little free time he has left should be spent with his family.

I don't know.

I can't find an answer.

I fix the second, weaker cup of tea and return to my chair by the window.

Serepta opens her limpid green eyes, stretches, yawns, and goes back to sleep.

The strays—I counted five of them out on the porch this morning—are curled up in the homemade cat condos on the back porch. Soon it will be cold enough to turn on the lamps set above their beds, as the clear plastic sheeting protects them from the snow and biting wind but offers no real warmth, and the single-bulb lamps help chase away the chill.

I'm so afraid of the day I can no longer afford to care for these cast-offs and orphans and will have to make myself turn away and ignore them milling around out there, cold, skinny, and starving, begging and calling and never understanding why I'm not answering their pleas for help.

Never understanding at all why I am failing them.

Chapter 5

Hanna

Connor is all over me—I swear he memorized my schedule like I memorized Seth's—so I'm trying to avoid him without being mean, and at the same time, now that I don't want to see Seth and the Rodent, all I ever do is run into them. There they are kissing, there they are getting high, there they are walking down the hall holding hands.

I give up.

Well, not really.

I just hate seeing her leaning against him with her bed hair swishing all over and her pointy little rodent face right there waiting to be kissed.

I wish I had bed head and a rat face, too.

No, no, no.

They sit at their own table in the cafeteria, chairs facing each other, her legs slid between his . . . ugh. It's so bad that I can't even go in there and eat anymore.

Love, I have decided, is hard.

I slept over Sammi's last night. Her little brother wouldn't leave us alone as we were getting dressed for Connor's party and kept whining,

"Where are you going?" but luckily her mother had a date and believed us when we said we were walking down to the diner and maybe the strip mall.

Anyway, we walked to Connor's since it was only like a mile away.

The love couple wasn't there, but somehow that made the night even worse because Connor kept cornering me with this hopeful puppy-dog look, which made me feel bad because I just don't like him back, so right before we left I ended up giving him a mercy kiss in the back hallway for like one minute. Then he tried to ask me something, but I checked my watch and was like, "Where's Sammi? We're past curfew!" and ran.

Why do the ones *I* like never like me? Why do I always get the ones I don't want?

Seth, you jerk. You give me a giant pain.

Seth came up to me at school while I was heading for the bathroom and with this big cheery grin said, "Hey, I hear you're going out with Connor."

And I said, "*What?* I am not! Who told you that?"

He stopped smiling. "Connor."

And I said, "Well, he's wrong."

Then Seth got this cold look and said, "Well, you better tell *him* that because he really likes you and he's telling everybody you two are going out and now he's going to look like a fool."

And I was thinking, *How is that* my *fault? I never said I'd go out with him!* But I hated the way Seth was looking at me like I was some kind of user, so I just said, "Look, I was with him for *one minute* at his party but that's it. No big deal."

That was the wrong thing to say.

"Maybe not to you but it was to him," he said snottily.

And I was like, *You know what, I don't need this.* But only in my head, of course. So I just gazed at him, dying inside, and he said, "Forget it. I'll handle it," and walked away like he couldn't leave fast enough.

Now they're both ignoring me, but so what? There are tons of other guys here who flirt, and to tell you the truth, I like that best because it doesn't mean anything. It's talk, words, a game, and everyone knows it and no one gets hurt.

Fuck you, Seth. You could have had me but you didn't want me.

Why didn't you want me?

"Well, that was fast," Sammi murmured, nudging me and motioning with her chin to the cafeteria table where Connor and his new girl-friend Teresa sat snuggled together. "How long did it take him to get over you? Three days? A week?"

"Who cares," I said absently because I had more important things on my mind, like what Seth and the Rodent had been arguing about when I passed them in the hall this morning. It had looked bad—the Rodent's face was red and her tone hot and furious, and Seth had a distant look in his eyes like he wasn't even there—and I was dying to know what was up.

Luckily, I didn't have long to wait.

Sammi caught up with me between classes and, seizing my arm in a death grip, steered me into a cove between the lockers. "Nutria broke up with Seth because he cheated on her with that girl who broke his heart—"

"Bailey?" I said, wide-eyed.

"Yeah, I guess. Anyhow, he's going back out with her now—"

The warning bell rang.

"Shit! I've got to go. I can't be late to Brother Gary's class or he throws a fit. I'll call you later." She released me, turned, and took off.

Well.

I stood there staring after her for a moment, then turned and headed to algebra with a giant smile on my face.

Seth had cheated with Bailey, the one girl who was bound to screw him over again, and when she did I was definitely going to be there to catch him.

My father got laid off today. He's union, and work always slows in the winter, but it's bad timing this year because of my school tuition and the heating bill and all. He told me if I needed money to buy Christmas presents, I'd better think about earning it, so I applied for a job at a pet store being a Santa's helper to the pet photographer.

If they hire me, I'll get an employee discount and can surprise Gran with all kinds of cat stuff for Christmas.

She's been on my mind a lot lately, mostly at weird times (like in the middle of US history class or English) when I can't do anything about it.

Like this morning: I dropped my scarf on the way down the driveway to wait for the bus, and when I turned back to pick it up, I got a clear view of Gran's house through the bare trees in the little woods. There was a light on in the living room, right where our reading chairs were, and I got this awful pang in the pit of my stomach, almost like being homesick, and then this really strong flash of memory.

"You got here right in the nick of time," Gran said cheerfully as I trudged up the back porch steps. "Here, I just finished making this for you."

"What is it?" I asked, sniffling and wiping my damp cheeks on the back of my hand. It had been a bad Sunday so far—my parents had been picking at each other from the moment I'd woken up—and so I took the little red bag she offered without much enthusiasm. It was made of felt, the drawstring a thin white silk ribbon trailing from the top, and when I looked inside, it was empty.

"A talisman," Gran said, pushing herself up off of the back porch step.

"Come on, let's go stroll the deer path and see if we can find anything to put in there."

She explained more as we walked, told me how red was a power color for strength and confidence and that whatever I chose to put in the bag should mean something to me, make me feel safe and happy or stand for something important.

"Okay," I said, crouching and picking up a smooth, round brown acorn. "Here, what does this stand for, Gran?"

"An acorn is the seed of the oak," she said. "So I would say an acorn stands for potential, growth, new beginnings, and—"

"That's good," I said and dropped it in my talisman bag. "Let's look some more."

We wandered farther and before long the bag contained a piece of mica—fool's gold, Gran called it, because the glittery outside made people think it was worth far more than it really was—a blue jay's feather for plainspokenness, and a little stick from the catalpa because that tree was old and sturdy and weathered, a place of comfort and shelter, questions and truths.

Gran and I had spent a lot of time sitting under that tree.

I shook my head, smiling, and picked up my scarf. Straightened and, on impulse, not even knowing if she was actually even sitting in the window, raised my arm, waved, and then turned and hurried to the road to catch the bus.

Seth must really be in love with Bailey because he stopped me in the hall to supposedly just say hi but ended with showing me a picture of him and Bailey lounging out in her living room. She had on a really short, tight low-rise skirt and an ankle bracelet and was wearing this smug, totally cocky smile. I wanted to vomit on the picture but only said, "Oh, she's cute," when what I *really* wanted to say was, "She has a nose like a bulldog and one helluva lazy eye."

Not that she does, but anyway.

A senior named Wynn has been sitting with me and Sammi at lunch and walking with me between classes. We went out to the courtyard with me wearing his jacket, and Seth was there with Connor. Seth was sneaking glances over at us the whole time, too. I could tell from the corner of my eye.

I liked the idea of Seth seeing that somebody else might like me, so I flirted hard with Wynn whenever Seth was somewhere in the background and even went to the movies with him once to see if we could be more than friends.

Wynn must have been thinking that way, too, because at the end of the night he said I was cool but a little too young for him.

Uh, *okay*, but I wasn't the one snickering through the movie's love scene, was I?

Still, word got out that we went, and Seth sat with me at lunch today. He ate half my French fries and even fed me one.

I don't understand him at all.

Oh my God, I can't even believe this day happened.

It was beautiful out, one of those freak fifty-degree mornings, and me and Sammi were in the courtyard before the bell rang when Seth got off his bus, stretched, spotted me, and started over. Sammi stepped hard on my foot and hissed, "Stop staring!" and I managed to break the lock Seth had on my gaze.

I swear, with the sun on his hair and that smile on his face, there was nothing in the whole world but him.

"Hey, stranger," he said, bumping his shoulder against mine.

"Hey," I croaked.

"Hi," Sammi said warily.

"God, it's great out here," he said, stretching. "Way too nice to spend in this dump."

"Mm," I said but my heart was going crazy. "I know."

He looked at me like he was searching for something, some kind of answer. He must have found it because he grinned and said, "Want to cut out?"

"No," Sammi said, giving me a hard look.

"And go where?" I said, ignoring her because, oh my God, this was it.

He shrugged. "I don't know, anywhere. Just hang out and enjoy."

"We can't," Sammi said, bugging her eyes at me. "We have a history test third period, remember Hanna?"

"If we leave before the bell rings we'll be marked absent," Seth said.

"And how're you gonna get home then?" Sammi said, elbowing me and scowling.

"We'll come back last period and hang here for the buses," Seth said. "No big deal."

"Yeah, no big deal," I said, giving Sammi my answer with one burning look.

She sighed, shook her head, and said, "Well, if you're going to do it, you'd better go before one of the teachers sees you." And to me, in a whisper, "Call me!"

So we went. We just turned around and cut across the side lawn to the road, which wasn't real easy for me in heels, but Seth said, "Here, hold on to me," and we picked our way across, with me expecting to have a nun snag us at any second . . . but no one did.

"I can't believe I'm doing this," I said when we got to the sidewalk and were out of sight of the school and could relax.

"You never cut out before?" Seth asked, taking off his suit jacket and slinging it over his shoulder.

"Nope," I said.

"So I'm your first," he said with a mischievous smile.

I blushed and gave him a hip bump. "Don't advertise it."

He laughed, slid an arm around my shoulders, and squeezed me to him. "Hanna, Hanna, Hanna, what am I ever going to do with you?" he said, and kissed the top of my head, right in my hair. "C'mon, let's go to the diner. My treat."

That alone would have been enough to make the whole day worth it. But there was more.

We got a booth in the back, ordered OJ and waffles, and while we were waiting for the food I got all kinds of shy and couldn't even look at him because I was afraid I would start crying with happiness or something totally geeky like that.

"So are you still seeing Wynn?" he said.

I shrugged and, tracing the design on my place mat, said, "Are you still going out with Bailey?"

"Yup," he said.

"This is so bizarre," I said, shaking my head.

"What?" he said. "I think we should have done it a long time ago."

"Really," I drawled because he was flirting, and if that's how he wanted to play it, then I could do that. "What else should we have done a long time ago?"

His smile widened like he was thinking something delightfully perverted, and suddenly the air in the diner got hot and close, and everything else receded and there was nothing but him and me.

"You should ask me over," he said.

"You should ask to come," I said, drowning.

He nodded, never breaking the gaze. "Yeah, I should."

And then the food showed up, which was good because I had to breathe again but bad because it completely changed the mood.

He told me about his guitar and his music theory class and all these songs he was learning from the sixties on up, stuff I'd never even heard of but made a mental list to download as soon as I got home.

"So are you in a band?" I asked.

"Nah," he said, coating his waffles in syrup. "I don't know if I want to get into a band or the studio side of it, like maybe an audio engineer."

"Right," I said, wishing my stomach would stop jittering so I could eat, too, but all I could think about was where we would go after this and what would happen once we got there. Would he ask me out? Would he kiss me without asking me out? Would I let him? That would make me an affair girl, almost like a slut, and I didn't want to be that, but what if kissing finally made him realize he really liked me and—

"Hey, cool, the Cowboy Junkies doing 'Sweet Jane,'" he said, nodding up at the ceiling where the speakers were playing a slow, dark, heartbeat-sexy song. "This song never gets old." The singer's voice was sultry, summer-night hot, and Seth watched me, playing air guitar and murmuring the lyrics like he was singing them to me.

Is it possible to bloom and die of love at the same time? Yes, because I was doing it, especially when I felt his legs stretch out on either side of mine under the booth and rest against me. I sat spellbound, watching his fingers slide over invisible strings, his hair slipping forward into one eye and him flicking it back without taking his gaze off me.

I don't think I even breathed until he leaned back at the end and smiled a slow, spontaneous smile that was *real,* that stopped time and erased place and graced me with happiness so pure it was too big to hide.

"Good song," he said finally and, breaking the gaze, picked up his fork.

"Yeah," I said and slipped my trembling hands off the table and into my lap. "I never heard it before but I like it."

He looked at me again, studying me like he was trying to figure something out.

"What?" I said.

"Nothing," he said, glancing down and poking at the last hunk of cold waffle. "Maybe I'll play it for you sometime. If you want, I mean."

"That'd be good," I said and wiggled my feet under the table. They bumped his legs, which were still sort of wrapped around mine and he quickly withdrew them.

"Sorry," he said without looking at me.

"No, I didn't mean to kick you," I said, and I hadn't. "My foot just fell asleep."

We hung out awhile longer, finishing our OJ and doing the dumb word games on the place mats, then he looked at his watch, stretched, and said, "You ready?"

"Sure," I said, because that was an understatement.

He paid and I lingered close enough so that everyone in the place would know we were together. He pushed the door open, and thanks to Wynn holding the door for me, I thought Seth was holding it for me, too, so I started through but I guess he wasn't because he started through at the same time and it was really embarrassing because I'd already said, "Thanks," and basically ran right into him. He got kind of snappy and said, "Well, go, then," like I'd humiliated him on purpose, which I hadn't.

I felt like kicking Wynn for getting me used to guys holding the door open for me.

And then Seth pissed me off by saying, "So I guess Wynn's a real gentleman, huh?" But he said it in this mocking voice, so I said, "Yeah, he is." And Seth snorted and said, "Well, I'm not Wynn," and I snorted back and said, "No kidding."

Talk about a strained ten minutes of walking.

I was starting to feel bad and even panicky for blowing it. I mean, so what if he didn't open the door for me, and okay, so mocking

Wynn wasn't the greatest thing to do but why did I have to get snotty back? Wasn't this chance bigger than one quick payback?

Finally, I couldn't take it anymore and stopped walking. "Look, do you want me to just go back to school and you can hang out on your own?"

He turned and shoved his hands in his pockets, ambling backward and watching me, moving farther and farther away. "Do you want to go back?" he said finally.

"Do you want me to?" I said, staying planted there by sheer force of will.

He shrugged. "I want you to do what you want to do."

Okay, now he was pissing me off because I'd ditched school to be with him and he wouldn't even give me one inch of reason to stay. "Well, good, then stop walking so I can beat you over the head with my shoe, all right?"

His jaw dropped and his face cleared and he laughed.

"Stop walking," I insisted, and bent to pry off my heels. The sidewalk was chilly under my stockinged feet and I picked up the shoes by the straps and let them dangle from my finger.

"Oh, hell no," he said with a mischievous grin. "I'm no fool."

"Matter of opinion," I said, lifting my chin and walking toward him, blood tingling at the laughter in his eyes. "Now stand still, you big chicken, and take your punishment."

"Girl, if you're gonna punish me, then you're gonna have to catch me and hold me down to do it," he drawled, still walking backward away from me.

"I'd like to hold you down," I muttered, swinging my shoes like I hadn't a care in the world. It threw him off for the one second I needed to lunge, but he recovered fast and, laughing, turned and took off at a jog down the street toward the little park.

"Pretty lame fake out," he called back.

"It's what I do best," I said under my breath.

"Come on, you'll never catch me walking," he taunted.

"Well, then, I guess I'll never catch you, Seth, because really, do I *look* like someone who runs?" I said with attitude.

His gaze dropped pointedly to my chest and his grin widened. "Hey, a guy can dream."

"Perv," I said, sauntering closer.

"You wish," he said, ambling onto the grass.

And, oh God, I *did*. I wished for everything, for him and me together, for the right to touch and kiss him, and for him to want me even one *tenth* as much as I wanted him—

"Damn, you're slow," he said and, with a cocky grin, headed for the swings.

Not always, I thought and, taking careful aim, hurled one of my shoes. It grazed his arm and he turned, astonished, while I aimed and threw the second one. If he hadn't ducked, it would have nailed him right between the eyes.

"Oh, you are so seriously gonna pay for that," he said, dropping his jacket and loosening his tie.

"That's what they all say," I said as, eyes sparkling, he started toward me.

I let out a shriek and, laughing, headed across the grass toward the slide, yelling, "This is home! I call you can't touch me!" but maybe I garbled the words because all of a sudden his arms closed around me in a tackle, but instead of driving us forward he somehow swung me around, and when we fell, I landed on top of him with my back on his chest, his arms locked high around my ribs and our legs tangled boy-girl. I immediately started to squirm off and he tightened his arms and said, breathless, into my hair, "Stop. Relax."

So I did, heart pounding, afraid I was too heavy, afraid he could feel the heat in my blood, the want in my heart, afraid he'd hate the smell of my sandalwood oil, my shampoo, my skin, just afraid he would find a reason to end it.

He was breathing against my neck, warm, heavy breaths that smelled of maple syrup, and somehow I began to breathe with him, lying there on the verge of everything, eyes closed against the wide-open sky, body tensed and waiting, and little by little the arms locked around me eased open just enough to free his hands, leaving his fingers on my ribs, his thumbs nestled against the bottoms of my breasts, brushing the curves under the ugly blouse and the thin lace bra, and oh God, I didn't know if he didn't realize his thumbs were there or if he was doing it on purpose, didn't know if I should say something or leave it be, because he was breathing deeper now, breaths that lifted his chest and me on it, breaths that somehow slid his arms down across my stomach and his hands to low-rise territory, where they settled on my hips, holding me without effort, sinking me into him without moving, without him rising or me falling, with just the heat from where the back of my skort pressed against the front of his khakis.

And I think he felt it, too, because he shifted beneath me just a little, but it was a reaching shift, an upshift that hollowed his stomach and tightened his thighs and suddenly we weren't just playing anymore.

I don't know what would have happened if we hadn't heard little kid chatter coming down the sidewalk toward the park.

"Shit," Seth said, releasing me and sitting up.

Face burning, I quickly slid off him and became very busy smoothing my shirt and hair and skort. I was so dazed that I didn't know what to say—was there anything?—or how to act or what to even think.

"Come on," he said, giving me a hand up. He wasn't looking at me either, releasing me fast and turning away, bending to pick up his jacket as I retrieved my shoes and purse.

"Where are we going?" I said as we passed the mom with three kids heading for the swing set.

"Hell if I know," he said with a wry smile and ambled across the grass to the sidewalk.

I took a deep, shaky breath and caught up with him.

It's the weirdest feeling, walking next to someone you just laid on and yet still being so careful not to let your hand touch his while he's being just as careful not to touch yours, feeling so huge and aware of how awkward it is, and that awareness makes it even harder to walk normally. Your face feels hot and fake and obvious, and you can't even decide if your expression is right.

Nothing is in harmony, nothing is in sync.

"Look, don't worry about it," he said as we stopped at the corner and got ready to run across to the mall. "I mean technically nothing really happened so you should still be all right with Wynn."

And then the light changed and he started across the road.

I just stood there with the wind knocked out of me, watching him moving farther and farther away without turning to see if I was following, without waiting to see the effect of his words.

Technically, nothing really happened.

Technically?

Oh, God, my stomach.

All these people stopped at the light, watching me stand there humiliated and stricken.

He made it all the way across and turned to see where I was.

"Hey," he called, shading his eyes. "You coming?"

My heart was pounding in a hollow place, telling me to leave, to walk fast and faster until he could no longer see me, and then to crawl into a dark hole and curl up and bawl. To pick up the tiny, trampled scrap of pride I had left and get out, and I wish I could say I did, but all I could think was that if I made a stand now, I would have to leave and my day with him would end, and he would *let* it end and that would be it, forever.

"What happened?" he said when I finally jogged across, still carrying my heels and with my purse banging against my hip.

"Nothing," I said and, grabbing the light post for support, put my shoes back on. "Okay. Let's go."

So we cut across the parking lot to the mall, where, in a show of faith that we could still have a decent day, I bought a pair of pants and a shirt on sale for like 70 percent off and put them on so I wouldn't have to walk around in my uniform anymore.

"You got quiet," he said while we were sitting side by side on the ledge of a giant planter in the food court, drinking Orange Juliuses. "What's up?"

"Nothing," I said, skimming my straw along the top of the drink and sucking up the foam.

He snorted. "Right. Every girl I know says exactly the same thing when she's pissed and you ask what's wrong. 'Nothing.'"

"I'm not every girl," I said, swirling the straw around.

"Why do you guys do that, anyway?" he continued. "Why don't you just come right out and say what's bugging you, like, 'Look, asshole, you're really pissing me off.'"

"All right: Look, asshole, you're really pissing me off," I said sharply.

"Yeah, like that," he said, nodding as if satisfied, and gazed out over the food court.

I waited. And waited. "Well?" I said finally.

He glanced at me. "Well what?"

I stared at him, incredulous. "Well, aren't you even gonna ask me why?"

"I *knew* it." He heaved a sigh. "Okay, Hanna. Why are you pissed off?"

"No, forget it now," I said, insulted. "You don't really want to know, anyway."

"Oh my God," he said weakly. "Look, I'm asking, so just tell me already. I swear I really want to know."

"Well, that's too bad because I don't want to talk about it anymore," I said.

He stared at me, mouth agape, and kind of shook himself. "Well . . . okay, then."

I looked at him. "'Okay'? That's it? Are you kidding?"

"Holy *shit*," he breathed, and started to laugh. Caught my high-eyebrow haughty-bitch look and tried to stop, but the more he tried, the harder he laughed until he was bent over and spilling the last of his Orange Julius all over the polished floor.

"You know you're very weird," I said, trying to sound cold, but the snicker burst out, and oh, God, it felt so good to just stuff the hurt away and go back to this.

"Yeah, well, look who's talking." Grinning, he slid an arm around me in a quick hug.

That was the last time he touched me, and we didn't get personal again either. We went outside and hung out on the wall of the cement planter against the building, but he was back to flirty Seth, cute but separate, like he was holding himself at a distance even though he seemed in a decent mood. I caught him checking out other girls but I couldn't say anything so I just started watching other guys. There were more girls willing to look back at Seth and disrespect *me* than there were guys willing to disrespect Seth, so that only made me sink even more.

I hit rock bottom when a girl with a hatchet jaw and better highlights than mine paused and looking straight into Seth's gleaming eyes, stopped to bum a cigarette. She glanced at me—I guess she could tell we weren't going out or maybe she didn't even care—and then I swear she actually eased in between us, perched a skinny hip on the cement wall, and turned her back on me to face him!

Did he say, "Hey, you're blocking Hanna," or anything like that? No. He just kept flirting with her like I wasn't even there, and oh my God, I can take a lot of punishment and still keep my eye on the prize, but this was just so out of line that I don't know what I would have done—cried? Screamed? Threw a fit and strode off in a huff?—if a big, gleaming black Harley hadn't rumbled up to the curb with karate guy straddling the seat.

"Hanna," he said, pulling off his helmet and shaking out his beautiful, poisonous dreads. He had on a black T-shirt and his rude ink was right out there for all to see. "What's up?"

"Hey!" I cried, beaming and launching myself off the cement wall, totally ignoring the surprised silence next to me and, at that moment, crazy in love with karate guy. "Oh my God, where have you been?" I pranced over and stood so close he practically *had* to put his arm around my waist. "What a gorgeous bike! Is it new?" Turning my back on Seth, I gave karate guy an intense, pleading look like *Please play along. Please?*

His gaze shifted past me to Seth and the girl, and then back to me. He quirked an amused eyebrow, stroked his goat, and nodded like he got it, like he wanted nothing more in the world than to play stupid baby games with high schoolers. "I bought it because I knew you'd look hotter than hell riding on the back," he said with a lazy grin, twinkling at me and loud enough for Seth and the girl to hear. "Whoops," he said, ducking as I blushed and slapped at him. "Did I say that in front of your old man?"

"My what?" I said as if I had no clue, then turned and glanced at Seth. "Him? Oh, no. He's not my boyfriend, he's just . . ." I cocked my head like I was deliberating, then shrugged and said, "Some guy from school." And I turned away again, stung by the sight of hatchet girl and her skinny-hipped, S-shaped stance, groin out, boobs level with Seth's nose, and Seth's hand resting way too close to hers.

"Cool," karate guy said, "then hop on. I'll take you for a quick ride. Unless, uh . . ." He glanced at Seth again, eyebrows high, like he was giving him one last chance to step up.

"Oh, no, he doesn't mind, he's busy," I said with a dismissive wave as if I didn't give one shit about him picking up a girl while he was with me. "I'll be back," I said over my shoulder, took the extra helmet, and squeezed it down over my ears. And karate guy, who seemed to be enjoying the drama way too much, waited till I climbed on and then, twisting around to face me, buckled my chin strap and tucked my hair in around my cheeks. As if that wasn't enough, he touched the tip of my nose with his finger and said in a low, mischievous voice, "You want me to give 'em even *more* to talk about?"

"No, you're doing just fine," I said with a wicked look from under my lashes.

He laughed, which surprised me, as down at Crystal's he always seemed too cool to actually laugh but it was a good sound and I loved that Seth got to see an older guy treating me nice.

"Later, dude," karate guy said, smirking at Seth and completely ignoring hatchet girl.

I settled my hands low on his waist, he checked behind us, and we took off.

I glanced back—I know I shouldn't have but I couldn't help it—and hatchet girl gave me a knowing look like I was just too obvious and turned to Seth, who was already looking away from me.

Damn.

The bike was sleek and cool and scary as hell. Karate guy took me around the parking lot and out to the road. He waited for a break in traffic, then said, "Hold on," and in a rumbling surge of "holy shit" power, gunned it.

"Oh my God!" I cried, laughing as we roared away. "This is amazing."

"First bike ride?" he threw back.

"Yeah," I said, squinting over his shoulder at the road.

"Cool," he said. "Then enjoy." He turned off the congested main drag, and meandered through side streets, shaded lanes, and out onto an empty road where he opened it up and took my breath away.

"This motorcycle makes a very distinctive sound," I yelled at his helmet, in the spot where I figured his ear should be.

He laughed and shouted, "Never heard it put that way, but yeah, she does." And then, "So you into that dude back there or what?"

"Is it that obvious?" I said.

"Yeah, you were looking pretty miserable. Glad I showed up."

"You and me both," I said and squeezed him a little tighter. "Thank you." I laughed forlornly. "And how weird is this, anyway?"

"What, you and me?" he said. "Why not?"

He wasn't serious. He couldn't be. "Are you serious?"

"What would you say if I was?"

And it was the smile in his tone that freed me, that took me one step past who I *thought* he was and delighted me with who he was being right now, so I said, "I'd say you have no idea what you're getting yourself into."

"Suppose I said I'll take the chance," he said.

I bit my lip and snickered. "Well, then I'd invite you to my sixteenth birthday party in May so you can meet my parents."

The bike swerved, and cursing, he righted it and steered over to the curb. Turned and gave me an astonished look. "How old?"

"Fifteen, same as Crystal," I said with a cheery grin. "What, did you think I was older?"

"Uh, *yeah*." He stared at me. "I could go to jail for you. Like, right now."

"Nah," I said airily. "You're what, eighteen? That's no big deal."

"It is to the law," he said.

"That's dumb," I said. "First of all, everybody knows girls mature faster than guys, and second, you haven't done anything but give me a ride."

He gave me this look, half amusement, half disbelief, and shook his head. "You're gonna get me in trouble, girl." And then his eyebrows rose like he'd just thought of something else. "Isn't this a school day?"

"Mm-hmm," I said. "But it was so nice, we cut out."

"Oh, Jesus," he said. "C'mon, let me get you back to Romeo."

"Wait," I said, tugging on his dread. "Does this mean you're not coming to my birthday party?"

He laughed. "Ask me again when you're eighteen."

"You got it," I said and smiled because he was making it so easy to like him.

When we got back to the mall, not only was the cement planter where we'd been sitting abandoned but the bag with my uniform in it was gone too.

"Looks like lover boy got pissed and left," he said, as the bike idled at the curb. "Now what?"

"I don't know," I said, panicking. "I mean, I don't care about him but, oh my God, where's my uniform?"

"Think he took it with him?"

"No," I said immediately. "I think he would have said, 'I'm not babysitting her shit,' and left it there! Oh my God, my father's gonna kill me if I lost that uniform!" I hopped off the bike and ran over to see if maybe he'd tucked the bag down inside the planter.

Nothing.

Then I ran to the garbage can and tried to look in. I couldn't see, so I had to lift the whole top off, which was humiliating, but there was no bag in there either.

"Oh my God, where is it?" I said, stopping and staring around the parking lot.

Karate guy glanced at his watch. "I have to be at work in forty-five minutes, Hanna, but I don't want to just leave you here. What do you want to do?"

Kill Seth. *Kill* him.

"Can you give me five minutes?" I said, wringing my hands. "Let me just run in and see if maybe somebody left it at the lost and found? Please?"

"Go ahead," he said and cruised over to a parking space.

I ran to the first counter in Macy's and asked if anyone had turned in a bag.

No.

Bolted down the center of the mall, not even looking for Seth, and was almost past the food court when someone called, "Hanna."

I skidded to a stop and spotted him alone at a table. Frowning, I scanned the area but didn't see my bag. "What're you doing in here? Where's my stuff?"

He leaned back and shrugged. "Isn't it out there where you left it?"

"No! I only left it because I thought you'd watch it," I said. "Seth, my uniform's in there!"

He looked at me, eyes cool and face expressionless. "Well, you weren't too worried about it when you left, so I figured . . ." He shrugged again and glanced over to the pizza place where hatchet girl was in line. "Try lost and found. They probably have it."

I couldn't even begin to say what I wanted to, because if I did, I would have hit him, cursed him out, or burst into tears. Probably all three. So I just whirled and ran to lost and found, where yes, the bag was waiting. I took it and ran back past the food court, past him and hatchet girl, through Macy's, and out to karate guy, who, good as his word, was leaning against his bike waiting.

"Can you drop me off at home?" I asked. "I'll give you gas money, I swear."

He surveyed my face. "Guy's an asshole, huh?"

I nodded, near tears.

"Sure," he said. "Climb on. And don't insult me with the money thing again, okay?"

So I did and he got me home before noon. My mother wasn't there, she was over at Gran's, so I changed into sweats and crawled into bed, and when she came in, I told her I'd felt sick all morning and had stayed in the bathroom, never even went to homeroom, and finally got a ride home. I said I had a bad stomachache, which I did, and I must have looked like hell because instead of asking me all kinds of questions, she blamed it on the homemade sun-dried tomatoes she'd put in last night's salad, told me to rest, brought me a cup of hot tea with honey, and left me in peace.

Sometimes my mother's so good.

I saw Seth coming toward me down the far end of the hall the next day and I could tell by the slow way he was walking that he didn't really want to run into me, so I just took the side staircase, and problem solved.

Chapter 6

Helen

Lon and I loaded the car with the candied yams, a butternut squash casserole, two pumpkin pies, and a gallon jar of pickled green tomatoes and drove over to the Thurys for Thanksgiving dinner.

"Go slow," I said, balancing the pies on my lap as he pulled out of the driveway.

Freshly shaved, salt-and-pepper hair neatly combed to the side, the thin navy blue stripes on his favorite dress shirt making his eyes look even browner, he glanced across the car at me and said, "Well, will you look at that: a pretty woman with a pile of food sitting right there in my shotgun seat. Talk about having something to be thankful for."

"Oh, really," I said but couldn't help feeling pleased because I *had* taken pains to look nice, digging out the cranberry-colored blouse I'd worn back when I worked in an office and pairing it with my black slacks. I'd even put on earrings, something I hadn't done in years as I didn't have pierced ears and the levers on the backs of the shiny gold buttons always left painful scallops in my earlobes. "Stop trying to butter me up and keep your eyes on the road, old man."

"Impossible," he said and, with a cheeky grin, reached over and squeezed my knee. "Want to go parking later?"

"I'm not allowed," I said primly and, when he removed his hand, "Oh, hell, I didn't think you'd give up that easily."

"I haven't," he said, waggling his eyebrows. "Just wait till the ride home."

"I know what you're doing, you know," I said after a moment.

"Oh?" he said, sounding far too innocent. "What am I doing?"

"Distracting me," I said and smiled when he met my gaze. "Thank you."

"Don't mention it," he said gruffly and, reaching across the seat, took hold of my hand. "You're shaking. Do you want me to turn up the heat?"

"No," I said. "It's just nerves. I haven't seen her in so long . . ."

"Who, Hanna? Helen . . . my God, don't tell me that's what you've been so worried about?"

I hesitated—missing Hanna was one thing but not *all* things— then nodded.

"Well, you can stop because she's going to be as glad to see you as you are to see her."

"I hope you're right," I said softly and turned my gaze out the window, watching as we drove past the woods and around the bend that would lead us to the Thurys.

❧   ❧   ❧

He *was* right, and not even Hanna's curious look at my trembling or the catastrophic moment during dessert could tarnish the glow on the day.

Hanna met us at the door sporting flushed cheeks, bright eyes, and a beaming smile, looking taller, older, and rebelliously lovely in her antiholiday outfit of jeans, the opossum-patterned socks I gave her last Christmas, and a scoop-neck black sweater.

She hugged me hard but I hugged her harder, and when I finally stepped back to look at her, I found she was doing the same to me.

"It's trite and awful but I'm going to say it anyway," I said, laughing and wiping a shaky hand across my damp eyes. "I can't believe you're so grown-up!"

"And I got a job, too! Oh my God, Gran, I missed you so much," she burbled. "You look so pretty! You should wear earrings all the time. I'm serious. They make your—"

"Ahem," Lon said good-naturedly from behind me on the porch stoop. "I hate to interrupt, but these yams aren't getting any younger . . ."

"Oh, no way, you brought *yams*?" she said, and when I nodded, she snickered and said, "I can't believe you remember that! He's probably still working there, too, the jerk. Hi, Grandpa, come on in!"

Melanie and Wes came to greet us and take the food, although Hanna refused to surrender the gallon of pickled tomatoes and insisted on lugging that out to the kitchen herself. "I swear I've been dreaming about these things," she said, setting the jar on the cluttered counter and wrestling with the lid. "I'm serious. You don't know how bad I was hoping you'd bring them, and I was even gonna call and ask but . . ." She bit her lip. "I feel kind of mean for not helping you this year."

"Well, I missed your company, that's for sure, and a phone call would have been nice, but I managed to make it through," I said lightly, not wanting to spoil the day.

"So you're not mad at me?" she said.

"No," I said and laughed as she blurted, "Oh, yay!" and hugged me again.

That moment alone would have made the day perfect, but there were more, so many more . . .

Melanie, catching me before dinner, slipping a gift card into my hand and saying they'd won a drawing for a week's free groceries but hoped I would take it and put it toward the ingredients for all those delicious Christmas cookies I baked every year.

The expression on Lon's face when Wes offered him the chair at the head of the table, handed him the knife, and asked if he'd do the honor of carving the bird.

Hanna looking around, looking at me, and with a satisfied sigh, saying, *Cool. Our whole family is here.*

Wes asking if Saturday would be a good day for him to come and cut us some wood.

Hanna and I working side by side in the kitchen, her loading the dishwasher, me scraping the leftover turkey bits into a container to take back to the cats.

"So tell me about your boyfriend," I said and grinned at her sudden blush. "Oh-ho, so you *do* have one, then, hmm? Come on, let's hear it. *I know:* He's an egghead named Waldo who collects bottle caps and wears itchy argyle socks, right? No? Then he's one of those underfed goth boys who insists his name isn't Harold but something intense like Storm-Ominous, with fake black hair and little porcelain fangs he puts in to creep out the cafeteria ladies." I went on this way, making her laugh even as she protested that no, she didn't have a boyfriend, but okay, okay, there *was* someone she was mad at right now but she still might like and he might like her, too, but he was already going out with someone.

This dilemma, according to her, would be resolved with time because he went out with a lot of different girls, seeing as how he was hurt bad by the first girl he ever loved and now he never wanted to love anyone again, so basically all she had to do was hang in there and sooner or later she would get her chance to show him how perfect they'd be together.

I asked her why she thought they'd be perfect together and she stopped, gave this look, part puzzled, mostly irritated, and said, *Because I just know we would,* leaving me certain he was a raging fool who didn't deserve her but unable to say it because the happily ever after she was targeting was so far beyond anything I could give her.

෴   ෴   ෴

And it was during dessert, while Melanie was serving the coffee and I was handing out huge slabs of pumpkin pie topped with whipped cream, that Hanna sat up straight and said, "Hey, Gran, I know! Tell the story about how you and Grandpa met." She glanced at her mother. "Do you know it, Mom? Oh my *God*, it's so romantic."

I stared at her, stricken, and Lon went still, and the silence stretched and gradually the anticipation on Hanna's face turned to bewilderment and then embarrassment and she said, "What?" and I didn't know how to answer because no matter how frantically I searched my brain, I couldn't remember what I'd told her, what fairy tale I'd made up years ago because the truth was too raw to put into words, and finally Lon cleared his throat and, looking paler than normal, forced a weak smile and said, "Helen's busy serving the pie. Why don't you tell it, Hanna?"

"No, that's okay, forget it," Hanna said, staring down at the table. "It's not important." She pushed her plate away. "I'm done. 'Scuse me." She slid out of her chair and hurried from the room, pounding up the stairs and shutting her bedroom door behind her.

"Ah, the joys of a moody teenager," Melanie said after a moment, and her awkward laugh hung in the huge silence. "Last week I humiliated her by telling Sammi she'd gone to bed early. It seems I should have said something cooler." She shrugged. "She'll get over it, Helen. No harm done."

And I smiled and nodded, forced myself to hand Lon the slice of pie I'd been holding and swallow a few choking bites of my own, to make stilted small talk as if everything was fine while listening for the sound of a door that didn't open and a footfall on the stair that didn't come.

෴   ෴   ෴

We left soon after that, with Melanie calling up to tell Hanna we were leaving and Hanna shouting back in a monotone, "Bye, Gran, bye, Grandpa. Happy Thanksgiving," without even sticking her head out of her room.

"Helen, what the hell did you tell her?" Lon said as soon as we were shut safely in the car. "You didn't tell her the truth—"

"*No,*" I said, clenching my hands in my lap to try and still their shaking.

"Jesus Christ," he said on an exhale. "Then what did you say?"

"I don't remember," I said and burst into tears.

Chapter 7

Hanna

Wow.

I think Gran's losing it.

It's the only possible answer. How else could you ever forget the way you and your true love met?

No wonder she looked so freaked. I'd be freaked, too, if someday my granddaughter asked me how Grandpa Seth and I met, and I couldn't even remember. And no wonder Grandpa Lon scolded me. I bet he was embarrassed for her.

Now I feel kind of bad.

I should have just told the story myself. It would have been perfect for today, with Gran being seventeen and going to that Thanksgiving dance at the church, and Grandpa being twenty-two and driving through town on his way somewhere else, getting a flat tire, and going into the dance to see if anyone had a jack, taking one look at her dancing to *Moonlight Serenade* in her red taffeta dress with the wide neckline, and falling head over heels in love. Asking her to dance—they did a thing back then called cutting in, where if you were dancing with one guy and someone else wanted to dance with you, all he had to do was tap on your partner's shoulder and say,

"May I cut in?" and if the guy you were dancing with was a gentleman, he had to let him.

I think that's cool.

So Grandpa cut in and Gran said he was breathtaking, a handsome stranger with snowflakes melting in his hair and a strong, steady grip that felt like he was never going to let her go.

When their dance was over, he said, "I have some things to do but I'll be back to see you home, so don't leave without me." And she said, "You don't even know my name," and he said, "I don't know what it is now, but next year I'm hoping it will be Mrs. Lon Schoenmaker."

Oh my *God*, that's so romantic.

I wish there was some way to let Seth hear that story.

Maybe he would get the hint.

Right.

Chapter 8

Helen

There was a message from Hanna on the answering machine when we got home, saying she was sorry for putting me on the spot and that I shouldn't worry if I didn't remember how I met Grandpa because she's pretty sure that memory loss happens to a lot of old people—

"Good Lord," I said, hitting the pause button and staring at Lon, aghast. "She thinks I'm going senile!"

He stared back at me, lips twitching.

"No! I am not going to let that girl think I'm a doddering ancient who has to write her address in her underwear just so she can find her way home again," I said, tossing my purse onto the chair and struggling out of my coat.

Lon reached past me and hit play on the machine.

"—and it's totally natural, so I'm sorry I got all weird and I'll see you guys soon," Hanna said cheerfully and hung up.

I stood a moment, then reached up and yanked the clip-on earring from my dented, aching lobes. My hands were still shaking and the gold buttons rattled in my cupped palm. "Will you feed the cats for me, please? I'm going to bed."

"It's only seven thirty," he said.

"Well, I've been up since five and I'm exhausted," I said, pausing for a second to lean against him as I made my way past. My knees were trembling, my legs felt leaden, and I didn't know how I was going to make it all the way upstairs.

"She didn't mean anything by it," he said, sliding his arm around me. "She was just looking for an answer to something she didn't understand and that's what she came up with. Don't take it to heart."

"I won't," I said and, gripping the banister, crept up step by step, listening to the sounds of Lon going into the kitchen, putting away the food Melanie had sent home with us, and finally opening the back door and calling the cats into the porch to eat.

❧ ❧ ❧

But I *did* take it to heart, to the deepest core of my heart while lying awake for hours watching my foot twitch under the cover and being unable to stop it.

I thought of the research I'd done and of the possible causes of this palsy.

None were very promising.

Most were terrifying.

Then I thought that since no one but Lon knows the real reason behind my refusal to go see a doctor you, Hanna, will someday be forced to make up a reason, to decide my reluctance was sheer pigheadedness or cheapness or, God forbid, that insulting catchall senility.

It made me angry and then sad because I'd always believed I'd have time to clear up the lies I'd told you, that someday when you were grown and married with a little one of your own we would sit on the porch in the afternoon sunlight, watching as your baby played with my newest batch of stray kittens, and you would understand when I explained why I'd buried the truth and woven you so many happily ever afters, because you had a daughter of your own now and would do anything to protect her.

You would understand my need to preserve your faith in me, to live up to that shine in your eyes that said I was your hero, and to fight the fierce sickness that filled my heart at the thought of ever letting you down.

You would understand me then, Hanna, and you would forgive me, oh God, I hoped you would, and your love wouldn't lessen at hearing my terrible truths but remain as steady and strong as it was when you were little and you knew that Grandma Helen would rather die than ever let anything or anyone hurt you.

I thought we would have that time together, but now I see how badly I'd wanted to believe in fairy tales, too.

Chapter 9

Hanna

Black Friday and I definitely earned my salary today.

There was a long line of people who wanted their pets' picture taken with Santa, mostly dog owners who never stopped cooing, "Sit *down*, Tiara, and stop that bad-girl barking or Mommy is going to take you right home!" or guys doing just the opposite, jerking their dogs' choke collars and bellowing, "Knock it off!"

I felt bad for the dogs and worse for the cats in the carriers, hauled out and handed to a fat guy in a fuzzy suit while all around them dogs were going crazy.

What a mess.

Today is the first day of deer season.

The shooting is sporadic from dawn to dusk every day until the season pauses for Christmas, and then starts up again just in case there's still anything left alive in the woods.

I'm being sarcastic because this is not my favorite time of year.

My mother doesn't like it, either, and gets up at like 5 a.m. in the dark, lays out the fluorescent pink knit hats we're supposed to wear from now on whenever we go outside just so no one mistakes us for deer and shoots us because, yes, it does happen.

I wore mine at breakfast and cracked her up.

My father says the hats are *not* pink; they're Day-Glo orange, but just to tweak him, every time we see someone wearing one we say, *Oh, what a cute little pink hat!*

My father says someday our smart mouths are going to get him punched in the nose.

Our property is posted NO HUNTING and so is Gran's, because we believe everything needs at least one place in the world where it can rest and be safe.

There's nothing we can do about the guy who built the cabin next door, though. He shows up in his business suit late every Friday, changes into full-blown camo, and plays weekend warrior, building a blind to hide behind and putting out acorn blocks and other bait to keep the hungry deer around so he doesn't actually have to get off his butt and work up a sweat trying to kill them. He doesn't eat them, either. Just saws off the bucks' heads for trophies and leaves the does there to rot.

Gran and I found one of the carcasses once when we were out walking her property line during an early spring thaw. The doe's corpse was horrible—sunken, gnawed, and rotten—and heartbreaking, since it looked like she had been trying to get back to the safety of Gran's woods and just couldn't run fast enough.

She hates this guy for a lot of reasons but mostly because when the does are killed it means the fawns lose their mothers after having them for only maybe six months and are left to fend for themselves through winter, the harshest season.

She gets all freaked when she says it; her chin gets really firm, and she adds in a big voice (even though no one is arguing with her), "And since rut usually occurs before the season opens, the does they're killing are pregnant. How do you *gut* a pregnant doe, for God's sake?"

This is when my father and Grandpa turn green, mumble a lame excuse, and sidle out of the room so as not to attract any Amazonian woman outrage.

Sometimes before they leave, Grandpa will wink at me, then tiptoe over to Gran pretending like he's scared of her and either swoop down and give her a loud, smacking kiss on the cheek or pinch her butt, which drives her crazy, and then, laughing, hurry out of the room.

It's really cute and always makes Gran blush.

I hope me and Seth are that cute someday.

It started snowing today. Me and Sammi were out in the courtyard along with half the student body and Seth came over to us. He smiled, reached out, fluffed the snowflakes from my hair, and said, "You look like a snow bunny with big chocolate cupcake eyes."

While I stood there hopelessly melting, he added, "Merry Christmas if I don't see you again before the end of the day," and ambled away.

Oh, God.

Maybe I should just go back down to Crystal's and let karate guy throw me around a little more. I know it would hurt less than this.

Chapter 10

Hanna

Christmas was small but good.

Gran cried when I gave her the five cases of cat food, then cried harder when we gave her the giant bags of cracked corn and the extra veterinary gift card my parents had bought before my father was laid off.

She got even more emotional when she gave us our gifts, a home-made cookbook of all her favorite recipes for my mom, a batch of homemade peanut butter fudge for my father, and an excellent pair of fat white crocheted mittens and a scarf for me.

"What?" I said, crouching in front of her and taking her trembling hands when she started crying. "I love them, they're perfect, I swear. What?"

"I wanted to do so much more," she said finally, gripping my hands hard.

"Oh, stop, come here," I said, rising and giving her a hug because now I was starting to get all teary, and if I went, I knew my mother would, too, and then we'd all have a very soggy Christmas.

After we ate I went up and changed into the hot new black angora sweater dress Crystal left for me under our tree (I gave her the same dress in red) and my new pair of high-heeled black boots and headed down to her house.

When I got there she had her dress on, too, so we took pictures and were being so loud that her parents and her brother down in the family room yelled back, wanting to know what was up, so of course we planned an entrance, with her going downstairs first and me following her down the four carpeted stairs to her family room.

Except that when I stood at the top of the carpeted stairs, my boot sole slid over the edge of the step, my knees buckled, and I skied down on my shins, landing at the bottom in a humiliated heap.

Her mother ran to help me up, but Crystal, her brother, and her father were laughing so hard they were crying, and her mother kept trying not to laugh, but these moist giggles kept bursting out of her until finally she gave in and fell back against the wall, roaring.

Once I saw I was okay, I stood up, smoothed the dress, and started laughing, too. Crystal's mom hugged me and I had just stopped dying of mortification when somebody knocked and Crystal staggered over to let them in.

It was karate guy, who walked into the foyer without noticing me, shrugged off his leather jacket, and slung it over the coatrack. Shaking out his hair, he took one step into the room, spotted me, and went still.

I really liked that reaction.

"Whoa," he said as a slow smile crept across his face. "So *this* is where Santa left my present."

"Merry Christmas," I said. "You missed a great show. I just fell down the stairs."

But it was like he hadn't even heard me. "Damn, woman." He gave me a thorough up-and-down and shook his head. "Are you *sure* you're only fifteen?"

"Fifteen and a half," I said, laughing. "Want to teach me how to flip somebody again?"

His gaze met mine. "I'm pretty sure you already know."

And that flustered me because he was still smiling but his eyes were all dark and velvety and serious, and the room was hot and my knees were starting to sting from their downhill run, and the rest of me was tingling, and everyone was watching and—

"Another one bites the dust," Crystal's father said and snorted. "Keep it in your pants, Jesse. She's jailbait."

"Dad!" Crystal said, whacking the back of his head. "Don't be disgusting."

"What's disgusting about that?" he said, surprised. "I was young once, too, you know."

"Mom, will you make him stop?" Crystal said. "He's grossing me out."

"Come on, handsome," Crystal's mom said, prodding her husband to his feet. "Let's go into the kitchen and you can talk dirty to me while I spice the cider."

They left, the guys left for a party, and I followed Crystal back upstairs, where I found out that karate guy's full name was Jesse Yennet and his mom had been our fifth-grade art teacher.

I was like, "What's his deal?" and Crystal gave me this interested look and said, "Why? Do you like him?"

"No, he's just always nice to me and I'm curious, okay?"

"Mm-hmm," she said and laughed. "What? I think you guys make a cute couple."

"Sure, especially since once my parents see his big 'fuck' tat, my father will tattoo his work boot against my butt. Are you *kidding*?"

And then she said Jesse got it from some hole-in-the-wall place after his mom was diagnosed with ovarian cancer and almost died, because that was pretty much how he felt about the world.

"When was this?" I said.

"When we were in sixth grade, don't you remember?" Crystal said. "She left in the middle of the semester and took like a year's leave of absence because she was so sick. Jesse was what, a freshman or a sophomore?"

"But she made it, right?" I said.

"Yeah, but he thought she was going to die and his dad was totally focused on her and Jesse just kind of got lost trying to deal with it. He started partying way too much and dropped out of school in junior year and got arrested for driving without a license but they went easy on him because of his circumstances—"

"You knew all this and you never told me?" I said.

"Why would you have cared?" she said, amused. "Everybody's got a story behind them, Hanna. You know that. You read."

"Well yeah, but that's fiction. This is like, *real*."

"Well, don't feel sorry for him because his mom's okay now and he quit partying and got his brown belt in karate and his GED. He's an apprentice stone mason and that's union so he makes really good money. And he's got that new bike and . . . oh, yeah, you already know about that part," she said, nudging me and grinning.

"Yeah," I said absently.

Can you even? I mean, I had no idea there could be so much to karate guy.

Jesse.

ↄ৩   ↄ৩   ↄ৩

I got home as Gran and Grandpa were just leaving so I changed and walked the deer path with them, putting down the corn and some apples as a holiday treat because the second wave of deer-hunting season began at sunrise, the day after Christmas.

On the way back I couldn't help wondering if peace on Earth really *was* supposed to be a sentiment people meant for only a day.

And right as I crossed through the gap in the little woods between our properties, I got a text from Seth.

Merry Xmas.

I stared at it with growing wonder, and then, shaking a little from both cold and happiness, replied, *Merry Xmas to you, too.*

A pause, and then: *Party at Connor's NY's Eve. Want to go?*

I clapped my hand over my mouth, eyes huge, and let out a muffled half laugh, half sob, then, getting a grip, punched out, *What about Bailey?* Freaked, deleted it, and replied, *I need a ride.*

I'll come get you.

I said, *OK,* and danced all the way home.

❦ ❦ ❦

I called Sammi and told her how he might come get me on New Year's Eve.

"Do you believe him?" she said. "I mean, I'm not trying to jinx it or anything but . . ."

"I know," I said because she didn't need to say it: What if he said he was coming and then just didn't show up?

❦ ❦ ❦

Seth hasn't texted me again but I've been operating as if he *is* going to come over and maybe even hang out for a while before the party, so I spent an insane day cleaning my room, trying to find a way to make it sexy and alluring and comfy and a major reflection of me all without letting my mother know that's what I was trying to do.

Well, I mean the sexy and alluring parts.

"So who is this guy that I've never met or even heard mentioned that I'm supposed to let upstairs into my fifteen-year-old daughter's bedroom on New Year's Eve?" my father said, lowering the paper and arching an eyebrow. "Want to fill me in on this, Hanna, or am I going to have to grill him when he gets here?"

"Mom," I said, giving her an impatient look. "You said you wouldn't let him do that!"

"Really," he said, sounding interested and glancing at my mother, who had covered her face with her hands and was shaking her head. "What else am I not allowed to do in my own home when Prince Charming is here?"

"Call him *that*," I said, freaking. "And please, *please* don't wear those dorky reading glasses or do that killer-grip handshake thing or make two thousand trips upstairs to get dumb things, because it's *so* obvious—"

"Good," he said, nodding. "I *want* it to be obvious. No hanky-panky—"

"*Mom!* That *word*!"

"You're not allowed to say *hanky-panky,* either," my mother said, giving him a twinkling look. "But don't worry, it's not only you. I'm not allowed to wear my bunny-head slippers—"

"*God,* no," I said, shuddering.

"Or sing any of my lame songs or . . . what was the last one?" she said.

"Ask him if he's thought about what he's going to go to college for because that's just so . . . ugh . . . I can't stand it," I said, not missing the wry look they exchanged. "And don't wear your ugly mom jeans, either, okay? Wear the newer ones."

"You getting all this?" my father said.

"Let me write it down," my mother said, smirking and reaching for a pen.

"No!" I hollered. "Then you'll leave it out on the counter or something and he'll see it and know it's a big deal and he can't know that *ever*."

"Oh my Gawd," my father said, clapping a hand to his chest. "He'll *know*."

"You guys give me a pain," I muttered, but I wasn't really mad and they knew it, so I grabbed the Pledge and ran back up to my room to give it an overhaul it hadn't seen since I'd graduated eighth grade.

     ᙓ   ᙓ   ᙓ

Every shirt I own is stupid and ugly.

All my jeans make me look fat.

My new sweater dress is too dressy, but Crystal got a nice, tight plum-colored hoodie she said I could borrow, so maybe that with black cords and my new black boots?

He should call so I know what time he's coming to get me tomorrow before I go completely over the edge.

What if he met somebody else and made plans with them and I just don't know it yet?

I think I would have to quit St. Ignatz and go back to public school just so I would never have to see him again.

     ᙓ   ᙓ   ᙓ

He called and he can't get the car but his buddy Phil said he'd drive us to the party if Sammi came, too.

I said, "Oh. And what did you say?"

He said, "I said it's good with me as long as it's good with Hanna and Sammi." Silence. (And thank God he couldn't see me writhing around on my bed and biting my own arm to keep from shrieking with joy.) "So do you think she'll go?"

I pulled my gnawed-up forearm from my mouth and, wiping it on the comforter, said, "Oh, yeah, definitely." I was so over the rainbow that I almost forgot to give him my address but he reminded me, and that made it seem all the more real.

The last thing I said was, "And if something happens and you can't come—"

"I'll let you know," he said and it sounded like he was smiling. "Okay?"

Oh, yeah.

I think I'm in a dream.

Or maybe it was the shot of blackberry brandy on an empty stomach.

Whatever it is, I don't want it to end.

It was so easy having Seth and Phil, the good little parochial schoolboys, come in, say hello to my parents and back up my 'going to the movies and out to eat' story without a hitch, then climbing into the backseat with Seth and leaving poor Phil alone up front while we drove over and picked up Sammi.

Seth had his arm along the back of the seat behind me and only moved it to smoke a joint. I didn't smoke because I didn't want to forget any of what would happen tonight or say anything stupid or miss my chance by moving too slow, but there was plenty of secondhand smoke, so that's probably why the first part of the night seems a little blurry.

Walking into the party with Seth, having everyone there see his arm around me and mine locked around him was almost too intense. My knees were weak, my face hot, and I couldn't stop trembling with excitement. Finally, Seth looked down at me, smiled, and said, "Cold?"

The place was like a steam bath but what was I going to say? "No, I just can't take being close to you"? so I nodded and he pulled me closer, which only made it worse, and that was why I decided on the brandy.

Anything to help me ease down a little and get some self-control back.

So we hung out and he talked to some of his friends, and me and Sammi kept exchanging excited eyeball messages across the room. There was food but I didn't eat because I didn't want to get caught chewing if he ever decided to kiss me. I know we talked but all I could focus on was his hand, warm at the back of my neck under my hair, sliding across to one shoulder, then down over my bra strap to the curve of my back right above my low-rise cords, like he was exploring my landscape, and my God, I was dying.

Finally, he leaned down, put his mouth against my ear, murmured, "Come on, it's too crowded in here," and led me through the knots of kids, up the stairs, and into the first unoccupied bedroom.

He closed and locked the door, turned to me standing there trembling in the dark, and with a smile in his voice, said, "Where'd you go?"

"I'm here," I whispered, and then his arms came around me, and an exhale swept out of me carrying all the strength I had left. I melted against him and lifted my face, and his mouth found mine, and oh, God, the sweetness was unbearable. I think he felt it, too, because he just kept kissing me as we found the bed and sank onto the edge of it, as he eased me back and stroked my arm, my hair, settled a hand on my waist and slid it to my stomach. I tensed when he did that, not on purpose but because he was making my whole body crazy for him, so he moved his hand back to my waist. I put my arms around his neck and pulled him down, wanting to feel his heartbeat against me.

I don't know how long we kissed but I was nearly senseless from the heat when I felt his hand ease up my side to my ribs, and it was like a drop of cold water plunked right down on the center of my sizzling delirium, not enough to put it out but just enough to wake me up a little. I brought my arm down, trapping his hand from advancing, and he smiled against my mouth and moved his hand, only to slip it back up again a few minutes later.

I stopped him again and made a low *un-un* in the back of my throat without ever breaking the kiss. He drew back slightly, searching my face and murmured as if surprised, "You're not like I thought you were."

"No," I whispered, gazing back, half hurt, half thrilled, because he saw me now, the real me, not the flirty school Hanna but the *girl,* and then he smiled this wry little smile like the joke was on him and kissed me again.

We talked for a little bit, nothing big, just teasing stuff, and about ten minutes later got up and went back to the party in time to watch the ball drop in Times Square, yell Happy New Year, and kiss right there in front of everyone. I went into the bathroom afterward, brushed my bed head (finally, Seth-induced bed head!), and put on fresh gloss, but there was no way to tone down my pink cheeks or the brilliance in my eyes.

Sammi caught me in the hall and, pulling me aside, whispered, "Oh my God, did you do it with him?"

"No, he didn't even get up my shirt," I whispered back.

"Well, that's not what it looks like."

"Well, I can't help that," I said and was so happy that, when we went back downstairs and I saw Seth sitting in the corner of the couch, having a beer and talking to a couple of guys, I didn't even really mind that he'd put himself in a place I couldn't get to. Instead, me and Sammi started talking to two guys from Connor's block and it didn't take long for Seth to come put his arms around me and start joking around and feeding me potato chips. I was flying so high that I stood on tiptoe and whispered, "So now you're my love slave, right?" and waited for him to laugh, and he did, well, it wasn't a laugh exactly but he gave me that same wry smile and his gaze went all distant. So I quickly told him I was only kidding but it lessened something some-how, and nothing I said or did after that brought the connection back to that same heady level.

And it killed me because I want to know him, *all* of him, every-thing about him, and I want him to know about me, to ask me all my thoughts and my dreams and what I love and hate . . . everything. All the real, true love things below the surface, all the secret hopes and stuff you never tell anyone but the people you really trust, the ones you know won't use it against you.

I wanted me and Seth to be like that more than anything.

He got Phil to drive us back to Sammi's at two and kissed me good night, but it gave me a gray feeling, like I'd finally had my chance and blew it, which was, in fact, the truth, as I had apparently been good enough to be with but not good enough to formally ask out, and that just broke my heart.

Gran and Grandpa came for New Year's Day dinner but they didn't stay long because Gran didn't feel good. She's stopped waitressing part-time because she's kind of shaky and she even brought her own travel mug because she says it's the best way to drink without spilling.

She asked me if I'd read any good books lately and when I said no, because I hadn't been over to peruse her bookcases in a while, she offered to lend me one of her book club selections and I said sure, okay, because I didn't have anything better to do and, let's face it, the phone wasn't exactly ringing off the hook.

So I went back with them after dinner was over and while I was there she asked me if I knew how to list things on eBay, because she was thinking about selling her collection of Hummels, as she couldn't dust them anymore and they were probably worth something.

I said sure, why not, and spent the rest of the day writing descriptions of old-fashioned, foreign-looking knickknacks and showing Grandpa how to navigate the auction site.

How do I get roped into these things?

Chapter 11

Helen

I am in the pantry sorting the remaining vegetables and removing any that shows signs of spoiling when Lon appears in the doorway. "Helen."

"You're in my light," I say absently, examining the last of the beefsteaks.

"Helen," he says again, and this time I hear the tight wheeze in his voice, the urgency, and the beefsteak rolls from my hand and onto the floor with a soft, dull plop, and I hear myself say, "Lon?" in a voice I would have never thought was mine. "What is it?"

He sags against the door frame, one hand pressed to his chest, and struggling for breath. "Call the . . . ambulance."

Chapter 12

Hanna

Gran called my mother and said Grandpa had another heart attack and was in the hospital. She said they're monitoring him and having visitors would be too stressful but asked if I would go over to their house before dusk every day and put out the deer food, feed the stray cats, and fill the bird feeders, because she'd be spending most of her days there with him. My mother told her I would.

I hope Grandpa gets well soon, because my mother said Gran would be lost without him.

That's so sad.

I hope someone will be lost without me someday.

Serepta is lonely without Gran and follows me around while I get her food and water, so of course I have to sit in my chair and pet her before I put out all the other cat food.

Good thing Gran left written instructions because I have to open seven cans, put them out on plates around the yard, then refill the water and dry food bowls.

At first I thought it was a giant pain, going through all this work every day just to feed some wild cats, but when they started inching toward the food, I changed my mind. They're thin and scraggly and so wary, like they think I'm going to kick them or something. It makes me wonder what kinds of terrible things happened to them before they found their way here.

Most of them were dumped by people, and if it wasn't for Gran, these cats would have died of starvation a long time ago.

Talk about *real* community service.

I did some research on feeding deer, just for the fun of it, and found out that giving them corn in the winter isn't such a great thing, and that if they really need food to survive it should be hay, or even cutting down a few trees so they have fresh browse.

Feeding them corn when it isn't a natural food supply for the season can actually do more harm than good.

Hmm.

What's that old saying about the road to hell being paved with good intentions?

Gran's going to hate knowing that all this time we might have been hurting them more than helping them.

I think I'll tell her later, when she's not so stressed.

In the meantime, I'm going to ask my father if we can get some hay.

Sammi finished her community service requirement. She thinks I'm nuts for not letting guidance know I fell off the list, but I'm not telling them now. God, then I'd have to go to stupid summer school or something to make it up, so forget it. I'll worry about it next year. I can always do double the time if I have to. I told Sammi that and made her swear on her mother's life that she would never mention the phrase *mandatory community service* in front of my parents because I don't want to remind them of it, either. She swore but she still thinks I'm crazy.

I'm not crazy. I just want to be available in case something wonderful happens this summer.

es   es   es

The first day of spring.

Seth stopped at my locker, picked up a strand of my hair, tickled my nose with it, smiled, and said, "Just don't want you to forget me, pretty lady."

I could kill him for giving me just enough to get all hopeful again, every single time.

Chapter 13

Helen

I come to the hospital every day and the nurses in the ICU are very helpful. They bring me a chair and a box of tissues, lower the lights, and leave me alone to sit beside Lon.

"I love you," I say quietly and try to stop shaking before touching his arm but it's impossible. He looks so old and frail in the hospital bed, so caught in the tangle of IV lines and monitors, so far away from me in his sedation that I don't know how to reach him. He's never been out of reach before—not since the beginning anyway, when I wasn't supposed to fraternize with him—and this separation terrifies me.

"Don't you leave me, old man," I whisper, holding his hand, bending my head, and letting the tears fall. "You told me you would never leave me, so don't you do it. You have to rest and get well, Lon. You have to come home. You do."

He has to, because I don't know how I could live without him.

Chapter 14

Hanna

Tomorrow is my birthday. Sammi is coming home with me after school and then we're sleeping over Crystal's, since her brother is throwing the first keg party of the season and we're invited.

My mother woke me up with the same song she always plays on my birthday, some dinosaur named *It's a Beautiful Morning*. I used to love it when I was younger and she made a big fuss over me, but come on, I'm sixteen now, okay?

Still, she dances in, invading my room and opening the blinds, but no matter how crabby I act, she just keeps singing until I peek an alligator eye out from under the covers and she knows I'm up.

Okay, honestly? I love my birthday.

It's a day when *anything* can happen.

When I got to school Sammi was waiting in the courtyard with a shiny red *Happy Birthday* balloon that only lived long enough to tell the world (including Seth) that it was my big day before a bunch of seniors grabbed it and sucked out the helium.

I didn't mind because at least it had gotten the word out, and that was the whole point.

The only dark cloud is that me and Seth haven't really talked lately, and once again, I don't know why. I *never* know why with him. He doesn't look mad when we bump into each other, or disgusted or anything, he just sort of recedes and does his friendly but distant thing where something is off but I can't pinpoint what.

It's maddening.

And according to Sammi, who saw him in the hall with his current girlfriend Solange this morning, he has a big hickey on his neck almost hidden under his hair.

That's not good birthday news.

Anyway, Sammi bought me pizza in the caf, which was nice, and we brought it out to the courtyard and hung out on the curb eating and keeping an eye out for Seth, who of course never showed up.

Maddening, I tell you.

"What if nothing good happens?" I said, leaning back on my hands. "I mean, this is my *birthday*, Sammi. *Something* has to happen."

"Maybe he'll dump Solange," Sammi offered, drawing up her legs and resting her chin on her knees. "That'd be a good present, right?"

I shrugged. "Only if I was next."

"Do you really still want to be?" she said, glancing at me.

"Yeah," I said without hesitation.

Sammi sighed.

"What?" I said.

"He dumped Solange," she said and met my startled gaze. "I heard it in the pizza line."

"Oh my God, why didn't you tell me?" I said.

She shrugged and reached for a pebble.

"I knew it," I said, jumping up and brushing pizza crust crumbs off my skort. "I *knew* this was gonna be a good day."

"Where are you going? Like I don't already know," she added in an undertone, tossing the pebble back onto the driveway.

"To give Seth a chance to give me my birthday kiss," I said, nudging her with my foot. "Come on."

She shaded her eyes with her hand and peered up at me. "Why don't you wait until *he* comes to *you* for a change?"

"Because you know he won't," I said, shifting impatiently.

"Right," she said. "Isn't that kind of the whole point?"

"Not on my *birth*day," I said, scowling. "God, Sammi, I have *one wish,* and why should I just sit around *hoping* it happens when maybe I can do something to *make* it happen? You know I'm not exactly the sit-back-and-take-whatever-comes-to-me type."

Sammi arched an eyebrow. "Except when the whatever is him."

"*No,*" I said coldly, but that was a giant lie and we both knew it, so I abandoned my snotty self and resorted to begging. "Come on, Sammi, come with me. Pleeease?"

She did but I lost her outside the media room to some junior guy, so I told her I was headed for the upstairs hall if she wanted to catch up. And then I walked and looked and, finally, right before the next bell rang, I spotted Seth and a bunch of seniors climbing out of a car in the parking lot. I stepped down the hall out of sight, listened to their approaching laughter, and right before they came in, set down my purse and crouched to fuss with my shoe.

They swept in reeking of pot and having some kind of sports argument.

I picked up my purse and rose, searching out Seth in the mix. He was talking to the guy next to him and didn't seem to see me, so I said, "Hey," as he passed.

He glanced my way, eyes bloodshot, and said, "Oh, yeah, hey, how're you doing?" and went back to his conversation.

I ducked to search for something in my purse, just in case anyone turned around, but no one did. And I should have left, I should have but I didn't, because I thought maybe he'd come back, and that's when the voices drifted to me, one kid saying, "Man, she's been dogging you all year. Why don't you just do her already and get it over with?"

Seth's response was too low to be heard, but the following burst of laughter wasn't too low at all.

Neither was the single sharp crack as my heart broke.

I couldn't even think for the rest of the day. All I could do was sit there replaying the laughter and getting sicker and sicker. Teachers called on me and I just said, "I don't know," to whatever they asked. Sammi asked me what happened and I just shook my head and said, "I'll tell you tonight," because I couldn't bear to say all the things that were rising into my mind.

I thought I'd been so careful, secretly restructuring hall routes, just happening to be in all the places he was, occasionally dating other guys so he wouldn't think all my hopes and dreams revolved around him . . .

But they knew.

Stoned guys, deaf and dumb to all but sports, partying, and their dicks, knew.

And if *they* knew, then everyone else knew, too.

Seth knew.

I hadn't been subtle, I'd been obvious.

I'd been *dogging* him.

Oh, God, just the word made me want to puke.

I was so miserable that I never even noticed the thousand-year-old nun who creaked up and snagged me for being out of uniform with my black stockings, so I had to buy a brown pair from the office, which apparently carried only the Original Yodeling Goatherd Brand of Thickest, Ugliest, Lowest-Hanging-Crotch Panty Hose in the Entire Free World, and put them on.

Wynn passed me in the hall and said, "Hey, happy natal day!" and gave me a big smile. Connor's girlfriend Teresa stopped and asked if I had anything good planned, and in the heartbeat before I answered, I realized that whatever I told her would get back to Connor and then to Seth, and if I ever wanted to make a stand and end this before I had no pride left at all, it would have to be now.

"Oh, yeah," I said, studying my reflection in my locker mirror. "Me and Sammi are heading down to an all-night kegger some guys I know are throwing for my birthday." I fluffed my hair. "Ought to be a blast."

"Sounds like it," she said. "Is it an open house or invite only?"

"Invite only," I said without hesitation. "They're not from this school and they're kind of older. Sorry."

"No problem," she said, smiling. "I just figured it was worth asking, since we're always up for a good party. Well, have a great time and don't do anything I wouldn't do."

I snorted a laugh and said, "Then it had better be a short list, Ter."

And she grinned and walked off.

I shut my locker and headed in the opposite direction.

Chapter 15

Hanna

"Where have you been?" Sammi said when she caught me at my locker at the end of the day.

I shrugged and jammed my books onto the shelf. No homework this weekend. Not on my birthday.

"Hanna." She grabbed my arm and leaned in close. "What happened? Seth came up to me and said he was trying to find you to wish you a happy birthday but you were, like, gone."

"Yup," I said. "I am. Gone and done."

She drew back, eyebrows high. "What does *that* mean?"

"It means that everybody in this place except you can kiss my ass, okay?" I said, slamming my locker. "I'm done with all of them." I gave the leg of my granny tights a vicious yank. "We'll be out of here in like three weeks, and you know what? Nobody's gonna be asking me out or calling me over the summer to see if I'm even still alive, so why am I putting myself through all of this? How long am I going to beat my head against the wall, getting all excited, getting my hopes up every time he looks at me, Sammi? I'm like a bad joke. I get stepped on, I come back for more. I get shoved aside, I come back again. What the hell am I doing waiting for him? I have to get it through my thick head that it's *just not going to happen*."

"I didn't mean it would *never* happen," Sammi said, touching my arm.

"Yeah, well, you know what?" I said, shouldering my purse and starting down the hall. "I'm tired of waiting. I'm tired of the whole stupid thing. So I'm done. Period. The end."

Sammi caught up and walked beside me. "Really?"

"Mm-hmm," I said. "Do you have to go to your locker?"

"Yeah, my overnight bag's in there," she said.

"Good, then let's go this way," I said, veering off to take a staircase we never used.

"Oh my God, Hanna, I can't believe you just did that," she said in a low voice after I kicked open the doors and strode through into the empty vestibule. She grabbed my arm and looked back over her shoulder. "Didn't you see him?"

"Who?" I said, clattering down the stairs.

"Stop!" she hissed, yanking on me. "Seth! He was coming right toward you—"

The doors flew open on the landing above us, and I looked up to see Seth leaning over the railing, grinning down at me.

"Hey," he said.

I arched an eyebrow.

"Happy birthday," he said.

Sammi nudged my ankle.

"Thanks," I said and started to leave.

"Hey," he said again.

I paused, teeth gritted, and looked up.

"I owe you a birthday spanking."

I snorted and kept walking.

"Hey."

"What?" I snapped and stopped again.

"You mad or something?"

And the absurdity of it, the fact that two hours ago I would have given anything to have him thudding down the stairs toward me, looking curious, maybe even puzzled, giving Sammi the chance to mutter, "Meet you at my locker," and leaving me there alone with him in this unpopular, unused staircase, wasn't lost on me. Neither was the fact that I was just dead inside, squashed flat by chronic disappointment.

"No, not at all," I said. All emotion had receded, pulled out like low tide, leaving my brain an empty ocean bottom.

He studied my face. "Yeah, you are. Come on, I can see it. You have a glass head, Hanna. I can read you, and you are seriously pissed off."

"Really," I said, because that just made it worse. "Well, think what you want." I turned to leave, but he grabbed my arm.

"Hey," he said, frowning. "You don't have to get shitty. I just wanted to say happy birthday, okay? God."

And that's when the tide returned, swept in like a boiling tsunami at that chiding *God,* as if I had been surly and ungrateful, like I was wrong for not being a happy, eager puppy leaping for any scrap, for daring to have a will and an opinion of my own, for biting the hand that, when he felt like it, might pet me.

I could feel the tears gathering behind my eyes and my nose starting to sting, and if there was one thing I didn't want to do, it was start bawling, because that would show him that he could hurt me and he didn't deserve that kind of power.

"I have to go," I said without looking at him.

"Not until you tell me what's up," he said.

"*Nothing,* all right? It's my birthday and I'm going to a party and you know what? I can't wait. I can't wait to get out of here and be with people who aren't just out for what they can get!" My voice cracked. "Now get *offa* me." I wrenched free and stalked out.

I waited until we were home and safely ensconced in my room to tell Sammi all of it, from the minute I left her at lunch to my parting words to Seth.

"If he can read me, Sammi, then he's known since the first day that I liked him and he's been playing me all year," I said, dropping my vest on the bed and unzipping my skort. "Got nobody to talk to? Wait one second and Hanna will show up. Want to cut out? Ask Hanna; she'll risk everything just to follow you around for a day."

"You weren't that bad," Sammi said, shaking her head in amusement at the sight of my saggy-crotch panty hose.

"No, worse," I said grimly, peeling off the geriatric tights and flinging them toward the wastebasket. "I hate him so much, I can't even say."

"No offense, but I've heard that before," Sammi said, opening her bag.

"Yeah, well, this time it's true," I said, yanking the ugly yellow blouse up over my head and tossing it onto the laundry pile in the corner. "I'm done following him around. In exactly"— I glanced at my watch—"two hours and forty-three minutes, I will be born, and I've already decided this is going to be a stellar, Seth-free year."

"Well, good, because that's exactly what I got you for your birthday," Sammi said, lips twitching. "One of those kick-ass T-shirts with a big red circle and a slash through his name that says 'This Girl is a Seth-Free Zone.'"

"Oh, shut up," I said, snickering and shoving her onto the bed.

∞   ∞   ∞

We had Chinese takeout because moo shu shrimp was my food of choice.

"You're welcome to come back on Sunday, Sammi, when we do

the cake and presents," my mother said, handing out fortune cookies. "I invited the Schoenmakers, too, because I think the outing will do them good. They haven't been anywhere since Lon came home from the hospital, and frankly, I'm getting a little worried. Helen was always so fearless, going everywhere, doing new things, zooming around town in that big old Buick she used to have, and now . . ."

"Now she's like an old lady," I said, thinking of how bad Gran had been trembling the last time I'd seen her.

"I think Lon's heart attack really knocked her for a loop," my father said, cracking open his fortune cookie and pulling out the slip of paper. "Hmm. 'The smart man prepares for the unexpected.'" He frowned. "I hate these things."

My mother's said, "'Flattery will go far tonight.'"

"Hey, somebody's getting lucky," Sammi said without thinking and, at my mother's astonished look, clapped a hand over her mouth and fled the table, laughing.

"Sure, keep right on teaching them sex education," my father said drily. "They won't use it, they just need to know. Nice Catholic school. Right."

The rest of the fortunes were useless, but the good part was that since it was my birthday, I didn't have to load the dishwasher, so me and Sammi escaped to get ready to go down to Crystal's.

"You're sure Crystal's mother is all right with hosting the two of you?" my mother said when we clattered back into the kitchen with our party wear stuffed in our bags and our faces innocent of all anticipated wrongdoing.

"Oh, yeah, she doesn't care," I said. "And we're good, anyway."

"Mm-hmm," my mother said, giving me an amused look. "You'd better be."

"We will," I said, scowling. "God, Mom, nothing like being suspicious."

"Mm-hmm," she said again. "Just remember that I was young once, too, okay?"

"I know, I know, now bye, Mom," I said, hustling Sammi out the door and into the gorgeous May twilight. "Come on already. No, don't walk so fast, just in case she's watching."

We set off at a casual pace, talking and laughing, until we were camouflaged by the woods, and then picked it up because the party started at nine and it was almost eight and we still had to get to Crystal's, change our clothes, and do our makeup.

We made it to Crystal's within the half hour. Sammi and Crystal had met before and even though they were different kinds of people, they got along well and cracked each other up, which was excellent.

There's nothing as good as best friends.

Crystal gave me a killer black top almost exactly like the plum-colored one I'd borrowed to wear to Connor's party, except this one was a light, silky material instead of a sweater.

"Oh, I'm definitely wearing this tonight," I said, modeling it.

Then Sammi gave me a beautiful black cord choker with a really artsy, hand-carved tiger eye butterfly hanging from a delicate gold loop in the center.

"I would have gotten you the earrings, too, but I ran out of money," she said and, grinning, lifted the front of her shirt to reveal her pink and tender-looking new belly button ring.

"Oh my God!" I said. "When did you do it?"

"Three days ago," she said, admiring it in the mirror.

"I hope you're wearing a crop top tonight," Crystal said.

"Oh, yeah," she said.

I told Crystal what happened with Seth while we finished getting dressed—Sammi in pink with her sexy new piercing, Crystal with her glossy, wavy black hair hanging loose down her back and wearing peacock blue to match her eyes, and me in black and tiger eye—and by the time the story was done, she and Sammi were in perfect agreement about one thing.

"It's your birthday, you get to go wild," Crystal said.

"There's got to be *somebody* good here tonight," Sammi said.

"I'll be your designated bodyguard," Crystal said. "I'm not really drinking, so I can watch out for you if you get drunk."

"But I get to hold her hair if she pukes," Sammi said, laughing.

"Trust me, the place is going to be crawling with cute guys," Crystal said.

"Seth can go to hell," Sammi said.

"He doesn't deserve you," Crystal said.

"All right, already, I get the idea," I said, grabbing my purse. "Seth is out, anyone else is in. It's almost nine thirty. Let's go!"

So we did, and I drank four beers really fast and got pretty stupid, seeing as I'm definitely a lightweight. The clearing was jamming, the music loud but not loud enough to have to yell over or get us busted, and the campfire in the fire pit threw a toasty, flickering glow. I ended up mingling a lot, going from group to group, talking, flirting, and then moving on.

"Oh, come on, you can't tell me you haven't seen *one person* you want to be with," Crystal said when I careened back and collapsed next to her on a log. She was sitting outside the ring of light thrown by the campfire, nursing a beer and watching Sammi show her belly button ring to some shirtless guy wearing a do-rag. "There's got to be somebody, Hanna."

"Nope," I said mournfully, leaning against her. "Only Seth."

"Oh, no," Crystal said. "It's too early for this."

"He's very cute, Crystal," I said and gave her an earnest look. "Truly. And he can be really nice but mostly . . ." I heaved an enormous sigh. "He's not. He's a gigantic asshole."

"Now there's an image I didn't need," she said, sounding strangled.

"I wish *every day* that he wasn't," I said. "I do. Every day I say, 'Dear God, please let Seth not be such a gigantic asshole,' but every day he still is." I shook my head, bewildered. "I don't really know what to do about that."

"Hot coffee, cold shower?" Crystal said, snickering.

"It's not funny," I said, scowling and struggling to sit up. "I think . . ." I pushed myself straight, brushed the hair from my eyes, and got distracted watching the fire ripple and pulse, throwing molten colors into the black sky, turning everyone golden and, for a moment, totally primal. "Is it hot in here or is it me?" I stuck a finger into the neck of my top and pulled it back and forth.

"Hey, look who's here," someone said.

I looked up into the darkness. "Karate guy!"

"Oh, God," Crystal moaned and hid her face in her hands.

"Well, *somebody's* having a good time," he said, lips twitching.

"Yes," I said, puffing out my chest. "That would be *me. I* am having a good time because . . . hey, guess what? It's my birthday! Here." I slid sideways, clutching Crystal's arm to keep from falling off the log. "Sit right here. There's room. Come on, you're not fat. As a matter of fact, you have a very cute booty." I leered up at him, pinching two fingers together. "Could I? For my birthday, I mean?"

"Oh, shit," he said, glancing at Crystal, who was wiping her streaming eyes.

"Oh, yeah," she said. "Could you stay with her for a couple of minutes while I run down to 7-Eleven?"

He looked at me.

I gave him a toothy grin because I really was very happy to see him. "C'mon, be a sport. If I get too fresh, you can just"—I made a tossing motion—"flip me right over your shoulder."

He looked away like he was trying not to laugh and rubbed a hand across his chin. "Okay, sure. You go ahead, Crystal. I'll babysit the birthday girl, here."

"You must need your eyes checked, because I'm *not* a baby," I said when he sat down in Crystal's vacated spot. "Look closely." I sat up straight and swooshed back my hair. "See?"

"Yeah, I see," he said, smiling.

I gazed back at him, caught by how sweet and tempting his mouth looked, with that plummy bottom lip and that cute little goat. . . . "I have a question," I said, swiveling so my knees were against his thighs.

"I'm sure you do." He watched as I picked up one of his dreads and touched it to my nose, then stroked it down along my cheek to my chin.

"Yes." I touched it to his cheek, smiling when he smiled. "Would you give me a birthday kiss?"

His eyebrows rose. "What?"

"Just one?" I said, abandoning the dread and laying my hand on his muscled forearm. It tensed at my touch and I liked that.

I liked it a lot.

"Sure," he said and leaned over and kissed my cheek. "Happy birthday."

I smiled expectantly, certain that was just the warm-up for the main event, and when nothing further happened, said, "That's it? That was the whole thing?"

He quirked an eyebrow, amused. "You complaining?"

"Oh, hell *yeah*. I could have gotten *that* from my grandmother." Scowling, I shook my head and leaned closer. "I want a *real* kiss, a totally hot, wicked, knock-my-socks-off—"

"No can do, darlin'," he said. "You're a little too out of it—"

"You're a stingy kiss miser," I said.

He grinned. "And still a little too young for me."

"Oh, crap, that is *so* not true," I cried. "I'm like the most mature girl in the *whole school*." My hand was still moving on his hot, damp forearm, feeling him from the crease of his elbow down to his wrist. "I *have* experience, you know." God, his arm felt good. It was all I could do not to lower my head and bite it. "And I would like to have more."

"I'll bet you would," he said, lips twitching. "But maybe another time, okay?"

"That's right," I said, nodding and tilting sideways until my head was resting on his shoulder. I peered up at him, the bridge of my nose grazing his jawline. "You smell good."

"You smell blitzed," he said and heaved a sigh. "What're you doing?"

"Not a lot," I said, pressing my mouth against his neck. I licked his skin, just a little, just to get the taste of him.

It was good.

"You taste good, too," I said.

"Come on, you can't do this," he said and then in a mutter, "shit, *I* can't do it."

"But it's my birthday, and good things are supposed to happen," I said, closing my eyes and sinking even further into him. "So far it's been really sucky, though, and I don't know why."

"Hanna, you have to sit up." He slid his arm around me, but instead of shifting me up, it sort of cradled me closer. "Come on."

But I didn't want to move, not at all. His body was so sweet and hard and perfect that moving was unthinkable, unless it was to lay him down and crawl on top of him.

I hadn't realized I'd said that out loud until he laughed, low and husky, and said, "Jesus, what're you trying to do, kill me?"

No, I was trying to do a lot of things, but kill him wasn't one of them.

"You don't like me," I said sadly.

"You know I do," he said, rubbing his forehead.

"No, you don't," I said, slumping. "Nobody does. Seth, the guy from the mall . . . he just plays me—"

"He's an asshole," he said.

"I *know*, and then there's you . . ." I peeked up and was surprised to see his mouth quivering. "What?"

"God," he said, laughing. "You are so fucking subtle."

I frowned, not sure what he meant.

"Relax, it wasn't an insult," he said, patting my back. "I would never insult the birthday girl."

"Yeah, but you won't kiss her, either," I said, sulking and writing my name with my finger on his thigh.

"Careful there," he said, shifting as the second *N* ended very close to the center seam of his jeans. "You're getting into dangerous territory."

"I still have an *A* to go," I said.

"Yeah, well, you're going to have to write it somewhere else," he said and moved my hand back into my own lap.

"Why, because you already have a girlfriend and that's her private property?" I said, tilting my face up again so my nose was against his jaw and my cheek on his shoulder.

"Nope, no girlfriend," he said.

"Oh." I thought a minute. "Are you gay?"

He snorted. "Not hardly."

"Good." More bright ideas tumbled in. "You know, you should come see me. But if you do—which you should—you have to hide your tattoo, because my parents would have heart failure, so you could just wear a long-sleeve shirt and then it would be fine. Okay?"

"Sure," he said. "Where the hell is Crystal, anyway?"

I knew where Crystal was. I'd seen her return, catch sight of us, grin, slip across to the other side of the campfire, and disappear into the dark. "Why, do you want to leave? I *knew* it. You don't want to be with me, either."

"Want has nothing to do with it," he said, gazing out toward the fire.

"Then how come you won't even *look* at me?" I said, tugging on a dread.

He exhaled long and slow. "You're making this really hard."

"No, I'm not," I murmured, my head on his shoulder, my mouth close to his ear where the skin was soft and hot and everything I yearned for here in the dark. "*I'm* making it very, very easy. Just one . . ." I kissed his neck . . ."little" . . and again . . ."kiss."

"Damn," he muttered on a husky laugh. "I'm gonna kick myself in the morning but . . ." And lifting a callused hand to the curve of my cheek, he lowered his mouth to mine, his dreads slipping forward like a slinky black curtain to shield us from view.

The first kiss was brief, his lips light and feather soft, rose petals and sweet plums, ripe and irresistible, tempting me, making me bloom inside, but when he tried to end it and ease back, I followed him, willing him to go on tasting, touching, teasing. He tensed, hesitated, and I sighed low in my throat and his breath swept my cheek, and then his mouth opened and mine opened, too, and his heart was pounding through his T-shirt, and I slid my arm up around his neck because he was so sweet, so hot, and God, I couldn't get close enough. Each time his breath hitched I molded closer, shifting, and finally sliding my leg over his, crazy to drown in him, to climb on top of him and—

"Whoa," he said raggedly, gripping my hips and stopping me, holding me almost straddling his thigh and pressed so tight that our breath rose and fell together. "You've got to stop. I'm not kidding. I can't do this."

"Do what?" I murmured, nuzzling his collarbone. "You're doing just fine." I shifted farther onto his thigh, and oh, yes, that felt good.

It must have felt good for him, too, because he groaned and pulled me the rest of the way into him, tucking my thigh tight into his groin and burying his face in the front of my shirt.

I kissed his forehead, his eyes, his mouth, kissed him with no boundaries, no thought, kissed him the way I felt, excited and aching and wanting until I was delirious and his hands were holding my butt tight against him, my thigh tight against him, until I was yearning for him and somewhere in the back of my mind warning signs were flashing, but they were nothing compared to the rush of being on him, with him, against him.

"I'm back, in case anybody's interested," I heard Crystal say from far away and would have ignored her had Jesse not started and cursed and pulled away but still held me, with his damp forehead pressed to mine and his breathing heavy.

"I'm going to get a beer, but I shall return," she said, sounding amused.

"Shit," he said, pulling back. "This wasn't supposed to happen."

"Well, it's okay, really," I said, gasping and putting a hand on my thundering heart, still too dazed to think straight. "I mean technically nothing did, right?" And the whole thing hit me, the unsatisfied hunger, the lingering sweetness, the gain and the loss, and I started to laugh and, yeah, to even cry a little, and he slid me off him and waited until the storm passed and I was okay again. "Oh my God," I said, wiping my eyes and giving him a shaky smile. "Now that was a serious birthday kiss."

"Yeah." He ran a hand over his dreads, folded his arms across his knees, and looked out toward the campfire. "It was."

I bit my lip and waited for him to say more, but he didn't. "Are you mad at me?"

He laughed without humor and shook his head. "Not hardly."

"Then what is it?" I said in a small voice, as the beautiful, full blossoming inside of me began to fold in on itself. "Did I do something wrong?"

"No." He looked at me then, his gaze dark and serious. "I don't know what to say."

"Say anything," I said a little desperately.

He thought a minute, then gave me a crooked smile. "Happy birthday?"

"Thank you," I said, and maybe it was because I knew he wasn't going to be my boyfriend or because he seemed so much older but not in a bad way, in a more mature way, like at nineteen and out of school he was so far beyond me that I could just say stuff without having to worry about how he would take it that I added, "You know what? Even though I only got one kiss today, I'm glad it was from you."

He blinked. "The feeling's mutual."

And then his eyes started to twinkle again and my smile returned and there it was, that sizzling bolt of black lightning arcing between us that made me blush and go all soft inside, made Crystal's return the catalyst he needed to rise, do that jean-tugging guy thing, look down at me, and with a wry smile, say, "Next time I see you, you'd *better* be eighteen," and I laughed and gave him a wicked look and he left, shaking his head.

"Sorry I had to interrupt, but it was starting to look pretty intense," Crystal said, plopping down next to me and giving me a knowing shoulder bump.

"Could everyone see us?" I said, only slightly alarmed because there were plenty of other kids making out and half of them were sitting right in front of the campfire where you couldn't miss them.

"No, it's pretty dark over here," she said, and then lips twitching, she added "so, how do you feel? Still buzzed?"

"No, and shut up," I said, flushing and laughing.

"Don't like him at all, huh?"

"Shut uuuuup," I said, laughing harder and burying my face in my arms.

"Don't look now, but he's standing by the keg, talking to some guy and pretending not to look over here," she said in a low, teasing voice.

"How do you know he's pretending not to look if he isn't looking?" I said, lifting my head just enough to peek.

"Because you can tell," she said. "See? He keeps messing with his dreads and watch . . . see? It's like he's trying not to smile. He's self-conscious."

"Hmm," I said, resting my chin on my hand. "Think he can see us?"

"Nope," she said. "Why, are you gonna flash him or something?"

"Hell no," I said. "If I ever lift my shirt up, it's not going to be when he's too far away to do anything about it."

So we wandered back into the party in time for Jesse to smile at me before he left, and then me and Crystal cruised past Sammi, who was making out with do-rag guy, took the path down to 7-Eleven so I could buy a soda and use their bathroom, and then it was my turn to find something to do, because the guy Crystal had been crushing on for like a month finally showed up and came right over to her.

I didn't feel like drinking anymore, and I didn't want to sit on a log in the dark because those were occupied by couples, so I drifted, talking to Crystal's brother and other people, just hanging out and enjoying the glow.

It must have been around two when Sammi came back into the fire-light and maybe three when Crystal did. I was tired by then and the crowd had thinned and everyone left was lounged out on the ground, so we decided not to stay all night, which, I found out, Crystal's mother hadn't said we could do anyway, so we left and snuck into her house, and her parents were sleeping, so our getting home so late wasn't a problem. Sammi took the sleeping bag on the floor while me and Crystal took the bed. I found out that Sammi and do-rag guy were going out, and, she said, if her mother ever saw him, she'd probably ground her for life, but she didn't care because she really liked him and what was so wrong with a gold tooth, anyway.

Crystal said her crush had asked her out and so she was a girlfriend now, too, and that was cool.

And I said Jesse gave me my birthday kiss, and Sammi was like, *OMG, really?* And Crystal was like, *Oh, yeah,* did *he,* but I got shy and didn't want to share all the details, so I only said, *No, we're not going out,* and, *Yeah, I'm okay with that.*

I thought about that last part long after they fell asleep and tried to decide if it was true. It was, so I fell asleep, too.

And that was the keg party.

On Sunday the Schoenmakers came over and we had a little party. Gran made my favorite carrot cake in the world and I made a wish— *Please let sixteen be my dream-come-true year*—and blew out all the candles.

I got some good presents. Gran gave me a really pretty pearl pendant and I think it was something she was passing on to me because there was no way they could have afforded to buy it new, and my parents gave me gift certificates to book and clothes stores, seeing as how my mother knows she can't pick my clothes for me anymore.

The only sad parts were that Grandpa had to have his cake without the cream cheese icing because of his new heart diet and that Gran was so shaky she actually spilled coffee on my pile of birthday cards and got all stricken about it, even though my mother mopped it up so it didn't even matter.

For a minute I actually thought she was going to cry, and I looked at my parents like, *Do something,* and my mother gave me this look like, *What?* and I didn't know, so all I could think to do was ask how many new baby fawns she'd seen so far this year, but for some reason that seemed to make it worse, and then I really didn't know what to do except offer up my biggest humiliation to distract her from hers, so I said, *Hey, remember those new boots I got last Christmas? Well, did I ever tell you that the first time I wore them I fell down the stairs in front of everyone?*

And that turned the tide because I told it in a way that made everyone laugh, and then my father started telling one of his funny trip-and-fall stories, and my mother smiled at me across the table like she was saying, *Thank you, Hanna,* and yes, all in all it was a very good birthday.

Chapter 16

Hanna

Memorial Day weekend

There was a parade in town and we went with Gran and Grandpa.

We brought lawn chairs and sat on the curb, watching the scouts, fire engines, and politicians, and the Lions, Moose, and Elks clubs go by.

When the old VFW soldiers marched into sight, Grandpa pulled out a hanky and mopped his eyes, and when the band went by and played the "Star Spangled Banner," he actually took off his cap and put his hand over his heart.

At first I was embarrassed because *nobody* does that, but then my mother looked like she was feeling it and Gran had taken Grandpa's arm and my father looked really solemn. I was like, *Oh my God, they're killing me,* so I gritted my teeth and finally the band moved past.

The town always gives out free hot dogs in the park afterward, but Gran's knees were too bad to walk that far and my parents wanted to go home and get our own picnic going, so I said I'd just walk through real fast—and it would *definitely* be fast because I was alone, and hanging out alone is no fun—and I'd meet them back home.

So they left and I walked down to the park, where the cliques were in full swing, which made it kind of boring except that Crystal's brother told me they were having another party in the woods Monday afternoon if I wanted to come.

"Sounds good," I said and decided to leave because there was really no one there I wanted to see, so I cut across the park and was heading up the sidewalk when a Harley appeared over the hill, and yes, it was Jesse.

My heart gave this weird leap, and at first I thought he wasn't going to stop at all, then I thought, *Okay, maybe he's just going to wave and keep going,* so I tried not to take it personally, but then at the last minute he pulled the bike to the curb and shut it off.

"Hi," I said, unable to stop smiling.

"Hey, Hanna," he said and gave me this quirky smile, like he was kind of bemused at seeing me in the daylight. "What's up?" He took off his shades, hesitated, and then pulled off his helmet. He had on a red bandanna underneath it.

"Nothing much," I said, beaming.

He shook his head and gave this laugh, a good laugh, and just looked at me. "You always this happy?"

"No," I said, laughing. "It's you. Every time I see you, I just . . . I don't know. You make me smile."

"Well, that's good," he said, grinning.

"Yeah, it is," I said because, oh my God, it was the *best* feeling. "So, you going to the park?"

"When I get there," he said, putting down the kickstand and relaxing. "You leaving?"

"I was," I said with a shrug. "Nobody's really there but Crystal's brother. He said there's another party in the woods on Monday afternoon." I smiled again; I couldn't help it.

"Oh, yeah?" he said, looking away and smiling. "Too bad I'm working."

"On a holiday?"

"Double time plus," he said, nodding. "So where you headed?"

"Home," I said. "We're having a picnic with the neighbors. I'll be the only one there under forty." The minute I said it, I wanted to take it back, because there was no way he could bring that tattoo to a family picnic. "I mean, I don't really care . . ."

He let it go. "No Crystal or your other friend?"

"No, they've got boyfriends, so I hardly see them at all," I said, wedging my hands in my back pockets and cocking my head. "I'm kind of on my own now."

He nodded. "Staying out of trouble?"

My smile widened. "Not of my own free will."

He laughed and we kind of hit a stalemate.

"Well . . ." I said after a minute.

"I didn't bring an extra helmet, or I'd give you a ride home," he said.

"Oh, that sucks," I said, making a face. "Riding's fun."

He gazed at me as if deliberating, then looked down at the row of bikes lined up at the edge of the park and the guys gathered around them. "Well, Granger's down there and so is Big Steve. You want me to see if I can borrow you one?"

"Okay," I said happily.

"Jesus, Hanna," he said, laughing again. "Sit tight and I'll be back."

I watched him rumble off, and he was back in a minute with a candy apple red helmet tucked under his arm.

"You can thank Steve's girlfriend for this," he said, handing it over and glancing back down the hill toward the cluster of bikes.

I followed his gaze and, on impulse, stood on tiptoe and waved even though I had no idea who I was waving to.

From the center of the crowd, an arm rose and waved back.

"Cool," I said and pulled on the helmet. It fit snug and smelled like flowery shampoo, and I climbed onto the back of the bike like I was born to be there, which made him smile again, and slid my arms around his waist. "Ready."

"Then let's roll," he said, and we rumbled away from the curb. "You in a hurry?"

"Not really, but I can't be too late," I said. "Why?"

"I figured we'd take the scenic route down along the canal," he said. "It's maybe an extra ten minutes."

"Perfect," I said.

It was beautiful meandering through the cool woods and along the sparkling water, just riding without even talking, with my hands settled on his sides at his belt, and every so often him resting a hand on my knee.

"You okay?" he said, following the curve in the road and steering wide of bicyclists.

"I could do this all day," I said. "You're a good driver."

"Thanks," he said.

But the canal road finally ended and we had to turn onto the road to my house.

"You don't have to pull all the way in," I said, getting nervous. "You could just stop at the end of the driveway and I'll jump off."

"Your parents don't like bikes?" he said.

"I don't know," I said, praying no one was out on the front porch. "The last time you brought me home, no one was here, so they never knew."

"Okay," he said, flicking on his signal light to make the turn into my driveway.

I didn't see anyone on the porch, so they were probably all out back, but this area was so quiet except for the birds that they probably heard us coming a mile away. The key was to get him out of here before anyone came around and waved us toward the house. The key was to keep that tattoo, and all they would interpret it as, out of sight.

He pulled in and did a half-moon at the edge of the driveway.

I fumbled with the helmet, yanked it off, and handed it to him. "That was fun. Thanks for the ride home." I glanced at the house and saw my mother standing in the front door, watching. Still, the combination of the motorcycle engine plus the acre between her and me would let me pretend that, even if she called, I wouldn't hear her.

"Sure, no problem," he said, glancing at me, then past to my mother, then back at me. His smile deepened. "Have a good one."

"You, too, and you know, I'm probably not even gonna go to that party on Monday now," I said in a rush, flushing as his smile grew quizzical. "I mean . . . I don't know. I might have something else to do. Stop it," I said, laughing and giving his arm a playful whack. "Go already or who knows what'll come out of my mouth."

He laughed. "That could be interesting."

"Go," I said and waved as he pulled out.

My cell phone rang.

I pulled it from my pocket. "Hi, Mom."

"Since when do you know boys with motorcycles?" she said.

"Oh my God, I only know one," I said, waving to her.

"Who is he?" she said, coming out onto the porch.

"Jesse Yennet," I said matter-of-factly, walking up the driveway toward home. "His mom used to be my fifth-grade art teacher, remember?"

"Yennet," my mother said musingly. "Ohhh . . . she got sick, didn't she? Uterine cancer?"

"Ovarian," I said.

"Terrible," my mother said, sinking onto the porch swing. "Yes, I remember now. My God, her husband was a basket case and—"

"Did you guys eat yet?" I interrupted because if I didn't, she'd go on forever.

"No, we were waiting for you," she said, rising and giving me a look. "We'll talk about this when you get here."

"Okay," I said and stuck the phone back in my pocket. Waited until she went back inside, then did a wacky little happy dance right out there for the world to see.

෭ ෭ ෭

I never went to the party on Memorial Day. Crystal wasn't going to be there and the only other reason would've been to dig myself up a boyfriend and I just wasn't into it.

Weird, I know.

But get this: on Tuesday, Seth showed up on one of my new hall routes, not his usual path at all, and said, "Hey, stranger, where you been?"

So I was nice back, not crazy in love like before, where everything he said was funny and every move he made adorable, but friendly, and I could tell he didn't know what to make of it because he said, "So who're you going out with now? Do I know him?"

And I laughed and said, "Nobody. I'm free as a bird." And gave a very strange but totally spontaneous little skip, caught his surprise, and said, "What?"

"You tell me," he said. "Why so happy?"

"Why not?" I said with a shrug. "We've only got like four days of school left—"

"Yeah, that reminds me," he said. "You doing anything this summer?"

"What, like a vacation? No, I'll probably just be hanging out," I said. "Why?"

"Well, if I hear about any good parties, you want me to give you a call?" he said, stopping and leaning against the lockers.

"Sure, that'd be cool," I said, and my voice didn't even waver.

"Okay," he said and ambled a few steps backward. "Well, I have to give Bailey a buzz now, so I guess I'll see you . . ."

"See you," I said and headed off in the opposite direction, only then realizing that he'd done it again.

School is out. I made it with one A, two Bs, a couple of Cs, and two Ds, and no one caught the mandatory community service thing, either.

The funny part is that I don't see anything so much more superior, character-trait-wise, between the kids who did the service and me. I mean, I serve who I want to serve without being graded on it; I plant Grandpa's tomatoes and feed the cats and in the fall and winter walk the back acre route with Gran, pulling the little cart filled with food for the deer, and I do it to help them, not because I need a good grade on it to pass school.

So what good is it if they *make* you do it? Isn't the whole idea to want to help on your own, and if you don't, you just don't?

I don't know. Maybe it's me, but I'll tell you this: if you're only doing it because other people are watching, then what is it really worth?

Well.

Crystal called and told me Jesse left on a monthlong cross-country motorcycle trip with a couple of friends.

"Oh," I said. "Wow. That's half the summer. When did he leave?"

"Yesterday," she said. "You didn't know?"

"Why would I know?" I said, but yeah, he could have mentioned it on Memorial Day weekend or something. "We're not going out or anything."

"Well," she said. "He called, and before he talked to my brother, he spent all this time telling me about the website he set up where they'd be posting pictures from the trip, and I was thinking, yeah so, who cares, but now I wonder if he was telling me so I would tell *you*."

"What's the url?" I said.

So she told me and I went there and it was a black screen with a few biker graphics and a couple of shots of him and two other guys packing gear and then riding out of town. There was one picture of him, though, where he was next to his bike and looking straight into the camera with this gorgeous smile that I swear made me feel like he'd meant it for me, so I copied it off his site, printed it, and stuck it in my wallet.

It never hurt to have a cute guy around for company.

Chapter 17

Helen

I sit on the back porch in the shade petting Serepta and watching Hanna come and go. She's so busy these days, so lively, and I'm happy for her, I am, because her world *should* be expanding, she should be meeting new people and having new experiences, only . . .

I miss her.

Lon has taken to napping through the hottest part of the day. The heat drains him in a way it never did before, and that worries me because we have no air-conditioning and can't afford to have it put in. I have a fan set up in the bedroom and another in the hallway and he says this helps, but it's still stifling up there.

And when he sleeps, the silence that settles over the house scares me.

I go up to check on him often, forcing my knees to take the stairs and avoiding the creaky spots in the hallway. I ease the door open, and if he isn't snoring, I watch his silhouette in the murky light until I'm certain I can see his chest rising and falling, then go carefully out and back down the stairs.

I should go out to the garden and weed or pick cucumbers or walk the deer path or hang some clothes but I don't want to be too far away in case he needs me.

I would never forgive myself.

Chapter 18

Hanna

I got a new job!

I am now a counter girl at this ratty little sub shop outside of town that caters mostly to construction workers, so I'm definitely flexing my flirt muscles and earning big tips.

The owner, some crabby old lady named Olympia, trained me and then left me alone to fend for myself with nobody but her *father*, Antonio, an ancient, wizened little peanut of a man with chipmunk cheeks and crippling arthritis who putters around all day washing the dishes and cutting the moldy parts off the sub rolls. He has a heavy accent and I can't always understand him, but he's nice, so it's cool.

There was a keg party down Crystal's after the Fourth of July parade.

I went, thinking maybe Jesse would be back by now, but he wasn't. His last website post had said, *Riding hard for home,* and that had been two days ago from wherever they were, along with some new pictures of the Rocky Mountains, the Grand Canyon, and one of him and some girl with huge boobs and a bottle of Jack Daniel's standing on the bank of the Mississippi River. He looked beautiful, tanned, lean, forearms muscular and body relaxed, straddling the Harley, and

I don't know, maybe it was because I was getting older, but the whole thing kind of bemused me, knowing I'd kissed him and it hadn't ruined anything because we were pretty much just flirting anyway.

It was cool. We were cool.

That girl with the boobs, though . . . she bugged me.

Jesse came into the sub shop today.

He must have been working at a construction site because he came in with the normal group of guys and almost dropped his teeth when he saw me behind the counter.

"Hanna," he said, stopping dead in surprise.

"Hey," I said, crouching to pick up the wad of boiled ham I'd lost hold of when he walked in and handing it to little old Antonio, who would trundle it into the kitchen, wash it off, and use it for a takeout order. "You're back."

"Yeah," he said, running a hand over his bandanna and flushing under the gleaming-eyed scrutiny of the other construction guys. "I didn't know you worked here."

"Mm-hmm," I said with a noncommittal smile and waving at a guy behind him that always left me a great tip. "Hey, Ronnie."

"Hey, gorgeous," he said.

"So how was your trip?" I said while motioning to the guys to spew their orders. I wrote them down as fast as I got them—most of these guys ate the same thing, the same way, every day—and said to Jesse, "What're you having?"

"I don't know, it went right out of my mind," he said.

"Yeah, she has that effect on all of us," one of the guys said with a grin.

"Speak for yourself, Huey, I'm married," someone else said, winking at me.

"Well, it looked like your trip was a blast," I said.

"You checked out the website?" he said.

"Oh, yeah," I said and, thinking of boob girl, hauled a long slab of salami out of the refrigerated case, stuck it on the meat slicer, and proceeded to lop off about six inches in slow, even, determined strokes. "Let me know when you decide what you want, okay?"

"Uh, okay," he said and stepped back to let the regulars pick up their orders.

It was mayhem for the next ten minutes, and in the midst of it, he finally ordered a number four, so I whipped his together, too, only I saved his paying for last.

"I still can't believe you're working here," he said, pulling a wad of cash from his pocket and peeling off a damp ten. "Sorry, it's a little sweaty."

"Aren't we all," I said blandly, taking it and making change.

"Keep it," he said when I offered it to him.

"No, I still owe you gas money," I said, trying to hand it to him.

"I told you to forget that," he said, shaking his head.

And here is where poring over all those biker thumbnails on his website finally served me.

"I can't forget it," I said and, cocking my head, recited, "'Gas, grass, or ass, no one rides for free.' That's the big rule, right?"

His jaw dropped, the guys eavesdropping at the next table choked on their potato chips, and I just stood there, eyebrows high and cheeks burning.

"Jesus Christ, Hanna," he said finally, lips twitching.

Oh, God, I so didn't want to smile but there was no way to stop it, and I ended up shaking my head and laughing and waving him away. "Go eat your lunch, and if you want to give me a tip, you have to leave it on the table just like everyone else."

He nodded and found a seat, and I went about my job wiping counters and slicing tomatoes and shredding lettuce and making more subs for more guys and joking and laughing and stuffing my apron pockets with tips, and when the hour was up and the first crew was leaving, Jesse paused at the counter and smiled and said, "See you tomorrow."

"See you," I said lightly.

And you know what? He'd left me a five-dollar tip for a four-dollar sandwich.

෮ඁ   ෮ඁ   ෮ඁ

Interesting.

No Jesse today.

According to Ronnie, who just couldn't wait to trumpet out the news, Jesse had planned on coming, but some girl had shown up at the site looking for him right as they were about to pull out, and she'd brought Burger King, so he'd stayed to eat with her.

"Well, that's nice," I said. "BK's always good." I pulled out my pad and pen and said, "Now, what'll you have?"

I'm getting good at pulling the curtains shut around my "glass head."

I don't want to be read anymore.

Not by Seth.

Not by anybody.

We got robbed.

I keep thinking, I'm okay, I'm okay, but then I just start shaking and crying all over again.

I told the cop the guy must have known our busy time, because he came in early before lunch when there was no one there but me and little Antonio. I was slicing tomatoes and Antonio was sweeping and singing "That's Amore," making me laugh by dancing and pretending his broom was someone named Lola Brigitta, and then this guy came in wearing a hoodie, and I remember thinking, *Holy crap, it's August!*

I wish I hadn't put my tomato knife down, because something just didn't feel right, but I put it down anyway because, I mean, really, what was I gonna do, carry it to the counter just because he was wearing a hoodie? For all I knew he'd had chemo or something and was embarrassed because he didn't have any hair.

I don't know! I never met a criminal before!

So I grabbed my pad and pen and went to the counter and was like, *Can I help you?* And he just whipped out this box cutter and grabbed my shirt so hard, it was like he punched me in the chest, and yanked me half over the counter and said, *Open the register.* This surge of hot terror washed through me and I started shaking and I couldn't hardly stand because his eyes were flat and he didn't care at all, I was like *nothing,* and he threw me at the register. I stumbled and hit my mouth on the edge and started to cry and he didn't care that I was bleeding he just said, *Open the fucking register before I kill you, bitch,* and he would have, he would have, but I couldn't because I was shaking so bad . . .

. . . And then Antonio was coming up behind him with the broom, but the floor creaked, so the robber just turned around and . . .

. . . He cut Antonio's face—just slashed it—and his skin opened across his mouth and up to his eye, and it just split and gushed blood and looked like meat inside, and I couldn't even breathe but I was hitting all these buttons on the register, going crazy trying to make it open, and it finally opened, and when Antonio fell, that guy kicked him in the chest and he didn't have to do that, he didn't, because the register was open and he could take the money, he could have just taken it, but he didn't, he stopped to kick Antonio again . . .

. . . And then he just swung a fist and bashed me in the face so I would get out of the way, but I was already trying, I was trying, and he didn't care, he took the money and then he ran and left us there on the floor.

My head was spinning and all I could hear was the cord on the ceiling fan clicking against the blades, and then I heard a car door slam and started freaking and tried to get my cell phone out, but I was shaking too bad. The door opened and I started going, *No no no,* and I heard somebody go, *Shit!* and then, *Call the cops!* And it was Ronnie, one of the construction guys, and he got down next to me and said, *It's okay, Hanna, don't move, you're gonna be fine,* and that just made me cry even more because I hardly knew him but he stayed with me anyway . . .

. . . I think Antonio is dead but I don't know, I don't know.

Why did he have to kick him? Antonio never hurt anybody

He was just a little old man.

The whole side of my face is purple. Blood vessels burst in my eye so it's like one big red blood spot and the lid is swollen. My lip is split, my tooth is loose, and I have a giant knot on my head. My breastbone is bruised and there are fingerprints squeezed into my arm.

Antonio is alive but he might lose his eye, and his heart is all messed up.

I'm home from the hospital. My mother made me a bed on the couch because she was afraid I'd get dizzy and fall down the stairs.

People are calling and sending flowers and balloons.

It's surreal.

I'm surrounded by people who care about me and all I can think of is the look on that guy's face.

If I hadn't gotten that register open, he would have killed me.

I would have been over forever, murdered by some guy with a zit next to his left nostril, scabby knuckles, and blond eyebrows, a guy maybe six years older than me, wearing a gray USC hoodie and jeans.

He would have taken my life. *Taken* it.

Death by box cutter. Death by fists. Death by stomping.

It's unbelievable that someone I don't even know would touch me, not to mention punch me in the chest and the face. That making me bleed was *less* than no big deal.

I don't even know how to get my mind around this.

If he had killed me, my heart would have stopped while I was wearing a smeary apron, jeans, and an Olympia's Sub Shop tank top. I would have never seen my room again or laughed or said hi to my parents or good-bye to anybody or gone any farther, in *any* way, than I already had.

I just would have ceased. Exhale. Period.

I get cold sweats when I think of it.

He would have killed me for the twenty-three dollars in the register.

He *hit* me for twenty-three dollars.

It would have been more, but he left the change.

○○   ○○   ○○

Sammi's mother brought her down to visit. She came in, took one look at me, wailed, "Oh, no!" and burst into tears.

My mother was ready to send her right back home, but I was like no, it's okay, because that's how I felt, too. Crystal came and started crying, too. Then I started crying and it stung my face, so I kept trying to stop, but then my mother started and poor Gran came and got all white like she was gonna faint and had to sit down, and Grandpa and my father looked like they were gonna go hunt the guy down and kill him.

My mother finally pulled herself together and took everyone but Sammi and Crystal out into the kitchen for coffee.

Crystal gave me a sealed envelope after they left and said Jesse had stopped at her house to find out how I was and had asked her to give the envelope to me.

"He didn't stay long," she said. "He just said he'd heard what happened from the guys at work and told me to let you know he was thinking of you and hoped you were okay."

"That was nice of him," I said, because he didn't have to do it, we weren't anything to each other, not really, not friends, not going out . . . not nothing.

"I ran into Connor down at McDonald's this morning and told him what happened," Sammi said and blew her nose into a tissue. "Sorry. That was gross, I know. Anyhow, I figured you'd want to know, just in case you hear anything from you-know-who."

I shook my head and slid the envelope under my pillow. "That's not gonna happen."

Sammi shrugged. "Well, just in case."

We sat around for a while but they were antsy, I could tell, so I asked them if they'd walk down to Rita's and get coconut gelatos. My mother gave them money and they took off. I lay back like I wanted to rest just so everyone would leave me alone. When my mother got the hint and left, I slid the envelope out from under my pillow.

It was a card, not a funny get-well card or a cutesy, cheerful one or anything like that, but one of those thick-paper art cards with butterflies on the front and blank inside except for what he'd written.

> *Chin up, Hanna.*
> *You're a trooper. You'll make it through.*
>
> > *Keeping the faith,*
> >
> > *Jesse*
>
> *p.s. I'd come see you but I don't own a long-sleeve shirt.*

I smiled, but it hurt doing it.

The juvenile crime detective told my parents that I should talk to a psychologist because posttraumatic stress disorder is common, but I think I'd rather stay here and become a hermit. You never read about hermits getting beat up, only sending letter bombs and living in squalor. I can be a hermit without the bomb thing, no problem, and the squalor might actually be fun.

Crystal wants me to come over but I keep making excuses.

My bruises are fading and my lip looks a lot better, but my eye is still pretty ugly, and besides, they haven't caught the robber yet.

Gran fell down and the ambulance came and rushed her to the hospital.

Grandpa wanted to ride in the ambulance with her but they told him to follow them instead, so my mother drove him because he was totally freaked.

I locked all the doors when she left, but then I started hearing noises and broke out in a cold sweat and couldn't breathe too well and ended up sitting on the floor in the corner of the kitchen, shaking and crying like a big baby.

I think I just had one of those posttraumatic stress flashbacks the detective had warned me about.

When my mother came home, I asked her to make me a psychologist appointment.

Crystal keeps saying I have to go out sometime, but it's easy for her to say, as she's not the one who was attacked and almost died.

Plus, I've been eating so much ice cream that I'm starting to gain weight. I should stop because it isn't making me feel any better but I don't have anything better to do.

Pathetic.

I don't feel very "chin up" at all.

I feel lonely.

I told the psychologist that life keeps moving for everybody but me. I'm stuck. There's prerobbery Hanna and there's postrobbery Hanna; my life is halved now. Pre Hanna was so sure of her world she just, like, I don't know, strode through it like there was nothing she couldn't find a way around, like there was nothing she couldn't handle.

Post Hanna knows better. She doesn't stride, she hesitates, because now she knows what it feels like to be hit in the face by a guy who thinks she's less than nothing.

These are the kinds of thoughts I have now, like nothing is certain anymore, like I could peel up a thousand layers for answers and still never find one absolute.

The psychologist, an older guy with a potbelly, ragged cuticles, and a waiting room full of twitchy people, yawned and said how I feel is perfectly natural and that I must grieve for the Hanna I lost and learn to love the more experienced Hanna I've become.

Normally I would have told Gran what he said and we would have spent time dissecting it and trying to turn it into something I could actually use, but she was still in the hospital, so I told my mother instead.

She frowned slightly, as if trying to make sense of it and said, "Well, he *is* a psychologist, so I have to assume he knows what he's talking about, although I was hoping for something a little more concrete."

Talking to my mother is just not the same as talking to Gran.

೧೨ ೧೨ ೧೨

Gran is home again. My mother said she was so shaky because she has Parkinson's disease and the doctors diagnosed her within half an hour of her getting to the hospital. She's starting medication and is going to be okay.

Good.

Now Grandpa doesn't have to worry anymore.

I wish I could stop worrying, too.

My mother took me to see little Antonio, who is out of the hospital and back at work. She didn't want to take me—I think maybe she thought I'd go catatonic or something, but I didn't.

We went right before lunch when I knew the construction guys would be showing up because I wanted to thank them for the big bouquet of wildflowers they sent, but all that went out of my head when I walked in and saw Antonio, looking so small and fragile, sweeping near the jukebox.

"Hey, look who's here," he sang out, and then he set the broom aside and turned so I could see his black eye patch. When I started to cry, he gave me a big grin and said, "What, you don't think I'm cute like the pirate Johnny Depp?"

And that made me laugh, tearfully, yeah, because he'd lost his eye, but then he came limping over and wrapped a gnarled hand around my mother's arm and the other around my hand as if drawing us all together, and looking hard into her face, he said, "You're a lucky lady, Mrs. Thury. This nice girl, she makes the whole place bright like the sun." And then he looked at me and said, "So, when you coming back to work?" And there was a smile in his voice but the look in his eye was serious, like he was saying a lot more, and my mother said, "Well, school starts soon so I don't think—"

And he said, "I'm sorry for interrupting, but I gotta say that *figlio di puttana* took my eye and stole a young girl's . . ." He paused, struggling for words. "Peace of mind. That's not a man, that's a *stronzo* and you don't let a *stronzo* tell you how to live." He released us, hands shaking, his eye fierce and the scar puckering his cheek red and angry looking. "You hear me? You don't let him win! You say"—he slapped a hand down into the crook of his bent arm—"right here and put it behind you and keep going."

I nodded, even though I didn't know what half of his words meant, and he nodded in return and hobbled back to his broom. We said good-bye to Olympia, who was kind of reserved because my parents had asked her to pay my hospital bills and her insurance company was giving her a hard time, so she was really worried that we were going to sue and she was going to lose the sub shop. (We didn't and her insurance company finally paid. I was glad because it wasn't her or Antonio's fault that some shithead kid lost his mind.)

He's the one that should be sued.

Too bad they're probably never going to catch him.

On the brighter side, we ran into the construction guys in the parking lot and it was cute how polite they were in front of my mother. Ronnie gave me this awkward hug and they all wished me well, smiled, and then went in to eat because even though I might have died, they still had only an hour for lunch.

My psychologist visits are over. The psych told me he was proud of how well I was doing, which I guess was good because the HMO insurance paid for the appointments but not an unlimited number of them, so we both knew I had only like six visits to get right with everything.

I could have said a lot more, but time ran out, so I guess I'll just have to live with it.

Sammi came over and surprised me with a pair of excellent new shades she said I was going to wear to Crystal's brother's party to cover my eye so I would have no excuse not to go. She'd already talked it over with Crystal and they both would watch out for me and leave whenever I was ready, but since I was going to have to get out and catch the school bus within the next two days, they figured I had better have at least one dry run getting off the couch, away from the TV, and into real life again.

I must have been ready because I didn't need too much bullying to go take a shower, and get ready.

And the party was easier than I thought, with no crying or extreme paranoia or anything bad.

I didn't drink, so I was more aware of what everyone was doing, though, and maybe somewhere in the back of my mind I was listening for that cold "I'll kill you, bitch" tone, but of course it wasn't there. That would have been too easy.

Nobody made a big deal about my shades either, so I ended up taking them off and just hanging out, watching everybody party.

That's what I like about Crystal's.

You can just be.

My parents are starting to get on my nerves. They're being too nice, like I'm some kind of freak who's going to implode at any second. My mother keeps trying to get into discussions with me and even suggests more counseling, saying we could pay for it ourselves, but I'm like, *Mom, I'm fine, will you just let it go already? It's over, okay? I don't want to think about this forever, I just want to move on and live my life.*

God.

Then my father asked if I wanted to go to self-defense classes and I was like, no, because I don't want to be where people are fighting all the time, okay?

It gets tense, and the best thing I can think of to do is either read or go hang out at Gran's. It's like my refuge and we can get into good conversations if we want to, not like we *have* to. She always looks out for me but she doesn't try to make the world pretty and bright when it's not always that way. She's honest and when I told her how much I've always loved that about her, she started to cry—I mean *really* cry—and then I started crying, too, and it felt great to just let go.

Chapter 19

Helen

After Hanna leaves I go inside, sit with Lon, and tell him I can't take it any longer, that our secrets can't stay secrets, and even if it destroys us, I have to find a way to reveal the truth because we cannot die and leave Hanna with nothing but lies.

And Lon, who has loved me steadily and completely, who has never once let me down, and who has kept good care of my heart even when it cost him everything, dries my tears, eases my anguish, and says, *All right, Helen.*

All right.

୧୬ ୧୬ ୧୬

Writing the truth is hard.

I sit at my desk every day, force myself to place my fingers on our old computer's keyboard, and order myself to start.

The words don't come.

Not like the memories do.

They break in waves, in waking nightmares, and often I push away from the desk and pace the house, telling myself I have to begin but not doing it. Instead, I fret and walk, holding on to the backs of chairs, door frames and countertops as I go because my legs have become untrustworthy and I don't want to fall again.

At one point I decide I will never be able to write the truth and, maybe, if Hanna will come and sit still long enough I could speak it to her, but when I call she's out, and the relief is so intense it makes me weak.

I will write it. I will tell her all I've been ashamed of and all I've lied about but I have to do it in a way that she will listen to without prejudice. I couldn't stand seeing her get up and walk out before I finished explaining.

So I make myself begin and write every day I am able, shaking, weeping, raging, and missing Hanna, but at the same time glad she isn't visiting as often or staying as long because the stress of confessing has accelerated my illness.

I am disintegrating, losing control, and there is no hiding it anymore.

Hanna doesn't know I am dying, but that, I think, will be the least of the revelations.

Chapter 20

Hanna

I got into a wicked fight with my parents and now I'm grounded.

Seems my father ended up behind Crystal's brother in 7-Eleven yesterday, and of course Crystal's brother had been drinking, so he smelled like it, and then he was dumb enough to say something to the counter guy about throwing one more kegger in the woods before it got too cold, so my father came home and started questioning me about what type of behavior went on at Crystal's house, anyway.

I shrugged. "I don't know. Me and Crystal have our own stuff to do."

Then he said, "Well, I don't want you going down there for a while. If you want to see Crystal, you two can hang around here."

And I should have let it go, because it probably would have slipped his mind, but like a jerk I didn't. "I don't want to hang out here. There's nothing to do."

"You can do the same things here that you do there," my father said, and now he was starting to sound testy because it was suppertime and he was hungry and tired from work and, I don't know, maybe he just expected me to fold and turn into some meek kid, but that's not how I felt.

"Why are you punishing me? I didn't do anything wrong! God, what am I supposed to do, just die here alone? "

"Hanna," he said in a warning tone.

I glanced at my mom and she gave me a look that said, *Be quiet,* but I couldn't. "It's not fair! You guys already *chose* your life, and now what, I'm not allowed to go out and find mine? I don't want to get stuck here doing stupid boring things! I want to go out!"

"I know you do," my mother said. "We understand, Hanna. We were young once, too."

I hate when adults say that. I do. They always say it when they're trying to shut down your life and stop you from having fun. I mean, if they know what I want, then why do they keep getting in the way?

I could be so much worse, and it's like they don't even *know* it. They get so surprised whenever they realize that I might not be exactly who they think I am, that there are parts of my life that are *mine, my* secret hopes and dreams and hurts and tragedies, things that, if the robber guy had killed me that day, they would never have known because I've never even said them out loud, or that there's stuff about me that only Crystal and Sammi know, or experiences I've had that only Jesse or Seth know about.

They only know the Hanna I *want* them to know; they're only allowed to see what I show them, and all the life-changing stuff—except for being robbed—is my own personal business.

I'm not a little girl anymore.

I want my *own* life and yeah, I'm probably going to make mistakes, but they're *my* mistakes. I don't try to hurt anybody or lie or anything, but sometimes I *have to* just to get what I need.

And if they really remembered what sixteen was like, they'd remember that, too.

Anyway, the argument got stupider and I got more frustrated and really mouthy and my father got really mad and grounded me for a week.

Joy.

I'm still grounded but I'm allowed to go over to Gran's to help feed the animals, so today I did because I ran out of stuff to read and figured I'd see if she had anything good, because she belongs to like five book clubs and gets books in the mail almost every day.

Well, I found out she had to quit all of them because she doesn't have the money thanks to crappy insurance and her medication being so expensive, which really sucks because now all she's reading are Parkinson's real-life stories and back-to-the-land biographies written by people who ditched civilization and were apparently supremely happy living independently in the country.

I *already* live in the country and right now I'm not very happy, so I borrowed a couple of old murder mysteries from the bookcase instead.

When we wandered outside, Serepta came, too, although she gave me a puzzled look like she'd never seen me before and crept under a shrub.

"She's getting old," Gran said, holding on to the porch railing and gingerly lowering herself to the step. Her knees crinkled and crunched and her hand was making this unnerving rolling motion that I was trying to pretend I didn't notice until she noticed me not noticing her.

"Horrible, isn't it?" she said, holding up the hand and watching it quiver. "I hate it."

"Does it hurt?" I said cautiously.

"What doesn't?" she said and shrugged.

I didn't know what to say, so I just leaned against the railing and gazed out at the pond. "Look, the does are back there."

"They don't even know how little time they have left." She scratched her knee. "Do you think it's worse to know it's coming even though then you have time to make arrangements and say good-bye, or is it worse to die quick and unexpected?"

"Quick and unexpected," I said without hesitation, adding silently, *And in a greasy Olympia's Sub Shop apron.* "I would rather have time to say good-bye."

"I guess so," she said and, sighing, glanced at the hunting cabin next door. "I hate knowing there's nothing I can do to save them, not even for an hour, not even for a day."

"At least they're safe here," I said and then finally remembered to tell her about feeding the deer hay instead of corn in winter. She didn't get as upset as I thought she would, only nodded and so we hung out a little longer, but we were both in quiet moods, so I left soon after that and followed the path through the break in the woods separating our back acres from theirs.

There was no wind and I could hear my footsteps. I could hear each falling leaf touch down. I could hear the wasps buzzing as I passed the dilapidated old wood barn. The sunlight was thin and the air still, the trees still, and I got the oddest thought—*It's a helluva thing*—but I didn't know what that meant, only that it felt like the land was waiting. Just waiting, like it knew everything was changing, and that was a dumb thought because of *course* it did, the birds knew, the animals knew, and so did the plants and trees, because it was autumn for God's sake, and soon it would be winter . . . but still.

By the time I made it up our back steps and into the house, I'd started feeling like I was waiting on the change of season, too.

Last day of grounding, so I took the books back to Gran. It was chillier today, there was a wind, and the wasps were gone. I passed her garden and scared up a flock of finches who must have been feasting on all the flowers and weeds and old tomatoes gone to seed.

This was the first time I can remember that Gran didn't open her door wide and automatically invite me in. She was in sweats and slippers and she looked like she'd been crying, which freaked me out because I'm so used to her being strong that I didn't know what to say.

It didn't really matter, though, because she took the books—she was shaking bad—and said she hoped I didn't mind but she wasn't feeling up to company. So of course I was like, No, no problem, and on my way back I walked up on a doe standing motionless in the tree line without even seeing her until she broke and ran, with her big white, fluffy tail waving to signal danger. I wanted to tell her, No, stop, I'm not one of the dangerous ones, but she didn't give me the chance.

It's a weird time. Or maybe it's just me.

I sliced a chunk of skin off my shin this morning shaving my legs. It bled and hurt so bad that I can't even imagine what it must feel like to have a razor-tipped arrow slice right into your guts.

I hate bow-hunting season and I hate waking up in the dark. I hate walking down the driveway and the wooded parts of the road to the bus stop in my stupid pink hat, afraid that someone just a little sleepy or nearsighted might mistake my hair for a deer and draw a bead on my spine. (Because for some reason, that's always how I think of it, as an arrow shattering my spine.)

I don't know what's wrong with me.

I don't know why I'm thinking of the robbery again now, too, when the mornings are so cold and dark, and triumphant hunters drive by the bus stop hauling bloody carcasses with lolling heads in the beds of their pickup trucks.

Grim.

Chapter 21

Hanna

I think Seth might finally like me again.

He had a free period, so he stopped by my locker, and I cut class, so we ended up hanging out in the upstairs hall, leaning against the window ledge next to each other. The whole time I was absorbing his details, the shape of his hands, his fingertips callused from playing the guitar, the way the bottom of his wavy hair was summer-sun blond, mingling threads and fading up to a darker winter blond, his eyes, not a clear blue but a smudgy one, and how, even sitting, my shoulder was inches below his, perfect for resting my head against if the opportunity ever came up.

A lot of kids passed by on the way to the staircase, gave us interested looks, and said hi, which was kind of funny after a while because we both know so many people that we started making bets on who the next one would be, one of mine, one of his, or an unclaimed neutral.

"So what do I get if I win?" he said, giving me a dangerous smile.

"Ummm . . . a hearty handshake?" I said brightly.

"Get the hell out of here," he said, laughing.

"Okay," I said, pushing off the windowsill like I was leaving.

"Get back here," he said, catching hold of my wrist. "Am I gonna have to hold on to you just to keep you from running out on me?"

"I don't know. Let me go and let's find out," I said, cocking my head and giving him a sparkling look from under my lashes.

"I don't think so," he said, sliding his fingers through mine and holding my hand. He caught sight of a couple of guys heading toward us, and grinning, he raised our linked hands and said, "How you doing?"

"What's up, Seth?" they said, giving him these really cheesy guy-congratulatory grins.

"Three more for me," he said smugly when they passed.

"Maybe, but you're starting a rumor," I said, giving our hands a pointed look.

"So?" he said, glancing at me. "Do you care?"

And what I wanted to do was shout, *Make it more than a rumor! Make it a reality!* But what I actually did was shrug and say, "Hey, if you don't care, I don't care."

"Okay, then," he said and waved our linked hands at kids four more times, which put me three kids behind him, and the bell rang before I could recoup my losses.

"Woman, you are now *my* love slave," he said, rising and releasing me.

"I'll think about it," I said, fluffing my hair and tucking it back behind my ears. "What's the job description?"

He laughed and fell into step beside me. "You do whatever I want you to do."

"Hmm. So far, no good. Pay?"

"None."

I snorted. "No wonder you're having trouble filling the position. What about benefits?"

"You want benefits, too?" he said, grinning.

"Well, yeah, because so far, I don't get anything at all," I said.

"You get me," he said, nudging my arm.

My heart skipped and I caught my breath and, for a second, all sound stopped and the air shimmered and I almost said, *okay,* I almost showed my whole hand and I would have if some dippy sophomore in blue eye shadow hadn't bumped into me hard and knocked me right out of the moment.

"Sorry," she mumbled, ducking and slipping past.

"Nothing like watching where you're going." Shaking my head, I crossed the hall to my locker and got my history book. "Well . . ."

"Oh, no, you don't," he said. "You're not getting away that easy. Come on, I'll walk you to class."

So he did and even though I didn't see him again for the rest of the day, the last thing he said was, "You know I won fair and square. That should get me *some*thing."

"Oh, I'm sure it will," I said. "I just don't know *what* yet."

"I do," he said with a slow, sexy smile.

"Bye," I said, laughing and heading into class.

I can't even believe it.

All I have to do to *get* him is pretend that I don't want him.

Seth was stoned in school today and Connor told me he had to go sit out in Phil's car just so he wouldn't get snagged and suspended. Then he told me that Seth was having a hard time at home and his parents were thinking about taking him out of St. Ignatz and sending him to public school instead.

"Wow, that would suck," I said.

Connor looked at me hard, like he was trying to gage something. "You should go out and see him," he said finally.

"Me?" I said, surprised. "Why?"

"Do me a favor and just go," he said. "I think he needs a friend right about now."

A friend.

Great.

But I went, of course.

Seth was lying down in the back of Phil's car, so I climbed into the shotgun seat.

"Hey," he said, not even bothering to sit up. "Where you been hiding?"

"Oh, I've been around," I said, more than a little freaked at how out of it he was. "What's going on with you?"

He grunted and closed his eyes. "Too . . . much . . . shit."

"Do you maybe want to talk about it?" I said, leaning over the seat and nudging him into opening his eyes. "I'm a decent listener." And a fool because, yes, I still wanted him.

"You're a decent everything," he said and then shook his head and gazed up at the ceiling. "I'm pretty fucked up." He laughed without humor. "It runs in the family."

"Mm?" I said, settling my chin on the back of the seat and watching him.

"Oh, yeah," he said and then was quiet for a while. When he finally spoke, he didn't look at me. "I don't get you."

"What's not to get?" I said lightly.

He snorted and this time he did smile, still without looking at me. "Forget it."

"No, really, what?" I said, leaning over and poking him. "Tell me."

He caught hold of my arm and then slid his hand down to cover mine. Gazed at our hands as if debating, then ran his thumb gently across my knuckles. "You're nice."

"Is that a bad thing?" I said, watching him.

"You always look happy," he said, frowning.

"And . . . ?" I said.

"You are *definitely* not who I thought you were."

"So is that good or bad?" I said and waited, heart thumping, to discover my fate.

"I don't know yet."

I must have made a little noise as the blade sank into my heart, because he blinked and glanced at me, saw my face, and said, "No, I don't mean that in a bad way, not to you. I mean it to me." He shook his head. "Shit, I really didn't want to . . . look, it's not you."

"Okay, I get it." My voice was rusty. "You don't have to say anymore. Just forget it."

"No, you're thinking wrong, I can see it. You're nice, Hanna." He stopped and seemed to struggle with something. "*I'm* not, okay?"

"What, nice?" I said, surprised. "Yes, you are."

He shook his head, refusing to meet my gaze. "Every time I go to ask you out, I think, *Yeah, okay, she's a major flirt, she knows what's up, she knows how to play the game,* and then you give me that big smile or you say something that totally throws me a curve, and then I'm like, *Shit, maybe not,* and . . ." He cleared his throat.

"So you're saying I'm too nice," I said flatly.

"*No,*" he said, looking at me now. "I'm saying you're nice and I don't want to fuck that up, okay? And if we go out, I *will,* because I always do." He looked away again and ran a hand through his hair.

"Then why did Connor even send me out here?" I said.

He was silent for a long moment. "I told him to."

"Why?" I said.

"I almost didn't," he said in a low voice.

"But you *did,*" I said, laying my hand on his arm and smiling when he finally looked at me, because there was something there, I could feel it, and if it took all I had, I wasn't going to let it go. "So why?"

His smoky blue eyes grew shiny and he muttered, "Oh, *Christ,*" and looked away, but he was laughing a little when he did it, like he was embarrassed and then he swallowed hard, I saw his Adam's apple bob, and he said, "You sure you want to do this?" and I said, "Do what?" and then he laughed to himself again like he couldn't believe he was going to do this, and my heart started pounding so loud I could hardly hear him when he looked at me and, with a crooked, bittersweet smile, said, "So do you want to go out with me, Hanna?"

Yes.

Chapter 22

Helen

It's done.

The truth I've never dared speak to anyone but Lon is actually down now, in writing. It was Lon's idea to send it away and make it into a real book because Hanna always borrows those.

The thing is, she doesn't read nonfiction, and so I had to think further.

I wanted her to listen.

I wanted her to understand.

And because I was doing so poorly and missed her so much, the fear of losing her fell under the need to sit with her through this story just like I had when I'd told all those other stories.

This was the one that counted, and so I sent my words, my secrets, to a narrator, and they came back as an audiobook.

Chapter 23

Hanna

We spent the rest of the day in Phil's backseat.

My *yes* did something, unlocked him somehow, and he dropped his distant-Seth self and turned into . . . I don't know, a sweet, sexy Seth who wrapped me in his arms and blew my mind. All those pent-up emotions came out in sighs and whispers, in touching and stroking and murmuring each other's names and laughing softly and being able to lean against him the way I'd wanted to for so long, to feel his arms holding me so tight it was like he would never let me go, hearing him say things like, "I can't believe I'm doing this," and they came out kind of hesitant at first, like he was wondering at it, and his bewilderment made me a little sad for him and also love him all the more.

We talked some, too, during those up-for-air moments, and I told him all kinds of important things about my life because I wanted him to know about me and I wanted to know about him, too.

I told him about my parents separating when I was little but how they were okay now, and the sub shop robbery, how Gran had come to be my grandmother, and about how she and Grandpa had met. I told him about her stray-cat condos on the porch, and he said, "So she's a crazy cat lady," and I said, "No, not at all," and tried to explain why taking care of them mattered and how we had kind of a sanctuary there for deer, too, but halfway through he started kissing my neck and I lost track of everything but him, which I think, when it comes to true love, is exactly how it should be.

I don't know what I love more: being Seth's girlfriend, or the surprise on peoples' faces at school when they see us with our arms around each other.

Sammi's been tracking all the reactions, and in these last two days it's ranged from bets that we won't last a month to some sophomore wearing blue eye shadow crying in the bathroom after we walked by on that first day with our arms around each other.

Bizarre.

We met between classes, used each other's lockers, ate together, hung out together, and were pretty much inseparable. It felt amazing being able to walk into the caf and meet his gaze, to be able to write *Hanna & Seth TLF* all over my books, to be able to turn to someone and say, "Have you seen Seth?" when I was looking for him or have somebody in class nudge me and to look to the door to see him standing out in the hall, smiling and waiting on me.

On our one-week anniversary Seth bought a blue secondhand SUV. He had to get a job to pay for gas and insurance, so he's going to be working in a bowling alley out near his house four nights a week and, unfortunately, Saturday daytime—but, we now have a place of our own where we can be alone, as long as we can find a private place to park it.

Making out in lust is great, but making out in *love* is stellar, the two of us wrapped together in the backseat, his hand slipping under my jacket, under my shirt, pushing up my bra and finally closing around me, all the while straining against me and me against him, wanting but not taking because it wasn't just something to do but me and him, and it mattered what we thought of each other when it was over.

At least it did to me, because what he'd said to me that day—how I knew how to play the game, how I'd been around—had never actually left me, and sometimes when I saw him smiling at other girls or walked up on him joking around with them, or he walked up on me joking with other guys, I thought about that, about the difference between a guy's reputation and a girl's, and yeah, it bothered me.

So even though all I really wanted to do was say I love you and rip his clothes off and let him rip mine off, I went slow, and I have to say it was a blast.

We had our first fight.

I guess it *was* my fault, because he's right, I know how he is and I shouldn't have come up on him and that blue-eye-shadow-wearing sophomore Lacey McMullen with such a bitch attitude, but it's too late now.

You know how you can look at the same thing every day for weeks and think nothing of it but then all of a sudden something in your mind clicks, and you realize there's something very wrong with this picture? Like while you were busy thinking nothing of it, your subconscious knew otherwise and was connecting dots so you would finally realize the threat?

Well, what I noticed was Lacey McMullen, with the giant, sparkling cow eyes rimmed in bright blue eye shadow, a substantial set of boobs, flushed cheeks, a perky, eager smile, and a very strange tendency to be hovering on the outskirts every time I turned around.

No, not every time *I* turned around.

Every time I was with Seth and turned around.

And the worst thing was . . . I knew that look.

It was anticipation, even though the odds were against you.

It was being ready and waiting for that instant, unexpected opportunity.

That did not bode well, especially after I pointed her out to Sammi, who said, Yeah, she's the one who was crying in the bathroom when she found out you two were going out.

Great.

The only good part was that he didn't seem to know she existed, or so I thought until I got out of gym early, walked into the caf, and saw him leaning against the wall with his hands in his pockets and her standing in front of him, laughing and wrapping his necktie around her finger.

I strode over, eyebrows high and wearing a serious bitch face because flirting was one thing but touching quite another.

She saw me coming, let go of his tie, and stepped back but didn't leave.

That irritated me even more, so I looked at him and said, "Am I interrupting something?" which turned out to be the absolute wrong thing to say.

"Well, yeah, actually you are," he said coolly, and that was like knives in my stomach because she was still standing there soaking it all up, so I gave her a look that said, *Get the hell out of here* now.

She looked past me at him.

He nodded and said, "I'll catch up with you later," and *then* she sauntered off.

I couldn't believe it. "Take a walk with me?" I said with a tight smile.

"Sure," he said with absolutely no warmth in his voice at all and ambled out of the cafeteria after me, not even trying to catch up or hold my hand.

laura wiess

"So what was that all about?" I said, pushing open a door and stopping in an empty stairwell.

He shrugged. "Nothing."

"Really," I said and hated the shaky hurt in my voice.

He must have heard it, too, because his remote expression faded. "What do you want me to say, Hanna? Oops, you caught me talking to another girl? C'mon." He pulled me into his arms and I went, stiffly and filled with frustration, but I went. "It was no big deal. She's just a kid—"

"Who has a crush on you," I mumbled, and bingo, that was another wrong thing, because he laughed and said, "Yeah, I know, but so what? That doesn't mean I have a crush on *her.*"

"Hmph," I said, unwinding enough to put my arms around him.

"So I hang out with her sometimes, so what? It doesn't mean anything," he said, tilting my face up and catching sight of my tear-filled eyes. "Oh, c'mon, don't." He kissed me. "Shh, c'mon. Don't you know that I love you?"

I went still and searched his gaze. "Really?"

"Yeah," he said, laughing as I threw my arms up around his neck. "Yeah, yeah, yeah, Hanna, baby. I do."

Two nights later, parked in our spot, he slid a hand down into my jeans and put my hand into his, and it was tight maneuvering on both parts, so we actually unzipped, and I got my first real feel of him. He put his hand around my hand and showed me how to move it and then he slid his hand back down into my pants and started kissing me wildly. My hand was moving and his was moving and both of us were breathing loud and his hand hit the right spot on me in passing and I arched up into it and I guess that really made him crazy because maybe four seconds after that he totally lost it and collapsed on me, gasping and laughing. He brushed my sweaty hair from my cheeks and looked into my eyes and said, *You're so beautiful,* and then, with his hand still down there, said, *Now you,* but I got shy and would have said no if he hadn't started kissing me again.

It got so hot that I actually put my hand on his and showed him where and how, and when it happened, he was exultant and said he'd never done that for anybody before.

I said, *Me neither,* and that meant we had a real first together.

My father was called back to work and my mother says that when there's more money coming in, maybe we can start fixing up the basement so me and Seth can have a place to hang out.

Plus, my mother says Gran has discovered books on tape, and now Grandpa goes to the library for her and brings home as many audiobooks as he can check out. She's still into books about Parkinson's, back to the land, or homeopathy, but she's been branching out to oldtime biographies, too.

I haven't been to see Gran in a while—too long actually—and while I'm really not into the audiobooks, she does still have bookcases full of regular novels I haven't read yet. They're going to come in handy, because Seth practices the guitar a lot when we're together, so I have a feeling I'll be reading just to pass the time.

It's kind of cool to be that comfortable with each other so quickly.

We had Gran and Grandpa over for dinner Sunday and it was quiet as my father was tired from working overtime and my mother was concerned about Gran, who was having trouble forming words fast enough for anyone to connect them into a sentence.

Grandpa stayed close by her now, always there in case she needed him, doing some kind of stepping thing in front of her when her feet froze in position and she couldn't make herself walk, supporting her when she first got up because her balance was getting really bad, and the sight of her made me want to cry, which I did but not until later when I was alone.

I think I'm going to go over to Gran's and ask her if she knows why my parents separated way back when. I mean, I get the idea that it wasn't because of cheating, but then what else could it have been? Money? We've never had a lot and they worry about the bills and stuff but that doesn't seem like such a big deal, either.

So why, then?

❧ ❧ ❧

I called first to see if she was up for a visit and I could tell just by how long it took her to form each slurred word that it was not a good day, so when she finally said no, I was disappointed but not surprised.

"Then can I ask you a quick question?" I said, getting up off the bed and shutting my bedroom door just in case my mother came upstairs.

"Sure," Gran said after a moment.

"Okay, well, remember back when my parents separated? Do you know why they did? I don't need all the details or anything, but nobody ever told me *why*." I sank to the edge of the bed and waited, gazing at my reflection in the full-length mirror on the closet door.

"Ask them," she said after a long pause.

I shook my head. "No, I can't. That's, like, *never* talked about. I mean, what if I bring it up and it starts something bad all over again? I don't want to do that. Can't you just tell me? Please?"

"Why dig up the past?" she said finally.

"Because it's my past, too; it's my family history and I think I'm old enough to know," I said promptly, because I was ready for that one.

"Then ask your mother," she said, struggling hard with each word. "It's not my story to tell."

I pulled back, looked at the cell phone, and stuck it back to my ear. "What?"

"Only they know the real reason," she said. "Do you understand?"

"No," I said, because I couldn't believe that out of all the stuff we'd talked about, this was the one thing she was not going to tell me. "C'mon, Gran. Please?"

"I can't," she said. "I don't know."

Oh my God. "Well, then, why do you *think* they split up? I mean, can you at least give me a clue?"

"Hanna." She said my name on a sigh, like the conversation was ending.

"Wait," I said frantically. "Was it because of cheating?"

"No," she said. "Life."

"What? What does that mean? I don't get it."

"Ask your mother," she said, sounding exhausted. "I have to rest. Bye."

"But . . . okay, bye. I guess." I sat there for a long time after she hung up, trying to figure out what the hell had just happened. Gran had never put me off, never not answered my questions—any question, especially an important one like that. Why had she told me to go ask my mother? I couldn't ask my mother, it was too dangerous a subject and could cause some type of subterranean rumble beneath what had felt like pretty solid ground ever since they got back together.

I didn't know what to do, so finally I just got up and tried to shut the closet door but it was too jammed with stuff so I gave up, leaving the door cracked open, and went downstairs to set the table for supper.

Chapter 24

Hanna

I swear to God, I could *kill* him.

I can't believe he did this to me.

I was still off the stupid mandatory community service list—and was happy about it because my plans to do it all in senior year had not changed—and stupid Seth finds out and decides that's irresponsible of me so he goes and talks to Mr. Sung, my guidance counselor. There was this big mess and now I have to do my sophomore and junior community service *this second,* instead of in senior year when Seth would have already graduated and been at college and I wouldn't have missed any time with him.

He *told* on me.

I can't believe it.

So then I had to tell my parents, and my father sided with him, but my mother said, yes, it was irresponsible, but it wasn't Seth's business to *fix* her daughter. That set off a big argument about how I was spending an awful lot of time with him and maybe that should change, too. I was like, oh my God, if he had just minded his own business, none of this would have happened in the first place.

The most hurtful part is that with him doing his community

service out in his town and then working at the bowling alley, and me now having to do double time, there's no way I can spend time with him, too, not any decent time besides at school. He said it was worth the sacrifice because his parents were on him now that it was senior year, and his father wanted him to go to *his* alma mater and his mother to *hers,* and he was holding out for Rutgers because it meant he would still be near enough to see me on weekends and all, but it just really pissed me off because if *I'd* overstepped my bounds and done it to him, he would've had a serious fit.

He brought me a rose to school, though, and acted really sorry, but there was something off about it . . .

I don't know, maybe it was me.

So now I have to make up, what, sixty hours of community service before winter break?

That's just great.

Without saying anything to anyone but my parents and the Schoenmakers, I designed my *own* community service idea and presented it to Mr. Sung, who I like very much because he's a big supporter of the rights of the individual and the pursuit of happiness.

But most important, Mr. Sung never gives me a pain about my cut slips. (Him: "Too many this week, Hanna. You had more free time than classes again, I see"; Me: "Well, I'm sorry, Mr. Sung, but if I went to all my classes, I would have never seen Seth"; Him: "You are going to end up shoveling manure for a living someday, Hanna"; Me: "I already do that here every day, Mr. Sung") and then he cracks up and so do I. He tries to look at me like I'm a grave disappointment but is no good at it because his eyes are always merry and he just seems so glad to be alive.

It's refreshing.

So anyway, I knew my idea was going to be a tough sell, so I bought a smoothie and a bagel with cream cheese from the caf and went into guidance with a big smile and a very obvious bribe. "Hey, Mr. Sung, you look happy this morning," I said, setting my offering on his desk. "Here, I brought you a present just because you're so splendid." I pulled up a chair and sat down, grinning because I knew he knew what I was doing, but that was okay. "Have I mentioned how handsome you look in burgundy? You should always wear it. I hear the nuns go crazy every time you walk by. But don't tell them I told you or I'll get in trouble."

Mr. Sung leaned back in his chair, lips twitching. "Ahhh, Hanna, every year I'm blessed with a challenge, a student who somehow manages to circumvent the rules, flaunt the requirements, ignore the classes, and who still leaves the faculty not only happy to see her but willing to find ways to help her squirm through. Congratulations on making it two for two." His grin widened. "I'm pretty sure you're going to set some sort of St. Ignatius school record."

"Well, I try," I said demurely, making him laugh. "No, but seriously, this stupid mandatory community service thing: I need to complete, what, sophomore and junior service by winter break?"

"That's sixty hours," he said. "I don't see how—"

"Well, actually," I said, and then made an apologetic face for interrupting him. "Sorry, but I already found a perfect worthy cause that would work really well and it'll give me all the hours I need. Since I have to do it and there's no way around it, I mean."

He chuckled and shook his head. "Why does this not surprise me? All right, what's the big plan? You're going to run a blood drive for senior Greenpeacers on a Save the Whales ship while teaching English as a second language?"

"Oh, you're a real wise guy today," I said, giving him a look and going on to explain how my neighbors the Schoenmakers sort of ran an animal rescue sanctuary and Gran had Parkinson's and not only did they need help caring for the rescue cats but Grandpa worked as a crossing guard to supplement their social security, which, as we all knew, was like a pittance compared to what they needed in real life just to afford her medication and all—

"Isn't she in a nursing home?" he said, frowning slightly.

"No, and that's the whole point," I said quickly, because I knew it was against the rules for students to volunteer in private homes. "She doesn't want to go into a nursing home, but they've used up the free day-care help from the church and all, and Grandpa is there with her every day except for the hours he needs to be a crossing guard, so—"

"Hanna," he said.

"Oh, Mr. Sung, please, just listen outside the box for a minute, okay," I said, giving him anxious spaniel eyes because I was not above using what I had to get what I needed, and besides, it always amused him whenever we tried to persuade him into supporting outlandish ideas. "They can't hire babysitters because they have no money and they've already put in formal requests to all the high schools to be considered for the community service lists and were turned down but *it isn't fair.*"

"Explain," he said and sat back like he was ready to enjoy the show.

That was a very good sign.

"Well, if Gran was in a nursing home, then I could spend every single day there getting pinched by smelly old bald guys with waggly eyebrows and giant hairy moles, and breathing in every hideous geriatric germ known to mankind, and the school would still absolutely give its blessing, right?"

He covered his face and waved me on.

"But here's someone in a private setting who *isn't* a burden on society and who *isn't* draining the system of resources . . ." I paused, waited until he looked at me again, and then gave him a knowing look because I was very proud of that phrase and wanted to make sure he caught it. "And so she gets told no, you're not allowed to have any help because *you* won't spend the rest of your life the way *we* think you should! That's not fair."

He glanced pointedly at the clock.

It was almost time for homeroom, so I gave it all I had. "I *know* this family, Mr. Sung. I've known them since I was born and I've been in their house a thousand times—who do you think lends me all those books you always see me reading? Gran, that's who! Back when they had money she used to belong to maybe five book clubs, but now . . ." I sighed and shook my head. "Well, now she can't even *hold* a book anymore—and how sad is *that*?—so Grandpa gets her audiobooks and she listens to them and they're actually kind of boring now because she's only getting these back-to-the-land biographies by old hippies . . ." I caught his amusement at my digression and rallied. "Anyway, it's perfect. My parents are totally behind it, I can do my homework while I'm there with her, and they really, *really* need help. I mean, isn't that the whole point of doing community service, anyway? Helping people who really need it and not just sitting around pushing papers or stuffing envelopes?" I sat up straight, nodded, and gave him my brightest smile. "So, what do you say? Will you go to bat for me on this? Please?"

Score.

     ✣   ✣   ✣

There was more to it than that, of course—there always is whenever you have to ask permission for something—and Mr. Sung said he'd have to go out to the Schoenmakers' to make sure they really did exist and it wasn't actually something like Schoenmakers' Billiard Parlor or Tanning Salon (he really is a wise guy) but it was as good as done.

     ✣   ✣   ✣

I waited until I got the official nod and then told Sammi, who thought I was nuts for not going for the easy envelope-stuffing job at the local politician's headquarters, and Seth, who just gave me a smug grin and said, "See? Now that wasn't so bad, right?"

I felt like punching him and said so, and he laughed and kissed me.

I really do love him. I complain, but it really is great knowing he cares enough to look out for me.

Chapter 25

Hanna

I don't know if I can do this.

Do my community service at Gran's, I mean.

When I thought of it, I hadn't been there in a while, so I didn't know how bad it was, but oh my God, poor Gran is falling apart. I mean, she can't even talk anymore.

I can't think about it or I'll start crying.

The place is a wreck. I mean, Grandpa is doing what he can, I guess, but there's no way he can do it all. Just no way.

I mean, she can't even *talk*.

And she scared me. This disease is scary. It's like it's taken her over and she's totally out of control.

I came home, looked at my mother and burst into tears.

"Why didn't you tell me?" I cried.

"Tell you what?" she said quietly, leaning back against the kitchen counter and watching as I collapsed in a chair. "That poor Lon is going to work himself right into another heart attack if he didn't get some help with Helen? That when you ask him how he's doing and he says, 'Well, it's been hard sometimes,' it's the understatement of the century? That Helen will have this disease for *years,* Hanna, for the rest of her life, and the medication may slow the progression, but it'll never cure it because there is no cure. Oh, sweetie." She crossed the room and crouched beside me. "Tell me."

So I did once I stopped crying . . .

❧ ❧ ❧

The bus dropped me off in front of my house, but instead of going in, I headed around back and through the little woods to Gran's. I had to walk fast because Grandpa had to get down to the grade school for his crossing guard job, so I followed the deer trail up toward the old farmhouse.

I felt pretty damn good at being so noble and doing something *real* for my service, something one-on-one, and as I passed the garden, I said hi to all the stray cats watching me warily and the bird feeders, which definitely needed filling. I skipped up onto the porch, knocked twice, and heard Grandpa call, "Come in!" I did, and oh my God, I was in the middle of saying, "Hi, your friendly neighborhood volunteer is—" when I saw Gran in a wheelchair by the window and Grandpa pulling on his crossing guard vest and checking for his wallet.

It's a good thing he was in a rush, because I was so shocked by the sight of both of them, how small they had gotten and how old, that I don't even know if I could have spoken.

"Her medication is wearing off, but there's a church volunteer here with you today, so she can show you what to do," he said, taking my hand and looking into my eyes. "You're a lifesaver, Hanna. I don't know what we would have done if you hadn't come to help. Now, I have to run."

He left and I took a deep breath and slid my book bag off my shoulder, then went over and touched the woman in the chair whose arms and hands and feet were twitching and jerking. "Gran? Hi, it's me, Hanna." I waited because I knew she was moving slower, and she finally turned her head maybe an inch. I figured that meant she knew I was there, because after all, she wasn't deaf, so I said, "Um, do you need anything?"

"She can't talk," someone said, and I turned and saw an older lady with sleek gray hair coming out of the kitchen and wiping her hands on an old striped dish towel. She glanced at it, wrinkled her nose slightly, and said, "Well, Lon says he can still understand her, but I believe that's wishful thinking on his part." She smiled and smoothed her hair. "She's had some applesauce and I changed her diaper and she has a sippy cup full of water, and Lon says he's been putting on one of those books on tape for her every afternoon and she listens to a couple of chapters, so if you don't have any questions, then I'll be off."

"I . . . uh . . ." I didn't like this lady, I didn't like how comfortable she was here or the way she said Grandpa's name, like they were best friends or something, and I really didn't like the way she told me she'd changed Gran's diaper, because, oh my God, that wasn't something I'd even thought of, and it was private and she just said it right out loud without even caring that Gran had heard her . . . but this lady *was* a grown-up, and once she left, it would just be me and Gran, and I honestly didn't know if I could handle it.

"Well, I'm sure you'll be fine," she said briskly, picking up her purse and heading for the door. "Just be careful not to let her slide out of the chair and fall. Bye now."

"Bye." I waited until I saw her headlights sweep out of the driveway, then looked at Gran.

She looked back blank-faced, no expression, but her eyes, oh, they weren't blank at all, they were full of sadness and fear and all the things I knew she was dying to say but couldn't. I felt my own tears rising, and tamped them down fast, because who knew what would happen if she cried? Could she blow her nose, even if I held the tissue, or would she choke on it?

"Well, I'm glad *she's* gone," I said into the silence, watching her watch me, hands waving and jerking, body trembling, legs twisting and feet in spasms. It was bad, really bad and the longer it went on the more I wanted to beg her to stop, *please stop,* because my Gran would never scare me like this, would never leave me standing here in shock, lost, shaking and near tears without opening her arms and holding me safe. This gaunt, twisted old lady with the messy hair and stone face, this silent woman hunched over in the wheelchair was a stranger, someone I didn't know, could *never* know . . .

And yet I *did* know her, I did, and so I sank down on the otto-man across from her and caught hold of one of her fluttering hands, surprised at how warm and soft it was. I kept it between mine, feel-ing it strain to fly free but I didn't release her, only held her gaze and she held mine and I smiled, overwhelmed and said, "Did I ever tell you that I love you?" Her eyes filled with tears and I realized what I'd done and yelled, "Crap!" and jumped up, released her and grabbed a tissue. She blinked and two tears fell but she was still breathing okay so I said, "All right, let me put your book on and then don't tell my mother or she'll make me do it at home, too, but I think I'll straighten up for you and maybe do some laundry."

Grandpa had put their little old-fashioned stereo unit with a tape player and CD player right near her, and there were two CD cases next to it. One title was *How It Ends: A Love Story* and the other *Country Home Blues,* and that second CD was already in the player so I switched it on and half listened as the narrator started telling a story about maple syrup season in Vermont.

I made sure Gran was belted in okay, gave her some water from the sippy cup and waited until she swallowed each minuscule drop, found her ChapStick on the tray table, and put that on her too—and let me tell you, that was rough because her head wouldn't hold still, so I ended up getting her on the cheek, then the chin, then the nose, and I didn't want to laugh, but I did because it was so silly, a terrible situation but also an absurd one, and I think (I hope) I saw laughter in her eyes, too, but maybe it was wishful thinking because mostly I saw fear, and then nothing.

I kept an eye on her and listened to the book (which was kind of dull) while getting the cat food ready for the strays. I didn't talk as I did it, figuring she wanted to hear the story, but when the chapter was over, I chatted some, nothing big, just the kind of stuff you say to fill a silence.

I finally put the TV on because there was only one chapter of *Country Home Blues* left and then only one audiobook left and I figured we'd need that for tomorrow, so I did homework waiting for Grandpa to return because I couldn't put out the cat or deer food until there was somebody to stay with her.

And then I started thinking about that, about how if Grandpa wanted to, he could just put her in a nursing home tomorrow and there would be nothing she could do about it because she couldn't talk, couldn't e-mail or IM or protest, couldn't even stand up and run away. She was trapped, totally and completely, and the more I watched her tremble and writhe, twist and sweat, my God she was sweating so bad, the more horrifying it got because it wasn't ending. She couldn't change it, couldn't shake it off, stand up, and say, *Whew, I've had about enough of that!*

She couldn't stop it. *Ever.*

And *that* freaked me out even more because that meant she would never bake me another carrot cake for my birthday or walk the back acres or tell me a story, crochet mittens or even get up to go to the bathroom or reach across the table for another biscuit at Thanksgiving.

This wasn't an attack from someone else, someone who wanted your money and would beat your face in to get it; no, this was yourself attacking you from the inside out, and you could never escape yourself.

෩   ෩   ෩

And that's what I told my mother, sitting at the kitchen table, the words falling low and hoarse and still stunned because in a world where *every*thing could be changed, could be bought, begged, borrowed, or stolen, it was too incredible to think that *this* could not.

I wanted to believe that if she just tried hard enough, she could stop it, if she just hoped hard enough, it would change and she could *save* herself but she just wasn't trying hard enough. . . . But it wasn't true.

She had no choice.

I tried to tell Seth about last night but when I got into the heart of it, when I said, "Can you imagine just waking up one day and not being able to talk and thinking, *Oh, it'll pass,* but it never does and then realizing, Oh my God, whatever words I said last night were the last I'll ever be able to say? What if they were nothing words like *See you later* or *I washed your blue shirt* or *Don't forget to set your alarm* and all the things you figured you had plenty of time to say, all the questions and answers and things you were holding on to, just waiting for the right time to say them—"

"All right, already, I get it," he said, holding up a hand and cutting me right off.

I looked at him, astonished.

"Come on, Hanna, it's depressing and I don't want to get depressed, I want to enjoy being with you," he said, putting his arm around me but avoiding my gaze. "She can't talk. I get the idea. Now, can we move on?"

And without waiting for me to answer, he did move on, talking about stuff like his work and how people couldn't bowl for shit and some new song he was learning on his guitar while I sat there full of words and with no one to receive them.

かわ   かわ   かわ

I tried again later to tell him how it felt to see her helpless but he cut me off again, this time annoyed and was like, "What the hell? I already told you I didn't want to talk about it; do I have to come right out and *say* I don't give a shit? I mean I feel sorry for her, I do. She was a nice lady—"

"Was?" I said. "Seth, she isn't *dead*."

"Well, you know, maybe that'd be better," he said, running a hand through his hair and avoiding my horrified look. "Would you want to live all fucked up like that? I wouldn't."

"Well, no, but it's not that simple," I said, groping for the words to explain how I felt. "Maybe it's only bad from the outside, the part we can see, you know? Maybe inside, in her mind, she's still okay with being able to see the yard and the deer and—"

"Yeah, okay, all right, Hanna, you're getting a little too intense," he said, leaning away from me and staring off across the courtyard. "I mean, I just want to be with you, okay? Have some fun, you know? Remember fun?" He glanced at me and smiled, put his arm around me and pulled me close. "I get what you're saying, but there's nothing you can do and it's getting you all freaked out. Just keep your distance and do your time there and put it behind you when you leave." He dropped a kiss on my head. "She's old, you know? Shit happens."

And we sat until the bell rang, with him smiling and joking with people going by and me smiling and wondering how I could love someone and he could love me, and I could still feel so alone.

Chapter 26

Hanna

I went back to Gran's to continue my community service because I had to.

When I got there Grandpa was distracted and running late again. He told me Gran was having a pretty good day, that she *could* still communicate but only sometimes, very slowly and by blinking—one for yes and two for no—only it didn't always work, so I shouldn't take the blinks for absolute truth.

He said he'd gotten a little baby food into her—baby food, oh God—and put the next audiobook in, too, but not to play more than a chapter or two a day because she would fall asleep somewhere in the middle and miss parts and she hated that.

He squeezed my hand and hobbled out. I took a deep breath and was going to try to be cheerful, but that would have been fake and I just couldn't do it, so I just said to Gran in a shaky voice, "I hope you don't mind but I'm not really in the mood to talk, so I'm just going to put on the tape. I hope that's all right."

I waited, watching her face, and there was one slow blink and if it was on purpose it meant yes, so I quick hugged her (and got whacked in the ear with an involuntary backhand for my trouble), then laid out my homework, started the next audiobook and sat down to work.

"How It Ends: A Love Story, *by Louise Bell Closson,*" the narrator said smoothly. Her voice was low and held an intriguing hint of intensity, and I looked at Gran, who sat listening all alone, and I thought about how many books we'd shared and talked about and so I put down my pencil and curled up in my chair next to her wheelchair.

"I would not willingly peel back the scar tissue protecting the deepest chambers of my heart and reveal the bruised hollows pooled with the blood of old wounds—the terror comes just thinking about it—but now, facing darkness, I am left with no choice. I love you, and because of that I am going to try and raise the dead."

"Wow," I said, pausing the CD and glancing at her. "You sure you want to hear this? It doesn't sound exactly cheerful."

She blinked once, slowly.

"All right," I said because I wasn't exactly cheerful, either, and even though the last thing I wanted to hear was someone else's happily ever after (or from the sound of it so far, bloody bruises) it was still better than silence.

I reached out, hit play, and settled back in the chair.

A Love Story

If you really want to hurt someone, if you're the type of person who smiles as you grind your heel down onto the white-knuckled grip of the desperate dangling off the edge of a burning building, then do this: tell your victim a devastating secret about a loved one, something that will change the way she thinks of them forever . . . but do it only after the loved one is gone, so she can never go back and ask them the truth.

The perfect time would be right after the graveside service, when she has to be half carried, wailing and inconsolable, out of the barren January cemetery, still reaching for the thirty-one-year-old mother left behind in the casket, and dragged back to the boardinghouse where she and her mother had rented a room from Kitty, who hurried ahead to set out a postfuneral buffet for the friends of the deceased.

Do it after the thirteen-year-old, now motherless child, dazed and heartsick, is herded into the bedroom to rest while downstairs the adults shed coats, blot drippy noses, and uncap the Rock and Rye to toast the deceased.

Sit the shattered girl on the edge of the same bed she shared with her frail, tubercular mother. Ease her stiff body down onto her side exactly as she was on that fateful morning four days ago when, feeling the faint warmth of the thin January sunlight on her face, she opened her eyes to find her mother lying beside her only inches away, stretched out and staring back, her lifeless, murky gaze fixed, sunken, and discolored, her skin slack and dusky purple, the bloodstained hanky clutched in a frozen claw, the dried trickle of rust staining the embroidered pillowcase beneath her cheek.

So go ahead, press the quaking child down to rest and tuck the blanket in tight around her, tuck it tight like the sheet turned shroud they wound around her mother while the child writhed and begged, and the landlady Kitty held her back . . .

And then pull down the shades and turn off the light, shut the door, and leave her to nap where the chill of death mingles with the sweet, familiar scent of Evening in Paris talcum powder, and her mother's pink velvet bathrobe hangs limp and defeated from a hook on the open closet door.

Become too busy to check on her as the hours pass and the party continues, as the mourners gather in pockets throughout the house, maybe even outside the bedroom where the child lies rigid and wide-eyed, afraid to move, afraid to sleep. Yes, let the mourners go on drinking, laughing, trading stories, reminiscing about good ol' Evelyn Bell, oops, you mean Evelyn Bell *Closson*, another one of those *war widows* who just can't seem to find her marriage certificate, and let the laughter follow, hearty laughter with a tinge of malice, not much really, just enough to wrinkle the girl's forehead, to cause her to search out the beloved souvenir photo in the cardboard frame from Ciro's nightclub that has sat on the table next to the bed for as long as she can remember.

The black-and-white photo, taken almost fourteen years ago, is of her parents, eighteen-year-old Evelyn Bell and twenty-one-year-old Walter Closson, on the night they met.

Their whirlwind romance has always been the child's favorite
bedtime story, the magical tale of how Evvie Bell, a pretty, vibrant
eighteen-year-old who had gone to Hollywood to make her fortune,
became a sophisticated cigarette girl at Ciro's and was discovered
not by movie mogul Louis B. Mayer but by movie-star-handsome
PFC Walter Closson, a GI with twinkling eyes, a wicked smile, and
a casual, irresistible grace. The tall, dark, and confident Walter spotted young Evvie across the crowded room and fell head over heels in
love, calling her to his table again and again, buying pack after pack
of Winstons, until the camera girl came along and he'd convinced the
dazzled, rosy-cheeked Evvie to pose with him for a photo.

That began their thrilling three-day romance, a fairy tale of dining,
dancing, an orchid corsage, and a champagne-hazy Army-chaplain
marriage outside the back of the club. This was immediately followed
by a one-night honeymoon at a nearby motel, Walter shipping out,
and Evvie being fired from Ciro's.

Within two months, Evvie, now alone, broke, and pregnant, decided Hollywood was no life for an American GI's wife, so she packed
her belongings, took her souvenir photo, and came home to Plainfield
to move back in with her grandmother Bell and wait for her husband
to return from war.

"And then came the saddest news of all," the child's mother would
say, the tip of her nose turning pink and her soft gaze far away and
glistening with unshed tears.

"Daddy was killed storming a bunker, and the grenade blew up
everything but the letter you wrote telling him about me," the child
would say when she was little, snuggling close to her mother, resting
her head on her chest and winding a strand of her mother's fine brown
hair around her finger. "And the envelope wasn't even opened yet, so
he didn't even know he was going to be a daddy."

"That's right," her mother would say, stroking the child's cheek. "And then you were born—"

"And then Grandma Bell died without ever finding Clark Gable's shoes under her bed and we moved here to Kitty's house and lived happily ever after," the child would say in a satisfied voice. "The End."

And her mother would kiss her and run a thin, work-roughened hand over the child's thick dark hair—her father's hair—and rise from the bed they shared in the rented room. Sometimes she would place a scarf over the lamp so the light wouldn't fall across the child's face and sit in the chair in the corner, mending socks and listening to the radio. Other times she would leave the child to sleep, close the door, and join Kitty and the other boarders in the parlor for coffee and company.

By the time she was thirteen, the child, Louise, knew her life. She understood it, and all the pieces fit; she'd been born a war baby to a war widow, and even though the war was long over, they still lived in a neighborhood of workingwomen and fatherless children, the block a collection of ramshackle shotgun shacks and female-owned boardinghouses, places with sagging, neatly swept front stoops, sparkling windows with paint-chipped sashes set beneath dented downspouts, and tidy former victory gardens in sight of single-seat outhouses.

A place where clothing was handed down and around, and harried mothers with distracted gazes, empty change purses, and mouths to feed worked days at the grocery store and nights at the factory while their children peeled potatoes and made beds, did homework, cut paper dolls, and played Hide and Seek, Tag, and 1–2–3 Red Light.

Occasionally a new boarder would arrive or an old one would leave, a baby would be born and there would be laughter and booties and scavenged lace for trimming bonnets, or a child would die and there would be tears and solemnity and dark clothes. The few little old men left living on the block would stand at the curb as the casket went by and hold their worn Sunday fedoras over their hearts, mop their rheumy eyes with rumpled hankies, and bow their heads in sorrow and respect.

It was a small life and for the most part a steady one, where once a month Louise and her mother would go to a movie matinee, a gala musical or snappy, sophisticated comedy, and they would eat red licorice and Sugar Babies, and laugh or cry together. Her mother would stifle her cough in one of her many hankies, and once the movie was over they would walk home, Louise singing or dancing along the sidewalk, always careful not to step on any cracks, her mother quiet and thoughtful until they came to their block, when she would suddenly look at her daughter, smile and say, "Who needs all that Hollywood glamour? We live our own way and ain't it grand?"

And yes, it was until four days ago, when Evvie lay down next to her daughter in bed, intending to rest a moment before letting out the hem on Louise's new hand-me-down winter coat, and while indulging in the simple pleasure of watching her daughter sleep, felt her heart flutter and then quietly, without fanfare, stop.

So if you want to destroy the child, to reveal a secret that can never be forgotten or slash a wound in her soul that will never heal, then say *this* outside her bedroom door on the afternoon they bury her mother: "Oh, for Pete's sake, if Evvie and Walter really *were* married, then why does the kid's birth certificate list the father as John Doe? Yes, I've seen it. Evvie showed it to me last New Year's Eve and made me promise never to tell."

And if the child's heart isn't already pounding close to bursting, then top it off with: "So the kid's not only an orphan now but a bastard, too. Who's gonna break *that* news?"

"The state will clue her in. They're sending somebody out to collect her tomorrow."

And despite the laughter and the noise of the party, the thin, terrified mewl that escapes the child is heard through the door, heard by

Evvie's friend Kitty standing outside, who blurts, "Oh balls, don't tell me she's awake?" and swings wide the door to reveal the child's stricken face in the shaft of light, wide-eyed, tearstained, and utterly lost.

The best friend of her late mother, flushed and tipsy on too much rye, does not say, *Oh, honey, I'm so sorry,* or, *Can I come in and keep you company?* but rather, "Jesus Christmas, don't look at me like that, Lou Lou. I'm not the one who's been lying to you your whole life. Now go to sleep!"

And then the door swings shut and the voices fade.

Moments later the child's cold hand, *my* hand, slips out from under the blanket, closes around the Ciro's souvenir photo, and tucks it beneath my undershirt, over my heart.

Exhausted, I sleep.

"Oh my *God,*" I said, looking at Gran. "Are you *sure* you want to hear another chapter?"

She blinked once, and one tear slipped down her cheek.

I blotted it with a tissue and hit play.

How It Ends

The lady from the state home came midmorning while I was sitting in the kitchen tracing the boomerang print on the laminate tabletop and trying not to look at Kitty, whom I was too numb to hate and too scared to lose.

The state lady was thin and abrupt, wore brown tweed, and smelled of cold, fresh cigarette smoke. She accepted coffee from Kitty, who had quickly shed her apron and straightened the kerchief tied over her rollers, and sat at the table across from me. Other than asking my name and raising an eyebrow when I mumbled Louise *Closson,* though, she spoke almost entirely to Kitty. She explained the official procedure, paused and blew on the steaming black coffee, then informed Kitty that I was allowed to bring one valise or cardboard box of necessaries but it couldn't be heavier than I could carry.

Kitty, either still hungover from the funeral party or maybe even a little ashamed of the secret she'd revealed the day before, rubbed her eyes, exhaled, and without looking at me, said gruffly, "Run down to the liquor store, Louise, and see if they have an empty box you can have."

"It was my understanding she would be ready to go," the state lady said, glancing at her watch. "I do have other appointments today——"

"Go, Lou," Kitty said and, as I slid out of my chair onto wobbly legs, added, "I'll get your things ready in the meantime."

So I went, stumbling weak-kneed and dumb in a thick, foglike fear through the cutting January wind, plodding down the frost-heaved sidewalk with the cold chapping my wet cheeks, absently pulling my benumbed fingers from my coat pocket to touch the home-base oak as I passed, skirting the remains of the hopscotch board chalked onto the cement from our last game before Christmas, detouring into the street past the dilapidated house with the chicken-wire gate and the dog who hated everyone.

The old foreign lady who lived there always smelled like cabbage and liniment, and when she smiled, her whole face would wrinkle like an accordion. Her hands were gnarled and covered with liver spots, and she scrimped all year to save enough to make the most delicious *kiflis* at Christmas, the prune, nut, and apricot filling moist and the powdered sugar drifted as high as sweet, dusty snowbanks. She had always liked my mother and me, always pinched my cheek, and for a moment a wild thought cut a chasm across the fog, a thought that said, *Maybe you could live here with her, maybe you could just walk right up those sagging steps and knock and when she answers you could beg her and she would hide you until the state lady left, maybe . . .*

But then the dog rushed the gate, snarling and barking, skinny and cranky on a diet of boiled cabbage, bread crusts soaked in bacon grease, and old soup bones, and my feet carried me past the house and around the corner to the liquor store with its smudged glass, crooked sign, and dead flies on the windowsills. I'd been in here twice before— all us kids always ran errands for the adults, eager for the nickel they'd give us—but I didn't know the man with the empty, pinned-up shirt-sleeve reading the newspaper behind the counter.

"Hey, kid, what do you need?" he said finally, glancing up when I sniffled.

The store was too warm, making me woozy, and stank of stale smoke, sweat, and sour wine. I shuffled forward and stopped in the hollow near the register, a dip in the floor where the linoleum pattern had been worn smooth by countless feet and asked for a free box.

"How big?" the guy said, motioning behind him to the jumble of empty liquor boxes piled in the corner.

"I . . . I . . ." I stammered and, because I didn't know, said, "I need to be able to carry it myself," and then everything blurred and the tears spilled over, running quick, hot, and without pause down my cheeks.

"Sure, I get it, sister," he said quickly, heading for the pile. "Don't take it to heart. Lotsa kids have to get rid of the puppies. I mean, what're you gonna do, keep 'em all? Can't do that, right, or they'd eat you out of house and home."

I sucked in a deep, hitching breath.

The guy nodded. "That's right, I had to do it myself once. Loaded up a box of the sweetest little mutts you ever wanted to see and dragged 'em door to door for three days. Got rid of all but two and I couldn't bring 'em back home because I knew my old man would drown 'em so I took 'em down to the park and left 'em in the box on a picnic table." He glanced at me. "I figured anybody going on a picnic's gotta be happy, you know, and puppies make people happy so I figure somebody would take 'em home." He studied a box, cast it aside, and reached for another. "This oughta do." He held it up, nodded, and handed it to me. "Listen, if I was you, though, before I went door to door I'd take 'em down to the grocery store or the butcher's and sit out there with 'em, looking real pitiful. I mean, what broad can resist a kid and a puppy, right? Heck, I'd take one myself if my landlord wasn't such a rotten old bastard, if you'll pardon my French."

I sniffled and wiped my face on my sleeve.

"Just . . . whatever you do, don't leave 'em in the park, not even on a picnic table. They got clowns out there who think it's funny to throw puppies in the pond to see if they can swim." He shook his head and, grimacing, rubbed the shoulder stump where the empty shirtsleeve hung. "Must be gonna snow." He gave it one last rub. "Okay?"

"Okay," I mumbled and, when he didn't say anything more, made my way out of the store and back down the block to Kitty's.

♥ ♥ ♥

When I returned, the state lady was on the phone in the hallway and Kitty was upstairs in my room, standing in front of the closet mirror holding my mother's best black velvet dress with the rhinestones on the collar. When she spotted me she turned away, hung it back in the closet, and said gruffly, "You shouldn't sneak up on people that way. There"—she pointed to a pile of clothes on the bed—"I got your things ready for you."

I stared at her, unsure of what to do. She'd been in our closet, in our bureau drawers, and was standing here in the middle of our *home*, touching all our things. If my mother was alive, she never would have done this—although when my mother was sick Kitty had come in and straightened up, brought her hot tea and toast, swept the carpet and put away the laundry, so maybe it *was* all right?

And suddenly it didn't matter to me that she was in here and my mother wasn't because as long as *someone* who cared about me was here, then I could be here, too. I set the box on the bed next to the stacks of clothes, winter sweaters and skirts and pants . . . and noticed my summer shorts and tops, the playsuit my mother had made me for my birthday, and my summer pajamas in the piles, too. I stared at them, heart thudding, and said in a small, wavering voice, "When do I get to come back?"

Kitty, on her way out the door, paused without turning and sighed. "Come on, Lou, you're a big girl. Don't make me spell it out." Silence. "You don't come back, okay? You're gonna go live somewhere else now."

"Oh," I said as the world narrowed to a pinpoint and a weird ringing started in my ears. The fog returned, sapping the strength from my knees, so I felt behind me for the bed and sank onto it. The room was stifling, and I clawed open my coat and scarf.

"I can't keep a kid. I have to get this place cleaned out and rented. I didn't mind carrying your mother all those times she was sick because I knew she was always good for it, but this last month she was sick more than she worked, and if it wasn't for the church taking care of the burial, well, I don't know what would have happened."

I gazed at her stocky, blurred figure and all I could think was that my mother's beautiful velvet dress would never fit her. Never.

"Besides, I hear the state home's a real nice place for an orphanage," she said in a hearty voice. "Somebody even said the kids get ice cream twice a week. Now, hurry up and pack your box, and I'll see you downstairs."

I watched her leave, then looked slowly around the room. The ache in my chest was sharp again, almost as bad as it had been that last moment in the graveyard when they pulled me away from the casket and made me leave my mother there alone. I put my hand to my heart, felt the blunted corner of the souvenir cardboard Ciro's photo beneath my undershirt and pressed it to my skin.

How could I take only what I could fit in the box? My whole world was here and it wouldn't all *fit* in the box. What would happen to the things I couldn't bring with me? Would people steal them? Would Kitty sell them or hand them out to the neighborhood?

No, that didn't make sense. It was my stuff. My *mother's* stuff. No one could just take our stuff and give it away without us saying so.

I looked at the clothes stacked next to me, the white underpants and undershirts, the school pants and dungarees, shorts and blouses and skirts, the sweater and oxfords, the socks and pajamas. I looked at the bureau, at the top two drawers that had been my mother's.

I wasn't supposed to take my mother's things. No one said I could.

They'd said, *Pack your own things, Louise.*

No, actually the state lady had said "a box of necessaries" but if I brought those things and left my mother's, they would be stolen right out from under me, all of them, and I would never see them again.

I glanced at the door. Rose on trembling legs and, avoiding the creaky spot in the carpeted floor, eased the door closed. Hurried to the bureau, opened the drawer, and slid a hand beneath my mother's lacy nylon slips, not sure what I was searching for but finding an envelope. Inside it were pieces of an old brown, crumbling pressed flower.

Shaking, I took it.

I grabbed the almost empty bottle of Evening in Paris cologne, too, because my father had given that to her on their wedding night. I opened her jewelry box and took the stickpin with the fake pearl, the sparkly costume earrings, broaches, and necklaces, the matching sets she'd loved, and hands full, I dumped it all on a pair of underpants, rolled it up, and set it in the bottom of the box.

I was crying now, as every piece I took made me a terrible thief, but if I didn't steal my mother's things, they would be laid out, worn, torn, and pitiful, for the world to see.

The thought filled me with such panic that I ran back to her underwear drawer and found the two old bras with the safety-pinned straps and put those in with my undershirts, found the blue and the pink nylon panties with the rust stains that would never wash out, the polka-dot pair with the saggy elastic, the green pair with the hole on the side and added those to the box, found the lumpy, badly darned woolen socks that had always made my mother's ankles itch and threw those in, too.

Those were my mother's secrets. *Those* were, not my father.

I wrenched open the closet door and nearly fainted as the scent of my mother billowed out. I leaned into it, breathing deep, every cell raw with yearning, stepped into the row of dresses and sweaters and skirts, pressed my face into the soft fabrics, wrapped my arms around them, weeping and begging God to please *please* make them into my mother just once, just for a moment, just one more moment.

But he didn't, and Kitty would call for me soon, maybe come up to see what was taking me, so I sank on watery knees and reached back past the shoes to the turquoise box where my mother kept our photos. The box was too big for the liquor store box, so I dumped the contents into my box, just dumped it and then stuffed a pair of pants and a skirt on top of the pictures.

I couldn't reach the top shelf of the closet, where my mother always hid the Christmas presents, so I dragged over her chair and, for the first time ever, stood on the tapestry cushion and felt around until I found another envelope, a bigger one, and so I took that, too, took it without even opening it, because I knew if my mother had hidden it, then she hadn't wanted anyone to see it.

What else, what else? I looked frantically around the room, ran to the bookcase and fumbled out the *Treasury of Best Loved Stories.* Went back to the closet to my mother's winter coat, dug the soft angora mittens with their happy kittens pattern from the pockets and pushed those into my coat pockets, and then I took the scarf and the hat, too.

I jammed it all in the box, covered it with pajamas and a sweater, and as I searched for more, I knew that my mother really was gone, because if she were alive, if there were any chance at all that she would be back, then I would never be doing this, but she was gone and I was alone now, a bastard *and* an orphan, and the knowledge tore terrifying rents in the fog, leaving the pain and shame to sear sharp, stark channels into my heart.

I took all the leftover hand-me-downs Kitty had piled on the bed, stuff I wasn't taking, and jammed them back in the bureau drawer so she wouldn't see what I'd done.

"Louise?" Kitty called from downstairs. "Come on. It's time to go."

"Coming," I said, gazing around—what else, what else?—and finally seizing on my mother's hairbrush and reading glasses.

It was all that I could carry.

I paused the CD and looked at Gran. She was still awake, arms twitching and writhing, legs jerking. "One more?"

I waited and when she finally blinked, it was twice, so I asked again and it was once.

I hit play.

The first month at the home was a terrifying haze of unfamiliar adults and new rules, giant rooms filled with cots and girls with blank faces, of waking up one morning in pain and finding blood, *blood,* not on my pillow but lower, destroying my nightgown and underwear, staining them like my mother's had been stained and *knowing* it was tuberculosis, knowing I had the same bleeding from down there as she did and I couldn't stop crying.

They came to take me somewhere and I fought hard because I had heard of sanitariums for the dying. They held me down, faceless people in white who were chewing clove gum, and I heard a man say I was *hysterical,* and I heard them say, *Mother deceased, no father or other living relatives . . . illegitimate . . . kindest thing . . . state is legal guardian,* and then I woke up with different pain and two small gauze bandages on my abdomen, and all I remember asking the nurse was, *Is this a sanitarium?* and she looked surprised and said, *No, you don't have TB. This is a hospital ward and you've just had a little operation to make you feel better,* and that made me cry with relief, and I said, *I'm not going to die? No,* she said, *but you must eat your Jell-O.*

I parted the confusion one more time to ask why I was there, but the nurse just patted my head and said, *Never you mind, doctor knows best,* and since I was afraid to make them angry, I didn't ask anything else, only slept and wept and did whatever they told me to.

When I was sent back to the home, I arrived as a bruised and broken nobody, stripped of my mother, my last name, my home, all my things, my friends, my school, and my familiar, child's body.

I would lay in bed in the girls' dormitory at night, tracing my two little scars under the covers and staring into the dark until my eyes ached, begging my mother to manifest like a ghost in the movies or a gentle, invisible hand ruffling the curtain, and I would know it was her, loving me from somewhere I couldn't get to.

And all the time, this new empty, lonely silence surrounded me. The funeral was over, the party thrown, the grave closed, and the orphan disposed of. Evelyn Bell Closson was dead and the world had moved on, all except for me. I wore the loss like a heavy, impenetrable cloak stitched with grief and pain, woven with disbelief, shame, and betrayal.

ෆ ෆ ෆ

I began wishing that I would fall asleep and never wake up so I would never again have to relive that gruesome moment when I looked at my mother and she didn't look back. I didn't want to dream of those murky eyes or the blotchy purple skin, didn't want to wake up with my empty hands reaching and never finding, with this ache so huge it cracked my ribs and produced tears that would overflow whenever and wherever they wanted to.

I didn't care what I wore or what I ate. I didn't care about anything at all.

The home sent me to finish freshman year at the local high school, a huge, noisy place that rang with laughter and hundreds of footsteps pounding down stairways and echoing through halls. I could have disappeared there—they were used to seeing the poorly dressed state kids, I guess, scuttling along the edges of life and had learned to ignore them—but the home had registered me as Louise *Bell* instead of Louise *Closson* and I was so shocked the first time the English teacher took attendance and called, *Louise Bell,* that I blurted, "Closson! Bell was my mother's maiden name."

The realization of what I'd said, of what it *meant,* hit me at the same time the teacher's lips tightened. The boys in the class snickered and the girls' eyes bulged and they quickly edged their desks away as if I was contagious.

I was sent down to the office for a meeting with the assistant principal, who, stiff with disapproval, said that while only crude people would stoop to calling me a *bastard,* there was no denying that the unfortunate circumstances of my birth did in fact make me *illegitimate,* a child whose parents had never been married and that when the time came for me to look for a husband, I must be honest and confess this, as most men would feel duped if they unknowingly courted a young woman (not *lady*, but woman) of questionable background.

I didn't blink when he said this. I couldn't. I couldn't even see him, so blinding was the humiliation. And then he made it worse by adding that any young woman indiscreet enough to volunteer such shameful information before a class of impressionable young students would be watched closely in the unhappy event she became too friendly with the boys. He said I must strive to overcome my dubious legacy, maintain a pristine reputation, and be thankful the state had given me a home, clothes on my back, and three solid meals a day.

All I could think of while he was speaking was, *Please, God, let me wake up and find out this was all a nightmare, a terrible, awful mistake and that my mother's been back at Kitty's all this time, going crazy searching for me. Please, I swear I will eat all my vegetables and dust the furniture without complaining. I won't even argue about bedtime only please, please, let me go home.*

I was dismissed with that warning but I wasn't invisible at school anymore. Now I was snickered at and whispered about, bumped into, shoved aside, and on one terrifying occasion, caught in a stairwell by a pair of hulking, freckle-faced seniors, who trapped me between them and laughed as they groped my behind, ignoring my panicked struggles until I started to cry, and then they let me go and disappeared back into their crowd.

I told no one because there was no one to tell.

But I dreamed about the encounter, and somehow it became a good dream where the groping softened to holding and hugging, and I woke up sick at the residual happiness and longing the physical contact had left me with. I'd felt cared for in the dream, wanted and protected, important to someone, and it left me so hungry to be touched.

There was no affection between the limited home staff and the crowd of children, no spontaneous hugs or squeezes, no one to lean against or a hand to hold, nothing. Approval was expressed with nods and smiles, maybe a rare pat on the shoulder, and while the staff wasn't cruel, neither were they kind. They didn't fraternize with the children, didn't take the little ones on their laps or listen to personal problems or breech the invisible walls between those who had families and those who didn't.

There were too many of us, too many unwanted, unclaimed faces, some upturned and eager to please, some downturned and creased with sullen bravado, the mask of the unloved. Some kids became the mothers they didn't have, cuddling the younger children, seeking love and acceptance in their needy embraces. Others grew hard and mean, pinching the smaller kids, pushing them around, socking them, or stealing their stuff, pleased to be dreaded by the home's ward mothers, to be called down for a one-on-one scolding, to lose privileges and brag about it.

I fell prey to the bullies at the home, too, and over the months, the box that contained my life was slowly emptied, stolen piece by piece. My mother's hairbrush disappeared and reappeared in someone else's hand, her earrings clipped to someone else's ears, the photos cut for paper dolls. The last straw came when I walked into the dorm and saw one of the big girls holding the bottle of Evening in Paris. I went blind with rage and threw myself on her, punching, kicking, and biting until the ward mother pulled us apart.

As a result, what was left of my mother's things—the last few drops of cologne, some photos, and the few flimsy brown pieces of the dried orchid—were confiscated and locked in the home's office along with the contents of the big envelope the state lady had taken from my box on the very first day.

The only thing I had left was the cardboard souvenir photo from Ciro's, and no one tried to steal it once the bigger girl, sporting a black eye, bloody nose, and fearsome bite marks on her forearms, told the other kids to steer clear of me because I was nuts.

The staff labeled me incorrigible, a rebel who insisted on clinging to the past instead of putting it behind her and moving forward.

And I was fine with that because I didn't *want* to put my mother behind me. I didn't *want* to forget I'd had a real home once and a life where I wasn't an orphan and a bastard but a girl with a mother, and a father who'd died in the war.

While my heart didn't move forward, other parts of me did, and I developed a real waist, hips, and large breasts. With those came my second period, perhaps originally delayed by shock and occurring some months after the first episode.

I'd woken up one morning feeling awful and gotten dressed only to have the ward mother take me aside on my way to breakfast and say, "There is a blood spot on the back of your skirt, Louise. You're going to be fifteen soon, you're a young lady now and must practice better feminine hygiene."

"Blood?" I whispered, because I'd heard stories of course, but they had been vague references to the arrival of an Aunt Tillie, and there had been pale girls who held their stomachs and were excused from gym class, and those white Kotex dispensers in the lavatories, but none of that applied to me—

"Follow me," the ward mother said, leading me into an empty stairwell. "I didn't realize you missed the girls' health film." She cleared her throat and focused somewhere past my left ear. "Your menstrual cycle is your body's way of preparing for a baby. The nurse will give you napkins and a belt you must wear until the flow stops. You mustn't swim while you have your monthlies, and you must change the napkin often or you will smell unpleasant." She glanced at the arms I had crossed protectively over my tender breasts. "You'll be given deodorant and a razor, and this afternoon you'll be fitted for a brassiere. No more undershirts. It will be your responsibility to wash your brassiere in the sink nightly, along with your underpants. Young ladies must be modest, clean, and fresh at all times. Keep your finger-nails trimmed and your hair combed. No one likes a dingy girl.

"Boys will be paying attention to you now, so you must be very careful not to encourage them. Always sit with your knees together and your ankles crossed. If you have any questions, you may come and see me during your free time, all right?"

No. Yes. I didn't know. What was this heated river rising inside of me, so grateful for her instruction, for her taking the time to talk to me one-on-one and for knowing my name? Throat aching, I reached out and touched her arm. "Thank you, Mrs. Sanders."

"You're welcome." The ward mother nodded, stepped back, break-ing the connection, and said briskly, "I'm glad you're finally coming around. Now please go down and see the nurse."

And the moment, as fragile as a bath bubble, popped.

        ❧   ❧   ❧

Two months later, only a week after Christmas, a doctor from a rural community upstate queried the home about fostering a neat, quiet, able-bodied girl to help around the house and keep his invalid wife company.

He arrived for an interview on New Year's Eve, and some hours later, they sent me home with him.

I paused the CD and glanced at Gran.

Her eyes were closed, so I turned off the player, did my homework, and when Grandpa finally returned, loaded the deer food, opened the cans of cat food, and did what I was supposed to do.

It was cold and gray out, a depressing twilight, and most of the stray cats were huddled in the three-story cat condo. Normally there would be little electric heaters or lamps glowing inside to bring heat, but I guess they couldn't afford it anymore, because the heat wasn't on.

When I walked into my house, fingers numb from the cold, nose running, I looked at my parents and said, "If I died tomorrow, what would you do with my stuff?"

"Garage sale," my father sang out, but when I didn't laugh, he glanced at my mother.

"We would keep it, of course, because you loved it and we love you," she said, watching me.

"Good," I said hoarsely and made it up to my room before I started crying.

Chapter 27

Hanna

Seth and I can't mess around at my house because my mother's always home in the afternoon, so we usually go straight to his house after school and stay in his room until his parents get home from work. I don't know how his classy, sophisticated-looking mom can breeze in, look at me sitting on his bed reading one of the many paperbacks I always keep in my purse and him sitting on the floor playing his guitar, and not know we were all over each other, sometimes only minutes earlier. How does she miss this?

I can see how his father misses it, because he's kind of absent-minded but not in a cute way, more like a rumpled, grumpy bear irritated at being woken from a lifelong hibernation way. He doesn't talk much, only comes home, takes off the top part of his suit and tie down to his T-shirt, puts on moccasin slippers, and watches TV, grunting occasionally or making arrogant comments. Seth's mom chatters at him but he hardly ever does anything but mutter back.

Still, he's nice in his own way to me, so I have no complaints.

It's been three weeks now, and I'm kind of becoming a permanent fixture in his house, which is very cool, although my being there so much has also brought me some pretty weird information.

Like one night when his mother went out shopping with the girls (she does that a lot) and his father was watching TV, Seth drank some vodka, got way too chatty and showed me things in his room, like the smudge on the wall behind his bedroom door, which was a souvenir left by Bailey's—who was out in Arizona in rehab—sunless tanner the first time he did her standing up, a dent he'd kicked in the wall near his desk when Bailey had dumped him that last time, and the scratch the hatchet-faced mall girl's studded bracelet had left on his headboard.

I didn't say anything, just listened and felt sick because he sounded so proud of it all, especially the little notches he had scratched on the back of the headboard where nobody could see them, and so I said, "Is mine up there yet?"

And he grinned and said, "Nope, not till we do it," and then he started kissing me.

I had to remind him that the door was open and his father could come along any minute. He snorted and said, "Don't worry about it; he doesn't see shit around here. If it ain't work, it ain't important."

So I asked him what his father did and he said he was an engineer, and that sounded boring, so I didn't ask any more because I really didn't care. Besides, I had a lot worse things to think about, like how many girls had been here before me, and even more hurtful, if he had loved any of them besides Bailey.

Even stupider, I had the urge to leave my own mark, but I didn't use sunless tanner or wear studded bracelets, so the best I could do was put on lip gloss and kiss the top left-hand side of his dresser mirror, leaving a perfectly hot lip print.

It wasn't much but it made me feel better.

Seeing those hidden notches started me thinking, though, especially about how he'd said I was the only girl he'd ever made orgasm just by having a hand in my pants. It made me wonder (and not in a good way), what he actually thought of that, and of me for letting it happen. Hell, not only *letting* it happen but pretty much showing him how to *make* it happen.

Hmm.

I probably shouldn't do that again.

I wore the pearl pendant Gran had given me for my birthday to her house today, thinking maybe she'd be happy to see it again, and I'm pretty sure she was as her thrashing was quieter and she managed to swallow four sips of water before I settled into my chair and hit play.

How It Ends

I didn't want to be a foster child. It meant the home actually had the power to give me away. I didn't want to leave the only familiar place left and be sent away with a man I didn't know to a place I'd never been, but I had no say in the matter. Out of the eight girls the staff had discussed with Dr. Thaddeus Boehm before he arrived, he had chosen four to meet, and I was one of them.

He rose when I entered the ward mother's office. He was a tall, dark-haired, distinguished-looking man in a dapper gray suit, topcoat, polished wingtips, and thin gray driving gloves. His hair was graying at the temples, his mustache neatly trimmed, and his gaze cool, sharp, and assessing. He smelled of rich, sweet cherry pipe tobacco and, beneath it, something . . . spoiled, like the vaguest hint of rancid lard.

"And this is Louise," the ward mother said, giving me a look that said, *Smile.*

"Louise . . . ?" the man said, closing a docket with my name on it and watching me.

"Bell," the ward mother said.

"Closson," I said at the exact same time.

His mouth curved into a chilly smile. "I see. Well, it's nice to meet you, Louise. I'm Dr. Boehm." He nodded but didn't offer his hand, so I said, "Pleased to meet you," and clasped my hands in front of me, not sure what I was supposed to do next.

"Louise has been with us almost a year now," the ward mother said, giving me a warning look. "She grew up an only child caring for her sickly mother, so she is used to having responsibilities and is a very bright, well-behaved girl."

I forced a smile.

He gave me a clipped nod. "Thank you, Louise. It was very nice meeting you."

"You too," I said and, with a peek at the ward mother, who looked disappointed, spun on my heel and left.

A half hour later the ward mother found me, told me to pack my things and come to her office immediately.

Dr. Boehm had chosen me.

❧   ❧   ❧

He drove a shining black Chevy Bel Air with sparkling chrome and a spotless black-and-white interior. The only thing he said when I arrived clutching my sad little box of hand-me-downs donated by the local church and my Ciro's souvenir photo tucked safely in my purse was, "This is everything?"

I looked at the ward mother, wanting to ask about the Evening in Paris bottle and the last few things of my mother's.

"We keep the children's documents and possessions for six months after placement, so once we're certain she's a good fit for your family, you may call and request we send them on," she said.

The doctor nodded, unlocked the trunk, and set my box down in the corner near the spare tire. He closed the trunk and glanced at me. "The passenger side is unlocked. Please wipe your feet before you get in."

I was careful to do so, as the floor mats were white and nothing I owned was as perfect as the interior of this car or even the blanket covering my side of the seat.

We said good-bye to the ward mother and I gazed desperately at her for a moment, wishing she'd snap her fingers and say, *No, I just remembered you can't have Louise, we need her here! Pick someone else instead,* but she didn't, only nodded and stepped back, so I glanced at the girls clustered in the windows. I didn't smile because I wasn't triumphant; I was scared and worried and shy at being in a car alone with a strange man. I had no idea what the rules were or what would be expected of me.

"We have a two-and-a-half-hour ride ahead," he said, pulling away from the home and onto the street. "If you have any questions, you may ask them."

"Thank you," I said nervously, smoothing my skirt down over my knees.

He waited a few miles and, when I didn't speak, told me why he had chosen me, that despite my unfortunate circumstance of birth, which had not weighed in my favor, he had been encouraged by our brief meeting as I appeared to be a neat, clean girl with good manners and modest expectations. He had carefully reviewed my file and my health records, and while my mother dying of tuberculosis had been troubling, the experience I'd gained caring for her had tipped the scale in my favor.

"Do you have any questions?" he said.

"No, thank you," I said and stared unseeingly out the window as the last of the familiar places passed and the unfamiliar began.

✎ ✎ ✎

He spoke again about an hour later when we stopped for gas and to use the restrooms. He bought himself a cup of coffee and me an icy bottle of Coca-Cola, and as we stood outside the car in the cold drinking them because even a small spill might stain the seat, he told me he had a handyman who did all of the outside work and a woman he referred to as Nurse, who not only assisted in his practice but for the last ten months had also taken care of his wife and, when the office was closed, acted as a live-in housekeeper.

"Naturally this is too large a burden for any one person to carry, hence the decision to bring in additional help," he said and sipped the steaming black coffee. "Nurse will still be responsible for my wife's medication and intimate personal care but her other duties must come first, so in addition to companioning Mrs. Boehm, you will be expected to assist with the cooking and housekeeping. We're not going to enroll you in school immediately, either. We will reconsider once the influenza epidemic has run its course. I trust this will not be a problem?"

I looked out past the gas pumps to the highway where so many people in so many cars were traveling in so many different directions and said quietly, "Not at all," because I'd already been orphaned long enough to know that my fate could have been far worse and that I was actually very lucky.

There had been a girl at the home, a slim, pretty girl with a knowing way and a ne'er-do-well father who would reel in every payday drunk on Kentucky mash. He was a short, square-headed man with a lank Hitler mustache and a fringe of thin, mousey blond hair. He'd stand out front on the curb, dungarees sagging, eyes bleary, scratching at the pestilence plaguing his groin and calling, "Where's my little darlin'? Come on out here and give your old man a squeeze!" and she would come tripping down the stairs, smile wide and gaze hard, wrap her arms around him, and curve her hips against him, and the whole time she was cooing and squirming in his arms, her hands were busy in his pockets, scandalizing the entire state-home staff.

The home fostered her out four times, and four times she was sent back for inappropriate behavior. She got caught in the boiler room with the janitor on payday, then with the scrap hauler in the slaughter room at the butcher shop on payday, and finally, in a move that didn't surprise anyone, disappeared with her daddy on payday and never came back.

We heard later, via the whispers racing through the home, that they had been arrested in Le Claire, her for prostitution in the back of a car, him for renting her out and collecting the cash.

Hers was not the darkest story. There were others, nightmare tales of kids who were worked or starved to death, beaten, chained behind buildings and locked in root cellars. The stories were whispered rather than openly discussed, and any kid who had lived through the torment and returned to the home alive was always avoided, as if their fate might be catching.

Almost as chilling were the reports of whole families dying of influenza and the endlessly echoing ravages of polio, both swelling the home to capacity with the influx of newly made orphans.

So I decided then and there that if I had to leave the home—which I did—then I didn't mind being kept safe in the capable, gloved hands of the doctor and in the isolation of the Boehm residence.

ଔ ଔ ଔ

He spoke again after we'd finished our drinks and gotten back on the road.

This time he told me what to expect of his wife, a woman of fragile emotional status, an only child whose mother had died giving birth and who had been sheltered from life's harsh realities first by her late father, also a respected physician, and then by him.

She had come close to death thirteen years ago during the delivery of their only child, a little girl born with a debilitating infection and severe, inoperable deformities, and who had lived less than two days before succumbing to the inevitable.

Losing the child—he did not say her name—caused his wife to become inconsolable and, unfortunately, irrational. She demanded to see the newborn, which, because of its horrific appearance, had been withheld so as not to further disturb her.

Finally, hoping to ease her distress, he had brought her the infant, having taken care to completely swaddle it from head to toe, but his wife had insisted on unwrapping the body, and the shock of what she'd delivered caused her to collapse.

When she awoke some hours later, he discovered that the trauma had affected her mind, causing depression and spontaneous hysteria. He'd immediately had her moved from the maternity ward to a room of her own, affording her privacy and uninterrupted rest, but sadly, there was no measurable improvement.

She was treated with electroshock therapy only once, as inducing the grand mal convulsion had cost her several fractured ribs and a torn ligament in her left leg.

The pregnancy had also exacted a dire toll on his wife's physical health, and in addition to her fragile mental state, she was plagued with feminine health problems requiring several surgeries over the years, which he himself had performed. The last of these operations had been ten months ago, but instead of improving with bed rest and carefully controlled stimuli, his wife was still caught in the unrelenting grip of moodiness, fluctuating emotions, and bouts of depression.

He recited all of this in a very precise voice that didn't invite questions.

"Her father was a great mentor to me and I promised him that when Margaret and I married I would always keep her well; however,

I fear this last year has been an exercise in futility. Just the sight of me agitates her now." He tightened his gloved hands around the wheel. "In addition, the stress has exacerbated my own health issues and I've had to cut back on my office hours."

"I'm sorry to hear that," I said.

"Thank you. Unlike my wife, I'm of fairly robust constitution, thanks to my late father-in-law's edicts of fresh air and exercise, so that continues to help." He flicked on the signal light and exited the highway. "Some of his ideas would be considered old-fashioned now, but I never underestimated his wisdom and very much enjoyed our debates. We spent many an evening discussing the effects the female reproductive organs have on feminine mental health."

His voice was calm and deliberate with no hint of anything personal; however, I could feel myself blushing in the twilight and wished he would change the subject.

"He believed educating women would be catastrophic, as the body's energy could only effectively serve one organ at a time, and if a woman was redirecting hers to develop her brain, then her real purpose in life, to bear children, would suffer and her uterus would atrophy." He shook his head. "Again, old-fashioned perhaps, especially with this fellow Freud going around spouting theories, but who's to say my late father-in-law's theory isn't also valid? Margaret was an innocent, obedient girl when we married, but over the years— coincidentally just about the time she began reading books *and* desiring a child—her compliant nature began to change. Now a stranger stands in her place."

Dr. Boehm lit the pipe clenched between his teeth, and a roiling cloud of sweet-scented cherry tobacco filled the car. He fell silent, puffing as the sky darkened and the traffic on the two-lane road grew sparse, finally giving way to nothing but miles of thick woods, opossums trundling along the side of the road, raccoons peering out through the underbrush, and deer crossing ahead, their eyes glowing like tiny moons in the headlights.

It was the sight of a doe and a yearling poised in the center of the lonely road, watching our approach that made me lean forward and breathe, "Oh, look how pretty!"

Dr. Boehm slowed the car and we grew close enough to see the doe's ears twitch and her muscles bunch as she flipped up her fluffy white tail and, with the yearling behind her, bounded off into the trees.

"Game is plentiful this season," he said, accelerating. "I intend to bag my limit and improve my taxidermy skills. Have you ever eaten venison, Louise?"

"No," I said, "but my mother took me to see *Bambi* on Christmas when I was five."

"Ah, yes, your mother," he said after a moment, his tone slightly acidic, and so we didn't speak again until we arrived at my new home.

ﻌ ﻌ ﻌ

Nurse met us at the kitchen door and showed me upstairs, past the doctor's bedroom at the end of the hall, to my room, which had a connecting door—closed and locked now—to Mrs. Boehm's bedroom.

"I've never had my own room before," I said.

Nurse snorted. "It comes with a price," she said and muttered a few more things, none of them complimentary, and as I listened, I discovered that if Dr. Boehm was God to Nurse, then Mrs. Boehm was a silly, useless albatross around his neck, a woman who, thanks to her late family's money, might have been useful once by putting the good doctor through medical school but who had long since become an embarrassing burden with her feminine problems and weak, needy nature.

"Is it any wonder the doctor can't bear to be in the same room with her anymore?" Nurse said, nodding and closing my bedroom door behind her, leaving me listening to the heavy, unrelieved silence in the room beyond the connecting door.

ларе ларе ларе

Out of all the things Dr. Boehm and Nurse chose to tell me about Margaret Boehm before I was allowed to meet her, what I still find the saddest, even after everything that happened, is that no one told me she was dying of neglect.

ларе ларе ларе

When I went downstairs the next morning, I was told that Dr. Boehm had decided to keep me separate from his wife for an incubation period, a safety precaution, as I had, after all, just come from a state home teeming with *outcasts, urchins, the unwanted and unwashed,* and who knew what kind of maladies I'd brought with me.

So instead of tending to the invalid, for the next several weeks I cooked, cleaned, and absorbed the odd, tense rhythm of the household. It was different from anything I'd ever known, this life that revolved around a man, the rush to put him first, to fulfill his requests and obey his demands without question, especially a man who seemed to believe he was well within his rights to *expect* the servitude and, while a part of me chafed under the censorious looks and sharp tongue of Nurse every time I moved too slowly or gave the doctor a questioning look, another part of me was very eager to fit in and very grateful to have a home, even if it wasn't a happy one.

At first I thought the tension was because of Mrs. Boehm secreted upstairs, but as the days passed, I realized it was Dr. Boehm who was turning out to be more than a little eccentric.

One morning at the end of January he told Nurse to schedule all of his appointments on Mondays only, until hunting season ended, as his health was in sore need of the restorative powers of nature. She looked at him, eyes lit with wariness, but didn't argue, only said, "All right, Doctor."

He wore his surgical gloves everywhere, even to dinner, and had the odd habit of tucking them down between each finger, one hollow at a time, over and over as if to ensure they wouldn't somehow slide off if he wasn't vigilant. Nurse would watch, and after two or three go-arounds, she would clear her throat or ask him to pass the carrots or do something to interrupt the habit.

He cared for no opinion but his own and spoke cuttingly of the poor and indigent, especially the unmarried women with illegitimate children who always arrived as *Mrs.* Smith or *Mrs.* Jones and left knowing their coy pretenses hadn't fooled anyone.

The first time he told one of these stories, I kept my gaze on my plate, eyes full of unshed tears, refusing to blink and release them, face hot, soul sick and burning. I felt sure he was mocking my mother and I hated him for his supercilious tone and casual cruelty.

The second and third times, however, I took a deep breath and lifted my gaze, not to him, not yet, but to the window and stared out as if daydreaming, refusing to give him the satisfaction of knowing he'd wounded me. After that I listened with no reaction at all and later found out that despite his deep scorn for unmarried mothers and bastard children, he still treated them without charge.

He was a puzzle, arrogant, distant, and unpredictable, a man who spoke of his wife as if she were nothing more than an ongoing medical case and who went weeks without looking in on her but who on one sunny day above freezing, took an hour out of his schedule to show me around the property.

We passed the handyman's quarters and the shed where the gardening tools were kept, the salt lick near the tree line for the deer, and finally his workshop, a low-slung wooden outbuilding set at the far back end of the property.

It had an uneven cement floor and sturdy wooden worktables—long enough to operate on, he joked stiffly—and three small squirrel hides draped over curved and rusted meat hooks embedded in a support beam.

Against the wall there was a bench that held his scalpels, a box of surgical gloves, and a tool that looked like tweezers with handles that he called an *ear opener,* used to insert and separate the skin from the ear cartilage. He showed me a large assortment of knives ranging from a small paring knife to a skinning knife and beyond, scissors to trim around bullet holes or the insides of paws, and heavy-duty pliers used for skin stretching.

The flesher, an unhappy-looking device for removing layers of flesh clinging to the animal's skin sat separately, as did the degreaser, clay, a jumble of wire, containers marked with all sorts of noxious chemicals, vats, brooms, cinder blocks, and a ragamuffin pile of furred pieces that, upon closer inspection, contained rabbit faces with limp ears and eye holes, squirrel tails, tiny chipmunk skins with empty, dangly feet, and raccoon masks, again with eyeholes but no eyes.

The place was chilly and smelled as if something had crawled into the walls and died. The main table had deep, reddish black stains ingrained in the top and when he saw me looking at them, hastened to say that his next investment was going to be a steel-topped table or, at the very least, the biggest laminate table he could find.

From there he led me back across the lawn, kicking up snow with each stride, and into his study. I'd never been in here before, never even seen the inside, as when the doctor wasn't here, the door was kept shut and locked. I paused, gazing at all the bookcases, the tall, pure-white sculpture on his desk of a woman holding a child and the dead animals positioned on every flat surface.

"Come in," he said, motioning me forward. "Leave the door open."

I did and, when he indicated I should sit, perched on the edge of the closest armchair while he traversed the room, stopping at each preserved carcass—a patchy-furred raccoon, a pair of rumpled-looking mourning doves, a red fox whose mouth was twisted in a fierce rictus of what could only be pain or terror, a plaque displaying severed pheasant's legs, and most unsettling, a tableau of a mother chipmunk lying belly up in a strategically angled bowl of dirt, acorns, and fallen oak leaves, teats turgid and poking through her soft white belly fur, and little pink, hairless baby chipmunks, newborns, frozen forever in the act of squirming toward them to suckle—and told me the abbreviated versions of these, his taxidermy efforts to date.

He spoke with unbridled enthusiasm of his ongoing quest to create the perfect mounted specimen in a replica of life, of making beginner's mistakes with the raccoon like failing to plug the mortal wound and orifices with rags to prevent the bodily fluids from leaking out and contaminating the fur. He spoke of the difficulty of preparing the doves and how he would not attempt them again for they weren't worth the trouble. He spoke of hefting the scalpel and incising the fox from the base of her tail and up along the spine, gently working his gloved hands into the incision and peeling her skin loose from the muscles.

"Skinning the vixen's feet was difficult but her face presented the biggest challenge," he said, pausing and running a gloved fingertip along the fox's backbone. "One must coax the skin down off the skull, leaving certain tissue attached around the eyes, nose, mouth, and ears. I had some trouble around the eyelids and the tear ducts, but I don't believe it's noticeable."

"No, not at all," I said faintly.

He went on and on, relating the fleshing process, the debate between dry preservation, pickling, and tanning, the threat of bug infestation in the hide, the old-fashioned use of arsenic and the benefits of oxalic acid, and how unprocessed rawhide was nothing more than desiccated skin and, given an environment with a high enough moisture content, would rehydrate, breed bacteria, and putrefy like any other.

"Oh," I said, swaying and blotting my sweaty forehead with the back of my hand. "It's very warm in here, isn't it?"

"Put your head on your knees," he said, and when I could sit up again without reeling, he called Nurse and, with her in attendance, put the stethoscope to my heart, peered into my pupils, and took my pulse. "Do you feel congested? Throat sore? Any aches or pains? Stomach upset?"

"No, I'm fine," I said, embarrassed.

"Are you menstruating?" he said.

"No," I mumbled, blushing. "It was just hot in here and you were talking about skinning things and taking out their eyes and putrefaction—"

"All right, that's enough," he said coldly. "You may go now, Louise. You have reminded me most emphatically of how useless it is to try and educate a female in the fine art of perfecting and bringing the natural world to life."

I rose too hastily and had to steady myself against the desk for a moment, then hurried away before the burning words crowding my throat burst out.

Bringing the natural world to life? Those animals *had* been alive, they'd already *had* life, and no man with a fleshing machine could ever come close to improving on that.

ↅ ↅ ↅ

Two mornings later Nurse, apparently deciding I was sufficiently healthy, made a soft-boiled egg, handed me Mrs. Boehm's breakfast tray, and told me to take it up to her.

"I don't know about you, but I think this book is weird," I said, turning off the CD player and glancing at Gran. "I mean, you can already guess everything that's going to happen; either his wife is some taxidermied mummy and the orphan girl is next—and I swear if she falls down when she's running away from him, that's it, I'm done with this—or the nurse is really his wife or his mother or both and he's a lunatic or some serial killer or whatever . . . I don't know." I rose, restless, and paced the room. "I mean, I feel sorry for Louise, but she's not doing anything to get away! Well, not that anything's really happened yet . . . and it *is* winter, and okay, yeah, she doesn't have anywhere to go or anyone to call for help . . . but still. She must feel like *something's* wrong there, you know?" I looked at Gran, who was drooping in her chair. "And, yes, you don't have to say it, I know there's a plague going on and people are dropping dead, leaving orphans everywhere, and yes, she has no food or money but . . . oh, hell, all right . . . so maybe it doesn't seem as ominous to her as it sounds to us. Or maybe . . . oh, God, maybe it was so bad back then that it really was better to stay than run away. What do you think? Gran?" I went over to her but she'd fallen asleep, so that left me no choice but to sit down and start my stupid homework.

જી જી જી

It was kind of creepy walking home alone through the back acres in the fast-approaching dark, and that was unsettling, because I'd never felt that way about our little woods before. I didn't know whether it was just a spooky night or if it was coming out of Gran's with that story on my mind and that horrible image of the doctor cutting open a spine and working his hands into the incision to loosen the skin from the muscle, but holy crap, when a leaf rustled, I took off for my back porch like the hounds from hell were after me.

And later at dinner, I said, "Did you know that electroshock therapy actually makes a person go into, like, an epileptic seizure and that it's so strong you can break bones and tear ligaments and stuff?"

"I'm eating," my father said, giving me a look over a forkful of spaghetti.

"Did you know that taxidermists use fleshing machines to—"

"Where are you getting all of this from? Don't tell me it's homework," my mother said, wrinkling her nose.

"No, it's Gran's audiobook, and it's supposed to be a love story, but did you know that doctors used to think that if a woman was educated, all her energy would go to her brain instead of her reproductive organs and her uterus would atrophy and then she would be useless?" I said, trying not to laugh as my father stared down at his plate in dismay.

"Seeing as how she was only good for breeding in the first place, of course," my mother said with a derisive sniff. "Don't get me started, Hanna." She twirled up a forkful of spaghetti and paused. "Ask Helen if I can borrow that book when you guys are done with it, okay? I'd like to hear it."

"Well, tomorrow we're going to find out if the guy has taxidermied his wife—"

"Eating," my father said weakly.

"Or he's some kind of serial killer who married his own mom—"

"That's it," my father said and, grabbing his plate, went into the living room to finish in front of a nice, simple alien-end-of-the-world sci-fi movie.

"Is he mad?" I said, looking at my mother.

She shook her head, lips twitching. "No, but someday, when you're in a mixed crowd, mention the word *uterus* and see how fast the guys clear the room. It's an interesting phenomenon."

"Can I use the word *atrophy* with it, too?" I asked, grinning.

"Oh, I wish you would," she said, and we both cracked up.

৩   ৩   ৩

My mother put her music on while we were clearing the table, and in the middle of it, she put a hand on my arm and said, "Stop for a minute and listen to this. Listen to the words, Hanna, and then try to tell me we don't just keep reliving the same feelings and problems as the people before us, over and over and over."

"What is it?" I said, leaning back against the counter.

"Janis Joplin singing 'A Woman Left Lonely,'" she said softly, turning it up and leaning next to me. "Tell me this isn't timeless."

And I listened and I heard the raggedy pain and raw yearning and bewilderment, heard the question and wanted to hear the answer, too, but the only one seemed to be neglect by a man and that made my heart as heavy as a brick, and I just shook my head and went back to clearing the table because I couldn't stand thinking that how bad I felt and how lonely I felt with Seth sometimes was not only timeless but . . . common.

Crystal's brother's keg party would have been better if I hadn't gotten the bright idea to bring Seth, too, to introduce him to Crystal and have him meet my other friends.

Bad idea.

He stiffened up the minute he saw all the guys with long hair and tats in the clearing, got a chip on his shoulder a mile wide, and partied so hard there was no way I could let him drive home, which pissed him off, so he started getting shitty with me in front of everyone there and only stopped when Crystal, wearing hard eyes and a hard smile, quietly reminded him that everyone here was *my* friend, not his, and he was making an asshole out of himself.

He went over and sat down on a log, smoking and sulking and glaring until I told Crystal we were just going to go.

"How?" she said. "He can't drive."

"I don't know," I said, because there was no way I could take him back to my house like that, so we took him back to Crystal's. She made him coffee, and I knew what she was thinking, but she never said it out loud, and she stayed while we poured a whole pot of coffee into him. I told her to go back to the party because I was going to walk him around until he seemed half decent, so she did.

I took him outside and made him walk with me, first with my arm around him, and then just next to me because he pushed me away and snapped, *I can do it*, so I was like, *Fine, then do it*, because I was so *mad* at myself for bringing him there in the first place.

"You think you know me, but you don't," he said, swaying and giving me a look full of disgust. "You don't know shit, so why don't you just get the hell away from me?"

"Why are you saying that?" I said, starting to cry. "What did I ever do to you?"

He blinked hard, focused on me, and sniffed. "Right, go ahead, cry. That's all girls ever do. Cry and lie to get out of it. You're all the same." He turned, fumbling with his fly and stumbled over to the bushes on the side of Crystal's house. That's when I heard a bike rumble up.

It was Jesse.

"Hey, Hanna, long time no see," he said with an easy smile, climbing off the bike and hanging the helmet. "You headed down to the party or what?"

"Actually, we're just leaving," I said, glancing around to make sure Seth wasn't lurching out toward me, because if there was one thing I didn't want, it was—

"Hey, how're you doing?" Jesse said, his gaze shifting to somewhere behind me.

"Sup?" Seth said, reeling up and slinging an arm around my neck.

I met Jesse's gaze, calm and dark and slightly amused, and just wanted to die, because he recognized Seth from the mall, I knew he did, and I felt like a fool. "So, uh, how's work?" I said desperately, dragging my hair out from under Seth's arm and wincing.

"In this economy I'm just glad for the steady paycheck." He tucked his hair behind his ear and cocked his head, eyes twinkling. "So how's school? Did you graduate yet?"

"No," I said, silently begging him not to go any further, and he must have caught my plea because he just smiled and said, "Well, hey, I have to get down to the party." And to Seth, "Good seeing you again, buddy," and ambled away whistling.

"So did you ever fuck him?" Seth said, loud enough for him to hear.

Jesse stiffened, paused, and turned, all traces of good humor wiped from his face. I caught my breath and managed a furious, "No!" to Seth, and after a second, Jesse kept going, and then I struggled out from under Seth's arm and said, "What is *wrong* with you? Why did you say that?"

"Because *he* wants to fuck *you*," he said, lifting his chin and giving me a cold look.

I looked away, arms wrapped around my waist, and I couldn't help it, I started to cry again. "Why are you being like this?"

"Tell me I'm wrong," he demanded.

"You're wrong," I said, avoiding his gaze.

"Bullshit," he said. "Were you ever with him?"

"What are you *talking* about?" I cried. "This is a *party* and he said hi, so what, big deal!"

"Were you?" he said.

And what I wanted to say was, *Yes, I was! There, are you happy now?* But I didn't because that would have made him even madder, and I was already humiliated, and all I wanted to do was walk away and leave him there, not forever but for now, but I couldn't do that because if I did, I knew he would never come back. He could do that, he could close himself down and turn it all off, and one stupid fight wasn't worth losing him over, so I didn't say anything, just stood there huddled and sniffling and wiping my eyes, and finally he sighed and said quietly, "Come here." I did and he held me and said he was sorry but he didn't like seeing me so friendly with so many scummy bikers—

"They're not scummy, they're my friends," I mumbled against his tear-soaked shirt.

"Yeah, well, I'm your *boy*friend," he said, holding me tighter. "Unless you don't want me anymore."

"Of course I do," I said, crying harder because I was scared. "Don't even say that!"

"Well, what am I supposed to think, Hanna?" he said, pulling back and making me look at him. "You're choosing *them* over me."

"I never said that," I said, hiccupping. "But Crystal's my best friend—"

"I thought *I* was your best friend," he said, sounding hurt.

It just got worse from there for another minute until I was really sobbing and saying, Fine, I wouldn't come down to any more parties at Crystal's unless he was with me, and then he hugged me and we walked some more and he finally got sober enough to drop me off back at my house. I was worried about him driving home but he said he'd be fine and he was, except for running over somebody's big plastic recycling bucket and dragging it for a mile before it finally shattered and broke free.

Gran is getting too skinny and I think it's because she can't eat anything anymore but mushed-up food because she chokes easy. Grandpa said if the food goes down the wrong pipe and ends up in her lungs, then it'll breed bacteria and she'll get pneumonia and probably die, so we have to be very, very careful about feeding her.

Plus, she never stops moving and that has to burn calories because she's always sweating, too, and I swear to God she looks so exhausted that I feel like tying her arms down or something, just to give her a break. The thing is, she'd still strain and twitch and jerk, only she'd probably end up with hideous rope burns, too, and that would make me an old-person abuser, so forget it.

I don't want to hurt her, ever.

How It Ends

I took a deep breath and, juggling the breakfast tray, opened the door to Mrs. Boehm's room. "Hello?"

"I was wondering when you would make an appearance," said a soft voice from somewhere among the pile of pillows on the bed. "Come in, please."

"I have your breakfast," I said and sidled into the shadowy room, trying not to spill the glass of grapefruit juice and cup of hot tea on the tray.

"Another egg," the voice said with a tinge of disgust.

I wasn't sure what to do with it and stood there until she said, "Well, bring it here, please, and then open the shades. I'd like to see who I'm talking to."

I did, setting down the tray and then going around the room pulling the shades. When I was done I turned and got my first real look at Margaret Boehm and the sickroom.

It was a woman's room, an elegant, magnificent private garden. The beige carpet over the cherry flooring was patterned with pink roses, violets, and blue forget-me-nots. The wallpaper was cabbage roses against a baby blue background with deeper blue morning glory vines twining throughout. The ceiling was high, the chandelier crystals twinkling in the thin February sunlight, the furniture a rich, glossy mahogany. There were old bisque dolls and lace scarves on the bureaus and the vanity was covered with cosmetics and an elegant rainbow of perfume bottles with stoppers. The vanity stool was pleated satin with clawed ball feet and the bedside lamp was pink with beaded glass fringe.

The bed was a double like the one my mother and I had shared, only instead of having room for two, one side was piled with novels and magazines, an ice pack, a hand mirror and brush, and a pile of white sheets waiting for decorative embroidery.

What struck me hardest at that moment was how everything in the room seemed to be flourishing except the woman supported by the mountain of flowered pillows, the small, pale, shrunken figure whose bony shoulders seemed too slight to support even the lacy straps of her nightgown. She gazed back at me, blue eyes rimmed with dark hollows and braided ash-brown hair slightly mussed from sleep. Bruises dappled the crooks of her arms, and the skin at her throat looked . . . withered.

"So you're the strapping young orphan come to distract me from my misery," she said, taking in my hand-me-down woolen skirt and the white blouse straining slightly at the buttons. Sighing, she picked up her fork and toyed with the runny soft-boiled egg. "I have no appetite for this." She tasted the tea and set the cup down with a faint grimace. "Chamomile cannot hold a candle to Earl Grey, especially without sugar. Dreadful."

I waited, not knowing what to say.

She nibbled the buttered centers of her toast and sipped her grapefruit juice, shuddering with each swallow, and then asked me to help her to the bathroom. I did, sliding a supporting arm around her hot, trembling frame as we crept across the carpet, and then waiting outside the door while she completed her toilette. I helped her back into bed, where she lay back, pale and sweating, closed her eyes, and didn't speak again.

For the next week, this became our morning routine.

Lunch and dinner, however, were very different stories.

es   es   es

By noon her pain had eased some, thanks to her medication, and she was relaxed, awake, and lonely enough to want to talk. She didn't require anything from me at first, speaking generally about the approaching spring and how the long, dark months of winter always seemed so ominous. She showed me some of the books on the bed, novels she'd bought years ago that were now helping to pass the hours.

"Talk to me, Louise," she said one afternoon, smiling slightly at my surprised look. "For this moment at least, I've grown tired of hearing my own voice." She eased herself up against the pillows, wincing, and pulled her long braid out from behind her and laid it over her shoulder. "My forehead aches so from the weight of the braid but I can't seem to convince Nurse that the pain is real. She believes I only complain for attention."

"Would you like me to brush out your hair?" I heard myself offer. "I used to do it for my mother and she always said it was very soothing."

She gazed at me a moment, as if searching for something, and finally nodded. "That would be nice, yes. Please."

I moved a wooden chair with a tapestry seat over to the window and then helped her out of bed, into her robe, and over to the chair. "Are you all right?"

"Yes," she said breathlessly, wincing. "I'm just sore."

I waited until she was settled, then untied the blue ribbon from the end of the braid and spread the clumsy weave. When I was finished, her hair hung to her waist.

"Oh, that's lovely," she murmured as I brushed. "I don't know how anyone can choose to avoid human contact. I find myself hungering for it constantly, and of all that's out of reach for me now, I believe being touched is what I miss the most." She leaned forward to peer out the window. "Look at all this snow still on the ground. It feels like winter will never end and I did so want to see one more spring."

My hand jerked and the brush grazed her scalp. "Oh, I'm sorry, Mrs. Boehm, but of course you'll see spring! My goodness, why would you even say something like that?"

She never answered, only gazed out the window at the workshop until she could no longer sit comfortably, and then I helped her back to bed and pulled the shades so she could sleep.

෨ ෨ ෨

"I have hired a new handyman," Dr. Boehm said that afternoon in passing. "Don't let me catch you fraternizing with him, Louise."

I stopped, openmouthed, and gazed at his retreating figure. He was listing slightly, and his hair, normally so thick and neat, seemed sparser and almost moth-eaten.

I sniffed the air but there was no alcohol scent, only the faint smell of chemicals and rotting meat.

෨ ෨ ෨

I did Mrs. Boehm's hair every day after lunch. If she felt strong enough, she would sit in the chair by the window; if not, she would shift slightly and lean forward just enough for me to angle around behind her. Sometimes she sang old songs like "I'll Never Smile Again" or "Only Forever," her voice soft and wistful, almost a whisper, and on those days I would brush as gently as I could while her gaze followed the path Dr. Boehm's footsteps had made from the house to the workshop and back.

෨ ෨ ෨

Dr. Boehm shot a doe and dragged her straight to his workshop. Although afterward he said he'd plugged her orifices with rags to prevent her bodily fluids from leaking out and staining her hair, I could still see the blood trail, scarlet-black smears against the snow, beginning at the tree line, where she'd come for the salt lick and had taken the shot in the abdomen, gone down thrashing and convulsing, and finally died, and ending at the workshop door, a scant hundred yards away.

౭ఎ   ౭ఎ   ౭ఎ

One afternoon when a fresh snow was falling and Mrs. Boehm thought the sky too bleak to look at, she said, "How old are you, Louise?"

"Fifteen," I said.

"Fifteen," she murmured. "Would it surprise you to know that I would give anything to be you?"

My hand faltered in midstroke. "You don't want to be me, Mrs. Boehm," I said finally, resuming my task.

"Why is that?" she said.

To my extreme mortification, that's all it took, the slightest show of interest, the merest polite question, for the floodgates to open.

I told her how worried I was about being a good companion, that I'd been warned she was of fragile health and was not to be upset for any reason or I might get sent back to the state home where I was nothing but one of a thousand unwanted and meant nothing to anyone, where kids were dying of influenza and everyone at the high school never let me forget I was a bastard and how I hated that word, *loathed* it like nothing else because it reminded me over and over again that the story of my parents' marriage was false, a fairy tale, and that my mother, who I loved more than anyone on Earth, had lied to me and then died and left me to learn the truth from strangers. She died before I could ask her what really happened, if she and my father had loved each other even a little or if it had just been the endless champagne or—

"Wait," Mrs. Boehm interrupted. "Who said I wasn't supposed to be upset for any reason? Was it my husband?"

I blinked, dazed at being pulled so abruptly out of my story. "Yes. He said you had a very fragile constitution and weren't to be upset for any reason."

"A fragile constitution," she echoed, leaning back against her pillows and smiling a cold little smile. "Oh, that's priceless. It makes me sound like a gardenia, something frail by nature rather than by interference and explains my decline so neatly, don't you agree?"

"I don't know what you mean," I said, hurt by her complete disregard of my story.

"No, I don't suppose you do," she said, sighing.

I could feel her watching me but became very busy polishing the hairbrush handle with the hem of my skirt.

"Louise." She touched my wrist, stilling my busywork. "Did you have a special beau before you came to us, someone who held your hand and told you he could never live without you and now is doing exactly that?"

"No," I mumbled.

"I thought not. A female moves differently after becoming the object of male attention. She becomes more . . . aware of herself." She fell silent a moment, fingers rubbing absently at the edge of the quilt, and when she spoke, her voice was low and careful. "I would like to tell you something important, something I believe your mother might have shared had you been a little older when she passed."

I glanced up, but her gaze had shifted and she was staring at the heavy gold band too big for her finger.

"I have gathered a handful of pearls, each begun as a tiny, irritating fleck of instance that slipped past the shell and settled in to sully the bed of the oyster. They're *my* pearls, my hard-won, misshapen little treasures, and no other living soul on Earth knows I've collected them. Up until this moment I believed they would go to the grave along with me and no one would ever benefit from them, but now . . ." Her gaze met mine. "I'm going to share them with you, and when you have them all, you will have the beginnings of your own strand."

"Mrs. Boehm, really, that's very generous of you," I said, uneasy at the strange light in her eyes. "But I'm not sure I'm allowed to accept such an expensive gift—"

And then she laughed, harsh and sudden, and when she looked at me again, there was no humor in her eyes, and the intensity had been replaced with compassion. "Oh, my dear," she said softly, shaking her head, "don't you know that you have no choice?"

I paused the CD and glanced over at Gran, glad to see she was still awake. "You know, I don't know if I like this lady or not. Want to hear one more chapter?"

She blinked once, so I hit play and settled back to listen.

How It Ends

She went on to tell me, as I brushed and brushed, about the day she and Dr. Boehm first met. As she spoke, her voice lightened, grew girlish and ultimately eerie in its unconscious parody of youth.

"It was May, and only Nanny, Cook, and I were at home. Nanny was upstairs resting and I was in the parlor putting the first spring lilacs in a vase when I heard the front door open and my father speaking to someone.

"I couldn't imagine what he was doing home in the middle of the day, as on Wednesdays he always made free house calls to the less fortunate and they always kept him so long that he never even came home in time for dinner in the evening!

"Naturally I became alarmed and hurried out to the foyer only to collide with . . ." She paused, as if expecting me to say something, perhaps guess, so I said, "Dr. Boehm?"

"Yes!" she cried, clapping her hands. "Only he wasn't a respected doctor back then, Louise, he was just plain Thaddeus Boehm, a filthy, skinny boy all spotty with scabs and splotchy from crying." She leaned closer to me, eyes gleaming. "And, oh, my dear, he smelled just *terrible.* Believe me when I say that if I hadn't brought the lilacs in with me, I most certainly would have gagged."

"Really," I said, pulling back slightly.

"Yes, but all I said was, 'Father, are you well?' before burying my nose in the bouquet. When I spoke, the boy lifted his head and looked at me, and when he did, his eyes grew round as saucers, and I promise you this is true, he looked at me like I was an angel," she said, and her voice began to tremble. "He *did,* even though I had on my third best blouse and my hair bow was slipping. He didn't see any of that, Louise. He didn't see *any* of my faults first that day." A tear slipped down her cheek. "Now despite all the years I've spent struggling to please him, my faults are *all* he sees, and since they're unforgivable, he chooses not to look."

"Oh, I'm sure that's not true," I said, alarmed by her tears and the rise in her voice. "You're ill, Mrs. Boehm, and naturally he doesn't want to excite you—"

"You don't know," she said, turning her face away and swiping a hand across her cheek. "Fix my hair now, please. Braid it neat and tight in the event he does decide to visit, and then please leave me."

I did as she asked because I didn't know what else to do.

❧ ❧ ❧

Late that night I heard the rumble of a truck, loud in the country quiet. I rose, went to my window, and craning my neck, followed its headlights around the back of the house, down the snowy stone driveway to the workshop, where, unless my eyes deceived me, a man met with Dr. Boehm and led two large, slow-moving deer out of the truck and into the workshop.

I mentioned it to Nurse the next morning and received a sharp "Mind your business." After that it seemed wiser not to ask.

❧ ❧ ❧

Dr. Boehm continued to disappear each day into his workshop or the woods or walked the tree line outside, talking animatedly and occasionally waving his arms while the new handyman Peter stood listening without expression.

❧ ❧ ❧

An unpleasant smell has pervaded the house, not all at once and not everywhere but in pockets, sometimes strong, sometimes faint, sometimes early in the morning when I first step out of my room on the way to the bathroom and less often late at night, when I've finished the kitchen work and am on my way up to bed.

It's different from the scent Dr. Boehm normally carries, and one I regret to say I've almost become used to. That's more a wild smell, bloated decay mixed with the panicked musk of a dying animal, feces, and urine, often threaded with the garlicky scent of arsenic or the sting of chemicals.

This scent is fainter yet fresher at the same time, the terrible sweet smell of infection, old blood, and bad flesh, and it scares me enough that I don't bring it up, that I catch my breath and pass through it swiftly like it doesn't exist because I'm afraid to think of what it could be and what it will bring.

I paused the player and looked at Gran.

Sleeping.

Damn it. We would have had time for one more chapter.

Sighing, I turned it off and went and got the food ready for the cats and the deer.

And when I slipped outside to collect all the old, used paper plates from the ground and lifted the lid off a garbage can that had been sitting in the sun, I got a noseful of the smell of old, rotting cat food and almost freaked out.

Seth told me to dress up because he was taking me out to dinner for our anniversary, so me and Sammi went to the mall after school and I found a really sleek little black dress and high heels.

My father looked askance at the dress and was like, "Where's the other half?" and my mother, who usually runs interference for me said, "What about with lower heels?" and I got all freaked because I *wanted* to look like I had legs a mile long, but I just griped some, went into my room, put on lower heels, and stuck my high ones in my purse to put on in the car on the way down.

Seth showed up ten minutes late, which annoyed me (he's late a lot, which sometimes I don't mind, but on our anniversary you'd think he would have made a better effort) and wouldn't you know that instead of walking in and whistling or something, he just raised his eyebrows at the dress, cleared his throat, and said, "Ready?"

And I was like, *Oh, you're kidding right?* But of course I didn't say it, not in front of my parents, so we left and of course I looked stupid trying to climb up into the SUV and keep my dress down at the same time but I finally made it.

Now, granted, he'd already said *Happy Anniversary* to me at school and given me a red rose that I had at home in water now, and maybe his family didn't make a big deal out of anniversaries, but this was our first one and where was the romance?

"Are you okay?" I asked when we got onto the highway and I was busy changing shoes. "You haven't even said anything about my new dress."

"Yeah, I'm a . . ." He made a face. "It's a little short, isn't it?"

My jaw dropped.

"I mean, I've been thinking about your reputation and all—"

"What?" I said, astounded. "What reputation?"

He shrugged. "I don't want all these guys thinking like that about my girlfriend. You know?"

I just sat there staring at him, still too shocked and, yeah, insulted, to say anything.

"So maybe you should just tone it down a little," he said, signaling and switching to the middle lane. "And maybe dress like that only when we're alone together because, yeah, you definitely look hot." Smiling, he reached over and took my hand, not seeming to notice my silence. "So, you hungry? They have great crab legs here and tonight's the all-you-can-eat buffet. Do you like crab?"

"Sure," I said, staring out the window at the passing scenery and trying to reason my way through this, because in a way, I understood what he was saying, but in another, that was really hurtful.

"Hey, when do you want your present?" he said, reaching into his pocket and flashing me a little foil-wrapped box. "Now, at dinner, or after dinner?"

"Surprise me," I said with a forced smile. He smiled back and leaned over a little so I could kiss him, and then put his hand on my leg and, teasing, said, "So what *do* you have on under there, anyway?" and I gave him a very wicked look and said, "That's for me to know, and you to find out . . ."

"Here, you go first." I gave him his gift, the one I'd spent days searching for online, rummaging through endless vintage car sites and auctions, scrabbling desperately to unearth just the right classic MG key ring for the year of the car he was trying to buy and he loved it. He gazed at it, jaw slack, and then laughed, held it up, and looked at me like I was amazing. "Holy shit, I can't believe it! Where the hell did you find this?"

"It wasn't easy," I said, laughing as he hugged me. "Do you like it?"

"Are you kidding? You just blew me away." He kissed me. "You're really something."

"Well, I try," I said demurely, and he laughed and kissed me again.

"Here," he said finally, putting the key ring in his jacket pocket and handing me my gift. "Now you."

Now me.

I ran a slow nail along the taped edge and unfolded the wrapping paper. Opened the little white box, heart pounding and blood thrumming with an anticipation that was way bigger than anything I'd felt before, even at Christmas, and as I lifted the lid I couldn't help hoping *gold ring* and—

"Oh," I chirped, staring down at the delicate silver chain with three plain silver balls nestled on the bed of cotton. "Wow. Look at that." I held it up, watching the tiny links twinkle as they caught the light. "How pretty. I don't have anything silver, either. Thank you." The chain looked too small for a necklace and kind of big for a bracelet but that was just one of the several shocked WTF thoughts whirling through my mind. "Uh . . . put it on me?" I handed it to him and held out my wrist.

He looked at my wrist, puzzled, and then grinned. "Sure." Ignoring my waiting hand, he shoved back his chair, bent, and grasping my ankle, laid my foot across his lap, never noticing my sudden stillness. "I should be a pro at this by now." He flicked his hair out of his eyes and, lowering his head, fumbled with the clasp. "Christ, you'd think they'd make them easier to put on, though. If I ever get it hooked, you're never going to be able to get it off again without breaking it."

I was glad he wasn't looking at me.

"There," he said, leaning back and smiling. "What do you think?"

And I looked at my ankle with the silver chain looped around it and the three silver balls and my eyes burned with tears, which turned out to be good, as he thought it was because I loved it.

Later that night we parked off a deserted, dead-end street and climbed into the way back of his SUV. It didn't take long for my dress to go up, but when he tried peeling off my panty hose, the ankle bracelet snagged on the sheer fabric. He tried tugging the panty hose off beneath it, swearing good-naturedly and squinting to unhook the clasp in the dim light. I laid there waiting, cooling off, letting him wrestle with it and listening as his muttering took a sharper turn, wondering if he'd notice my detachment and, if he did, what he would make of it.

"Think maybe you could help me out here?" he finally snapped.

So I sat up and, without a word, calmly peeled the panty hose off the other leg, leaving it bunched and torn under the bracelet, and laid back down.

He laughed softly, good humor restored, and eased back up beside me, kissed me, and ran his hand over my stomach, hip bones, and lower, down my bare thigh and up again, where he lingered as the windows steamed, the breathing deepened, and finally, when the hand I had on him didn't take him there, he stopped kissing me and urged my head south.

ಲ   ಲ   ಲ

I called Sammi when I got home.

"He got you *what*?" she said, sounding shocked.

"An ankle bracelet," I repeated.

"But you don't wear those," she said.

"I know."

"You don't even like them."

"I know."

"Does he know you hate them?"

"He should," I said. "I've said it a hundred times." Yeah, whenever he's admiring one on another girl.

"Why would he buy something he knows you don't like?"

"Because *he* likes them," I said, and then, feeling disloyal, added, "I mean, it's not *ugly*. It's silver—"

"*Silver?*" she blurted. "Oh my *God*, Hanna, has he ever even *met* you? You don't wear silver."

"I know," I said again. "What am I supposed to do?"

"Tell him to take it back and this time remember who he's shopping for," she said promptly.

"I can't do that," I said.

"Why not?"

"Because it's too late," I said, lying back on the bed and gazing up at the ceiling. "It would only hurt his feelings and make me sound like an ungrateful bitch. And he did try, Sam. I mean at least he got me something, right?"

"Yeah," she said, sounding unconvinced. "But he'd tell *you*, you know, if you got him something he never wanted and didn't even like. God, he'd tell you in a heartbeat."

"Maybe," I said, but my voice rang hollow.

Later that night I ended up cutting my panty hose off with a scissor so as not to disturb the ankle bracelet.

Chapter 28

Hanna

I took my ankle bracelet off, put on my panty hose, re-attached it, and wore it to school. Seth smiled when he saw it and hugged me.

The only thing that bugged me was that Sammi told me she'd seen Lacey McMullen haunting the upstairs hall near Seth's locker, looking all tragic.

What is it about Seth being stalked by lovesick girls?

I hate the irony of this, I really do.

Good-bye, virginity.

Hello, woman of the world.

He did it when I wasn't expecting it, was already inside me when I remembered about a condom, freaked, and stiffened up. He said, *Don't worry, I won't come in you,* and I was like, *You'd better not,* and it didn't take hardly a minute before he yanked it out in time, but I'll tell you this: I never worried so much in my life until I got my period and spent money I didn't have on two early pregnancy pee tests—both negative—that I had to take at school so no one but Sammi would know.

He tried to do it again two days later, and I was like, *No, not without a condom,* and he got pissed off and said I worry too much and he knew when to pull out. I was like, *Easy for you to say, you wouldn't be the one stuck with a really bad decision to make,* and it just got worse from there. I felt bad saying no because it was like rejecting him, but I also felt bad because I wanted him to understand that *I* would be the one who got stuck, not him, but I don't think he ever really got past the fact that he couldn't budge me on that.

Of course I ended up crying because I hate when he pulls away and won't talk and leaves me with all these unresolved problems. It's like he'd rather step out of it, and because he does that, it gets real quiet and we hit a stalemate. I can't stand the stalemate so I either get even more emotional trying to make him *respond* to me, which freaks me out because I'm not usually so high drama, and crying makes me feel weak and needy, like I'm begging. Sometimes I wish I could just say whatever I want to, like a guy does, just say it flat out, and *he* would be the one to have to humble himself to make nice and bring us back together, but it doesn't seem to happen that way.

I mean, I watch his mom and she's always chatty and cheerful, filling the silences with her words, and I don't know whether his father thinks she *likes* to talk to herself, but if he does, he's wrong. I bet she does it because she's trying to connect with him somehow, to make him look up and see her as a person, someone who is interesting and worth looking at and listening to.

Like the other day, when we were in his room, and his mom got home, I heard his father say, "Bull. Nobody goes shopping four times in one week, Ellen."

"You don't know much about women," Seth's mother said.

"I know about *you*," he said, and it didn't sound like a compliment.

"Seth has company," his mother said evenly. "Do you really want to start this now?"

"Come on," Seth said, grabbing his wallet and keys. "Let's go to Burger King."

"Okay," I said, because it was always embarrassing when they got into it.

"So what did you buy?" Seth's father said.

"*Window*-shopping! I was *window*-shopping—"

"You must think I'm really stupid, Ellen."

And we just kind of sidled out and Seth was in a distant mood that night, a bad mood, and he said something really mean while he was watching some group of girls talking and laughing and acting up a little out on the street, like, *See how slutty you look when you act like that?*

I didn't say anything and he must have been itching for a fight because he said, *What? You don't think every single one of us can be replaced?* And I got really quiet then and sad because I felt so bad for him and that seemed to deflate him because he just sighed and tipped his head back on the seat and looked at me and said, *Face it, Hanna; if it wasn't me, it would just be somebody else.* And it came out tired, but it was like an accusation, too, like I didn't love him and all the things that were so beautiful between us could have just happened with anybody, and that really hurt.

I'm watching my mother now, too, how sometimes when my father's cranky, she gets nicer, like to try and smooth his time at home and make it a place he wants to be instead of a place that's unpleasant, but I notice something else, too: when she feels something, she just says it. She doesn't dilute it so as not to piss him off, especially if it's a strong opinion. And he's apparently okay with it or, at least, he's *used* to it because most of the time he just shrugs and says, *You're entitled to your opinion,* and I've heard him say that for years, but I think I'm starting to understand what it really means.

The Schoenmakers do this, too.

Interesting.

I feel like the weak link in a family of Amazonian women.

For some reason Seth gets cranky when I read, especially when I read while he's practicing his guitar. He says he's playing for *me,* so I should watch and listen, and I *do* watch and listen for like fifteen whole minutes, but sometimes he plays for an hour, and there's no way I can sit there and do nothing but watch him for an hour. I told him that and he got pissed and said, *Oh, but you can read about people who aren't even real for an hour? You don't live in a fucking novel, Hanna, you live in real life,* and I was like, *Yeah, I* know, *but what's the difference between you disappearing into music and me into a book?* And do you know what he said?

"I don't do it to *get away* from you," he said.

Oh my God.

This is one of those tense spots we just can't seem to get around, but it's no big deal.

He's also working more hours at the bowling alley, almost full-time now, and he says I have too much free time, and that's irresponsible, and I should get a job, too, and save for a car and stuff. So I think I'm going to.

I told Gran that if she could stay awake a little longer, we could listen to a few more chapters of the book. I mean, I don't want to tire her out, but this few-chapters-a-day stuff is killing me.

How It Ends

Nurse has taken to scrubbing everything in the house with foul-smelling disinfectant as if she were driven by demons and will not stop to answer even the simplest questions.

❧   ❧   ❧

March brought the first crocuses of spring poking up through the snow, and my mother's birthday. I'd been near tears all week, missing her, remembering her last party, when we'd gathered around Kitty's kitchen table singing (oh, so stupidly) "Young at Heart," and then "Happy Birthday," pretending not to see the blue tinge to her lips and secretly hoping she'd have enough breath to blow out the candles.

I missed her and needed a way to mark the day, so while Nurse was busy scrubbing and Dr. Boehm was off in the woods with his rifle, I decided to go cut some of the forsythia by the shed, bring it in, and force it into blooming in her honor.

I found a pair of scissors and crunched my way across the bleak yard. I'd cut three slim branches when someone said, "Hello."

I turned, startled, and the handyman was standing there. He was younger than I'd thought, in his early twenties perhaps, with ruddy skin, dark eyes, and a tight, hesitant smile. He had an accent I couldn't place and very broad shoulders.

"Oh," I said, clearing my throat. "Hello. I'm Louise."

"Peter," he said, stepping closer, pulling off his work glove, and offering his hand.

I hesitated, not knowing whether I should take it or if shaking hands would be considered fraternizing, and by the time I decided it wasn't, he'd already lowered his hand and was turning to leave.

"No, wait, I'm sorry, it's just that . . ." I stopped, flushing. How could I tell him I wasn't allowed to talk to him without sounding ridiculous?

"The boss doesn't want us to get too friendly," he said with a twinkle in his eyes.

"He told you that, too?" I said, astonished.

"Sure," he said with a shrug. "But this is a free country, right?"

Before I could answer, a door slammed down at the workshop.

Peter winked and melted back into the tree line behind the pines.

I turned back to the barren forsythia bush and cut a few more branches, nodding at Dr. Boehm as he strode past me into the shed, reappearing a moment later with a large and lethal-looking pair of grass clippers, and returned to the workshop.

❧ ❧ ❧

I set the branches in a glass of water on the nightstand in my room. Took the Ciro's souvenir photo out from under my pillow and studied my parents' faces. My mother looked sparkly with pent-up excitement, my father handsome in his uniform, leaning back and giving the camera an arched eyebrow and a cocky smile.

Had it been love at first sight, an instant knowing that they were meant to be together? Had the hazy Army-chaplain wedding behind the nightclub been real or just a ruse used by a randy GI to take advantage of a young girl? And if it had been real, why hadn't my mother put Walter Closson on the birth certificate? I wish I knew.

I touched her face, the girl in the photo who was only three years older than me. Kissed it and pressed it to my cheek, then slid it back under the pillow and went down to make Mrs. Boehm's dinner.

That evening Mrs. Boehm told me of her wedding day and the night that followed.

❧ ❧ ❧

Margaret and Thaddeus Boehm had a beautiful ceremony, from the orange blossoms in the bouquet to the Viennese lace on her late mother's veil. Everything had been perfect. Twenty-eight-year-old Thaddeus, her father's protégé, had grown up to become a dashingly handsome, if not a touch solemn, young man, leading his class in medical school and wooing Margaret with charm, respect, and just the right degree of fervor.

But the wedding night, well, that had been puzzling.

Margaret, twenty and armed only with scant, skewed advice from the unmarried nanny; an abrupt, "Be a good wife, accept your lot, and do your duty," from her father, who had then turned and given Thaddeus a long, speaking look before wishing them well on their honeymoon trip; and pink-cheeked giggles from her second-cousin bridesmaids, had stood beside her husband at the Niagra Falls hotel desk trying not to blush when the clerk smiled, rang for a bellboy, and directed them to the honeymoon suite.

A week earlier (and without mentioning it to Nanny, who was a staunch believer in serviceable cotton nightgowns), Margaret had slipped away and gone back to the bridal store to spend two full, blushing hours trying on peignoir sets, beautiful gossamer silk and satin nightgowns with alluring lace straps and strategically placed inserts, plunging necklines and gathered bodices, all in drifts of clinging, nearly sheer fabric that was both frightening and thrilling.

She purchased three, one in white for the wedding night—a creation so angelically lovely and wickedly revealing that she hoped she'd have the nerve to wear it and nearly fainted imagining the look in Thaddeus's eyes when he saw her in it—a pink one with pin tucks, and a simple blue one with sheer panels across the bodice that she'd first thought too forward but afterward, in a frenzy of excitement, had run back for.

And because her father would be getting the bill, she asked the salesgirl to write the receipt as *wedding accessories* instead of lingerie, as that would have been terribly embarrassing.

The honeymoon suite was lovely, a living room with a bar and a TV, two bathrooms, and a bedroom with the lights low, champagne on ice, a double bed turned down, and chocolates on the pillows.

She had turned to Thaddeus, overwhelmed with love and nerves, happiness and hazy expectations, and he'd put a tender hand to her cheek, kissed her briefly, and said he had forgotten his pipe tobacco and would run down to the smoke shop in the lobby to get some.

She smiled, thinking he was giving her a chance at modesty. When he left she quickly opened her suitcase and shook out the dreamy white peignoir set. Rushed through a quick toilette, taking a sink bath with a fluffy washcloth and rose-scented soap, freshening up all the parts she thought might be necessary, then slipped into the shimmering rayon satin negligee and chiffon robe. She brushed her hair, dabbed Arpege perfume behind her ears and her knees, brushed her teeth, reapplied her lipstick, and taking a deep breath, opened the bathroom door and went into the bedroom.

He wasn't back yet and she didn't want to open the champagne without him, so she drank some tap water instead, just to ease her dry throat, and reclined on the bed in what she hoped was a provocative position.

And she waited.

He returned forty-five minutes later, his expression remote and unapproachable, his pipe full, and oddly enough, he had a smudge of what looked like—but certainly couldn't be—pancake makeup on the front of his trousers. "I'm sorry, Margaret, but I believe one of the wedding guests may have passed on some type of stomach flu and I was the unlucky recipient. I don't want you to catch it, too, so I'm going to sleep out here on the sofa."

"Oh, no, Thaddeus, please. I don't mind if we both get sick," she said, sitting up and giving him a shy smile. "It *is* our wedding night . . ."

"And you look lovely, but I refuse to taint you with this," he said, shaking his head. "No, don't get up. It will only make my removal more difficult."

"But, Thaddeus," she said, rising anyway and approaching him. "Won't you even—"

"Margaret, please," he said, suddenly stern. "A lady does not beg for affection and a wife does not embarrass her husband by demanding more than he can give. I'm not fit to be a proper groom tonight, so please go to bed and I'll see you in the morning." And nodding, he stepped out of the room and closed the door behind him, leaving her openmouthed and sick with embarrassment.

"He was ill for the entire honeymoon," Mrs. Boehm said, toying with the frilly edge of the coverlet and glancing at me from under her lashes. "I didn't know what to think, Louise, and there was no one I could ask, so I thought I'd done something wrong, that I was too eager or willing, that I should have been more demure and less . . ." She sighed and shook her head. "Accommodating, I guess. I don't know.

"Anyway, when we returned from the honeymoon, he carried me over the threshold into our first little bungalow and I thought maybe *now* we would become husband and wife in more than name only . . . but he had already instructed the movers to put our things in separate bedrooms. I know that's old-fashioned, and I said so, but he insisted. He said a physician kept irregular hours and he couldn't bear the thought of disturbing me every time he had an emergency call. I protested and said I didn't mind at all but . . ." Her voice faltered. "I seemed to be the only one disappointed by the plans, and so the arrangement continued." She looked away. "And continues to this day."

I studied the carpet, embarrassed by the intimate revelation and not sure what to say.

"I know Nurse considers me a failure as a woman *and* a wife, but I *need* him, Louise. He's the only man I've ever wanted. I know the sight of me as I am now is distressing and I try to make myself more attractive, but I so rarely get to see him. . . . I hear him walk down the hall and my heart, my whole body, just aches. . . ." She took a shaky breath. "You're too young to understand, but I *love* him and I miss him, I miss touching him and being a *real* wife. . . ."

She said more, I know, but I had started singing "Happy Birthday" to my mother in my head and so I missed it.

☙ ☙ ☙

Nurse was cleaning constantly now, scrubbing, waxing, boiling the bedding, lost in a world of disinfectant and invisible germs, in chewing the skin from her chapped bottom lip until it bled, and often appearing at Mrs. Boehm's door right after lunch, before I could begin brushing her hair, ordering me from the room, and remaining inside with the door closed and locked behind me.

Dr. Boehm quit shaving and spent his days dressed in stained and unkempt work clothes. He came in from the workshop at night wearing bloody gloves with bits of fat and raw, gray flesh clinging to his sleeves, with boots caked with fetid gore, with his gaze feverish, jubilant, angry, his hands shaking and a finger always worrying a raw sore on the back of his neck near his shirt collar.

He changed his gloves before he ate, though, and before deciding to move the two-foot-tall white plaster sculpture out of his study and onto the middle of the dining table. He would stare at it as if in pain throughout the meal, not even bothering to acknowledge me and Nurse anymore, muttering instead at the statue, a woman with the barest of facial features and cradling a young child in her arms. The child's head was nestled in the crook of her shoulder, and its arms wound around her neck.

It was a stark, beautiful piece, and while Dr. Boehm was very possessive of it, pausing to stroke the face or turn it slightly toward his place at the table, I touched it, too, when no one was looking because the statue's tender embrace made me think of my mother.

Nurse and I never questioned the statue's presence, supposing, I guess, that the centerpiece could have been far worse—the stuffed bodies of any number of animals—and even Peter, allowed inside to move the breakfront so Nurse could scrub behind it, paused when he saw the statue. He reached out, noticed his own dirty hand, and stepped back. Turned quickly away but not before I noticed tears gathered in his eyes.

I never thought of leaving them, of calling the home and trying to explain how they'd placed me in a household that was not what it had seemed. It would sound too dramatic and I could hear the impatience in the ward mother's tone: "Well, of course Dr. Boehm smells unpleasant after working on his taxidermy, Louise. I would venture he smells the same after leaving the operating room. This is no cause for alarm," or, "Cleanliness is next to godliness and Nurse should be commended for her vigilance in fighting illness. I wish we had more like her here, as the wards are full of sick children. . . ."

I could have called and begged to be returned anyway, I guess, but the fact remains that I didn't. I accepted, absorbed, and adapted to the whims of the adults because that's what a young girl does, especially one desperate to belong to someone, somewhere.

Chapter 29

Hanna

I was in the snack aisle down at 7-Eleven trying to decide between Nacho Cheese and Cool Ranch Doritos when a low, easy voice said, "Hey, this must be my lucky day."

It was Jesse and he was with another guy, both of them wearing dusty jeans and battered work boots. Jesse had on a mason's T-shirt and an open flannel under his denim jacket and his dreads were pulled back into a ponytail. He looked tired and grubby and gorgeous, cheeks pink with cold, dark eyes warm, and that delightfully plummy bottom lip curved in a mischievous smile.

"Hi," I said, and I don't know how long we would have stood there gazing at each other if his buddy hadn't reached past him, grabbed a bag of pork rinds from the rack, and said, "You ever eat these things, man? They're great, but Christ, they make you fart."

Jesse blinked, snorted, and turned away, shaking his head.

"That's it," I said, laughing and grabbing my own bag of Nacho Cheese Doritos. "I'm outta here. See you, Jess." I walked around the rack and was heading for the register when I heard Jesse say, "Nice timing, asshole."

"What're you talking about?" his buddy said, sounding puzzled.

I paid and left and you know what's interesting?

Every time I see Jesse, he always leaves me glad I did.

There's not a lot of people I can say that about.

Grandpa was just finishing up cleaning Serepta's litter box when I finally got there.

"She's not so good today," he said in a low voice. "Watch her close, all right?"

"Oh, Grandpa," I said and, crumbling, hugged him. Not long—he hugged me quick and put me aside, wiping a shaky hand across his eyes, and then grabbed his crossing guard gear and hurried out.

I looked at Gran. "He loves you a lot, you know."

I waited, but she didn't answer, of course, so I gave her a sip of water and hit play.

How It Ends

The snow melted and the sun returned, coaxing daffodils, then tulips and azaleas into blooming and brightening up the soggy, muddy yard.

Mrs. Boehm wasn't doing well; the pain and increased medication made her vague and moody, at times lucid and sweet, and at others backbitingly bitter. She insisted on sitting in the chair by the window when I brushed her hair, despite the fact that she was often in agony, saying she wanted to see spring arrive but actually watching the door of the workshop, stiffening whenever it opened and Dr. Boehm strode out, catching her breath, leaning forward, and placing her fingertips on the glass in a ready wave that he apparently never looked up and saw.

She was rail thin now, and worried, I asked Nurse if I could vary her diet and cook her special, tempting treats, but Nurse, busy scrubbing the bathrooms, said no, Doctor had put her on a specific diet and we must stick to it.

Mrs. Boehm's appetite waned even further, and her wedding ring began slipping off her bony finger while she slept, causing us a daily search among the bedding. Usually it was somewhere up amid her pillows, but the last time it wasn't, and I was forced to search further, to peel back each layer of quilt and blanket until I found the ring laying near her hip atop a stained mattress pad and giving me my first horrifying look at her bare, mottled thighs, twin sticks riddled with raging, weeping sores beginning at her knees and disappearing up beneath her silky blue nightgown, blackened, bone-deep holes with edges eaten raw and surrounded by necrotic tissue.

"Oh my God!" I blurted, dropping the sheet and backing away from what I then thought were the worst bedsores I'd ever seen.

Struggling, she pulled down her nightgown and cried hoarsely, "Don't look at me like that! Stop it, Louise. Stop it! Don't you dare turn away and pretend you didn't see! Sit down!"

So I sat, paralyzed by the shocking strength of her anger, ashamed at how quickly I'd turned away, at how desperately I hadn't wanted to see what festered beneath the beautifully flowered covers.

"I'm thirty-eight years old, Louise, and the simple fact is that I'm dying," she said, disregarding my stricken gasp and sliding the ring back onto her scrawny finger. "I have made less than five decisions of any importance whatsoever in my entire life and while it would be useless for me to regret them now, I have paid a heavy price for allowing others to decide my fate." A flash of annoyance crossed her face. "You look at me as if I'm speaking a foreign language. Is this so hard to absorb?"

"Yes. No. I don't know," I said helplessly. "Please, Mrs. Boehm, don't excite yourself. I don't want you to die!"

"Oh, Louise," she said, rubbing her forehead. "Please, don't try to stop me from speaking my mind for *once* in my life. It's difficult enough to try and find the words for the things I most urgently want to tell you, but to know that you, too, would rather I took this poison to my deathbed just to maintain this ridiculous façade is truly more than I can bear.

"So I'm going to speak and you're going to listen. You will not leave here armed only with the fairy tale that those who will someday love you will always act in your best interest and, because of that love, you don't have to think about your own future. *You will not.*" She paused, breathing hard, jaw clenched with pain, and then told me of a betrayal that has haunted me my whole life.

"My father was a brilliant physician and a kind, generous man but an arrogant one who believed men were superior and all else on Earth existed only to serve them," Mrs. Boehm said. "I was raised to be a good girl, to speak softly and be pleasing to the eye, to be gentle and innocent and agreeable, to be able to run a household and embroider and arrange flowers, and to *never* question a man's decision as I could not possibly understand the issue, anyway. I was not allowed to raise my voice for any reason other than a house fire, or be openly angry or state my wishes directly, as those behaviors were considered unbecoming in a female.

"I could, however, ask nicely for things, and the sweeter the smile or more submissive the voice, the more I was rewarded with approval. If, however, I asked bluntly or stated an opposing opinion, if my father thought my request was unnecessary or unseemly, I was simply not allowed to do it, whether it was looking something up in one of his medical books or having a second serving of tapioca pudding at dinner.

"I realized that my father loved me most when I was what he wanted me to be and was the most disappointed in me and the least loving when I exerted my own small will or did not do as he expected.

"So I learned early to put my own wishes aside and tend to him first, to believe that I could not make a decision because I was only an uneducated, overemotional female, subject to the whims of my repro-ductive organs—yes, I am finally saying that aloud!—and would ruin my life had I ever the misfortune to gain control of it." She stopped, pressing a hand to her mouth.

"Are you all right?" I said, half rising in my chair. "Should I make tea?"

"No, stay," she said hoarsely and reached for my hand. "Oh, Lou-ise, I *did* love my father dearly, and I feel like a traitor saying these things, but they must be said. They *must* if you are ever going to gain from them."

I took her hand, sat back down, and steeled myself to listen, be-cause if it was true, if she was dying, then I didn't want to be left once again with questions but no answers.

&ᴓ   &ᴓ   &ᴓ

She told me that despite her father's attempts to limit her exposure to the harsher side of life, he *was* a physician, a man who possessed fas-cinating stories, and she a curious child with a penchant for wending her way around the rules, so while she couldn't come right out and *ask* to hear the intriguing stories of his day, she did find another way.

&ᴓ   &ᴓ   &ᴓ

"My father never knew I knew this, but after hours, once I was sup-posed to be long asleep, he and Cook—never Nanny, because she didn't drink—would meet in his study, pour snifters of brandy, and discuss the events of the day." She gave me a speaking look. "Natu-rally this was highly irregular, but I'm assuming my father was lonely for female companionship, as he never did remarry after my mother passed. . . ." She fell silent a moment as if pondering, then shrugged.

"I discovered, purely by chance you understand, that if a person tiptoed into the spare bedroom, got down on her hands and knees and was very quiet, she could hear everything they said through the heating grate."

"Smart," I said.

"Thank you," she said with a dignified nod, and then resumed her story. "The night my father brought Thaddeus home, he said Thad was to be given a bath and put in the spare room off the kitchen. I knew from the look on Cook's face that she was going to have a few things to say that night, so I waited till Nanny had fallen asleep and then tiptoed into the spare room . . . " Mrs. Boehm paused, frowning, and glanced at the closed door.

"What?" I said, following her gaze.

"Nothing," she said after a moment. "I thought I heard something. Would you check, please?"

I rose, unnerved by her sudden stillness, and quickly crossed the room. Threw open the door and looked out into the empty hallway. The smell was there but the smell was in here, too, and Dr. Boehm's room was just down the hall, so I honestly couldn't tell if it was fresh or lingering from earlier. I sniffed again but didn't smell Nurse's telltale disinfectant anywhere, so I just shook my head, closed the door, and sat back down.

"All right," she said, shifting in bed. "Now, where was I? Oh, yes, eavesdropping on my father and Cook the night Thaddeus arrived. It was so frustrating, Louise, not to be able to ask who he was or why he was so filthy or what had prompted my father to bring him home. . . . So frustrating to be patted on the head and told to run along, that Thaddeus would be living with us now and I could always visit with him later but not to pester him with questions." She shook her head. "Is there any torment on Earth worse than questions without answers?"

"No," I said, and meant it.

"Well, I heard Cook say, *This boy has seen a hard life, Doctor. He's been beaten and badly used and I doubt he's ever taken a real bath in his life. He is . . . unclean.* Unclean! A word that could mean anything. Useless, Louise. Utterly useless." She gazed past me into yesterday, seeing things I could never see. "I heard my father give a heavy sigh, and then he told her what had prompted him to remove Thaddeus from his home. . . ."

Her father, she said, had sipped his French brandy and told Cook he'd been called down to a wretched section of town, tenements and slums, outhouses with wells right near them, a place where typhoid and diphtheria had once flourished and, based on what he'd seen, surely would again.

The hovel requiring his services had been the worst he'd ever seen. The man of the house was little more than a drunken, breathing, syphilitic shell sitting slumped against the wall, a bottle of whiskey in his hand, his forehead and most of his cheek eaten away by a runny, ravaging gumma.

"But, Cook, as astounding as it is, *he* wasn't the reason I'd been called out," he'd said.

The reason was a woman lying on the bed surrounded by filthy, scabby, spotty children, siblings, he'd later discovered, but none bearing any resemblance to the other. They were watching their mother, scrawny, deplorably filthy, covered with seeping sores and attempting to deliver yet another child.

"I shooed them all away except for the oldest boy, who I asked to heat some water," the good doctor said. "The rest of the children were cretins with dull eyes and deformed limbs, but this lad seemed aware and hastened to assist me.

"I wore gloves, of course, two pairs, as I made my initial examination of the woman, expecting to find her dilated and near to delivering the next poor bastard; however, she was *not* dilated, there was no fetal heartbeat, and she would not stop thrashing and moaning, so I had to ask the lad to restrain her. He did, crying, and she screamed, *Help me, Taddy, it's eating me alive,* which of course was an inappropriate thing to say to such a young boy who should never have been witnessing such an unhappy scene anyway, but I bypassed this because she was so obviously out of her head.

"The boy begged me to help her, but I couldn't deliver a baby that wasn't there, so I examined further and determined it was a very large malignant tumor of the womb and, given her malnourished state, the active syphillis she'd no doubt suffered her whole life, her irregular heartbeat, and the strain on her faltering body, measured out a dose of morphine and informed him that I was giving her something to ease her pain."

"And it did," Cook said.

"Yes," he said quietly. "Her heart stopped while I was explaining the nature of her illness to the brood, how it was inoperable and would continue to consume her, causing untold agony and a slow, miserable death. Only the boy seemed to understand any portion of what I said, or even cared.

"They had no telephone, of course, so I pronounced the time of death and packed up my things, intending to go and call the coroner, when the boy caught my eye. He had washed his hands and tried to comb his matted hair and was standing by his mother's body, weeping. He looked at me and said, 'My ma is dead.'

"I know, lad," I said. "I'm sorry.

"He looked past me and spotted my stethoscope on the table where I'd left it and returned it to me even though he could have sold it somewhere and probably gotten enough money to feed the whole wretched lot for a month. It was at that moment, Cook, when he handed it to me, that he said, 'I want to be a doctor, too, sir,' and it touched me so deeply, given his hopeless circumstances, that I . . ." He cleared his throat. "Well, you see what I've done. If he turns out to be mentally defective or his contagious legacy destroys him, then I've gambled on the wrong horse. If not, then perhaps he *will* defy his birthright and follow in my footsteps."

"But his scourge," Cook said. "Can you cure it so he's fit?"

"Perhaps not cure it, but I can certainly manage it," the doctor said. "Tomorrow I will begin treating him with mercury pills and we will watch for sores, tooth loss, and most importantly, obvious neurological damage, although that may not reveal itself so readily and may instead manifest over a matter of time. Unfortunately, we have no choice, so until I indicate otherwise, keep him from Margaret, feed him on separate dishes, and have him use the hired man's facilities. Find him a decent set of clothing, as I'm sure he'll want to attend his mother's funeral. It will be a potter's field affair, and I question my own wisdom in allowing him to attend, but he seemed quite attached to the poor wretch and feels guilty over her unhappy death. It was necessary, but I want no resentment at *me* spurring him through life." And quietly, "He has much to overcome, Cook. God only knows what he's already seen in his young life."

"He is a handsome boy, now that he's clean," Cook said. "How old do you think he is?"

"He says he's sixteen," the doctor said. "A young man so nutritionally deprived that he has yet to enter puberty."

"Oh my goodness," Cook said.

"Exactly," the doctor said. "You can understand now why freeing the mother to free the child was indeed an act of mercy."

Silence.

"Do you think he knew—"

"No," the doctor said abruptly, "and we will never speak of it again."

"Of course, my father made her swear she'd never tell me, so I had to act curious in the beginning so I wouldn't make her suspicious, but that all passed fairly quickly once Thaddeus settled into our house. So that's how he came to be the son my father never had, his prize protégé, a fine doctor, and ultimately, my husband," Mrs. Boehm said, giving me a level look. "Isn't that remarkable?"

I gazed at her, stunned.

"So you see, Louise, people always act in their own best interest and are rarely what they seem," she said, smoothing the covers over her lap. "Every person has a beginning, even those who would rather die than acknowledge it." She grimaced as a spasm of pain passed through her. "My husband has never spoken openly to me about the years before he came to us, and I'm quite sure it would destroy him if he discovered I knew of his unfortunate origin, so I would appreciate your discretion in this matter."

"Of course," I stammered, as more alarming realizations came to mind.

"Yes, I see I have given you a lot to think about." Her face was drawn, her smile tired, and her gaze bleak. "I'd like to rest now, so please pull the shades and wake me in an hour." And then she closed her eyes and lay stiller than death while I did just that.

Reeling, I went into my room, but all of a sudden the smell of rot was too strong, was everywhere in the house, and I opened my window but I still couldn't stand it, not along with what I'd just heard and still couldn't believe, with knowing that Mrs. Boehm was dying, that she would *die* right there in that bed, and then what would happen to me? I wouldn't be needed here anymore, would be sent back to the home to rejoin the sick and grief stricken, the crowded ward of teens that preyed on one another, would become one of the faceless, unwanted surplus who just kept coming . . .

The thought was unbearable.

I pulled on a sweater and went outside, standing by the back door a moment, hugging myself and gulping in the fresh air.

Peter came around the side of the house and stopped when he saw me. "Are you all right?"

I turned away, wiping my eyes, and nodded. "I'm fine."

"Why do you say that when it isn't true?" he asked, touching my arm.

"I don't know," I said helplessly.

"I'm leaving," he said after a moment. "I haven't told the boss yet, but I'm quitting on Friday."

"You're leaving?" I said, shocked. "Why?"

He shrugged and looked out toward the road. "This isn't a good place for me. I don't think it's a good place for anybody." He met my gaze. "I've already stayed longer than I meant to."

And there was an unspoken question in his dark gaze that tilted something inside me and brought a strange weakness to my knees. "Do you know where you're going?"

He shook his head. "I'll find something. I always do."

"But . . . to just go? To leave your home—"

"This isn't my home," he said with a grim laugh. "That was stolen years ago." And then he stopped abruptly and shook his head.

"Well," I said, feeling sadder than I should have, given that I hardly even knew him. "I guess we'll miss you. . . ." I backed up a step. "I should go back in now before anybody sees us talking. And besides, Mrs. Boehm needs me." I reached for the door. "If I don't see you again before you go, then . . . good luck."

"Louise," he said. "Have you ever thought about leaving here?"

"Leave? No," I said. "They're my foster family, and besides, where would I go?"

A door slammed at the back of the yard and I immediately opened the door to disappear inside before Dr. Boehm saw us.

"Wait," Peter said urgently. "I . . . the workshop . . . have you ever been in there?"

"Only once, way back in the beginning," I said, pausing. "Why, have you?"

"No, but he had me board the windows, and the smell around the place . . ." He gazed at me as if trying to gauge how much to say and, when I gave a nervous look toward the back of the yard, expecting to see Dr. Boehm striding toward me at any second, said hurriedly, "You don't want to stay here, Louise. It's not a good—"

"I have to go," I said and quickly slipped inside. Ran to the kitchen window and watched as Peter turned and walked past Dr. Boehm, who was muttering and rubbing his gloved hands together and didn't even seem to notice him.

Peter stopped and turned and met my gaze for a moment in the window, then walked back over, picked up his rake, and continued to work.

"Gran? One more?" I said, keeping my fingers crossed.

It took a moment, but she blinked once.

I woke up Mrs. Boehm and brought her a tea tray. We were sitting together in silence when a loud blast startled both of us. She dropped her spoon and struggled to the edge of the bed, motioning for me to help her to the window. I did and we looked out in time to see a scowling Peter striding over to where a deer, bony hips poking out through her sides and belly bulging, lay thrashing by the salt lick, and Dr. Boehm hurrying down out of his tree stand, rifle in hand.

"That's a pregnant doe," I cried, covering my mouth and looking away, sickened.

"He is consumed," she murmured, swaying in my arms. "And still he denies himself."

"The poor fawn . . ." I whispered, and then in a surge of fury, "It's not hunting season. Oh, how *could* he?"

"Does are pregnant during hunting season, too, Louise," she said quietly, without taking her gaze from her husband's raggedy, tottering figure. "If they have mated in the fall, then they are pregnant when they're shot. . . ." She closed her eyes and rested her forehead against the glass. "It is man's right to destroy all he surveys."

No, I wanted to say. *No, it's not,* but instead I just looked back out the window, near tears, and saw Peter, grim and hands clenched in fists, watching as Dr. Boehm knelt by the deer's body. The doctor said something, but Peter didn't move. Dr. Boehm glanced up sharply and spoke again, and with an angry, jerky movement, Peter bent and helped the doctor lift the doe's twitching body and place it on the cart Dr. Boehm commandeered alone and pushed doggedly toward the workshop.

ᘓ∽   ᘓ∽   ᘓ∽

I helped Mrs. Boehm back to bed and for the first time was unhappy at touching her, forcing myself not to shrink from the feel of her wasted muscles, hot under my hands, twitching and flexing like a pile of snakes. I wanted to leave the room, to leave the smell wafting from her whenever she moved, to wash my hands over and over again, to plunge them into Nurse's buckets of disinfectant—

"Come set my hair, Louise. Thaddeus will be proud of the kill and may decide to visit me tonight," Mrs. Boehm said breathlessly, grimacing at her reflection in the hand mirror and missing my astonished gaze. "I would like to be beautiful for him when he does."

ᘓ∽   ᘓ∽   ᘓ∽

So I sat for an hour winding her hair around rollers, and when we ran out of those, she showed me how to use strips of rags. While I was busy she told me about the intimate moment fifteen years ago that had changed their lives forever, the night of their fifth wedding anniversary when, desperate, she had ceased to be a lady and had become a woman.

I looked at Gran, and her eyes were open, but I wasn't sure if she was actually seeing, so I got up and knelt in front of her, just far enough away to avoid her flailing feet. "Can I keep going?" I waited but she didn't blink. "Gran? One more chapter, and then I swear I'll go get the animal food ready? Please?"

It took a moment but finally her gaze found mine and she blinked.

How It Ends

It was, Mrs. Boehm said, the deck of racy playing cards she'd found in his bottom bureau drawer one day when, home alone, she'd decided to weed through their clothes for the annual charity drive. The deck had been hidden beneath a pile of old dress shirts and the cards were dog-eared and curved as if shuffled often. The photos of men and women together were shocking and, upon closer study, answered many of the questions she'd had since her uneventful wedding night five years before.

She went through them again and again, studied the women who were hard and cheap looking, wore far too much makeup and looked the way she'd always imagined prostitutes would.

Feeling just a little sick and guilty, as if she'd been snooping on purpose, as if, five years after the wedding and still a virgin, she wasn't getting just a little anxious, just a little desperate to find the key that would unlock her husband's stern, distant affection, so she had trumped up a reason and gone rummaging through his personal effects, she shuffled the cards one last time, studying the men, their naked backsides (they only showed the men from the back or the side, never the front like the women) and their expressions that seemed to alternate between fierce concentration and a kind of dazed ecstasy.

The more she looked, the stranger she began to feel, making her want not only to look at these couples but to *be* one of them, she and Thaddeus, naked as the days they were born, a husband and wife without secrets or separateness, wrapped in each other's arms and marveling at what they'd been missing.

Yes, this was what she wanted now that she'd seen it, now that married love was more than twin beds, a movie screen kiss, and a fade to black.

She replaced the cards exactly as she'd found them, shut the drawer, rose, and left the room. She thought of the suggestive lingerie the women had been wearing, and without even pausing to run a brush through her hair or refresh her lipstick, she ran out and caught the bus down into the city, where she did her best to replicate the peekaboo bras (only pink or black, no red) and the lacy black garters and panties. She thought of the hair of the women on the cards and went to the wig department, leaving with a long, flowing Veronica Lake–style wig in a dazzling auburn, then headed straight for the shoe department for a wicked pair of black platform high heels with ankle straps.

From there, now slightly breathless, spurred by adrenaline and the images on the cards, she went to the liquor store, her first time ever inside of one, and bought their highest proof gin and several bottles of tonic, then on the advice of the clerk, stopped at the market for two fresh limes, two porterhouse steaks, two baking potatoes, and a fresh pouch of cherry pipe tobacco.

She caught a bus home and lugged her bags—so many!—up the block to their tidy little house. Tried to think of which should come first, the drinks and seduction or the meal, and decided first the fresh tobacco, then the meal, then when he was nice and relaxed, she would make them . . . no, first a predinner drink, a cocktail to relax him, and then the tobacco, the steak, the postdinner refill or two, and the seduction.

Yes.

She felt giddy with excitement because she had a plan now, she was doing something daring and unapproved, and later, when they were snuggled close and it was over, she would tell him how she'd planned this and he would lean back and smile and say, *That's my clever girl!* And she would bask, oh yes, she would bask in the glow of his admiration because she'd been waiting far too long to earn it.

So when he came home, she did nothing to alert him, didn't reveal even the tiniest glimmer of the excitement shimmering inside of her. She had taken a bath earlier and pinned her hair up (in secret preparation for the wig) but she was wearing a pair of slacks and a pullover, and she gave him her cheek to kiss like always, sent him in to sit in his chair and discover his surprise fresh tobacco, and said, while he sounded genuinely pleased at the gift, "Oh, and I read that all the up-and-coming young doctors are having cocktails before dinner, so I made us each a nice gin and tonic. Here." And she carried his, which was twice as strong as hers, in, and he put down the newspaper and thanked her for that, too.

By the time the steaks were ready, he had finished the first drink and was absently sipping a second.

She kept the conversation general during dinner, spoke of his many surgical triumphs, and the gin made him expansive, loosened him up enough to laugh and actually tease her, saying she looked ten years younger with her hair up and dressed like that, and she laughed along with him and kept her distance and when dinner was over she casually poured them another round of drinks, his strong, hers mostly tonic because she felt looser, too, and had to go easy or she would scare him away.

"Madam," he said, leaning back and giving her an owlish look, "are you trying to take advantage of me?" Luckily he missed her stricken look and, chuckling, hefted the glass and took a hearty swallow. "So tell me, my dear," he said, leaning back in his chair and smiling, "what else do brilliant up-and-coming young physicians do? Vacation in Cuba? Learn how to ski? Put in swimming pools?" He drained the rest of the glass and, still smiling, surrendered it for another. "Let's hear what the women's magazines have declared de rigeur for the cream of the medical-community crop."

"Better than that," she said, trembling as she motioned for him to follow her into the living room and sat him in the center of the couch, taking careful note of his wobbly gait and flushed cheeks, "stay there for a second and I'll show you." She handed him the drink and hurried into her bedroom, closing the door behind her.

"Ah, let me guess," he called. "You bought a new dress. No, a dress and shoes."

"Wrong," she called with frantic gaiety, shimmying out of her clothes and struggling into the cutout black bra, lace panties, and garter belt. The black stockings were the hardest, her hands were cold and clumsy, and it seemed to take forever to buckle the ankle straps on the shoes. "Keep guessing," she called, bending and pulling on the wig.

"A dress, shoes, and a *hat*. I hope they're green, Margaret. You always look lovely in green."

"Thank you, dear, but that's not it," she called.

"I know!" he announced, his words distinctly slurred. "You bought a fur coat! What kind is it, Margaret?"

"Don't be silly," she called back, dabbing cheap perfume everywhere, rolling on bright red lipstick, rimming her eyes with black pencil, and smearing rouge on her cheeks. She gazed at herself, astonished, almost sick with anticipation because she looked like someone else, like a woman who *knew* things, knew how to excite a man, knew

how to get everything she wanted, and so she turned on the phono-
graph and played the record album of boudoir music she'd bought,
turned on the bed lamp she'd covered with a sheer black scarf, and—

"I know," he said. "It's a mink! You bought a mink, you little
minx!"

She said a brief prayer, took a deep breath, and shaking, opened the
bedroom door and stepped out into the living room.

"No," she said and didn't know whether it was the shoes with their
sassy high heels or the fact that she was nearly naked in the main
room of their house or the gin or the deck of cards that had showed
her what she was missing or the fact that he was sitting there, mouth
open, eyes wide, staring at her with a look she had never seen before,
a riveted look that made her sashay straight over to him, lift the glass
from his slack hand, and straddle his lap. "The ladies magazines say
that all you handsome, brilliant young physicians should always have
your hands full after dinner." And when his fingers, cold and damp
from the glass, crept up and gripped her thigh, when his breathing
came heavy, she took his face between her hands and kissed him hard.

He only said no once, tried to hold back once when he was
propped above her on his knees and shook his head as if to clear it and
said, *Margaret, no, I shouldn't, you don't know*—

Do it, she'd said, pulling him closer. Touching and stroking him,
delirious, crazed by the powerful heat, yearning for this moment like
none other, ever, loving him with every cell, wanting him, and so he
did, and she locked herself around him and watched his face, saw the
fierceness and discovered the second expression wasn't concentration
at all but need, yes, need because she needed him and he her and this,
this was how they should be, laughing, tumbling, kissing, loving all
the time . . .

When it was over and he had collapsed, hot, sweaty, smelling of gin
and her new cheap perfume, gasping and mumbling and nuzzling her

throat, her neck, she whispered, *I love you,* and he whispered it, too, and fell asleep with his arms tight around her.

Right before she fell asleep, when she was lying there drowsing in a beautiful, dreamy haze, wondering at the miracle, hoping they had made a baby, her arm draped across his stomach and her hand settled at his hip, her fingers found a small, scab-covered sore on his side, ran idly over it, and returned to nestle in his chest hair.

She slept.

When she woke up the next morning, he was already gone and she spent the day in a delicious delirium, wondering what would happen when he got home. Would he sweep her up in his arms and carry her straight to the bedroom, or would they flirt with each other, prolonging the anticipation over dinner, and then fall into bed? Or maybe not bed at all, maybe he'd ask her to dress up again and they would use the couch this time instead of stumbling together into the bedroom like they had last night?

Oh, it could be anything!

Except that when he got home he ignored her upturned mouth, went straight to the bottle of gin on the counter, and poured it down the sink. "I will not have any more alcohol in this house," he said without looking at her. "I don't know what got into you last night but if it happens again, which I promise you it won't, I will arrange for you to see a colleague of mine who specializes in female disorders."

"What?" she'd whispered, hand at her throat.

"Last night's tryst was . . . tawdry," he said, still without looking at her. "You're the wife of a highly respected physician. You have a responsibility to remain above reproach—"

"Thaddeus, we're married," she cried. "What we did was between a husband and his wife—"

"I cannot reason with you when you're like this," he said coldly, turning away.

"Like what?" she cried. "Upset because for the first and only time in five years my husband made love to me and now he won't even *look* at me?"

"Lower your voice," he said, pausing in the doorway.

"Thaddeus, please don't shut me out," she said, coming up behind him and touching his arm. "I *love* you."

He stiffened but didn't pull away and when he spoke, his voice was stern but tired. "And I you, Margaret, but what happened last night cannot happen again."

"Ever?" she said, voice cracking.

He nodded once and went into the living room to smoke his pipe and wait for dinner.

          ೧೨   ೧೨   ೧೨

"And it hasn't, but, Louise, my God, it has to just one more time before I die," Mrs. Boehm said, blotting her eyes with a tissue. "It won't be the same, I know that, since this last operation, but if only he would lie down beside me and hold me again, touch me, and . . . I know I shouldn't say this to you, but there are other things a man and a woman can do besides intercourse. It's true. I've read about them."

I rose and went to the window, far too embarrassed by what she'd confessed to look at her. These were the most personal of moments, intimate interactions that no stranger should be privy to.

I didn't know what to do except to help her be beautiful and get Dr. Boehm up into that room.

"Argh!" I buried my face in my hands. "This book is making me crazy. One more chapter?" I peeked out at Gran.

Her eyes were closed.

Sighing, I rose and turned off the CD player.

          ೧೨   ೧೨   ೧೨

"If we ever get through this book on tape and you get a chance to listen to it, trust me, you're not going to believe it," I said to my mother after supper, and then, trying to gauge her mood, said casually, "If Daddy only messed around with you once in like eighteen years of marriage, would you have stayed with him?"

She stopped rinsing a plate and gave me a funny look. "Well, I guess it would depend on why."

"Because he had syphilis?" I said brightly.

"Because he . . . what the hell kind of book is that, anyway?" my mother said.

"A very intense one," I said, half to myself. "And not at all what I thought it was going to be."

"No serial killers or stuffed wives?" my mother said.

"Not so far," I said, retrieving the glasses from the table. "It's actually kind of sad. Women didn't have it so good in the olden days, did they?"

"Are you asking me because you think I was there?" my mother said, eyebrows high.

No," I said, cracking up, and then my mother highjacked the conversation and took me back to her glory days and we didn't get serious again.

But I thought about Margaret Boehm that night, doing everything she could to win her husband's affection and attention, and I really didn't like the way it made me feel at all.

It made me feel like I understood.

❧   ❧   ❧

I was helping Seth clean out his SUV because he finally found just the right classic MG online and needed to sell the SUV to buy it, and I found an earring—definitely not one of mine—under the back bench seat.

It came out in a handful of McDonald's wrappers, which made it worse because we always went to Burger King. I stood there staring at it, a small hoop with three little blue beads, kind of bent like it had been ripped from an ear, and he noticed my stillness and said, "What?" I held it up and said, "An earring . . . and it isn't mine," and he got all insulted and went into this rant, saying I'm so suspicious and what else does he have to do to show me that he loves me, and then I started feeling bad because he said it hurt every time I doubted him and he hated being blamed for things he didn't do. He was getting loud and that was embarrassing because we were out in front of his garage, so I was just like, *Okay, forget it,* but he said, *No, it's not okay,* and then I started to cry because he was so cold and distant, so I went over to him and whispered, *I'm sorry, okay? I do trust you and maybe the old owner left it, right? Maybe I jumped to conclusions,* and he said, *Yeah, maybe you did,* but he then put his arms around me and said, *You have to trust me, Hanna, okay?* And I was like, *Okay, I do.*

And I do, I do . . . I just . . . I don't know.

Maybe it's me.

I was setting the table for supper one night and my mother was making the pasta salad and I said real casually, "What would you do if Daddy ever cheated on you?"

And I don't know what I was expecting, but it wasn't her easy, "Divorce him."

"You would?" I said, shocked. "Just like that?"

"Of course," she said, giving me a curious look. "Why, what did you think I would do?"

"Well, I don't know, but not that," I said. "You would break up our family?"

Oh my God, my mother hit the roof, and I was so not expecting it that I just stood there with my mouth hanging open.

"I can't stand that you just said that," she said, grabbing a bottle of Italian dressing by the neck and shaking it like she was trying to kill it. "If your father cheated on *me,* then *he* made the decision to risk every single thing we had together, knowing that this would destroy us, so no, Hanna, it wouldn't be *me* breaking up the family, it would be him."

"But you could forgive him," I said warily.

She snorted. "Why? Why would I want to live with a deliberate cheater and a liar and a betrayer, with someone who was willing to hurt me like that just to get off?"

"Mom," I said, flushing.

"No, I'm serious, Hanna. Why would I? Why would I think so little of myself to do that? And how could I even stand to look at him, not to mention touch him? No," she said and twisted open the cap of the bottle, "we told each other way back in the beginning that there were several absolute relationship breakers and topping the list was cheating, so we both know that if either one of us did it, it would mean the end of everything."

"Really," I said, leaning back against the wall and watching her. "So that means if you cheated, Daddy would divorce you?"

"Absolutely," she said with a brisk nod. "And I would expect him to."

"Wow," I said, more than a little uneasy. "I never knew that. What about unconditional love?"

She shook her head. "Think about what those words mean, Hanna, and then you tell me. Unconditional love. Love without conditions."

"Yeah . . . ?" I said, not getting it.

"All right, suppose your father came in from work every night, screamed in my face, called me all sorts of vile names, beat the crap out of me in front of you, beat you, too, brought home hookers, and did all sorts of disgusting things—"

"Ew, stop," I said, scowling. "Daddy's not like that."

"Right, but if he was, and we had no conditions on our love, then I would still love and stay with him, right? Because with no conditions, then *any* behavior is acceptable, then I would just take whatever I could get, right? Do you see what I'm saying?"

"So there are conditions," I said.

She sighed. "If you don't believe me, go ask your father."

So I did, plopping down onto the ottoman in front of him and poking the newspaper until he sighed and lowered it. "Yes?"

"What would you do if Mommy cheated on you?" I said.

"Beat the crap out of the guy and then divorce her," he said matter-of-factly.

"Do you believe in unconditional love?" I said.

"Only for you, kiddo," he said.

"Okay," I said. "Would you ever cheat on Mommy?"

"No," he said with absolute certainty. "No roll in the hay is worth losing what I've got."

And that made my eyes sting, and in a little-kid move I hadn't done in I don't know how long, I reached over and hugged him, crushing the paper and making him grumble, but I knew it didn't matter because he smiled and hugged me back.

It took me almost two hours of frantic digging through my catch-all drawer and the memory boxes in my closet but I finally found the worn, red talisman bag Gran had made for me back when I was little.

An acorn, for growth and potential.

Mica, because all that glitters is not gold.

A piece of the catalpa tree, for us, together.

I wanted to bring it to her, offer it up and say *See? I still have it, it still means something to me,* but I was afraid she'd start crying and choke so I just tucked it into my pocket, and went to sit with her, and listen to the next chapter.

How It Ends

It would be an understatement to say it went badly.

We waited, Mrs. Boehm and I, from seven o'clock when we heard him come in from his workshop until almost ten, her with curls drooping and makeup fading, making pitiful small talk, indulging in busywork like cleaning off the other side of the bed just in case, and her lighting up every time there was so much as a creak in the hall.

At ten, angry and unable to bear her sinking hopes and humiliation anymore, I excused myself, went downstairs, found Dr. Boehm in his study poring over a taxidermy manual, and said as politely as I could, "Excuse me, Doctor, but could you come up and see Mrs. Boehm, please? It's important."

"Is she hysterical?" he said without looking up.

"No," I said, wanting to slap him. "Will you come, please?"

"In a moment," he said.

I waited, knowing what would happen if I didn't, knowing he would either forget or willfully dismiss the request as he had dismissed so many of her others, and when several moments had passed, I coughed. More moments, and I cleared my throat.

"Are you coming down with a cold, Louise?" he said finally, glancing up at me.

"No," I said, holding his gaze.

He heaved a sigh, closed the book, and rose. His gloves were stained with old blood and his clothes were rumpled and putting off that same unpleasant odor, but I didn't dare make mention of any of it, plus I knew Mrs. Boehm wouldn't care.

"Congratulations on the doe you killed today," I forced myself to say, and we made our way through the hall and up the stairs.

"Yes, well, she wasn't exactly what I was hoping for, but I can still use her," he said cryptically, pausing outside his wife's bedroom door.

I waited, watching as he hesitated, and then, when he finally drew a deep breath and turned the knob, I went on past to my room next door, not to listen but to be . . . aware.

I had just taken out fresh pajamas and unbuttoned my blouse when I heard voices rising, his harsh and hers wild.

I went to the adjoining door and put my ear to it in time to hear him say, "You cannot keep doing this! I've done everything in my power to help you, Margaret, but it won't work if you don't try!"

"Try for what, this horrible, sterile existence? Why would I want to live this way for another thirty years, Thaddeus? I'm dead to you already, you've all but buried me, and—"

"I won't do it, Margaret. I *can't*. I've had to live with what I've done for eighteen years now, and—"

"So have *I*, Thaddeus! Don't you think *I* have to live with it, too? Don't you think I deserve *some* small happiness out of—"

"I will not discuss this again," he said. "From now on any request you make to see me must come through Nurse to ensure it's for a valid medical emergency. Good night."

"Thaddeus." Her voice was flat. "I know."

Silence.

"Pardon me, Margaret?"

"I *know*," she said, and her voice was rising again. "I know everything about you. I know about your mother—"

"Margaret."

"And how my father found you—"

"Please." His voice was wire tight and shaking. "Don't."

"I know it *all*, Thaddeus, so yes, I think you *will* spend time with me, because I'm all you have, do you see? I know *everything*, even how my father treated your mother—"

"He eased her pain," he said automatically.

"Oh, yes, he certainly did that," she said with a strangled laugh. "You're a physician, Thaddeus; deep in your heart of hearts, you know what he did to your mother. You know and you just can't bear to acknowledge that your beloved mentor deliberately took her from you while you stood right there trusting him, isn't that right? No, do not turn away from me! I know about your family and their disease, and even knowing everything, every ugly, filthy little detail, I still love you and . . . where are you going? Thaddeus?"

I stepped away from my door right as hers clicked closed and held my breath, praying he wasn't going to call me out and punish me for my part in this. Instead, his abrupt footsteps passed and I heard the door to his room close.

And I heard Mrs. Boehm weeping as though her heart was breaking, so I knocked tentatively on the connecting door and called softly, "May I come in?"

The weeping didn't stop, didn't pause, and so I eased open the door and hurried across the carpet to the bed, heedless of anything but the wrenching sound.

"Shh," I said, perching on the edge of the bed and brushing her wet curls back from her face. "Everything will be fine."

She just shook her head, hands over her face, shoulders shaking.

"He's just surprised," I said, hating to make excuses for him, but the strength of her sobs was beginning to scare me. I did everything I could think of to ease her pain; rubbed her arms and stroked her hair and handed her tissues and shut off the overhead light and switched on the bedside lamp and wetted a washcloth and blotted her hot, streaked face, and when she finally opened her eyes in the dim light, her gaze was broken, disconnected, and feverish, scaring me even more, and when she took my hand in hers and whispered, *My heart is breaking, oh God, feel it,* and placed it over her breast and I stiffened in shock and tried to pull away, she whispered, *No, don't,* like she was carrying on a conversation with someone who wasn't there. I sat frozen as she whispered to herself and held my hand to her racing heartbeat, and sweating, I prayed she would release me so I could go.

⁓   ⁓   ⁓

What additional horror that lay beneath the covers should never have been shown to me, but in her delirium—and I *must,* I must think of it as a delirium or it will haunt me—she revealed the final operation meant to cure her unseemly desires, not a hysterectomy as I'd been told but a madman's artwork of amputation and stitching, the scar tissue shiny and tight and streaked red, the genital mutilation bringing a panic so strong that I wrenched free of her grip and wiped frantically at my hands and my arms as if ridding myself of a thousand insects, backed away, leaving her lying there, eyes closed, breath heaving, sinking in on herself.

I stumbled to the door and Dr. Boehm was there, eyes unfocused, bloodshot, and damp with tears, syringes in his bare, ungloved hands. He looked at me and said, "Go," and I went, I ran to my room, and while I was grabbing things, my Ciro's photo and for some reason a pair of bedroom slippers, I heard him say with infinite tenderness, "I'm going to administer something that will end the pain, Margaret, for both of us, and then I'm going to lie down beside you. Will you have me?" and her voice, cracking with joy, "Yes, oh yes, please . . ."

Oh, God, I ran, I ran down the stairs and out the door, and there was no one there. I saw a flashlight bobbing at the back of the property and it was Peter, saw him open the workshop and pause, then slip inside, and a dim light went on and I took off running to him. I smelled the place yards before I reached it and, unable to call, ran inside and skidded in a slick, spreading puddle, skidded into Peter, who stood frozen, and I followed his gaze . . .

The pregnant doe had been gutted and laid on her side on the table, her front legs parted and the fetal fawn laid in between them, front legs broken to form humanlike elbows stitched up to encircle the mother's neck, head tilted up as if nuzzling her nose. A doe skin lay in a heap on the floor, buzzing with flies and leaking terrible fluids, and there amid a pile of partially chewed entrails and awash in chemicals, lay one last starving, shrinking, terrified fawn, hiding its face in the wet carcass, jerking to rise and falling sideways, cringing and thrashing, and I shrank back because its belly was eaten open and its intestines—

"No," I whispered and would have gone down had Peter not grabbed me and pushed me back toward the door.

"Go," he said grimly, looking around the slaughterhouse and seizing a cinder block from the floor. "It's too late."

"No," I sobbed. "Wait, we can take it—"

"Go!" he shouted, voice cracking, and I went, and behind me I heard a terrible thud, and then the cinder block fall and he was beside me again, breathing hard and leading me across the yard and helping me into the front seat of his rattletrap old truck, and I couldn't stop crying and patting my pocket for the Ciro's picture, but it was gone, I'd lost it somewhere, along with my bedroom slippers, and as we pulled out I saw Nurse on her knees in a pale spill of porch light, disinfecting the cement lions flanking the front door, and she didn't even look up when we drove away.

I sat there a moment, shuddering, then reached out and shut off the CD.

Wiped my eyes. Wiped Gran's eyes.

Gave her a little Gatorade from her cup and wiped her nose.

Went into the kitchen and stood looking at the pile of apples in the fridge.

Took six out and, hands shaking, started slicing them for the deer.

Hunting season started in a little more than two weeks.

Seth wasn't in school today.

I tried calling him five times, but he never answered his cell so I finally gave up.

It was hard, not knowing if he was sick or if he'd just cut out.

Harder still not to go to the office to see if Lacey McMullen was absent, too.

But I didn't.

After school I all but ran to Gran's and it was funny how even with her so sick, being with her could still make me feel safe.

Heart,
are you great enough
For a love that never tires?
O heart,
are you great enough for love?

—Alfred, Lord Tennyson

How It Ends

"We've crossed the state line, Louise," Peter said quietly a while later, as I huddled silent and numb against the passenger door, staring at the dried blood on my shoes. "I'll either have to leave you somewhere or marry you now, whatever you choose."

"Marry me," I said dully, because I didn't want to be alone.

ల౩   ల౩   ల౩

We stopped in a little town and had a justice-of-the-peace ceremony. The details are hazy but I remember the justice asking if we were in trouble, and I knew by the way he said it that he was asking if I was pregnant, so I said yes and started to cry, and he married us in a real ceremony; I have the official marriage license to prove it.

ల౩   ల౩   ల౩

We got hot dogs at a drive-in joint and a room at a cheap motel. He took one bed, I the other. We slept like the dead.

ల౩   ల౩   ల౩

I moved through those first weeks in a thick gray cloud, barely speaking, plagued by nightmare sights and smells, always curled into myself, trusting no one, missing my mother and, even more, the Ciro's photo, barely able to think about what had happened at the Boehms', if either of them were still alive, if Nurse was still there or the state home knew or even cared that I was gone.

Peter was very kind and cautious with me, speaking quietly, watching me closely, teasing me into reluctant smiles, making sure I ate and even bought me a ring, a plain sterling-silver band he found in a pawnshop.

Good deals were necessary, as all we had was what he'd left with.

I, of course, had nothing.

We found a medium-sized town where newcomers weren't noticeable and rented a small apartment. He got a job working nights on the railroad loading freight and I waitressed days at the local diner. We saw each other briefly in the morning and again at dinner. I never realized it then, but now I believe Peter had done that deliberately to give me time to adjust, to get to know him without feeling threatened or obligated or scared.

Peter carried a story of his own, one I was too oblivious at that point to ask about.

I'd never worked for money before, never had even five dollars to my name, and the first night I realized I was allowed to keep the quarters I'd slid off the tables, I was ecstatic. I danced home, spread it all out on the counter in the kitchenette, and ignoring Peter's good-natured amusement, counted it out and vowed that if tips were left for good service, then I would become the best waitress in the country.

That was the first time I had ever seen him laugh aloud and was surprised to see he had two denture plates, one for his four top front teeth and one for his bottom front two, both held in place with metal that hooked to his side teeth. The moment he saw I'd noticed, he flushed and stopped laughing.

"Wait," I said, but he just shook his head and disappeared into the bedroom to get ready for work. I felt bad then because I knew I'd embarrassed him but didn't know how to make it right because other than his name and the fact that he was Dutch, I didn't know anything at all about him.

I know that sounds ridiculous now, in an age when nothing is sacred or private, when people go on talk shows and spill the ugliest parts of themselves, the darkest tragedies and the most degrading behavior, but it wasn't like that back then. There was a process, and yes, Peter and I jumped the gun by marrying, but then we backed up straight to the beginning and began the slow, steady dance of getting to know and trust each other, and falling in love.

Because we did fall in love.

After all I'd seen of love dying, it was a miracle to feel the joy of its birth.

ᥱᎻᢀ   ᥱᎻᢀ   ᥱᎻᢀ

Peter loved to fish and on Sundays I would pack a picnic lunch and we would drive out to a lonely stretch of the river and I would read (and sneak peeks at him) while he cast from shore. Sometimes I would open the bags with our lunch and find a little surprise from the five-and-dime—a bangle bracelet, a pretty little hand mirror, or a bottle of lily of the valley cologne—and he would smile at my delight, and yes, it did take me far too long to realize that he was wooing me.

The idea electrified me like nothing else ever had, pushing all the darkness and sadness aside and making me look at him, our apartment, my ring, the small amount of time we were able to spend together . . . I looked at it *all* differently.

Now the idea that, when I rose from the bed, he would tumble into it, into the warm hollow I'd created with my body became a thing of blushing intimacy, and I began wearing just a dab of lily of the valley cologne to bed so my scent would be there when he slipped under the covers after I left in the morning.

I noticed how the sun glinted off his thick, black hair, smooth and shiny as a crow's wing, and how he would sing when he was in a good mood or wanted to make me laugh, Sam Cooke's "Chain Gang" before he left for work at night, and in the morning, a little more tiredly but twice as loud and silly, as I left for work, he would stand at the front door and belt out Maurice Williams's "Stay," making me laugh and blush and half run down the street, always turning back to wave, always seeing him waiting there, watching me with a smile. People looked at me with kind amusement, men saying, "He's got it bad, sister," and women asking if he had a single brother. It made me dance all the way to work and smile at everyone, even the crabbiest customers who sent their food back or made a mess of their table and left me a nickel tip, but I didn't care.

He was singing to *me*.

I started setting aside tips each day because I wanted to buy him a surprise in return and decided on a transistor radio I saw in Woolworth's. That way our apartment would have music, and maybe he would sing to me even more, maybe love songs like "Put Your Head on My Shoulder" or "I Only Have Eyes for You." And maybe he would ask me to dance, only I didn't know how and the thought panicked me so much that I asked one of the other waitresses, Coral, how to dance, and she grabbed the cook out of the kitchen, a short, round little man with a five o'clock shadow and a cigar stub stuck between his lips, and fed the jukebox two whole dollars, playing slow songs just to teach me.

I bought the transistor radio, then went to the library and found a Dutch cookbook, got a library card, and brought the book home, poring over it in secret and trying to find something not too hard and not too expensive that I could make for him as a surprise. I decided on a rice pie, a wonderful-sounding yeast-crust pie with a vanilla-and-milk rice-pudding-type filling, and made it on Saturday so we could take it to the river with us on Sunday.

It was a beautiful Sunday and I took care with my outfit, wanting to look beautiful and desirable and feeling frustrated at my scant wardrobe. Still, my hair was curled and my lipstick perfect and I smelled of lily of the valley, and the pie and the radio had been secretly and carefully tucked into the picnic basket.

The riverbank was deserted as usual with only the occasional car of churchgoers passing by, and as we spread the blanket beneath the tree, he said he'd been thinking of taking on some extra work, not double shifts at the railroad but at a nearby construction site where they were looking for good, strong temporary laborers.

"We could bank that extra money, Louise, and when we have enough, maybe we could buy a little house somewhere," he said almost shyly. "I know you want a home of your own, and things would be pretty tight, we'd have to sacrifice, but I think we could do it." He shrugged. "I don't know, just an idea."

"It's a great idea," I said, overcome. "Oh, Peter, it's a wonderful idea!" And without even thinking I threw my arms around him, and the moment my body touched his, a bolt of electricity shocked us into stillness, but only for a heartbeat, because his arms came around me in a way that promised never to let me go, never to let me down, never to hurt me or betray me or live without me, and he breathed my name on an exhale as sweet as the sunny day, and I lifted my face and he lowered his and kissed me.

And kissed me.

And kissed me.

And probably would have kept on kissing me had a car not slowed on the road and a woman said, "Right out in broad daylight! Shameless! You young people have no morals at all anymore!"

And Peter, eyes bright, mouth curved in a wide smile, pulled back slightly and, winking at me, called, "I hate to break it to you, lady, but this young person is my wife."

"Baloney," an old man next to the woman snapped. "Nobody kisses his wife like that, especially out in public!" Scowling, he stepped on the gas, and the enormous old Plymouth chugged off in a cloud of dust.

We looked at each other and laughed and he kept his arm around me, and oh, the glory of nestling my head into the curve of his neck and shoulder, the absolute rightness of knowing all I had to do was lift my face and he would kiss it, of discovering that if I reached out, he would reach back, clasp my hand, hold tight, lift it to his lips, and kiss it, watching me, dark eyes glowing.

I gave him the radio and he got so quiet that I thought he didn't like it, but that wasn't it at all. He said that no one had bought him anything since his parents had been killed in the war and he was so touched that I started to cry because I hadn't known that, hadn't known that he was an orphan, too, and because of how miraculous it was that we'd ended up together.

Then, because our stomachs were rumbling, he switched on the radio while I laid out the food, and of course, the first song they played wasn't a beautiful, romantic love song but Brenda Lee's sassy "Sweet Nothin's," which of course he had to sing along to me, grabbing my hand and pulling me up to twist with him on the grass, and I was laughing and twisting and singing right back as if I'd lived my whole life for this one joyous moment and, oh, the freedom of being silly, of teasing and flirting and seeing the gleam of appreciation in his eyes.

Out of everything that has ever happened to us our whole lives, that one magnificent day with the sun and birds and the river and the discovery of the homemade Dutch rice pie, which almost made him cry, and the transistor playing in the background of so many kisses was, without a doubt, the most beautiful.

∽ ∽ ∽

We didn't talk of darker things that day, and we didn't run straight home and fall into bed, either.

No, we ran straight home and spent a hot, sweaty, panting hour kissing on the couch, an hour that left me dazzled and topless, left him frustrated at having to stop and get ready to go to work.

"You can't lay there like that," he said hoarsely, looking at me. "I'll never leave, Louise. I swear you have to put your shirt on or I'll stay and then I'll get fired and we'll lose our apartment and end up out in the street and—"

"Oh, all right," I said, giggling and pulling my crumpled shirt over me. "There, is that better?"

"No," he said with a weak grin. "I don't want to leave you."

"Ever?" I said, suddenly solemn.

"Ever," he said and gave me a tender kiss. "I knew that the minute I saw you."

"Really?" I said, gazing into his eyes and running a fingertip down his cheek.

"Would I lie to you?" he said.

"No," I said, and a smile that held all the happiness in the world blossomed.

∽ ∽ ∽

We made love for the first time that next Sunday on my sixteenth birthday, not out in the open at the river between eating, reading, and fishing, but there together in our bed with the rich, buttery summer sun melting in through the blinds, the transistor playing "Forever" by the Little Dippers, with his mouth sweet, hungry, soft, and everywhere, with his work-roughened hands slowly lifting my slip up over my head, unsnapping each garter and peeling down my stockings, easing off my bra and panties, cupping my face, and stilling my trembling, laying me down, hands sliding up beneath me, lifting me to meet him and whispering, *It's all right, I won't hurt you,* and then he did but only a little, and I understood the pain and knew it wouldn't last and it didn't, and we went on, and I discovered there is nothing in the world like being taken by a good man who loves you.

"Oh my God, the nice parts are almost worse than the horrible parts," I blubbered, laughing and grabbing two tissues, one for me and one for Gran because she was crying, too.

Seth had to work late again, so me, Sammi, and her boyfriend decided to go over to the bowling alley and surprise him, first time ever.

Too bad he wasn't there.

The girl at the shoe rental counter gave me a funny look when I said, *Hi, I'm Seth's girlfriend, is he working tonight?* And she said, *No, not till Monday, I think,* and this *bad* feeling washed through me, and I said, "Oh, okay, you don't by any chance know where he is, do you?" And you could see she knew something but she wasn't going to tell, so I pulled out my phone to call him, and then Sammi said, "Wait, isn't there a party at Connor's tonight?"

So we drove over there, and yeah, there was definitely something going on, and Seth's car—his new old MG—was there. We stopped and they waited in the car while I went to the door, and it was unlocked, so I just walked right in and it was a party all right. I saw Seth hanging out talking to Connor and Phil and this weird undercurrent ran through the room and Seth looked up and saw me, blanched, and then looked to the other side of the room to the keg where a whole mess of people were, including Lacey McMullen, the blue-eye-shadowed sophomore.

He got up fast, came right over, said, "Hey, what're you doing here?" and put his arms around me. I wished I'd asked Sammi to come in with me because I would have given a thousand dollars to see who he was looking at over the top of my head, but I didn't, so I never knew if it was Lacey.

"C'mon, let's go out to the car," he said, so we did.

I told Sammi it was okay, she could leave now, and I did it on purpose because that MG is a two seater and that shotgun seat is *mine*, and yeah, he might have come alone but how weird was it that Lacey was here, too, and I wasn't?

Sammi and her boyfriend left, and me and Seth got in his car. Thank God the top was up because I was so upset I was shaking, and said, *We went to the bowling alley to surprise you, only guess what?* And he said he was sorry, but yeah, he lied because he just wanted a night out on his own with the guys because he didn't have a lot of time to himself anymore, and he knew that if he'd just come out and said that, he would have hurt my feelings, so he thought it would be better to make up an excuse.

He held me and apologized and said he was glad I'd shown up because it wasn't that much fun without me. I didn't bring up Lacey and he didn't bring up Lacey, and when he kissed me, it started out so sweet and tender, then got so raw we were clinging to each other, bridging back to each other, and it ended the questions. Being there with him, in his arms, quieted my crying and dulled the hurt that he'd lied. We talked for a little, and he promised he wouldn't lie again and

I shouldn't, either—although when exactly have I lied?—and then he said, *Ready to go back to the party?* And he waited patiently while I put on my makeup, nodding at people going by, and in a beautiful gesture, got out to go around and open my door.

Right as he got out, I dropped my lip gloss and it fell down alongside the seat into the back. He'd stopped to talk to somebody—I don't know who, I could only see his bottom half—so I wedged my hand down to get it, but the gap was too tight, and there was a spiral notebook shoved back there, down in the gap, so I pulled it out thinking it was Seth's, only it wasn't.

It was someone else's.

And in that second I had a choice: Do not open it, do not look. Put it back and go on believing everything is fine. Or open it, see Lacey's name written in her stupid curlicue writing in the front cover, close the notebook, and get out of the car. Interrupt Seth talking to Connor and Teresa, hand him the notebook, watch as realization dawns in his eyes and then turn, rigid with sick, scalding fury, and walk away.

"Hanna," he said in a tone that wasn't pleading because there were too many people around and had a tinge of *Oh, shit, I'm in trouble* laughter in it. "Come on."

"You should go after her," I heard Teresa say worriedly.

"Hanna," Seth called again. "What're you gonna do, walk all the way home? Come on. Don't be stupid."

I almost stopped then, I did. I almost stopped and turned and let him coax me back, almost chose once again to believe him, but something wouldn't let me, not this time. I just kept walking and waiting for *him* to chase *me* for a change, listening for the sound of that little MG's engine to rev, for him to pull up at the curb and stop me from walking away, and the farther I got, the harder it was to call Sammi, to ask her to come back and pick me up, but I did it.

I did it.

Chapter 30

Hanna

Everyone at school knew we were in a fight but I don't know if anyone knew the real reason why. Lacey could have told them, Seth could have told them, I could have but I didn't. I was too miserable and the whispers were too intense and plentiful.

Seth must have gotten to school early that first morning because when I went to my locker, all the stuff I'd had in his locker was back in mine and all his stuff was gone.

I stood there numb, gray with shock, then tugged my first-period books free and turned to Sammi, who was sort of shielding me with her body and giving the rubberneckers her evilest *WTF are you looking at?* face. "Don't let him see me, okay?"

"Okay," she said without hesitation and steered me off on a brand-new hall route.

I don't remember much about that day or even that week, only the times I caught sight of Seth in the distance, and then the clawed fist gripping my heart would tighten and shoot red streaks of pain through the numbing fog, and I would have to go into the girls' room and, if it was crowded, shut myself in a stall and just sit there and breathe.

I didn't even know if we were broken up or if he was just waiting like I was waiting.

I wanted to blame Lacey—it would have been *so easy* to blame Lacey, to tell myself that she had offered, so *of course* he accepted, to make an excuse for Seth just so I could stay blind and tell myself it wasn't *him* who had done me wrong—but Lacey didn't owe me anything. *Seth* owed me his loyalty and betrayed me, and it was as simple and as complicated as that.

School. I hate it. I am gray all day.

Sammi said she saw Seth in the hall and he looked stoned but not happy.

He didn't look at her as they passed.

I went into the girls' room and came face-to-face with Lacey.

I stopped dead, blocking the doorway. She went totally white and sucked in her breath and her eyes got huge and terrified and the weirdest thing was that in that moment I could have been a hunter and she a yearling, or a robber and she a counter girl trapped and frozen and helpless, because even though my heart was pounding and my adrenaline racing, I had all the power and I knew it. I could hit her, kick her, shred her with words, hold her there, rip out her hair, and throw her purse in the toilet and she couldn't do anything back but cringe, crouch, cry, and in the end, hope I showed mercy and pray for it to be over.

I looked at her for so long that tears welled in and spilled out of her eyes. The sight of them cracked my bemusement and I stepped aside, out of the doorway, stepped far enough away and watched as she sidled by and slipped out.

And then I got a bad case of the cold sweats and had to wobble in and sit down on a toilet and put my head on my knees, thinking of how close I'd come to being something I would have hated.

"Seth cheated on me," I said to Gran. "I think we're broken up."

She trembled.

I hit play and cried silently, huddled in my chair with Serepta on my lap.

How It Ends

That Sunday night, after Peter gave me my birthday gifts—a single pearl suspended on a gold chain and a tiny little tin of Evening in Paris talcum powder—and I blew out the candles on my cake, we took the slices to bed with us, and while we were eating them, as if we had discussed it beforehand and decided it was time, we started to talk about our pasts.

Peter told me he had left Holland and come over to America alone at fifteen, two years after surviving the Hunger Winter of 1945, and that he hoped he never saw a sugar beet again for as long as he lived. He smiled when he said it but his eyes were bleak, and I was going to try and change the subject, but he shook his head and said, "You're my wife, you're entitled to know," and told me a brief story no one else knew.

Until you, now.

⌒ ⌒ ⌒

Peter told me that between the time he landed in America at fifteen and the moment he met me, he had feared nothing in this world, for the worst had already happened before he left Nazi-occupied Holland.

He was the son of a music teacher and a gunsmith, the youngest of three, with two older sisters. He was thirteen when the Hunger Winter claimed his sisters, thirteen and a half when the soldiers dragged the remaining villagers from their homes and made them stand at gunpoint and watch as they degraded the women, as his father lunged forward in animal rage and would have made it to his wife, half-naked and bleeding in the dirt, if he hadn't been shot in the back, as his mother mewled and sobbed, trying to cover herself, to reach his body, as a soldier, smirking with cold disgust, hit her with his rifle butt, opened his pants, pissed on her, and then fired one last round.

The worst had happened as Peter, big for his age even then, started for the soldier and was knocked down, made to crawl past his father's body—*don't look don't look don't look*—to his mother's, and when he closed his eyes, ashamed to gaze upon her nudity and defilement, his shame earned him a boot to the ribs, flipping him over and coming down hard on his throat, a boot caked with bloody mud . . .

And then a gob of spit and the rifle butt slamming down into his face, his mouth, shattering his teeth with an agony unlike any other, and in that instant his fear died. Later, when the soldiers had beaten others, killed two of his schoolmates, stolen their meager food supplies, ransacked their homes, and left, he rose, shaking, blood in his mouth, blood in his eyes and ears, and limped to his mother, covering her nakedness with his own shirt, lifted her, and carried her home. He set her gently in her bed and went back for his father.

No one helped him, as they had their own dead to care for, their own naked shame to cover. He laid his father next to his mother, drew the quilt over them, and closed the door.

He stayed in the house, lost, dazed, until the smell from the room with the closed door became too much, and then he dug up the few valuables the family had left—kept only because there had been no food to barter them for—and left the village to make his way out of Holland.

Two years later at fifteen and armed with a false set of documents, a new name, and little else, he stepped off the boat alone at Ellis Island.

He was silent and solemn, a young man of medium height who looked older than he was, with thick, black hair, a broad back, and corded forearms, with a quick gaze that saw and weighed everything. He never smiled, ashamed of the few shattered stubs of teeth left in the front of his mouth, and bore their frequent ache with stoic acceptance.

He kept to himself, worked in back rooms and docks, hauling freight, carrying boxes, doing heavy lifting, grunt work, hard, muscle-building work where the boss never spoke to you, never asked your name, and you never offered it because you were one of a sea of tired faces, hungry faces, desperate, dirty, drawn faces, those of immigrants who hid limps and old aches from badly set broken bones, men with withered arms, missing arms, with hungry children and crying wives, men who took the day labor and were grateful for the dollar, two dollars, five dollars handed to them at the end of the twelve hours.

"First thing I bought were these, and I had to put them on time payments," Peter said quietly, pressing a thumb to his front teeth and avoiding my gaze. "It took me three years to pay them off. I hope you don't mind I didn't tell you before."

"No, not at all," I said, humbled by what he'd gone through. "I just can't imagine how terrifying it must have been to leave your home and come to a whole new country—"

"It wasn't," he said, sighing and rubbing a hand over his knuckles. "Nothing was." He glanced at me, gaze solemn. "There's only one thing that can scare me now and that's the thought of losing you. That's the only thing in the world that would kill me."

"Well, then, you ought to live forever because you're never going to lose me and I'm never going to lose you," I said and quickly fed him a piece of my cake and kissed him, and little by little the terrible bleakness faded. He said it was my turn, so I summoned my nerve and told him my parents' love story, all of it, including the shock of discovering they might not have been married and how I hated the word *bastard* now, and he said, "So why ever tell anyone again, Louise? They're gone and you're a married woman in a place where no one knows you. Why not just say they were married? Who can prove otherwise?"

And that, in a nutshell, is how the reinvention began.

We worked hard the next few years, scrimping and putting almost all of our money into a savings account for our first home. We were very careful making love, as we both wanted children but not until we had a settled place for them.

Peter took extra work whenever or wherever he could find it and that became our living money while most of the rest was banked.

The worst fight we had was after Peter stopped in at the diner one day for supper and saw one of the regular patrons, a burly guy with a roving eye and a belief that waitresses expected to be mauled for their tips, reach out and slap my behind as I whisked by with a tray full of hot food.

I missed the initial contact but, when I heard the commotion, set the tray on the table, and turned, Peter had the guy up against the wall by the throat and with dead, cold fury said, "Don't ever do that again." He held the guy's bulging gaze, riveted with dead-on calm for a second longer, and then released him, tensed as the guy stared back, as the cook shouted, "Hey!" and came out of the kitchen with a cleaver, as I said, "Peter!" and the guy sneered and Peter waited, ready, and then the guy threw a couple of dollars on the floor, said, "Fucking immigrants can't even speak English," and sauntered out, and only my fierce grip on Peter's arm, I think, kept him from going after him.

He was angry at me that night, both for not telling him about the guy in the first place and then for holding him back. We had a terrible fight with me saying I could have handled it myself and him saying, *How, by smiling and ignoring it? By saying nicely, Don't do that, please, okay? You think that's going to stop a guy like that?* and me getting furious because he was right, I *had* already done both of those things and it hadn't worked, but I still didn't want him in there creating a scene, getting me in trouble and maybe even fired, and besides, the guy was way bigger than Peter. I made the mistake of saying that, and Peter lifted his head and narrowed his eyes and in a flat voice said, *I've handled worse,* and turned and walked out.

Ь Ь Ь

We didn't go out much, maybe for a burger once a week or to the movies once every couple of months, and we didn't do a lot of socializing because . . . well, because we were happy in each other's company. We *liked* each other, liked walking in the door and seeing the other's smiling face, telling stories or debating the stuff on the news or curling up reading or having tickling matches or French fries for supper.

We went on dates to the river (where we actually made love once in the water, out of sight of the road) and on Sunday drives, to fairs and carnivals and out for coffee. It didn't matter *where* we were so much that we were together.

And within five years, we bought our first cozy little starter house in a neighborhood of starter houses. We dug a big garden in the back and planted vegetables. Scoured the newspaper for garage sales and slowly but surely furnished the rooms. We got two free puppies, a boy who was part beagle, part schnauzer and a girl who was part German shepherd and part Afghan hound, named them Sonny and Cher and watched them grow into a pair of devoted, smart, and mischievous beauties. I took as many hours as the diner would give me and Peter worked at least one railroad double shift a week. He'd moved up to conductor now and was always bringing home anything left longer than ninety days in the lost and found.

We had more lost hats, gloves, and umbrellas than everyone else on the block, combined.

And finally, after two more years and a comforting sum in the savings account, we decided to stop being careful about making love and start a family.

ఆ&ఆ   ఆ&ఆ   ఆ&ఆ

Thirty-four periods and much heartache later, I finally scheduled my first and much-dreaded visit to the gynecologist, a gruff, elderly man I'd chosen because Coral the waitress used him and I knew of no one else.

He noticed one of my old abdominal scars while examining me—I remember distinctly the way his face changed when he saw it—then lifted the embarrassing paper gown and located the other one. Pulled down the gown, pulled off his rubber gloves (just seeing them made me want to run screaming right out of the office), pushed back the stool, and told me to sit up.

He asked me if I'd had any abortions or any children while very young, children of unfortunate circumstance that I might have delivered and given up for adoption.

The nurse's expression remained carefully blank, but mortified I said, "No, of course not!"

He asked me my IQ and when I looked at him, puzzled, and said I didn't know, he asked if I'd been put in special remedial classes or had attended a normal high school.

"A regular high school!" I said.

And then, eyeing me as though every single answer I'd given was a lie, he said, "Was your mother an unmarried woman? Were either of your parents criminals, declared mentally incompetent, or—"

"I don't understand why you're asking me this," I asked, voice shaking. "I came here to find out why I haven't conceived and you're—"

"Calm down, Louise." He exchanged glances with the nurse, patted my knee, and rose. "I see women all the time who were just not meant to have children, and I'm sorry to say that seems true in your case as well." He met my stricken gaze. "It isn't the end of the world. You and your husband can still have a somewhat satisfying life. Just think of all the shopping and traveling you can do without . . . "

Shopping? Traveling? What the hell was he saying?

"But . . . we want a baby," I said, hands twisting in my lap. "It's all we want, Doctor, a family of our own, wait, you don't understand . . ."

"Take all the time you need to compose yourself," he said over his shoulder as he headed for the door. "Nurse?"

"Coming," she said and, casting me a brief, sympathetic look, followed him out.

∽ ∽ ∽

Looking back, it's odd that I never equated those two small scars on my abdomen with my inability to get pregnant.

That terrifying, confusing time in the state hospital after my mother died was so hazy now that it seemed like it had happened to someone else, and although Peter had undoubtedly registered the existence of my scars, he never put two and two together, either.

Why should we have?

We'd never even heard of mandatory sterilization for the unfit and wouldn't for years, until investigative journalists exposed the practice, and by then I had sworn off doctors so completely that not even the idea of a baby could induce me to see one.

"Wow," I breathed, falling back against the chair and shaking my head. "They sterilized her when she was how old? Thirteen?" I sat there, foot tapping, scowling, scratching my eyebrow, and then drumming my fingers on the arm of the chair until I couldn't take it anymore. "What is it, exactly, about female reproductive organs that makes guys think they have a right to mess with them?"

Gran swallowed.

"I mean, where do they get off doing sh . . . er, stuff like that, anyway?" I jumped up and started pacing because first it had been Mrs. Boehm and now it was Louise. "Seriously, Gran, what the hell? I mean, I don't go around trying to regulate the contents of *their* testicles—"

Grandpa, who had just opened the door to walk in, winced, turned, and walked right back out again.

"Or decide who should be castrated because they're not worth *breeding,* so where do they get off being so obsessed with the contents of my uterus? I mean, just mind your own business already, and worry about your own organs instead of mine. I swear."

I railed at home, too, driving my father from the room and trying not to tell too much of the book so my mother would still want to hear it, only it really aggravated me, so I called Crystal and told her, and then Sammi, too, who said her boyfriend had been sitting next to her but I'd yelled *uterus* so loud that he'd quickly gotten up and left the room.

Good.

They should *all* leave the room and leave the fates of uteruses (uteri?) up to their owners.

ෆ ෆ ෆ

Sammi called and told me Teresa had gone to a party at Phil's and Seth had been there.

"With anyone?" I said, sinking onto the edge of my bed because if he had brought someone, if he had, then we were officially over.

"No, but she said he got so messed up that he had to stay at Phil's because there was no way he could drive," Sammi said.

"I don't suppose she asked him about me," I said.

"Well, yeah, she said she went outside to get high with him and while they were smoking she asked if you guys were still together, and he just looked at her real cold and said, *Tell Hanna if she wants to know that she'll have to ask me herself,*" Sammi said.

I sat silently for a minute, feeling the hot pain spark something less than anger but more than irritation and a weird stirring of excitement because he hadn't said *No, we've broken up.* Instead he had sent me a message, and okay, it wasn't exactly an apology on bended knee but he *had* broken the stalemate and that meant—

"Hanna?" Sammi said tentatively. "What're you thinking?"

I told her and she sighed.

"What?" I said a little defensively.

"I wasn't going to tell you this part but now I have to," she said, sounding upset. "She said he also tried to come on to her."

"What?" I said.

"She said—and don't tell her I told you because she didn't want to hurt you—when they were done getting high, he kind of backed her against the wall, and at first she thought he was kidding or she was imagining it, but then he put a hand up on each side of her and she was like, *Whoa, not gonna happen,* and slipped away. He laughed, but not in a good way, and then she went inside and he just hung out with Phil most of the night." She fell silent. "Are you mad at me for telling you?"

"No," I said, turning away from my reflection in the mirror. "It's better that I know, although I bet I know why he did it."

"Why?" Sammi said warily.

"Because he knew it would get back to me," I said and was completely unprepared for her response.

"How about just because he's an asshole and he doesn't care how much he hurts you?" she snapped.

Yeah, that could be it, too.

෨ ෨ ෨

I saw Seth today, not right up close but passing him in the hall. I don't know how that happened, because I've been so careful to avoid all his routes, but I was walking and trying to find something in my notebook, and I just got this feeling and glanced up. He was coming toward me in the flow of traffic, and he quickly averted his gaze before our eyes met. I knew people were watching so I just looked back into my notebook, and we passed and I smelled his beautiful scent and my knees actually got weak.

How long is this stalemate going to last?

෨ ෨ ෨

I haven't worn my ankle bracelet since the night I walked away and he didn't come after me. I wonder if he's mad about that.

I laid on my bed, stared at the ceiling and listened to "Sweet Jane" over and over, trying to figure out whether or not I should make the first move toward getting back with him.

All it would take was wearing that bracelet.

෨ ෨ ෨

Gran doesn't look good at all today. She's flailing all over the place and I'm afraid she's going to fall right out of her wheelchair, even though she's belted in.

Even worse, I think she might have peed herself, because I can smell it, but there is no way I can change her.

I just can't.

It would be a major violation and I wouldn't even know how to begin.

How It Ends

Peter, heartbroken that there would be no natural child, retreated into himself, and when I told him I was hurting, too, he held me briefly and said, "I know, Louise. Just . . . give me some time." It was his way, to retreat into a place I couldn't go, and, although it frustrated me sometimes because I never really knew what he was thinking or processing or had decided, trying to make him talk about it was like banging my head against a brick wall and only made things worse.

So we put our all into working and saving, but the times they were a-changing and our neighborhood fell to a never-ending wave of broke, stoned, braless, sometimes dirty and desperate, sometimes charming and cheerful, often earnest and always hungry, *free love, let it all hang out, don't trust anyone over thirty, do your own thing* hippies.

The kids weren't bad except for the occasional vomit on the lawn or porch, the casual appropriation of anything left outside that could be sold or bartered for pot, acid, or food and the nerve-wracking habit they had of just opening the door, flashing a peace sign, and wandering in whenever they felt like it.

Some of them were my age and a lot of the guys thought I should *quit being a tool of the man, fuck the establishment, and tune in, turn on, and drop out* with them, but I always told them that if I did that, then there wouldn't be any food *here*, either, and then where would they eat for free?

"Bummer," they'd mutter good-naturedly and, swiping a slice of cheese or an orange, wander back out to find the guy with the psyche-delics.

Someone, I never found out who, decided the dogs, our beloved Sonny and Cher would be happier *free, man, not locked up in the backyard like prisoners,* so they opened the gate while Peter and I were at work, removed the dogs' collars, and let them go.

We ran looking for them for hours, handing out hastily scrawled fliers, and posting LOST DOGS signs on the phone poles, asking everyone hanging out on the block if they'd seen the dogs and getting only slow, wide-eyed shaking of heads or vague memories of thinking they might have gone that way.

Or that way.

Or the other way.

It was awful.

I couldn't sleep, couldn't stop crying thinking of them out there in traffic, hungry, stolen, lost, maybe hurt and unable to find their way home. And what if they'd gotten split up? They did everything together—eat, slept, played, peed, dug holes, stole snacks—so how could they survive without each other? Oh, *why* hadn't I locked them in the house instead of leaving them in the yard? *Why?*

Exhausted, Peter hit me with that same question, and it salted the wound so keenly that I raged back, saying that it was *him* who hadn't wanted the dogs sleeping on the couch while we were at work and it was *his* rule, not mine, and so if they were starving or dead out there somewhere, then he had no one to blame for it but himself . . .

"You know what?" he said. "You're right. It's my fault. Everything that goes wrong around here is my fault."

"I didn't say that," I said, already regretting lashing out at him. "I didn't mean it. I'm just . . . I can't stand the thought of them lost out there all alone. . . ." And I started crying all over again, and this time, instead of pushing him away, I leaned against him, and his arms came around me, not tightly this time but there all the same.

Sixteen days after replacing the LOST DOGS signs with REWARD signs, a pickup pulled up and a dark-haired, moon-faced girl in tie-dye got out and knocked at the door.

"Hey, man, I think I found your dogs," she said, scratching the inside of her arm and avoiding my gaze. "They're in the back of the truck, but—"

I pushed past her, running down the steps and to the back of the pickup. "Sonny? Cher? Son—" I went still, gazing at the dogs, *my* dogs, lying on their sides on the hot metal, fur stretched over bones, too weak even to lift their heads, filthy, sunken, and I gasped, "Oh, *no*," and Sonny managed to twitch the tip of his stubby tail in a feeble wag.

I shouted for Peter and scaled the truck's tailgate, crying, crouching in there with them, running my hands gently over their heads, babbling, "You're home, you're home, you're going to be fine," and gagging at their filthy, sun-baked smell.

Peter took one look at them and, swearing, jerked down the tailgate and lifted Cher in his arms. "Open the car," he said, and I scrambled past him, past the girl who said, "There's a reward, right?" and I flung open the back doors of our car, and while Peter was laying Cher across the seat, I ran for water and wet a paper towel and squeezed some into her mouth while the girl said, "You said there was a reward, right?" and Cher licked my hand once and exhaled and never inhaled again.

I stared at the dog in disbelief a moment and then backed out of the car. Turned on the girl and in cold rage said, "Where did you find these dogs?"

"There's a rew—"

"Where?" I shouted, making her cringe back against the car. "Did you steal them?"

"No, man, I swear, they were chained up behind a pad down on Saxson," she babbled, scratching and scratching her arm. "Some bony dude brought 'em down there a couple of weeks ago, and then just, like, never came back—"

"Whose house?" I said.

"I don't know," she said, trying to inch away. "A lot of people crash at that place—"

"But no one remembered to feed the dogs?" I said, breathing hard. "No one heard them barking or crying or begging for food and water, no one—"

"Hey, you know, you're flipping out and I didn't have to come here," she said, flinging back her frizzy hair. "I could've just left them there—"

"But there was a reward," I said as I caught sight of Peter, standing slumped and head bowed over a limp Sonny in his arms. "Can't collect the reward if the dogs are dead, right?"

"Well, yeah," she said, shrugging a shoulder and looking away. "I mean bread's bread, and there's never enough, you know? You gotta eat."

I stared at her, incredulous. "Get out of here. Go, or I swear to Christ I'll—"

"Peace," she said and, scuttling past me, scrambled into the truck. It pulled a screeching U-turn, and as it blasted past, she stuck her arm out the window and gave me the finger.

We buried the dogs together next to the garden and I didn't cry until I looked up and saw some of the kids on the block, girls mostly but a sprinkling of guys, too, standing there in line, each with a flower and waiting to pay their respects.

The neighborhood wasn't good for us anymore, so we put our house on the market and sold it to a man of about forty wearing a terrible toupé, striped bells, and a crushed-velvet Nehru jacket. He came arm in arm with a skinny, gray-toothed woman who giggled and said, "Far out," when she walked into each of my neat, freshly painted rooms.

I hated them both.

By the time the house changed hands, I was more than ready to go.

Instead of buying in a neighborhood where our future children would have plenty of playmates, we bought a wooded piece of land with a big old farmhouse and outbuildings, where we could shut out the world and live the way we wanted.

The new place—*our* new place—changed almost everything.

₧ ₧ ₧

The house and the land embraced us.

The first moment I saw it, something inside my heart opened and whispered, *Yes, oh yes,* and kept on delighting as we explored the rooms, admired the giant hearth in the kitchen and the fireplaces scattered throughout, as we smiled at her white plaster walls, deep windowsills, and Dutch doors, as we stood under the towering catalpa tree in the back and gazed out across the gently rolling green lawn, the wild woods, and the little pond down the hill.

"It'll be a bear to heat in the winter," Peter said, eyeing the size of the place. "There's a woodstove and fireplaces, but the rest is electric baseboard. We might have to close off the rooms we're not using so we don't go straight to the poorhouse."

"Okay," I said, dazzled by the sight of a towering sugar maple beginning to turn red and a giant tangled knot of wild roses and blackberry bushes spreading alongside it.

He shot me an amused look. "I'm going to need to get a snowplow for the pickup, too. There's no way I'm going to shovel this driveway. I'll have a heart attack before I even get past the pines."

"Okay," I said, spellbound at the sight of a doe poised at the tree line down near the pond. She lifted her head and sniffed the air, then sauntered across the grass and started grazing. Another joined it, and a moment later, two more. *Oh yes, oh yes.* "Okay to all of it. To anything."

"Including the French maid?" he said, laughing when I smacked him in the arm.

"Do you see that?" I said, nodding in the does' direction. "It's an omen. It is. This is our home. It's true. I can *feel* it."

He watched the deer for a moment, tawny and graceful in the late afternoon sunlight and said quietly, "Me, too." His hand closed around mine. "I think we could be really happy here."

"Oh, yes," I whispered.

�%   �%   �%

Peter started singing again, not only when he left for work now, day shifts because he had some seniority under his belt, but when he came home. The door would open and he would great me with "Lovely Rita" and lift me in a hug and kiss me while I laughed and dangled and hugged him back, near tears because it felt so *good* to be happy again.

He tilled me two gardens, one for flowers and one for vegetables, as I'd learned something listening to the hippie chicks and that was about eating organic, and I wanted to try it. Peter didn't—he said he wasn't giving up chili dogs for anybody—and that was fine because it meant I could plant what I wanted and reap whatever I sowed.

Peter wanted to live off the land, too, but thankfully, while he did buy a shotgun and ammunition, that vision shifted to a less lethal one the first time a young buck at the salt lick, antlers fuzzy with velvet, lifted his head and stared back as we watched from the porch, breathless with admiration.

"Dr. Boehm thought killing and gutting them, then stuffing and posing them was bringing the natural world to life," I murmured, not wanting to frighten the buck away.

"Boehm was an asshole," Peter said, and went and bought a roll of PRIVATE PROPERTY NO HUNTING ALLOWED signs, which he stapled to trees throughout the woods, just in case the ones at the property line were disregarded.

From then on, although it was never defined to outsiders as such, our home became a sanctuary to any and all wildlife that chose to live there, and the shotgun, stored in its case in the closet, has yet to be used to kill anything.

❧   ❧   ❧

The place came with barn cats, three wily young males who took months to get close, and only then because I'd been feeding them through that first hard winter. I convinced Peter to take them in to be neutered, having read that fixed cats live longer, happier lives and were less likely to roam or get into fights.

And besides, by the time he did, we had two *more* cats, pregnant females who delivered a total of five sweet little kittens, and who also had to be caught and spayed once the kittens were weaned.

I'd never had a cat before, but we brought the females and their brood into the house to stay, as I couldn't bear the thought of those playful little fluff balls falling prey to the owls or hawks or even the occasional car speeding along the winding country road.

One kitten, a cranky-looking little tiger named Wren, with a tail that stuck straight up in the air and a perpetual scowl as if we existed only to thwart him, climbed up the couch and wobbled onto my lap one afternoon. He looked in my face and began kneading my leg, tiny needle claws making a pincushion out of my thigh, but the expression on his unhappy little face grew so sloe-eyed and dreamy that I sat, enchanted, as his kitten purr rumbled out and his kneading intensified until, finally, overcome by his own contentment, he collapsed, asleep.

Thanks to Wren, I fell head over heels in love with cats.

Money was tight that winter, and after being late twice on the electric bill, I decided to stop waitressing and apply for an office job instead. The benefits and pay were better, and it would be a relief to sit all day, so I went to a mortgage company in town and for the first time ever was asked to fill out an application. I read through the questions, heart pounding, and with a casual confidence I didn't feel, checked *Yes* next to *Did you graduate high school?* and when asked where and what year, wrote in the name of the high school back in the town I'd lived in before my mother had died, and the year I would have graduated had I been allowed to keep going.

I hoped, because it was out of state and so far away, no one would bother to check.

That night, when telling Peter about it, I discovered he'd *always* said *Yes* to that question, too, adjusting the date he'd arrived here to accommodate a high school graduation in Holland so as not to automatically be disqualified from his career.

"But we're lying," I said.

"Louise, do you think you're a stupid woman?" he countered, leaning back in his chair and running a hand over his hair.

"What?" I said.

"Do you think you're stupid?" he said.

"No," I said, frowning.

"No," he said as if in agreement. "You read everything you can get your hands on. You have an extensive history in customer service. You're used to making decisions on your own. You're a whiz at managing our finances, what little there is of them." He grinned at my look. "You're an independent worker who doesn't need a supervisor hanging over her shoulder all day just to make you perform. You speak well, you reason even better, and you'd be an asset to any company smart enough to hire you." His smile faded. "Now, you can go in there, offer them all of that and make them gladder than hell that they hired you, *or* you can check *No* and tell them you didn't graduate high school and watch how fast the door closes and you're out of there."

"Do you really think that's what would happen?" I said.

"You have an interview tomorrow, right? Well, if you want to test the theory, go in and change your *Yes* to a *No* and see what happens." He snorted. "Standards are set by people who have decided that you can't possibly be considered smart unless some fat cat sitting behind a desk at some institution somewhere decides you are, and rubber-stamps you to make it official." His voice grew bitter. "You know, Hitler's Youth was considered the best and the brightest once, too, and look at where all that lockstep conformity got them."

"All right," I said with a sigh. "I get the point."

So I left it as a *Yes* and got the position. The money was good but *I* was better, as I was determined never to make them sorry they'd hired me. I did so well processing mortgage applications that I was promoted to assistant supervisor of the department, and then supervisor. I attended training sessions and seminars and soon had framed certificates marching in rows across my walls.

I was proud of them but in a distant, impersonal way. They meant a lot to the fictional Louise who had *chosen* not to have children, whose parents had absolutely been married, and who had definitely graduated high school, not to the real me whose journey had started the morning she found her mother dead.

૭ઝ   ૭ઝ   ૭ઝ

With no children growing up and reminding us that we were getting older, time seemed inexhaustible, gliding by in whole seasons rather than days or weeks.

Fall into winter was the hardest for me, as the brutal snow, ice, and wind scoured the acres, driving some animals into hibernation and others into a desperate, daily search for food. I did research at the library, made lists of the types of plants the land would support and what the animals on it needed to help them survive, and in spring planted white oak and crab apple trees, easter red cedars, dogwoods, sumacs, hemlocks, and honey locusts.

More cats came, sad, scrawny, cringing souls dumped by people who told themselves that cats could survive in the wild without a problem because *Look, they have claws!* or lied to their children with *They'll find a good home on the farm* when instead, lost and terrified, they were often hit by cars, attacked by animals, or died of starvation because they were *domesticated cats,* not cougars, and simply didn't know what to do.

Peter called me a bleeding heart for feeding them, but what was the alternative, turning my back on their hunger and desperation just because I didn't *want* to see it? Ignoring it because their life-or-death struggle inconvenienced me?

Impossible.

If I hadn't learned anything else from Margaret Boehm, I'd learned that.

So even though Peter sighed and muttered about going to the poorhouse, I noticed he always scraped his plate into the scrap bowl or stopped to pet whoever was brave enough to wind around his ankles on his way out to the barn.

I loved him even more for his good heart.

We got three chicks for an ongoing supply of fresh eggs, and they grew into two hens and a rooster, who became Cindy, Lucy, and the rooster Brunhilda.

Peter laughed when I named the rooster, and for a while, every time he would pass the proud, muscular Rhode Island Red scratching in the yard, he would sing in a warbling, Elmer Fuddian–type opera voice, "Oh, Bwunhiwda, you so wuvwy . . ."

The rooster would pause, giving him a beady look, and I would call, "You're asking for it," but he would just laugh and keep going.

All that ended one fall afternoon when Peter was kneeling at the edge of the garden, sitting back on his heels and hunched over, deeply involved in planting a second crop of lettuce seedlings. His jeans, always hanging low on his hips, hung even lower in the back. His T-shirt had ridden up, too, exposing—at least from *one* bird's-eye view—a dark, alluring crevice that might have contained any number of fat, tasty grubs or scurrying beetles and must have seemed maddeningly irresistible in the ongoing quest for dinner.

I was washing the dishes, thinking that Peter really *did* need a new belt for Christmas and absently watching Brunhilda stalking around behind him. When I finally realized what was happening, it was too late; the big bird zeroed in, cocked his head and, eyeballing that intriguing new crack in the landscape, rammed his beak into the promising darkness.

It was electrifying.

By the time I'd wiped the streaming tears from my eyes and staggered out onto the porch, Brunhilda had found safety behind his girlfriends and was muttering at being so cruelly misled, and Peter was muttering back, twisting around, groping himself, and trying to make out the damage.

"Did you see what that crazy bird did?" he said, looking both bewildered and outraged. "What the hell kind of rooster pecks a guy in the ass?"

"He was provoked," I said, and then buried my face in my hands and howled.

∂ ∂ ∂

One summer, the last truly pure and happy one, on Peter's birthday I was upstairs getting dressed to go to work, standing at the back window in my slip, wishing for a cool breeze and debating whether to put on the dreaded panty hose when I spotted Peter standing out at the edge of the lawn looking at the pond.

He wasn't doing anything in particular, just standing there gazing at the water, a man whose thick, black hair was now gray at the temples, whose beautiful, summer-tawny skin was looser, and whose muscular arms were growing slack, a man whose accent still stumped me at times and who still sang occasionally but no longer the newest songs, preferring to stick with old favorites like "Let It Be." A man who once said, *I've crossed the state line, Louise. I can either leave you somewhere or you can marry me. Whatever you choose,* and who had then gone on to make me happier than I ever thought possible.

I don't know where it came from, the rush of love that rose and enveloped me, the sudden desire to be that girl again and him that young man who had kissed and danced by the river, those two who had taken such pleasure in learning each other inch by inch. . . .

I looked at the clock, then at Peter, who had turned away from the water and was walking slowly back across the lawn toward the house. Dropped the panty hose, ran down the stairs and out onto the back porch, scattering stray cats and causing him to look up in alarm.

"What?" he called, walking faster.

"Nothing, stay there," I said, half laughing, near tears as I padded down the steps and ran across the grass to meet him. "I just love you, that's all, and I wanted to say thank you for loving me back."

He tilted his head and gazed at me, eyes twinkling and his mouth curving into a wonderful, bemused smile. "You know you're out here in your underwear."

"Am I?" I said, leaning forward and kissing the spot beneath his ear.

"People will talk," he said, shivering.

"If they can see us, they're trespassing," I murmured, kissing it again and sliding my arms around his waist. "Let them tell it to the judge."

"What're you doing?" he said huskily, as I backed him toward a particularly thick patch of clover and sank to my knees.

"Everything I can think of," I said, tugging him down beside me.

"Watch out for bees," he said, and then with a small, wicked smile, "Maybe you'd better not sit in the grass, Louise. Maybe . . ."

"Maybe I'd better stay right up here," I whispered, hiking up my slip, and then his eyes got smoky and his hands slid up beneath the lacy silk, and mine fumbled with his button and zipper, and I knelt over him, kissing and taking him, and the sun burned my back and the clover stained my knees and he did get stung once on the thigh, and several of the cats crept closer and watched worriedly from the underbrush, and I laughed and touched the gray at his temples and the lines of his dear, sweet face and whispered, *Oh, yes,* because what I'd hoped to discover was true:

In our hearts we were still who we'd started as.

"I can't take this story," I said, turning off the CD player. "First it's a tragedy, then a horror story, then a romance, and now it's what, a back-to-the-land thing? It's a roller coaster, Gran, and no matter where I think it's going, it never goes there." I rose and, shaking my head, walked into the kitchen singing, "Oh, Bwunhiwda, you so wuvwy. . . ."

I wish *I* had chickens.

ɛ⁄ɔ ɛ⁄ɔ ɛ⁄ɔ

It was cold walking home across the back, and at the gap in the little woods I stopped and opened my cell, not because anything had come in but because this was where I'd been when Seth had texted me about the New Year's Eve party.

We haven't talked in more than two weeks. If we don't hurry, there might be no going back.

ɛ⁄ɔ ɛ⁄ɔ ɛ⁄ɔ

Sammi told me she saw Lacey and Seth talking in the upstairs hall-way at his locker. She said she was too far away to hear anything and couldn't really see their expressions but that Lacey looked more intense than Seth did.

I said, *Of course she did, she's the one who* wants, *he's the one who* gets, and that sounded really mean but at that minute it was exactly how I felt and it didn't matter that Lacey was the one who'd gone up to *him* like I had so many times in the past, tracking him down and making it easy for him, making myself available so he wouldn't even have to reach too far and maybe strain himself while *I* got shin splints from racing around the school every day just to be in the right place at the right time.

The whole thing put me in a bad mood; the stalemate, the worsen-ing weather, knowing deer season was coming again and now having the whole Boehm taxidermy weirdness in my mind and not being able to talk with Gran about it because she couldn't answer back. I'd had no idea how much I'd counted on her opinions until every one of them was taken away from me, and it was like someone had said, *Too bad, Hanna, you lose and there's nothing you can do about it,* and that same rotten, miserable helplessness and frustration and, yeah, fear, came back into my mood, not big and obvious but gray and seeping. Not even Mr. Sung stopping me in the hall and congratulating me on bringing my grades up and tearing through those mandatory hours, warning me to be careful or I would become a model student and then he'd be left without a challenge could make me really laugh.

ᙍ   ᙍ   ᙍ

I ran into bow-hunter guy from the property next door on my way home from the bus stop. He didn't have his black knit face mask on but I still knew it was him from the camo wear and the way he walked, and it left me feeling even weirder because he had a nice face, a regular, open face just like anybody else, and he smiled and said hi when he walked by. I said hi and *so much* wanted to ask why he didn't care that he was stealing their *one chance* at life just like *I* had one chance and *he* did, too, but I didn't because I was afraid he would just call me a Bambi lover (like that was a bad thing), and then get mad and go kill something extra like a squirrel or some doves just to pay me back.

So I said nothing just to keep the peace, and I hated it.

           ❧   ❧   ❧

Gran is not well. Even for her, she's not well.

Grandpa doesn't look so hot, either.

And then some shithead went and hit one of the stray cats and just left the poor thing lying dead in the road in front of the house, and I had to go out there with a snow shovel and a box and push its poor mangled, floppy body inside, carry it into the back, say a prayer and bury it.

It was almost a relief to go in, sit down, and hit play.

How It Ends

At first we called it a run of bad luck, shrugged, and kept going.

Later, we just dug in and took the hits as they came.

The town reassessed our place and the taxes almost tripled. We appealed and were turned down. We paid them for a while, but they became too much on top of everything else, so we were forced to subdivide the land and sell off the acreage in the back to a nice, hardworking family with a child and later the side acreage as a recreation spot.

Money was still an issue. I was laid off, the roof needed replacing, the furnace went.

And then, out of the blue, Peter had his first heart attack.

෴ ෴ ෴

He was in the hospital for two weeks, and in those two weeks I paced holes in every carpet in the house. I hated thinking of him under the care of doctors and nurses, and I was terrified that they wouldn't be good enough to pull him through.

I forced myself into the place, throwing up in the bathroom as the sweet, rotten disinfectant scent of the Boehms' clogged my throat. I held his hand and hated how suddenly frail he looked, how his menu was a sick person's menu and his food delivered on a tray, and my God, there were moments when I wanted to grab him and scream, *Get up! Let's get out of here! You know what'll happen if we stay!* And I'm sure he knew it because he would murmur, *Don't, Louise. I'll be fine. I told you I'd never leave you, never want to live without you . . . I meant it . . . just give me a little more time and I'll be fine.*

I would have stayed all night if they'd let me, if he hadn't said, *Go, you've got animals to take care of,* and gently tugged loose of my grip.

So I would leave, jaw like iron, teeth clenched as I strode down the endless hallway to the door, and I would burst through, and then start running through the parking deck to my car and fumble with the keys, climb in, slam and lock the door, and then lose it.

Nobody ever stops and asks you if you're okay when you're crying in your car in a hospital parking deck. They already know you're not because they're there, too, and chances are they're not okay, either.

෴ ෴ ෴

I've written our lives as though we had no friends and that isn't true. We had good friends from work and neighbors who shared their families, joys, and woes with us, and we loved them but there was no denying that the lives of those with children was very different from that of those without. Not better, not worse, just different, with different priorities and schedules and time allowances.

So yes, we had friends and loved ones.

Never think otherwise.

જ જ જ

Peter came home a different person. A sad person, quieter than he'd been before, more tentative about how far out of sight of the house he would go or what kinds of things he'd find to do in his time off. He was anxious about going back to work and was considering putting in for early retirement until I convinced him to stay out on sick leave for now, as we needed the health insurance. He didn't eat as much, but the good part was that I had already laid down the law and told him his diet was changing and nothing he could say or do was ever going to alter that.

He just gave me a listless nod, leaned back in the chair, and closed his eyes.

"What're you doing?" I said nervously, after a moment.

"Resting," he said.

"Are you okay? Do you have pain?" I went right over and would have put my hand over his heart if he hadn't stopped me. "What?"

"I'm fine, Louise," he said. "Why don't you go find something to do?"

"All right," I said, hurt. "I'll bake some low-fat blueberry muffins. You're allowed to have those."

He sighed and swiping a hand across his watery eyes, got up, and walked slowly into the living room.

જ જ જ

Little by little I got him to talk and discovered he was terrified of becoming a burden I couldn't take care of, that he would rather die

than be taken away from me and our home and all he loved, that his
deepest fear was to be put in an institution somewhere out of sight of
the world, because out of sight is where atrocities occur and he didn't
want to be left to die in a long, slow, agonizing decline.

Hearing him say those things out loud was like reliving an old
nightmare that had been dormant for years but now rose again,
stretching and showing its teeth, and he began to cry and that scared
me even more because Peter had never been afraid of anything and
now he was, and that alone was reason to fear.

I promised him I would never put him in an institution and became frightened now, too, because although I knew we were older, I
had never wanted to think we were *old*, and yes, we moved slower and
drove slower and had to step out of the way when youth rushed past
as if they didn't even see us. Our clunky old computer was still almost
as foreign to me as the first day I'd bought it and there was more we
couldn't eat than we could. We had taken to listening to old music, *our*
music, and sitting out on the porch delighting in the rhythm of the
land, because its constant regeneration brought hope and sweet peace.

But now his trembling words sparked a dark terror in me, too, so
I made him promise me the same, no nursing homes, hospitals, or
institutions, because I had been held captive once and would never
go back, had seen those nursing home exposés on TV, seen the ruin
and the wreckage, the unwanted and forgotten sitting dull and lifeless
on the edges of their beds, food cold and uneaten, limbs mottled blue
or red and shiny with burgeoning sores, and the footage had brought
back the nauseating scent of decay beneath disinfectant, and I'd
turned it off, but the scent had lingered in my nostrils for days.

ℝℝ ℝℝ ℝℝ

I drove him to post-heart-attack counseling as often as the insurance
would allow, and when it was done, he was diagnosed with depression

and put on more medication. His medications were expensive and the insurance didn't cover it all, so I began taking things down to a consignment shop to sell.

I went back to the diner and started waitressing again. Coral was gone but the owner was still there and glad to take me back even if most of the other waitresses were a third my age and cuter than puppies. I felt old and slow and lumbering, with my creaky knees and the anxiety at being away from Peter making me distracted.

Still, the tips were a lot better than they had been in the old days, even if some of the patrons were more condescending and the kids smirking brats who left holy hell messes on the tables for me to clean up.

That second stint at waitressing cured me of any lingering regret I'd had at never having children.

In the earlier days we'd talked about fostering, of course, and even adoption, but Peter had been strangely reluctant, mumbling about thorough background checks and tracking family histories and what were we going to say about those and what if the state home or the police still wanted one or both of us for questioning about what had happened at the Boehms'.

He said by making an adoption application we put ourselves right back up there on the radar, and did I really want to revisit all of that and maybe have it get out that my parents *hadn't* been married and I *didn't* have a high school diploma, and what if we were charged with fraud or asked to pay back years' of salaries earned for falsifying job applications, and on and on until I'd said, *No, you're right, let's just keep it the two of us. I'm happy this way,* and he'd breathed a huge sigh of relief and we'd lived on from there.

Thinking about it now made me wonder all over again, and so when I got home one night and collapsed in a chair, watching as he made me a tuna sandwich on whole wheat with low-fat mayonnaise and a low-sodium pickle, I said, "Is there any other reason you didn't want to get all involved with background checks, Peter? Is there anything you never told me?"

And of course, there was.

& & &

During the almost two years it had taken Peter to make his way out of Holland after his parents were murdered, throughout all the dark horrors a penniless young man on his own must endure to survive hostile territory, it seems he had done some brutal things while trying to stay alive that were best left unclaimed and undisturbed.

I'm going to leave them that way, too, as other than making him stronger, they have no real bearing on this story. I'll only add that he's the best person to have at your back, as when he said he wasn't afraid of anything, because the worst had already happened, he meant it.

We lived small, finding homes for some of the strays because we just couldn't afford to feed them all anymore, even with the cheapest food. We closed off half the house to avoid having to heat it, clipped coupons, accepted a new hand-me-down computer from a neighbor when they upgraded and spent many a frustrating hour learning how to use it. When we'd had enough of typing, we walked the property together, put out the deer food in winter, and sat by the pond in spring.

And it was during the course of him being frugal and still trying to find me what he called a decent birthday present that he found me the absolute best present of them all.

& & &

"Louise," he said, after I'd blown out way too many candles and cut slices of the low-fat apple cake for each of us, "do you know what *ephemera* is?"

"No, but, good God, Peter, don't tell me you have *that*, too," I said, stopping with my fork halfway to my lips and staring at him uneasily. He looked different; his eyes were shining and there was a strange sort of excitement coming off him in waves.

"Well, in a manner of speaking, I guess I do," he said, cocking his head and grinning.

"Then it must not be fatal because you're looking way too pleased with yourself," I said, setting down my fork and sitting up straight, preparing myself for the worst. "So are you going to tell me what it is or do I have to go get my medical dictionary?"

"No, I'll tell you." He leaned back in his chair and gave me an extremely smug look. "Ephemera is a category on eBay."

I gazed at him, wondering if perhaps he'd finally gone round the bend. "So?"

And then he explained further, how he'd been perusing the category since we'd gotten our first computer and even longer, actually, thanks to one of his conductor friend's new-fangled cell phone with Internet access, and the searches he'd done and the alerts he'd set up had finally paid off.

"Ephemera, to eBay, is old, historic paper goods," he said, handing me a flat box wrapped in paper printed with orchids. "Happy birthday, my love." He smiled. "Well, aren't you going to open it?"

I did, hands trembling because I knew it couldn't be it, it just couldn't be, and so I wouldn't even get my hopes up, wouldn't even let the thought cross my mind. Shaking, I lifted the box lid and parted the crisp white tissue paper . . .

And it was.

It was.

ᙀ   ᙀ   ᙀ

For the first time in almost fifty years, I got to see my mother's smiling face.

⚝ ⚝ ⚝

"So I guess you're not going to stick me in some old-folks home and run off with a spry, sixty-year-old whippersnapper now," he joked, blotting his eyes while I sat there, clutching the faded, rough-edged Ciro's cardboard souvenir photo frame, and cried.

"No, I guess I'm not," I said, burying my face in my napkin.

"I did good then?" he said.

"Yes," I whispered. "You did good."

We made love that night for the first time since his heart attack, gently and tenderly, in no hurry and with much care, and afterward he told me the photo had been part of a small lot of old papers listed as *Doctor's Estate Scandal 1950s Memorabilia,* so he guessed that maybe Nurse, in the course of her cleaning, had found the photo and bundled it into my things. He said he'd found something curious: a piece of correspondence on state-home letterhead regarding the doctor's pro bono surgeries.

"Did you know he did operations for the orphanage?" he asked, running a lazy finger up and down my forearm.

"No," I said and tried to remember why the thought disturbed me, but it was out of reach now, and so I let it go and curled my fingers in his silky salt-and-pepper chest hair and fell asleep with his arms around me.

Peter had a second heart attack two years later, and by then I had long suspected that there was something seriously wrong with me. Serious enough to make my boss at the diner ask me to quit so he wouldn't have to fire me, but then we compromised and he laid me off so I could at least collect unemployment for a while.

I had developed uncontrollable and sporadic tremors, my body moving on its own, and my balance was awful. I was losing track of things, paying bills late, confusing days, months, and even years, forgetting to feed the cats, forgetting I had food on the stove, losing my keys, putting incorrect orders in at work and having to take them back over and over, and quite often, losing my way driving home.

It made me furious, made me beat my fists down on the legs that would refuse to move when I wanted to walk and yet would twitch, pedal, and jerk like crazy all night long. My muscles locked up and some mornings I was brought to tears just trying to roll over to get out of bed. I began adjusting our lifestyle, bought satin sheets because I could slide easier and elastic waist pants and pullover sweatshirts so I wouldn't have to call Peter in and ask him to button me up, used a cane, and erupted in anger the one and only time Peter tried to get me to go to the doctor's.

"No! I never want to see another doctor again for as long as I live."

"Louise—" he began.

"Don't tell me I'm being unreasonable," I said, crying because my hand was moving again and I couldn't make it stop. I wanted a sip of orange juice but couldn't make myself reach for the cup and, even if I did somehow manage to get ahold of it, would splash the juice right out.

"I'm just trying to help," he said quietly, watching me with a compassion that was both embarrassing and oh, so welcome.

The thing was, he couldn't help because I'd already researched my symptoms, and come up with a short, terrifying list of incurable diseases that would spin round and round in my mind every day and never let go.

So I delved feverishly into home remedies, pored over organic cookbooks and homeopathic books and websites, found our old travel mugs and used them instead of normal cups so I could drink without spilling things, graduated to using a walker at home, and stopped driving, enabling us to sell my car and put the money toward what seemed like an ever-rising flood of bills.

 App   App   App

And I began to think about the end.

Obsess about it, actually, remembering the Boehms' choosing to die of morphine overdoses rather than endure the continuing physical and neurological breakdowns from untreated syphilis, and staring at my parents' photo, thinking of how it would have felt to die like my father had at twenty-one, blown up by an enemy's grenade, or like my mother, growing weaker and sicker every day until without warning she had just . . . expired.

And I wondered . . . did she really have no warning, had her body *really* not been telling her, in its own silent way, with its breathlessness and weakness and pounding heart and constant sickness, that it was floundering? Had she known the truth and just decided not to acknowledge it, choosing instead to die with her secrets and leave her daughter shocked and alone, with no one to turn to for anything, not comfort or belonging or even answers?

Had my mother deliberately chosen to ignore the dark cloud over her head, knowing my birth certificate would be discovered, knowing I would be devastated and would have anger and disappointment and so many questions, and just turned away from it all, perhaps unable to bear the way I would look at her—not always, but at that moment, full of betrayal and, yes, maybe even brimming with the righteous disgust of the young who *know* they know everything—and just been too weak and weary to deal with it?

And now I understood it but at the same time I still hated it, hated the lifelong frustration of questions without answers, hated knowing that when I died and Peter died and people we loved came to clean out our home, they, too, would find puzzling documents, that they, too, would try and match up dates and immigration records and make sense of a folder full of journalist reports about mandatory sterilization at state orphanages and the rampages of syphilis and tuberculosis and an old archived obituary of a woman named Evelyn Bell with an angry *CLOSSON* penciled in red after it and a slimmer folder of horrible, grainy black-and-white photos of the dead and dying during Holland's Hunger Winter and a recipe for rice pie, and would anyone anywhere be able to guess the truth or would they just disregard it because we were gone now and who cared.

Or even worse, would they just make up convenient truths to suit themselves, painting us as poor, uneducated liars, a sterilized bastard orphan and a savage immigrant who had run off with a teenager.

The thought was unbearable, leaving questions without answers, leaving loved ones to sort between the comforting lies and the shocking truth, so I sat down at the computer during the moments when my shaking wasn't too dreadful and began to write.

"I think that's good for today, don't you?" I said, switching off the CD and avoiding Gran's gaze because I didn't like where the book was going now, not at all, and wasn't it bad enough that she was stuck in the middle of it without having to hear about it in a book?

Or was I wrong? Was it better to read books about people who were going through the same thing you were, just so you knew you weren't alone?

I asked her, let the helpless question fall and lay there without an answer, watched her twist and writhe and drool, she had started to drool now and needed changing every day, but I still couldn't do it and when I told my mother, crying, she said quietly, "With all that poor Helen is going through, I don't think the indignity of being changed is the worst of it," but the next time I went over, I found my mother there and Gran was freshly washed and changed and wearing a clean sweat suit and her hair was brushed and her ChapStick on. I started crying because I loved my mother for helping me but I also saw all the things I hadn't done and I realized how much I still didn't know about taking care of someone.

Worse, my mother took me aside and in a shaky voice said, "It's no one's fault, Hanna, but I found two spots that look like they're going to be bedsores if we're not careful, and if she gets those, she's going to have to go back into the hospital because those are open wounds and—"

"No! She hates doctors ever since the Boehms'," I blurted, and then had a weird, woozy moment of trying to remember if it was Gran or Louise on tape who we were talking about.

"Who are the Boehms'?" my mother said, frowning.

"No one," I said, shaking my head and taking a deep breath, because that was not good, blurring the line between fantasy and reality, and I heard Seth's voice say, *You don't live in a novel, Hanna!* and for a minute there, I felt like I did.

The question is not, "Can they reason?" nor, "Can they talk?" but rather, "Can they suffer?"

—Jeremy Bentham

Parkinson's disease has no cure and no mercy.

Over time the disease would steal my ability to swallow, to control my body, its functions and movements, to walk, turn my head, change expression, to think, to remember, to laugh and cry, and most heart wrenchingly, to talk.

It would shut down my bowels, host Alzheimer's, and usher in depression. It would destroy my body *and* my mind, leaving me nothing but pain, terror, and a strong, beating heart trapped in a useless, bed-sore-ridden shell. It could be stalled awhile with drugs, but it could never be stopped. Research money was being divvied up and thrown around, but not enough, and not enough at Parkinson's.

In the meantime, as if to prove its power, the disease stole my balance one fall afternoon and sent me reeling down the back steps. I couldn't get up, couldn't do anything but lie there thrashing and gurgling, so Peter had no choice but to call the ambulance, had no choice but to place me in the hands of those I feared most.

 polygon polygon polygon

There's a lot I'm not saying about the sheer helplessness and frustration, the mortification of having to be wiped and diapered like an infant, of being unable to control yourself, of having to lay there in the hospital and have people touch you and move you and take your blood and give you pills and speak to you with the loud, perky, professional cheer of the whole and the healthy who know they will never end up like you, simply because these things only happen to somebody else.

The medication helped, giving me on and off times, welcome windows where I could rise and dress myself, where I could get the spoon to my mouth and if the food was liquid enough, swallow it without choking. It gave me moments when I could talk, one word, maybe two or three, delivered seconds, sometimes minutes, apart and always in a nearly unintelligible mumble. But still, it was a word and I'd spoken it, not that anyone but Peter and a few others ever had the patience to wait around long enough to hear what it was.

The medication was expensive and wouldn't halt the slow, miserable disintegration, but I took it anyway. I took it and suffered the side effects because the doctor wanted me to and I wanted more than anything to get out of that hospital and go home.

So I took it and I *did* go home, and just the sight of our house rising through the trees down past the bend in the road made me weep.

When Peter helped me out of the car and showed me the wheelchair ramp he and the neighbor had built alongside the steps, when the cats crept out and the sun warmed my face and the scent of the freshly mowed clover hit me, I knew that no matter what, I would never willingly leave this place again.

I had lived as I'd wanted to here, and I would die the same way.

I'm afraid of this book.

I want a happy ending.

I want the book to finish and me and Gran to look at each other all pleased and, yeah, maybe tearful because a good book always makes you cry, and I want to hear her say something, say one word, and I don't care what it is, but I want to hear one word, just one.

Just *one*.

ເ∕ວ   ເ∕ວ   ເ∕ວ

My mother tried to keep Gran clean and out of the hospital but she said it was a losing battle. The house was a mess and the strain of trying to do it all was getting so bad that she was afraid Grandpa was going to have another heart attack.

"And what if that happened?" she said one night at dinner, looking at my father and me with fear. "If Lon has a heart attack, Helen can't even get to the phone! He could *die* laying there waiting for help!"

"What about one of those medical alarms, you know, the 'I've fallen and I can't get up!' thing?" my father said, shoveling up a forkful of peas. "I'm working again and we could have the bill sent right to us."

My mother looked at him, eyes swimming with tears, and said, "That is exactly why I love you, you know that?" and then she got up and went around and gave him a bear hug that knocked his glass of soda into his plate and swamped his peas and stained his mashed potatoes purple, but he just smiled and hugged her back and didn't look like he cared at all.

ເ∕ວ   ເ∕ວ   ເ∕ວ

I didn't play the book on Thanksgiving, first because it didn't seem like anything to be thankful for, and second because my parents were there with me. We brought food over for Grandpa and pureed some sweet potatoes and stuff for Gran, but she was really, really bad and it was a terrible day because we all knew that sooner or later one of us was going to have to tell him that she needed to be put somewhere, that he couldn't give her what she needed anymore no matter how hard he tried, and that caring for her was killing him and we could see it happening.

The worst part was that no one brought it up because we were all trying to be at least a little cheerful, but right after saying our Thanksgiving blessing he looked up and said, *You know her heart is very strong, she has no heart problems at all,* and that was kind of scary because all I could think was, *Oh my God, what if* he *dies of a heart attack because he's got the weak heart and leaves her here? Are we going to have to put her in a home or will someone just come and get her and commit her without anyone's permission at all?*

ↁ   ↁ   ↁ

My mother came back with me Friday and Saturday, so while she changed the sheets on the bed, cleaned the bathroom and washed Gran, I loaded up the wagon full of deer food and made the slow U around the back of the quiet property, caught in a thick tension headache, caught in a limbo with the world, feeling that the last peaceful day was coming tomorrow, before deer season opened at sunrise on Monday, knowing the stalemate with Seth couldn't go on forever, that we had all these words to say to each other and neither of us would say them, that we were silent not because we *couldn't* talk but because we *wouldn't,* and sick at what a waste it was.

ↁ   ↁ   ↁ

I went back to Gran's on Sunday by myself, not because of the mandatory community service but because they needed me. And while I was busy filling Gran's sippy cup with water, I glanced up and saw a little faded red plastic tomato ornament hanging on a suction hook on the window. I'd made it for her back in sixth grade with a stained-glass paint kit, and the sight of it twisted hard inside me, ripped something loose, and I forgot about the sippy cup, forgot about everything but Gran and ran back into the living room where she was alone, slumped and shaking in the chair.

"Gran," I said, dropping to my knees in front of her and grabbing onto one of her flyaway hands. "Don't leave me, okay? Please?"

Her hand struggled in mine but I wouldn't release it.

"Stay, Gran," I said and I wanted it to be an order but it came out a plea. "I need you. I do." I didn't even try to stop the tears. "Who am I going to talk to if you go? You said you would never leave me, Gran. You said so. Please stay."

I wanted her to look at me, to smile and pet my hair like she used to when I was little, but there was nothing. She gave me nothing, and finally, still crying, I let go of her hand, wiped my face on my sleeve, got up, and hit play on the CD player.

How It Ends

I don't know how you say good-bye to whom and what you love. I don't know a painless way to do it, don't know the words to capture a heart so full and a longing so intense.

I don't know how to ask you to understand that sometimes the most loving lies are necessary to protect the innocent.

I started writing this because I love you, and it was time to give you truthful answers to all of those impossible questions you once asked. There will be more questions coming, you know—there always are— and by that time I pray you will realize that a happy ending is not the same as happily ever after and that fairy tales are fiction, but love, *true* love that is trustworthy, steadfast, and reliable, is not.

True love is real, and I have loved you since that first day, the best way I knew how.

I hope someday you can forgive me.

          ❦   ❦   ❦

Peter found me some home day-care women for a while, volunteers from churches mostly who swept in with determined good cheer and, occasionally, teeth-grinding platitudes about God's will and never being given more than we could bear, cruelest when said as they changed my soiled diaper or patted my back as I choked on a teaspoon of applesauce.

And while I hated having strangers see me like this, wandering through my home looking at my things or rummaging through my bureau drawers, I was also desperately grateful because we could never have afforded to pay them and caring for me was an exhausting job.

I worried about the strain on Peter's heart.

I worried about all the things I'd wanted to tell him in our golden years that now I couldn't form the words for or even remember.

I worried about the widowed volunteers, friendly, attractive ladies who made eyes at Peter while feeding him lunch and told him of wonderful senior-citizen sponsored bus trips into New York at Christmas to see the Rockettes or down to Atlantic City to gamble or out to Pennsylvania Dutch country to mingle with the Amish.

I would tremble with outrage when this happened, and my involuntary movements would grow agitated and spastic, and the nice volunteer would sigh and glance at Peter and say, *She's so lucky she has you,* and bless his heart, he would reach over and take my spasming claw and say, *I've always been the lucky one.* The volunteer would raise an eyebrow and say, *It's not every husband who would take on such a heavy burden,* and then Peter, gaze gleaming, would release my hand and let it flail, inevitably knocking over my drink cup or sweeping my plate from the tray, and the volunteer would hustle over to clean it up, and he would wink at me and I would try to smile and fail, and die a little more inside.

Because I knew what the volunteers said was true.

My pills had no refills without a follow-up office visit, but I would not go back to the doctor because I knew the moment he saw me he would either advise Peter to put me in a care facility or, if I looked bad enough, might even commit me himself.

It might have been my terror-fueled imagination talking, it might never have actually happened, but if it did, I knew I would never get out again.

Peter got the doctor to refill my medication once by phone anyway, lying and saying I'd knocked the open bottle into the toilet by mistake, but the doctor wouldn't do it again, so we were forced to begin cutting my pills in half to make them last longer, trying to stretch the time in between doses.

The results were a hell I wouldn't wish on anyone.

છ૩ છ૩ છ૩

Fall came, the days cold, gray, and bleak.

Peter closed off all the rooms but the few we were using downstairs. He slept on the couch, as we couldn't share a bed anymore and hadn't since I'd come home from the hospital. My involuntary thrashing had not only made it impossible for him to sleep but had also left him bruised and, once, with a bloody nose.

Most days he managed to get me into the wheelchair and set me by the window so I could see the deer and the cats and all I'd once loved, but I had stopped caring, wrapped in endless pain and confusing thoughts and a great, heavy weariness. I couldn't move, couldn't speak, couldn't tell him how sorry I was to have let him down like this, to be such a terrible burden and carve such deep anguish into his face, to never have said one last *Thank you* for gently brushing my hair or washing me or shouting only when the frustration of seeing me dying grew to be too much.

I wished I had whispered one last *I love you* while I still could or asked him to sing me one last song or could spend one last sweet night in his arms.

I wished I would die in my sleep like my mother had, wished I had thought to gather medication while I still could drive and speak, while I could have visited several different doctors for enough different prescriptions to amass the correct and lethal doses, but still, that thought terrified me, too, because what if I did manage to swallow enough pills—a gamble because I could barely swallow at all—but didn't die? What if I just went into a coma and was committed to an institution and left to lie there, to languish for another ten years? What if I ended up in worse shape than Mrs. Boehm had been in, because at least she was able to move and speak, at least she'd been in her own home in her own bed with her own husband when she'd passed . . .

I was trapped, caught between never wanting to leave and only wanting to leave, and being helpless either way.

And at night, tormented by insomnia and a claustrophobia born of being unable to escape the tight constrictions of my own body, the smell of decay rose around me and there was no escaping that, either.

દર્ભ   દર્ભ   દર્ભ

I watched the deer, the does and yearlings, grazing in the back and wanted to warn them that they're in mortal danger, that mothers will die and fawns become orphans, and nothing I can do or say will stop it or save them.

I've tried to protect them but I've failed.

Now, even in writing, my voice will be still. Peter will FedEx this to the self-publishing company I've chosen, and it will return as an audiobook, because so few people make time to curl up in a cozy chair and read anymore.

When the questions come—and they will—you will have answers.

I love you with all of my heart, and I would not leave you as I was left.

I waited, but nothing happened.

No more narrator.

No more words.

I looked at Gran, but she was thrashing and offered no answers.

Got up, grabbed the CD case, and wrenched it open, searching for another CD, because there had to be another one, there had to be.

There wasn't.

"No," I said, shaking my head, dropping the case, and glancing around the room, searching for something to make sense of this. "That can't be. No one ends a book like this! Oh my God, I can't believe it. That's it? Are you *kidding?*"

I was so freaked, I didn't know what to do, so outraged and let down and full of pent-up anger at such a total betrayal, at some stupid writer who would draw me in and carry me along and make me love her and be anxious for her and want *so bad* for a happy ending, for a miracle or, Jesus Christ, at *least* a comment at the end or an author's note or *something* so that I wasn't just left hanging, going, *Well, what happened? Did she live? Did she die? What happened?* that when Grandpa finally got home, I was just like, "Next time *I'm* picking the audiobook, okay? And it's going to be a nice, normal murder mystery because I can't take another book like this one!"

And he just smiled and slowly unbuckled his crossing guard vest and watched as I gathered up the food for the cats and for the deer's last feast and stomped out, and when I was halfway across the yard, he came out onto the porch and called, "Good night, Hanna." I stopped, still mad and caught up in all the infuriating, unanswered questions the stupid book had left me with, yelled, "See you tomorrow," and just kept going.

❧ ❧ ❧

"That book?" I said to my mother at supper. "Forget it. It has no ending."

"It has to have an ending," she said, looking puzzled. "Everything has an ending."

"Yeah, well, not this," I said crankily. "It's a stalemate, okay? It leaves you in total limbo with no answers, and what am I supposed to do, *imagine* what happens? Just . . ." I scowled down at my burrito and felt myself cracking.

"Hanna?" she said worriedly.

"Just don't read it," I managed to say and waved her away and went on scowling down at my refried beans because I had a pounding headache, and I started wishing Crystal's brother was still throwing parties because all I wanted to do was wipe my mind clean and just be happy with Seth and not caught in this horrible, bleak cycle where death was coming as soon as the sun rose again.

I googled *Louise Bell Closson* and got nothing. Went to Amazon .com and Barnes & Noble and Borders and Books-a-Million and every indie bookstore I could think of, looking for her or, in case I spelled her name wrong, *How It Ends* and got so mad even typing in the title that I just shut the computer down and went to bed.

❧ ❧ ❧

I didn't sleep for a long time that night.

All That Remains

Sounds: the finches squabbling in the pine tree, made anxious by the empty bird feeders. Lon whispering a promise. The constant, rhythmic swish of dry skin sliding across worn satin sheets.

Sights: the deer grazing out back along the path, their rich, tawny summer coats faded to the gray-brown of dead foliage. A prescription bottle marked NO REFILLS. The truth, confessed and titled *How It Ends* in its case on the table.

Smells: the comforting drift of Evening in Paris furled in grief. Lon's dependable Lipton-tea-with-honey-and-lemon exhales. The earthy, sun-baked straw scent of the shy, scrawny stray cats in for a visit.

Sensations: Lon's callused hands fumbling the damp nylon nightgown up over my head and the cool wash of air that follows. A thigh muscle seized in a rigid, trembling cramp. Choking, trying to swallow the lukewarm trickle pooled at the back of my throat.

Emotions: relief, like a silver ribbon of promise wending through a razor-thorn maze of despair. A merciless yearning for what was, and never will be again. Terror, a smothering, black hood stitched to a body bag, zipped up, locked down, and nearly sewn shut.

Chapter 31

Hanna

My alarm goes off before sunrise and I roll over, wincing as the remnants of last night's headache throb to life.

"God," I whisper, peeling back the covers and stumbling out of bed. I feel awful, thick and foggy, grim with a vague, low-level dread like a lingering nightmare, and I pause, frowning, trying to figure out why, and then remember. "Ugh. It's opening day." I plod into the bathroom to get ready for school.

The dull throb stays with me as I go downstairs. My stomach is roiling and something's wrong, something past the headache and the tension of hunting season, but I can't pull it out of the fog so I grab two aspirins and sit down at the table across from my mother, who's already well into her second cup of coffee.

"Happy days are here again," she says grimly and hands me the ugly pink fluorescent knit hat we'll both wear from now on whenever we go outside.

"Joy," I say, pull it on, and go over to the counter to pour a bowl of cereal. Pause, gazing out the window over the sink because there's a light on over at Gran's, and the ribbon of dawn is just beginning to thread through the trees.

❧ ❧ ❧

Lon Schoenmaker finishes the first cup of caffeinated coffee he's had since his original heart attack so many years ago and rises, wincing at his arthritis. He sets the cup in the sink and goes to the table in the living room, where a thick envelope of documents awaits.

He withdraws his will and then Helen's and lays them out on the table. Next the deed to the house, a life insurance policy, their birth certificates, and last, a Post-It note.

He picks up *How It Ends,* fastens the Post-It note to the front of the shiny red CD case, and sets it out on the back porch. Straightens, a hand at his back, and stands a moment breathing in the crisp air, the faint scent of wood smoke, the rich beauty of all he loves. Looks at the thin strip of daylight glowing through the bare tree branches, turns, goes in, and locks the door behind him.

I don't know why I'm pouring cereal, because I'm not even hungry, but I need something in my stomach to take these aspirin, so I pour the milk, and my stomach is sick, my head is pounding, and out of the corner of the window, over on the land next door, I see a hunter, flashlight and fluorescent hat bobbing as he weaves through the trees, and I could just cry because dawn is coming and the does are out there like they always are, grazing, living, standing with their yearlings, just trying to make it through, and they don't even know that death is on the march.

Lon walks into the bedroom and stops at the edge of the bed. Looks down at Helen, wide awake, trembling, twitching, head and neck, hands and arms, legs and feet twisting and writhing, unable to stop, her mouth moving without words, and he leans over, touches her face, strokes her cheek, and she sees him, she knows him, because her eyes fill with tears and her gaze clings to his, terrified but trusting him the way she's always trusted him to be there, to never leave her, and he won't.

He takes the Ciro's nightclub souvenir picture from the end table, shows it to her and, when he's sure she's seen it, smiles and lays it on the pillow beside her.

"Your medication is gone, Helen. There is no more." He says this quietly and watches her closely, sees the awareness in her gaze, the fear and the acceptance and finally the relief. He strokes her hair back as best he can because she's moving so violently and says, "No more, I promise. I'll be right behind you . . ."

And then he rises and goes to the closet and pulls out the shotgun that has never been fired, and like the gunsmith's son he began as, he opens the box of shells and loads it.

"The hunter's in the field next door," I say to my mother, dropping into my seat and toying with the now soggy cereal. I force myself to eat a spoonful because otherwise the aspirin will kill my stomach. "It's going to be an ambush."

Lon shuts poor bewildered Serepta in the bathroom and stands at the side of the bed gazing at Helen, seeing not the wreckage Parkinson's has wrought but the woman he's loved most of his life, a sweet, strong, doe-eyed sixteen-year-old girl, a graceful young woman who went off to waitress and who would turn, cheeks pink and gaze shining, as he stood on the porch singing her away, wooing her back, and so he tries to sing as the memories come, tries to sing her one last love song, but the only one he can think of is "All Things Must Pass" and sees the tears slip from her eyes, sees her in his memory, dancing light and lovely in her slip, luring him with a smile like sunshine and unashamed, unreserved love into her arms, a woman who sprayed him with the hose and ran shrieking when he chased her straight into the pond, a woman who held his hands to her lips when he said he would never stay without her, that he would take a bullet for her, that he would never ever leave her, and he whispers the words, *I will always love you,* and lays a hand on her cheek and she gazes at him, trusting, waiting—

I get up to put my bowl in the sink.

It's almost dawn.

I stare into the dark field but don't see the hat . . . no, there it is, settled in the branches of a tree stand. Oh God, my head.

Lon takes a steadying breath because he has no fear now, he has always done what had to be done to love her and save her, to save himself the way he couldn't save his parents, and the memory of all that came before this moment mixes with the sweet life that is almost over, and he draws one more ragged breath, stiffening his resolve, and puts the barrel to her forehead, but her forehead keeps moving, jerking and shaking, and he can't get a clean shot, he can't pull the trigger with her moving, because if he misses, if he misses . . . no, he can't miss because this is their agreement, they would not be put away to die long and slow and ugly, they would go as they lived, their own way in their own home, so he *can't* miss, but he can't get a good shot if she won't stop moving, and so he turns the shotgun, lifts it high, and smashes it down on her forehead, and she stops moving then, and sobbing, he turns the shotgun and presses it to her forehead and pulls the trigger

The deer lift their heads.

The shot explodes in the silence and I jump, dropping my bowl into the sink.

My mother snorts and says, "Well, somebody just jumped the gun and scared all the deer away. There's going to be a lot of pissed-off hunters out there this morning."

And my heart surges and my brain pounds and all of a sudden I know, *I know,* and I make a high, desperate noise and scramble across the kitchen, fumble with the door, fling it wide, and bolt out into the burning cold. I'm running and it's almost dawn but not yet, not yet, and the light is murky gray mixed with pink and I hear my mother behind me yelling, "Hanna! No! What are you doing?"

Lon Schoenmaker's legs give out and he sinks to the edge of the bed next to his wife's still form, turns the shotgun on himself and, closing his eyes, fires.

The second shot explodes and it's here, right here, echoing in my ears and my heart, and I stumble, ragged with terror and running as hard as I can through the break in the little woods, and I can hear the deer running, too, crashing into the woods all around me, and the guy in the tree yells, "What the fuck?"

I run past the empty bird feeders and the cats streaking everywhere and finally, panting and half-blind with tears, take the back porch steps on my hands and knees. See a CD near the door with a Post-It with my name on it and grab it.

> Hanna,
> This is how, and why.
>
> All our love,
> Helen Louise Bell Closson Schoenmaker
> Lon Peter Schoenmaker

I stare at it, incredulous, and then a wordless wail grates from my throat like a rush of ground glass, leaving a thousand little cuts in its wake. I shove the CD into my hoodie pocket, push myself up, and grab the doorknob, but it's locked, so I stumble to the window and the shade is down but the light is on inside, and frantic, I smear my cloudy breath from the glass and look harder, squint harder, and . . . *no no oh no* . . . and back away keening, holding my stomach, and clutching at the railing, and my mother runs up in her bedroom slippers and I cry, "Mom, Mom," and I reach for her and she's there.

℃   ℃   ℃

The police and ambulance come with sirens wailing, and the sun rises, and the deer run on, scattered to the winds, and no does or yearlings die here today, the only day in her life that Gran has finally been able to save them.

One faces the future with one's past.

—Pearl S. Buck

I didn't tell anyone about *How It Ends*.

I don't know whether I actually forgot about it amid the shock or what.

I really don't.

The newspapers screamed SENIOR CITIZEN MURDER/SUICIDE, and all these people who didn't even know Gran and Grandpa spoke to the press, presenting all kinds of stupid, half-assed theories, and the papers printed them, and people went online and asked, *How could this happen in our community???* like being private was an unforgivable sin and they should have advertised their intentions so they could have been deemed incompetent and put in a nursing home or under immediate psychiatric evaluation.

Others tsked about how Gran just hadn't believed in God strongly enough or decided there must have been abuse in the home because otherwise she would have been in a care facility like she should have been, and on and on.

Only one person was brave enough to say that if, like Oregon, the state allowed for physician-assisted suicides, then instead of being forced to resort to extreme measures for lack of options, Gran would have been able to pass away with dignity, to go gently and peacefully surrounded by loved ones, not miserable, desperate, and smashed to pieces.

The person who suggested it was roundly condemned and never returned to the newspaper's message board to respond, because really, what would have been the point?

Everyone believes what they want to believe.

The police had to keep watch on the house because there were actually ghouls who came out to stare at it, people who wanted to see where the murderer and his helpless victim had spent their days, trespassers who tried to walk the grounds and peer in the windows and see if they could identify what caused the snap so they could avoid it themselves, but I knew they would never find it because they were only looking on the *outside,* and the answers, all of them, came from the inside, the past, present, and future, the imprints, decisions, and experiences, the parts of us that we hold secret and dear, the pieces that no one will ever know unless we make a point of revealing them.

Someday, when all of this is over, I'm going to give my mother the audiobook so she'll have the real answers, too.

ç∂   ç∂   ç∂

Three times so far my mother has opened the front door and stood behind the glass storm door watching me, eyes red and lids swollen from crying, fingers knotted together, and the pain of the last two days forever stamped in the lines of her face.

Three times she's slipped out of the house, crossed the porch to the railing, where I'm sitting with my back against the post, touched my jacketed arm, and said, "Hanna? Are you sure you don't want to come inside and wait? It's so cold and you're not even sure he's coming. . . ."

And three times I've shaken my head, short, quick, full-body, trembling shakes that are an extension of the bone-deep shuddering that hasn't stopped ever since I raced through the predawn chaos. "He'll come." I clench my jaw to keep my teeth from chattering, curl my fingers up tight inside the thick white crocheted mittens, and gaze down across the acre of flattened, frozen grass toward the road beyond, watching.

Because he *will* come, I know it.

All I have to do is wait long enough.

"Have you called him?" my mother asked this last time.

"No," I said, because it's important, somehow, that I don't have to. It's important that he finds Sammi in the halls and asks how I am, and when he hears the truth, all else falls away and he comes.

It's important that I don't have to ask.

He has to do it soon, though, simply because he loves me and I need him, because I'm huddled here, wrecked and broken, and the wake is tonight and people will come to stare and question and whisper, and he'll know that standing beside me will mean everything.

So I wait for him because I always have, because out of all the moments that went wrong, I think there were just as many that went right, just as much love and heat and want as hurt, disappointment, and cruelty. I want to believe there's a balance here, that out of this tragedy will come some good, and there *will* be a happy ending.

And most of all, for all the times he's told me, *Get your head out of a book, Hanna. You don't live in a novel,* I want to show him that, *yes, yes,* I know all too well that real life is not fiction.

℥   ℥   ℥

My parents stand together at the front of the crowded wake. My father looks weary, defeated, and my mother, eyes red, lashes wet and spiky, is like a wounded sentinel, dazed by the sudden ferocity of death and the deluge of unanswered questions but still standing with chin up and gaze fierce, determined to protect Gran and Grandpa from the flood of bright-eyed, stale-breathed mourners who cheaped out on flowers but still came to feed on the shocking tragedy, gossip, and judge.

I heard he had an arsenal in the cellar.

Do you think he really kept her tied to the bed?

I want to know what they were doing with all those cats.

I can't believe no one knew.

And then they turn and look at me, but I keep my gaze fixed on the sparse scattering of floral arrangements standing behind the urns and give them nothing, because this bone-deep ache is mine.

The only thing I say when people bait me with comments like, "I can't believe this happened . . ." is, "Anybody who really knew them knew he would never stay without her," but it's like they don't want to believe in a love that strong, in a happily ever after that deviates from the fairy tale, and so they keep fishing for answers they will never get.

Sammi, Crystal, and their families come, Grandpa's old supervisor from the railroad comes and so does an elderly lady named Coral. People from my parents' work come and Mr. Sung from school comes.

Seth does not.

And it's in the last half hour when I'm exhausted and close to tears, heart sore from gazing at the urns and wishing, oh God, *praying* this is all just a terrible nightmare that I glance up and see Jesse standing in the back looking solemn, dreads in a ponytail, carrying a jacket over his arm, and wearing a long-sleeved white dress shirt so new that it still has the fold lines down the front.

I almost break then, I do, but instead I meet his dark, steady gaze and make my way to him, take his hand, bring him forward, and introduce him to my parents, and in that space surrounded by loss and sadness and the passing of something real and good and true, something else real and good and true is passed on, too, seeded with a moment of pain that could someday become a pearl.

Winter

I huddle on the back steps, knees drawn up, hands in my pockets, and toes numb from the creeping cold, watching the birds gathered at the feeders, cardinals and chickadees mingling with wrens, blue jays, and doves, all picking at the seed spread across the frigid January ground.

A shadow flashes past and I glance up, growing uneasy as the birds continue to feed, oblivious to a thin black slash in the sky that's coming closer, looming larger, sharpening into strong wings and a curved beak, circling unnoticed over the peaceful scene below.

It veers out of sight, and as I exhale, the birds at the feeders explode in a flurry, hurtling into the air as the hawk bullets in. They scatter, frenzied, panicked, and streaking toward me, hitting the false sky reflected in the window with dull, solid thuds and falling broken to the leaves below.

The hawk, fierce, beautiful, inevitable, plumage dark and shining iridescent, lands and stands motionless, ignoring the feeble fluttering of the dove trapped in its talons. I watch, paralyzed, as the dove's twisted wings flap uselessly against its captor, hear the triumphant keen as the hawk surveys its domain then dips its head to *peck, tear, peck . . .*

And then there's no sound at all but my own mindless *Have mercy, you took it, now kill it, don't make it suffer,* and when the numbing fog inside me finally burns away and I'm close to screaming, the hawk tenses, spreads its wings and, with the limp body caught firmly in its grip, carries it off.

The feeders sway, abandoned.

Buff-colored feathers, torn loose and stained bright ripple and twitch in its wake.

Trembling, I rise and search for survivors. At first I see nothing but casualties: four sparrows that were never the targets but still fell in the course of the assault.

Then I spot the fifth bird, a wren, lying beneath the window on a drift of matted leaves. It blinks, quivering and still too stunned from the shock of impact to fly.

I crouch, weeping, and gently close my hand around it, absorbing the residual terror fueling its tiny heart. Cradle it close for a moment, then place it on one of the stray-cat towels in a warped and weathered shoe box, close the lid, put the makeshift sanctuary on the step, and return to bury the dead.

The strays however, always hungry, always prowling, have already discovered the small, cooling bodies and carried them away.

The relief that comes from this shames me, but I'm still thankful because the birds who died quickly have not only been spared but have spared *me* the struggles of the mortally wounded, of kneeling helpless beside a body too broken to fly but not broken enough to die, beside living wreckage that cannot be healed and would never again be more than a twisted, flightless song trapped on the ground alone, defenseless, and forsaken by its own kind.

And so I wait in the chill of the thin, gray light until the tears dry, the lost have been mourned and the hawk forgiven, and then return to the porch, open my jacket, and tuck the shoe box in close against me to warm it, not speaking, not lifting the lid to see if the little wren is still breathing, just waiting while the faint flutter of a single taken dove ripples through me again and again, just waiting, keeping quiet watch over the wren in the bottom of the shoe box and wondering if it will ever recover enough to be released.

Where is home?
Home is where the heart can laugh without shyness.
Home is where the heart's tears can dry at their own pace.

—Vernon Baker

I walk through the little woods, Serepta at my heels, and together we travel the deer path to the old wooden bench under the catalpa tree. Sit in the shade of those generous, heart-shaped leaves and breathe in the scent of the delicate white flowers.

It is impossibly beautiful.

Serepta, slow and arthritic, gathers herself and leaps up to settle beside me.

Birds—robins, sparrows, and wrens, maybe even the one I know—flit through the meadow grass, and a worn, raggedy monarch, perhaps the first to return from the winter migration, flutters past us and along the wood line in the sun.

It's fawn season, too.

There are hoofprints in the mud along the pond's edge, and for a heartbeat I think I hear you whisper, *Wild horses, Hanna.* I know it's only the sweet breeze rustling through the catalpa, but today, on my eighteenth birthday, I very much want to believe it's you.

Because this morning I discovered you left me everything you ever loved.

I lift my head, listening to the faint sound of a motorcycle in the distance.

It's a Harley—it has a very distinctive sound—and it's headed my way.

I smile and wipe my damp cheeks on my sleeve. Lift Serepta up into my arms and, cradling her close, rise and start back along the deer path.

Wild horses, Gran.

I miss you so much.

how it ends

Laura Wiess

READING GROUP GUIDE

QUESTIONS FOR DISCUSSION

1. In the prologue we are introduced to Hanna and Mrs. Schoenmaker and learn about the history of their relationship. How does the prologue foreshadow the events of the novel and emphasize the link between Hanna and the Schoenmakers?

2. When Crystal tells Hanna Jesse's history, Hanna is shocked at what Jesse has been through: "I never knew anybody with such a sad story before . . . I mean, I had no idea there could be so much to karate guy." What surprises Hanna about Jesse? How does the way he looks contrast with his personality and background? How does this passage reflect a common theme in the book? How have people surprised you in your life?

3. How are Hanna's parents a good support system for her? How does their relationship influence Hanna?

4. After the robbery at the sub shop Hanna tells her psychologist that "There's pre-robbery Hanna and there's

post-robbery Hanna; my life is halved now. Pre-Hanna was so sure of her life, she . . . strode through it like there was nothing she couldn't find a way around, like there was nothing she couldn't handle." How else does the robbery change Hanna's life? How does it help to prepare her for some of the events that are still to come?

5. Talk about your impressions of Seth. What draws Hanna to him? Have you or anyone you know experienced what Hanna went through with him? Why does she continue to go back to him when he repeatedly makes her feel bad? Discuss the ups and downs of Hanna's relationship with him.

6. Consider the husband-wife relationships in the book. Think about Hanna's parents, the Schoenmakers, the Boehms, Seth's parents and Jesse's parents. What do these couples demonstrate about the nature of love? What does Hanna learn from these relationships? What does she not understand?

7. Discuss the Schoenmakers' relationship. What is unusual about their marriage? In what ways is their love story universal? Did their relationship alter your view of what constitutes romantic love? Can you think of other fictional or real life love stories that parallel theirs?

8. When Hanna runs into Jesse over Memorial Day weekend she tells him, "Every time I see you I just . . . I don't know. You make me smile." Why does Jesse make Hanna feel good? How is he different from Seth? Why do you think it takes her so long to realize how she feels about him?

9. Discuss the theme of reinvention in the novel. Consider the Schoenmakers, the Boehms, Hanna, Jesse, and others.

10. Louise shares some of Peter's background in the audiobook but also writes that "he had done some things while trying to stay alive that were best left unclaimed and undisturbed." Why does Louise choose not to reveal more details about Peter's history? What do you imagine he might have had to do?

11. What is the significance of the book's title, *How It Ends*? Why do you think Wiess gives her book and the audiobook Hanna and Mrs. Schoenmaker listen to the same title?

12. This novel contains some shocking moments, particularly toward the end. What did you think of Lon's actions at the end of the novel? Were you surprised? Do you think he did the right thing? How does his personal history affect the choices he makes?

13. Discuss the role that animals play in this novel. What do they symbolize? How do they help to drive the story?

14. When Hanna rescues the wren after the hawk attacks, she discovers stray cats have carried away the birds that died. "The relief that comes from this shames me, but I'm still thankful because the birds who died quickly have not only been spared but have spared *me* the struggles of the mortally wounded, of kneeling helpless beside a body too broken to fly but not broken enough to die . . . " What does Hanna mean? What is significant about this passage?

15. What does Hanna learn from her relationship with the Schoenmakers? How does it change her? How does it influence her ideas about her own romantic relationships?

16. Did you relate to Hanna? Did you like her? Were any of her experiences similar to yours?

17. Why do you think it takes Hanna such a long time to acknowledge the truth about the audiobook? Why might it be hard for her to face the truth? In what other ways does Hanna have trouble facing reality?

18. Louise writes, "True love is real, and I have loved you since that first day, the best way I knew how. I hope someday you can forgive me." What does Louise want Hanna to forgive her for? What else does the audiobook show about the nature of true love?

19. What did you think about the book's ending? How did you feel after finishing the book?

20. Discuss some of your favorite passages or scenes in the novel. What resonated most for you? Are there any other themes or topics that stood out?

A DISCUSSION WITH THE AUTHOR

1. *How It Ends* is extremely inventive and touches on a wide range of topics, from love and family to taxidermy, animal

rescue and women's reproductive rights. What inspired you to write this book? What kind of research did you have to do to incorporate so many topics in this novel?

How It Ends *began when I was wondering about the experiences people keep hidden in their hearts, thinking about how there's always so much more to people than we see, and what a huge mistake it is to believe we know everything there is to know about a person, whether it be a stranger, family member, or friend. It shifted into higher gear when two of the images I've been carrying around in my mind for years surfaced and wove themselves into the mix.*

The first image came from one of the stories my mother used to tell me, about how it was back when she was a little girl in the 1940s. She lived in a neighborhood where all the kids used to play out in the street, and although no one talked much about the kinds of men who offered candy to children, all the kids were warned by their parents not to go near this one house on the block where an old man and his invalid wife lived, especially if it was dusk or he called you into his garage for any reason.

The local kids ran away from this guy whenever he beckoned but one day there was a new girl of about fifteen living there, a state kid, an orphan, placed with them to live and work. She had no one, and so was trapped: on the surface the old man and his wife looked harmless but behind closed doors, it must have been an unimaginable hell. She was rarely allowed to come out and play with the other kids and did not even go to school.

I asked my mother—who had been maybe 9 or 10 back then—what happened to the girl and it turns out she got pregnant, and was sent away in shame for getting herself into trouble. Can you even imagine? She—an orphaned child—was an unpaid servant, denied an education, sexually molested, impregnated by her foster father, and then punished for it, whisked away as if it were all her fault. How convenient.

The image of this faceless, anonymous girl trapped in a house of horrors, has haunted me for years.

The second image was from a story I read years ago about a man who was supposedly a deer rehabber and an amateur taxidermist. (Anybody else see a conflict, here?) Wildlife rehab is a wonderful, difficult, heart-and-soul endeavor if it's done correctly and with the best interest of the animal in mind, but supposedly this guy had been taking in orphaned fawns and shoving them into a dark, dank outbuilding along with deer corpses in various stages of decomposition, dissection, taxidermy experiments, chemical treatment, etc., and basically leaving them there to die of starvation.

It was not a stretch for me to imagine the imprisoned fawns confused, hungry, scared, and locked into what could only be a living hell with no food or water, with the thick, unrelenting scent of terror, death, and rot all around them, no sun, no breeze, no grass, no freedom, laying in chemicals that burned through them, blood, feces, mud . . . I couldn't get such self-serving cruelty out of my mind and wanted to know why? Why would someone do this? So I began to imagine an answer.

Somehow the anonymous orphan girl and the fawns wove together, along with the idea that no one is ever all they appear to be, a fascination with the imprints we leave on each other throughout our lives, and wanting to explore how love is born and how it dies. These threads became the fictional How It Ends.

As far as research goes, I explored taxidermy, the old mandatory sterilization laws for the unfit, medical pieces regarding the treatment of women and the maladies supposedly born of their *reproductive organs, the Hunger Winter, mandatory community service, Parkinson's disease, physician-assisted suicide, and the right to die.*

2. How do you capture the lives and emotions of teenagers so realistically? Do you spend time around teenagers? Or do you just have a great memory of what it's like to be that age?

   Both, I think. What intrigues me most about the teen years—besides the fact that you're coming up and everything is new, you're jockeying for position and trying to feel your way through an unfamiliar world filled with hazards, pitfalls, excitement, and experiments—is "kid logic." I love kid logic even when it completely unnerves me. I remember it very clearly because my own kid logic sprung from wanting to get out there and live my life, and not get caught or get in trouble for doing whatever it was I was doing.

3. Some of your interests show up in this novel—you're an animal lover and rescuer and, like your characters, live in the country. Was this a conscious decision or did it happen as you went along?

   I think it happened as the characters became known to me, and their concerns placed them in an environment where the dreams they had left had room to grow. Helen and Lon, going through what they had in the past, needed space to live their own way. Helen was attuned to the suffering of those who couldn't speak for themselves and so she tried to find an active and ongoing way to help by providing food and shelter, spaying/neutering for the cats and a home base. Hanna grew up seeing this behavior as normal but when she had to fill in for Helen, she thought it was a pain. Then she looked harder, saw the need, stepped up of her own free will, and chose to help, too.

I see the place where Helen and Hanna live as the far, wooded outskirts of town—a small town—with the inevitable development creeping toward them but not quite there yet. There are still woods to support the wildlife, and it's still a place where people can live privately and have room to stretch out.

So no, I'm not surprised that living in the country has sort of bled over into this book. After growing up in central Jersey, living up in the mountains now is an ongoing adventure. Kind of a culture shock—no pizza delivery here—but it's worth it. I learn something new every single day—which of course means that I get to feel stupid every single day, too, because I don't know what I'm doing—and it's tickling me to death. I love it.

4. What else in your life informs your writing? How do you think you work best? Tell us about your writing style.

Lots of things become fictionalized and feed in: moments, issues or causes I find intriguing or am passionate about, things I learn along the way, emotions I wonder about and more. I have to feel what the characters feel as we go along, especially when I'm sitting firmly on one side of the fence and the challenge is to try and see a situation or a belief from the opposing side. Doing that opens new doors in my mind, helps me to understand different points of view and respect other sides, even if I still don't like or agree with them. It creates a wonderful chaotic jumble of thoughts.

I work best when I'm not interrupted, alone in my studio, sometimes with silence, sometimes with specific music playing low in the background. I do a lot of research in every direction that seems interesting, exploring whatever strikes my fancy, and let it all simmer together until something sparks and a character with a question is born. I never know what that character is going to be made of until they show up.

5. The reason for Hanna's parents' brief split is not revealed. Did you have an idea in mind of what they went through?

I don't have an absolute, but I know it wasn't any one big thing that split them up, more like they came together with two separate, naive fantasy ideas of what their young, happy lives together would be—eternal romance, eternal hot sex, no fuzzy slippers or baggy sweats or overdue bills, no zoning out in front of the TV or the dreaded, frustrated Um, honey? We have to talk *moments—and were not prepared for the ups and downs of reality or the warring expectations, which bred discontent and disappointment, resentment and the pain of watching love founder and almost die.*

I'm glad they found their way back to each other, though.

6. Did you do a lot of research while writing the story-within-a-story audiobook *How It Ends*?

Here's where growing up in a family of storytellers came in handy, as the old days—in glorious, vivid detail—were always offered up as a companion to progress. The stories were bizarre, funny and interesting, and I must have absorbed far more than I thought I did, because they're definitely coming in handy now.

There was serious research too, of course, especially when it came to things like mandatory sterilization for whoever was deemed unfit *(want to chill your blood? It was still happening in the 1970s)*, the Hunger Winter, Parkinson's disease, the right to die and more.

7. What are you currently working on?

   I have several stories in the works but there's a certain romantic comedy that seems to be a little more irresistible than the rest. . . .

8. Who are some of your favorite writers? Did any particular works inspire *How It Ends*? What did you most enjoy reading when you were Hanna's age?

   I'm bad at pinpointing favorites—they shift along with my moods—but at Hanna's age I liked funny, heartwarming family stories like Cheaper by the Dozen *(the original book by Frank Gilbreth and Ernestine Gilbreth Carey, not the movie), thrillers, Gothic mysteries, horror (Stephen King), drama, love stories, and nonfiction back-to-the-land books. Animal stories, too. Stories with characters that made me invest everything I had in their happiness, fret over them, and get really depressed when the book was over and I could no longer walk with them.*

   Hmm, come to think of it, these are still pretty much the books I reach for. Give me a character to love and I'll follow her or him anywhere.

9. There are some pretty devastating scenes in this book, particularly as we near the end. Were any of these scenes painful for you to write? Do you get emotionally attached to your characters?

Yes, the scenes you refer to were very hurtful to write. Being trapped with absolutely no escape, being inside the minds' of Helen and Lon, feeling the pain, desperation, and helplessness they felt, running panicked and terrified with Hanna . . . none of it was good. I cried a lot, because yes, I do get emotionally attached to my characters.

10. Even though this book is categorized as a young adult novel it is also appropriate for older readers. Do you consider yourself a YA writer? Do you write with any particular audience in mind?

    Based on the reader e-mail I've received so far, Such a Pretty Girl *and* Leftovers *both have a pretty wide audience, ranging from about fourteen years old to readers in their seventies. Those books are about* teens *but maybe not necessarily only* for *teens. But yes, I do consider myself a YA writer.*

11. Was there a message for young people you were trying to convey? Does writing for a YA audience lend itself to lessons?

    No, I hope no messages but rather questions asked, and for these characters, hopefully answered. How does love begin? Is any love good love? What do you bring to the partnership? What do you allow in the name of love, behavior-wise, and what do you reject? Is there sacrifice, and if so, why? How does love end? What about perfect, fairy-tale love? If we believe in that, are we doomed to disappointment or can it possibly survive reality? What if no one is ever really *who you think they are? What then?*
    I love questions, and I love them best when I can find some answers.

reading group guide

ENHANCE YOUR BOOK CLUB

1. Hanna and Mrs. Schoenmaker bond over their love of animals. In one poignant scene they discuss the migration patterns of monarch butterflies after Mrs. Schoenmaker gives Hanna a book on the subject. Find out more about monarch butterflies at http://www.monarchwatch.org/.

2. Give some of your time to someone who needs companionship. Sign up to help out at a nursing home or hospital or make cookies and have tea with a favorite neighbor.

3. Arrange a volunteer outing at an animal shelter or find out how you can help animals in need at http://www.charity-guide.org/volunteer/animal-protection.htm or http://www.hsus.org/pets/animal_shelters/how_to_volunteer_at_your_local_animal_shelter.html, http://www.aspca.org/.

4. Learn more about the author at www.laurawiess.com and www.myspace.com/gypsyrobin.